BENDING

TOWARD

the LIGHT

Katherine Winfield

ISBN: 1986280501

ISBN 13: 978-1986280501

The journey of a thousand miles begins with a single step
—*Lao Tzu*

To my children

1

S he wrapped her fingers around the heavy white mug, hoping that the heat would transfer onto her goose-bumped arms. A quick shiver ran down her back from the forced cool air but also from nerves. The sound of Scott Mackenzie's "If You're Going to San Francisco" melded together with the sizzle of the grill, the clatter of dishes being cleared away, and the hum of voices. *San Francisco?*

Rory swiveled the padded stool back and forth and thought that for the first time in her life, after forty-two years, she was free to go to San Francisco or any place else that came to mind. But then a knot tightened in her stomach. Could she do it? Could she really leave?

She was filled with a nagging question: What *did* she want?

"You want some more?"

A uniformed waitress stood in front of her holding a pot of coffee over her half-empty cup. Rory smiled and said, "No-thanks. I'm fine." The waitress nodded and went down the line, refilling the other patrons' mugs. The smell of grease hung in the air, and Rory wanted to shout out to her, *I'm not fine; help me!*

A dark-haired guy with tattooed arms two stools down in a khaki work shirt with a patch that said All-Pro Plumbing was eating a cheeseburger. He glanced over at Rory, and she wondered if he heard the shouting in her head. But then he looked away, wiping ketchup off his chin. Next to the plumber was an old man in a suit, reading the paper. Rory pictured him getting dressed each morning, putting on his tie with nowhere to go but the diner each day. She felt his loneliness, his need for purpose.

Why had she stopped at the diner? Having driven less than ten miles out of town, she knew a part of her was stalling from making her escape. That was what it felt like: she was escaping.

She placed a five-dollar bill on the counter, slipped off the stool, and walked through the diner, wishing she was invisible. Her reflection in the glass door—tanned, lean body clad in cut-off jeans and a white tank top—glared back at her. Everywhere she went people noticed her, but not for who she was inside. All they saw was her physical beauty. And she worried sometimes that there was nothing else. She was just an empty shell.

She pushed open the door, and the hot desert air enveloped her like a blanket. Removing the sunglasses from the top of her head, she glanced around the dust-covered blacktop of the parking lot, assaulted by the smell of asphalt. Everything in Arizona seemed to be covered in a film of dust, as if the land was constantly trying to reclaim itself from humanity's invasion. The urgency she had felt this morning rose again like a stone in her throat, constricting her breath, and she wondered what was next.

The late-August sun glinted off the chrome bumper on her 1965 Ford Falcon station wagon, a gift on her fortieth birthday from her brother, a mechanic, whose passion was restoring old cars in his spare time. It had a rebuilt 289 V8 motor, dual exhaust, and red leather seats, with white exterior paint and wood sides completely restored to their original condition. When her brother had given it to her, she had at first been surprised, then slightly hesitant: What was she going to do with an old car? But once she drove it, the car began to grow on her, and now she loved it, especially since it was all hers and hers alone.

Before getting in the car, she kicked more dust off her dark-brown hiking boots and thought about her older brother, Nick. Only eighteen-months apart, he had always been her closest friend. They had been confidants since childhood, knowing every minute detail about the other. He loved ice cream, but it had to be Breyer's vanilla. She knew the first time he'd kissed a girl—Erin O'Reilly, sixth grade, behind the elementary school. He and Rory had practiced kissing on their own arms beforehand, and he'd sworn Rory to secrecy. He knew she'd seen every *I Love Lucy* episode and that she used to dress up in their mother's high heels and act out Lucy's lines in the living room. And he knew the secrets of her past. But now the almost three thousand miles that separated them had reduced their relationship to phone calls and e-mails.

Putting the car in gear, she drove out onto the highway, still not knowing exactly where she was going other than west and away from where she had been. She rolled down the window, letting the dry desert air flow through the car. She hated air-conditioning. The radio played another oldies tune, this time the Beatles' song "We Can Work It Out." But Rory knew that wasn't always true. She'd tried so many times to make things work. A dejected feeling seeped into her bones.

As the song ended, she was reminded of her mother, an original flower child who always had the radio tuned to sixties music; she'd know what to do. Without thinking, Rory picked up her cell and then stopped. It had been over a year since her mother had died—why was that habit so hard to break? She missed her mom. When her mom had been alive and living on the East Coast, weeks had gone by where Rory hadn't spoken a word to her. But now that her mother was gone, she thought about her every day.

Her chest rose as she tried to force away the sadness pressing down on her. She needed support and thought about calling Nick, but she knew she'd only hear, "I told you so."

Her hands gripped the molded plastic of the steering wheel so tightly that her palms were sweating. Her knuckles were beyond white. This was for real; she was leaving a life and a house she had lived in for over twenty years. She glanced in the rearview mirror, catching sight of her belongings, and wondered how it was possible that after twenty-four years of marriage, all that really mattered fit in the four-by-six space in the back of her car.

She blew the breath she'd been holding through her pursed lips. A car horn blared from behind. She jumped and glanced in the mirror at the dark-blue Ford tailgating her. It looked like Derek's unmarked car. Her heart raced. Was he trying to stop her? Should she pull over? But the car whipped around her, and a stranger angrily waved his hand as he sped by.

Glancing at the speedometer, she saw she was going ten miles under the speed limit, which wasn't like her. She was known for her lead foot and had six points on her license to prove it. She pressed her boot hard on the accelerator, and the V8 engine shifted into a higher gear as she watched the red needle rise from fifty to sixty and then seventy. She wasn't going to turn back, even though a part of her wanted to.

Derek Jensen at one time had been her rock. He had stepped into her life at a time when the world she had known had been shattered beyond repair. He had helped her put the pieces back together. But somewhere along the way, things had changed. Like an eroding river bank, he had slowly chipped away little bits of her self-worth until she no longer knew who she was.

One morning several weeks ago, she had come into the kitchen to find the usual note from Derek taped to the refrigerator, written boldly in his neatly blocked print on the lined yellow Post-it, each item numbered. (1) Pick up dry cleaning, (2) Call cable guy, (3) Make deposit at bank…as if she were a child. It had always bothered her, but instead of saying anything to him, she had let it fester inside; it didn't matter—nothing mattered. She had forgotten how to feel. But ever since the death of her mother, something had awakened in her like a crack of light under a door, a tiny glimpse of how dead her own life had become. On the outside she was a master at making things appear normal—the perfect yard, perfect wife, perfect mother. She had kept busy, and there were times she had believed the act, telling herself life was good.

But over the past several months she found herself riddled with various aches and pains. One morning she woke up and all her teeth ached as if she had a million cavities. She worried she had mouth cancer, but by the next day the pain was gone. Then a week later it was her shoulder, and then her elbow. Each time she pictured a cancer growing inside. She knew it was because of her mother's cancer, and she was being irrational, but she couldn't stop herself. And then the pain settled in her back and this time it didn't go away. She had gone to see an acupuncturist, hoping he could relieve the constant pain. He had asked a battery of health questions, and then strategically placed needles all over her body. After removing them, he had made her lie on her back. He held a crystal pendant over her, starting at her head and working his way down her body. She had tried not to laugh, feeling foolish, hearing Derek's voice in her head saying things like "New Age crap" and "A sucker born every minute." But when the man had finished, he told her that her throat chakra was not well. She had asked him what that meant, was it cancer?

He had chuckled and said not the kind of cancer she was referring to. This was a cancer of the soul. And until she fixed the true problem the physical pains would continue. A part of her thought he must be a quack, her soul was just fine. It wasn't until she was gathering her things to leave that he stopped her and made her sit back down. He held her hand firmly in his and said, "All the needles in the world won't heal your spirit. You need to let your voice be heard." And it felt as if the door had been opened wide and the crack of light had become an intense sun, releasing all the bottled-up emotions she hadn't known were there. She had cried all the way home because she knew he was right.

His words had stuck with her, and that morning in the kitchen, she had stared at the note with anger rising inside. And she knew she had reached the end. Ripping the note off the fridge and crumpling it in her fist, she had thrown it across the room, expecting it to crash loudly like the cataclysmic explosion that sounded in her head, but instead it landed softly and silently on the tiled floor.

Now the Falcon whipped along the straight stretch of highway. The desert heat hovered in waves above the road. Giant saguaro cacti stood like sentinels, and she felt as if their arms were reaching toward her, giving her comfort. She no longer gripped the wheel; her hands had relaxed. Passing by a shop, she marveled at the large pots of yellow asters and brilliant red geraniums lined up in front and thought of how incongruous they looked against the desert backdrop—like forced inhabitants that didn't belong.

Was that what she was?

She remembered as a child hearing about the Iron Curtain. For nights afterward she couldn't sleep, picturing an actual curtain that trapped people inside, not letting them leave at will. Her marriage, in a way, had been her own personal iron curtain. But what had been keeping her? Had she stayed married to Derek because leaving seemed too insurmountable? Or was it because it would mean she was a failure? But then two weeks ago, her twelve-year-old yellow lab, Daphne, had died, and it had gotten harder and harder to get through the day. She had felt completely alone.

Mornings were the worst; she had time to think. Lying in bed listening to the drone of Derek's shower, she'd feel the pressing weight on her chest that her life was simply passing her by. She could die tomorrow, and what did she have to show for it? She had Jillian, the one thing she and Derek had done right. She smiled thinking about her. Jillian was in graduate school in Rhode Island, loving every minute of her life. Rory loved her daughter's independence, something Rory had instilled in her from the time she could talk. And she wondered now if she had pushed so hard for Jillian to be independent because she herself wasn't. Her whole married life had been spent keeping peace and making Derek happy, and somewhere along the way, she had forgotten what made her happy.

Last Tuesday had been no different from any other Tuesday or Wednesday or Thursday, but something had changed. She felt as if she was an outsider looking in, watching the scene from a stage, and she didn't like what she saw.

Derek had finished a case the night before, not getting home until one in the morning. But he had still woken at dawn with his usual morning routine: shower, shave, dress. Rory had been seated at the kitchen table, still in her pajamas and doing her daily crossword puzzle, when Derek had come into the kitchen dressed in a dark-gray suit and navy-blue tie, his blond hair, now peppered with gray at the temples, neatly combed back. The aroma of Drakkar Noir drifted over. She noticed the perfect crease in his trouser, and it made her want to scream. He was fastidious about his clothes. Sometimes she would imagine going into his closet and rearranging all his suits or balling up his shirts, thinking he was too orderly, too regimented, but then she would think maybe it was her. Maybe she was the one who wasn't right.

Pouring his coffee into his travel mug, he asked, "Doing your little puzzle?"

She hated the way he demeaned everything she did. *Little* puzzle. Just that one word said it all. She didn't respond.

He went on to tell her that his bicycle was ready to be picked up at the shop. He had a Labor Day tournament in ten days. She watched him screw the lid onto his travel mug, wanting to say, "Get your own damn bike," but she didn't. She had become a pro at biting her tongue. She was his personal assistant, not his equal, not his soul mate, just someone to run errands, schedule appointments, and keep things running smoothly.

He came over to the table and picked up the section of the paper that was folded in half with inked circles around several job-placement ads.

She knew what was coming, and she didn't want to hear it. She stared out the bay window at her roses…her favorite floribundas with names like Tuscan Sun and Marmalade Sky. She loved her garden. The overflowing pots of *Kallstroemia grandiflora* and *Agave ocahui*. They brought her peace. She hadn't wanted to tell him she was looking for a job. She had wanted to wait until she had one. In the past, he had managed to talk her out of going to work.

She had only had one job outside the home her whole marriage. When Jillian had first started grade school, Rory had gotten a job as a dance instructor. For almost two years, she had taught dance and loved it, but when the owner of the studio had asked her to run the new location that was opening up, Derek had convinced her that she was needed at home, that Jilly would suffer if she wasn't there.

Now she looked him in the eye. "I'm thinking of going back to work."

Derek raised his brows, and she saw the muscles of his jaw flex. "What for?"

She shrugged. "I need something to do."

He gave a short *hah* laugh. "There's plenty for you to do. You just finished renovating the kitchen. I thought you were going to paint the den. That should keep you busy."

8

She stood, not liking the feeling of him standing over her, and headed to the coffee pot. "I want a job."

"As a…" He looked down at the paper. "Sales clerk? When have you ever sold anything?"

"There's a first time for everything." She felt the vein in her neck pound. Why had she left the paper sitting on the table?

"And a receptionist…at a hair salon?" He flicked his finger at another circle on the page. "You really want to sit at a little desk all day and make appointments for old ladies to get perms?"

"Why do you do this?"

"Do what?"

"Cut down anything I want to do."

"Come on, Rory—this is ridiculous. You don't need to work." He tossed the paper onto the table.

"I do." She pushed her shoulders back. She wasn't going to cave in this time.

"We'll discuss this tonight." He picked up his keys off the counter. "Don't forget to pick up my bike. Oh, and this weekend is the banquet. We're going to be seated with the mayor. Why don't you wear that black dress?"

She watched him walk out the kitchen door. Standing at the counter, listening to his car pull away, she felt as if his hands were around her neck, squeezing the life out of her, because she knew he would wear her down. He always did.

Then this morning, after Derek had left for work, it had been as if a force was propelling her, and she had started packing, not thinking about what she was actually doing. She had left a note taped to the fridge. The irony of it filled her with satisfaction. "I'm leaving. I'll call when I've decided where I'm going. I need time to think."

Now, the monotonous desert hills whizzed past the car window, and she felt as if her life had whizzed by with them. For the past twenty years, it had been a routine of activities: laundry, grocery shopping every Thursday, taking Derek's suits to the cleaners, running Jillian back and forth to soccer practice, gymnastics, Girl Scouts. And now, at forty-two, Rory felt as if she had just woken up, and the clock was running out. She needed to live.

Passing a barren field filled with hundreds of wind turbines slowly turning in the dry air, she watched the huge orange fireball that hung low in the sky sink closer to the horizon. Soon it would be dark. She shifted in the driver's seat, placing her left foot against the dash, relieving a cramp that was starting in her lower back.

She pulled off the Ten and headed down Route 79 toward Temecula, California. Her old friend Charlie had moved to the town several years back. She had invited Rory several times to visit, but Rory had never gotten the chance; maybe Charlie was still living there. It was as good a place as any to stop. Her limbs were aching to stretch, and her stomach was rumbling for a meal.

As she headed toward the reception desk of the Palomar Hotel, her hunger was replaced with apprehension. She'd never stayed in a hotel alone before, except for the time when she had gone to visit Jillian at college, but that had been different. Jillian had met her in the lobby, and they had hung out together until Jillian returned to her dorm. Whenever she traveled with Derek, he had always taken care of the arrangements.

She took out her credit card and handed it to the clerk. An image of Derek tracing her charges flashed through her mind. Would he do that? Would he track her down and force her to come back? She wanted to ask the clerk if she could pay cash instead, but she was too embarrassed to ask.

2

He er lids opened with the slowness of a heavy curtain being drawn back. Staring at the unfamiliar ceiling, she tried to get her bearings. She lifted her head and peered at the black hands of the analog dial of the bedside clock—eight o'clock. Her mouth felt as dry as the Arizona desert, and her head was pounding. She lay back down and covered her eyes with her arm, trying to block the sun. Temecula. She needed water but getting out of bed was more than she could process.

Last night, she had ordered a bottle of wine from the hotel bar and drunk the whole thing alone in her room. There had been too many thoughts swirling in her head, and she'd needed to drown them out.

She lay in bed a few more minutes and then rolled over and slowly sat up. Padding over to the chair, she searched for some Advil in her purse and pulled out her cell. No missed calls, no voice mails. She was surprised Derek hadn't called. In the past, when they'd fought and she'd left, he would hound her with phone calls. She threw the phone back in her bag, popped three pills into her mouth, then downed the remainder of a water bottle as she headed to the bathroom.

She stood in front of the mirror, ran her fingers through her thick hair, and pulled it into a clip. Leaning forward against the antique pedestal sink, she touched the fine lines around the edges of her eyes, gently pulling back the skin by her temples. She smiled at the mirror, watching the crow's-feet deepen. She had her father's eyes, except his had been the color of the sky. Hers were an elusive color that changed like the sea—sometimes blue, sometimes green. She loved the way the lines around her father's eyes would crinkle when he smiled but seeing those lines on her own face made her feel old.

Her father had died when she was only eighteen. He had been forty-two, her age now. She felt sometimes like she'd lost her buffer zone once both her parents were gone. She was next in line.

She got dressed and ate at a small diner down the street, feeling human again. She usually wasn't a breakfast eater; at home, a cup of coffee was all she needed, but when she and Derek traveled, she loved eating breakfast out. She had ordered the works: pancakes, bacon, eggs, hash browns, and tomato juice. Now back in her room with her headache gone, and her stomach sated, she kicked off her shoes, pulled the clip out of her hair, and fell back onto the bed, closing her eyes.

Her cell rang, and she reached out to where she had tossed it across the bed after checking for the third time if Derek had called. It was Charlie. Rory had called her on the drive into Temecula, but she'd just gotten her voice mail.

She'd been worried that maybe Charlie would be upset with her. When Charlie first moved from Phoenix, Rory had vowed to stay in touch, and they had at first, exchanging e-mails and occasional phone calls, but the communications had slowly dwindled. Charlie had called a couple of times over the past year, but Rory's life had been in such turmoil that she'd never returned her calls. Now, Rory sat up on the edge of the bed when she heard Charlie's unmistakable voice on the other end, and in true Charlie fashion, there were no hard feelings. They talked for a few minutes and then arranged to meet for lunch at a winery Charlie suggested.

It was a little before noon when Rory pulled into the long, curving drive of Thorn Castle Winery. The setting reminded Rory of pictures she had seen of the French countryside. Rolling hills with rows of grapevines spanned out behind the stone building at the end of the drive. Red bougainvillea, her favorite, draped over the arches of the long breezeway as she followed the sign to Café Bordeaux. She gave the hostess her name, then walked around the gardens, taking in the beautiful scenery while she waited for Charlie.

Her sandals crunched along the pebbled path as she drank in the abundance of color: purples, blues, reds—and tried not to think of her own garden and who would tend to it. As a child, she'd learned the names of plant species from her mother, who had worked at a nursery. She ticked off the names in her head as she strolled past: Mexican heather, ranunculus, larkspur, phygelius. Water trickled from a pitcher held by a stone cherub. It echoed softly, and the scent of lavender that lined the stone steps permeated the air. She stared off in the distance to the vineyard heavy with grapes, suddenly feeling lost. Yesterday's urgency of having to get away was gone, and melancholy had taken its place. Was it because her dysfunctional marriage could no longer be hidden? She suddenly wanted to run across the lot, back to her car. Why had she come to Temecula? She wasn't on vacation, like the tourists who strolled the vineyard. She couldn't make small talk and laugh and drink wine with Charlie. Charlie knew nothing about her, because Rory had for so many years pretended her life was normal, never sharing her dark secrets.

She heard Charlie's throaty voice behind her. It was too late to run. "You really are here!" Dressed in tight jeans, an expensive-looking leather jacket, and black boots that added three inches to her perfectly-proportioned-petite frame, Charlie hurried over to Rory and gave her a giant hug. Her short blond curls bounced along with her personality. Rory inhaled Charlie's flowery perfume. Charlie stepped back, observing Rory. "You look fantastic as usual, girl."

Rory felt her cheeks burn, hoping it didn't show on her face that she didn't want to be here.

A few minutes later, they were seated at a wrought-iron table. "So you're getting married?" Rory asked, clutching the burgundy-colored, bound menu against her chest. Charlie had mentioned on the phone that she was flying that night to San Francisco for an engagement party her future in-laws were throwing.

"I know; can you believe it?" Charlie said. "His name is James Arthur Binghamton the *third*."

Rory laughed. Charlie always made Rory laugh, and she had forgotten how Charlie used to make Rory forget about her own life when she was with her. Charlie had enough energy for both of them.

"I think his great-grandfather was the earl of something over in England."

"He must be pretty special, considering how picky you are. You used to say you had commitment phobia. I remember—"

Their server arrived at the table with the bottle of wine Charlie had ordered, adeptly opened it with a tiny corkscrew, and then poured a small amount into Charlie's glass.

"Keep pouring—I know it's good," Charlie said, waving her hand at the server. The waitress filled both glasses and then asked them if they had had time to look at the menu. Rory was getting ready to say no when Charlie said, "We'll have two Asian salads." She looked over at Rory, patting her hand. "You'll love it. It's the best salad I've ever eaten."

Rory handed the unopened menu back to the server, amazed

14

at Charlie's assertiveness and self-confidence. She wanted to be like that. She hated feeling indecisive, wishing she didn't analyze things so much. Whether it was buying something for the house or ordering a meal, she could never make up her mind.

Charlie picked up the conversation again after the server left. "I don't know if I was a commitment-phobe. But turning thirty-eight this year did something to me." She brushed her curls away from her face. It's not just that, though; James is different. I can't imagine ever wanting to be with anyone else. I feel like we're soul mates." Charlie set her wineglass down. "I know that sounds so clichéd, but we really are made for each other, and it doesn't hurt that he's *loaded.*" Her deep, throaty laugh resonated across the table. "Seriously, though, I didn't even know he had money when I met him, and it wouldn't matter if he didn't. This is the first time I've been in a relationship where I wasn't trying to find flaws. I guess it's *true love.*" She dramatically swept her hair back off her face.

Rory smiled, but on the inside, the melancholy was creeping back. The sounds of glasses clinking and the murmur of the other voices around them suddenly intensified in Rory's head. She grabbed her wineglass with both hands to keep from squeezing her temples and screaming at everyone to shut up. She felt as if everything was closing in around her. All she could think about was the glaring reality that her marriage had been a farce, smacking her in the face as she looked across the table at Charlie. "I'm really happy for you," Rory said quickly, because she was, and she didn't want her sadness to show.

"What brings you to Temecula? You were very vague on the phone."

Rory took a sip of wine, forcing it past the lump in her throat. The wine had a clean, crisp taste. Charlie was right about it—it *was* good. She slowly rotated the stem between her fingers, staring at the pale liquid, wondering where to begin. "I left Derek." Saying the words aloud confirmed the reality of it. Her stomach fluttered with unease. The feeling surprised her. She had expected to feel free, not defeated.

"No way! You two were like the perfect couple. What happened?"

Rory made a little snorting sound. "It wasn't as perfect as you thought." Through all the times Charlie and Rory had gotten together in Phoenix, after yoga class, shopping together, or hanging out at Charlie's apartment, Rory had never talked about the problems in her marriage. She used to love hearing Charlie's amusing tales of her disastrous and sometimes comical dates. Rory hadn't wanted to change the tone by complaining about Derek. Instead she would talk about Jillian and her achievements, winning the school art show, getting accepted into Rhode Island School of Design. Charlie's joie de vivre would spill over to Rory, and she would temporarily forget how troubled things were in her marriage.

The server brought their salads to the table and refilled their wine glasses.

"Things haven't been good for a long time," Rory said. She felt her cheeks getting hot, as if she was sitting naked for the entire world to see. She hated admitting how terrible things were, and she didn't know why. What was she afraid of?

"Even back when I was in Phoenix?" Charlie tore off a piece of french bread and popped it in her mouth.

"Even then."

"Why didn't you ever say anything?" Charlie looked confused and hurt.

Rory pondered on the question, curious about the answer herself. "I guess a part of me thought if I didn't say anything to anyone, then the fairy tale was actually working." She hoped Charlie would understand.

"When did you leave?"

Rory chuckled. "Yesterday."

"Yesterday? How'd Derek take it?"

"I don't know. I haven't heard from him. I keep checking my phone." Rory told Charlie about the note she had left taped to the fridge.

"It's probably his male pride."

"Maybe. But he's got a big bike tournament this weekend; I'm sure he's focused on that."

"A tournament is more important than his wife leaving him?" Charlie's eyebrows shot up. "I'm sorry, but that's weird." She reached out and took Rory's hand. "Is there any chance of reconciling?"

"That's what I'm about to find out." Rory took a deep breath, trying to keep a smile on her tightly closed mouth, but Charlie's touch made her want to cry. She looked off toward the neatly rowed grapevines, willing away the tears. "I need some time. I've never been alone." She hated feeling fragile and exposed.

"You're not really missing anything."

Rory looked over at Charlie. "This wasn't easy. I've always felt if you make that commitment, you should try everything to make it work." Her eyes drifted to her salad, and she wondered why she felt the need to defend what she had done. Lots of marriages fell apart. But it was more than just a marriage that was broken. It was her. She was broken. And she had held herself together for so long that she was afraid of what she would find when she let go. "Sometimes no matter how hard you try, it's not enough."

Charlie held up her hand. "I know. And don't get me wrong. I know that being alone is way better than being with someone you don't really love." She furrowed her brow. "Is that what it is?"

"I've asked myself that so many times, and I don't know. I mean, after living with someone for over twenty years, it's hard to separate habit from love." Rory wanted to open up to Charlie, wanted to break down, spill her guts. Tell her that she felt battered and confused from Derek's manipulative verbal abuse over the years, that each vicious barb had sliced away at her self-esteem and, in some perverse way, had also tied her closer to Derek, making it hard for her to even think on her own. She pictured standing in the CVS trying to pick out a birthday card for Derek. That's when it would hit her the most. *To My Wonderful Husband- To The Man of My Dreams – Our Love Grows Each Year.* They never had a card for how she felt – *To The Man I Once Needed But Who Is Now My Destruction-* It was so complicated that even she didn't know how to explain it. Rory sucked in the rich, earthy air and leaned back in her chair. "Derek likes being in control."

Charlie snorted. "What man doesn't?"

"I liked it in the beginning. I was so young and naive. I didn't see him as controlling, just...I don't know...competent, experienced." Rory gazed out at the rolling hills. "It's hard to explain."

Charlie shook her head. "Well, you totally had me fooled. You seemed like you had it all together back in Phoenix. I never would've suspected there were problems."

"I had a way of making things look good on the outside. And he'd never berate me in public. It wasn't until we got home..." She looked down at her ring finger, the gold band staring back at her, and thought about all the times he'd tell her what an idiot she was for something she'd said. She twisted the band back and forth, the metal rubbing her finger. That was his favorite line. "I don't know why I put up with it. I guess I didn't notice it in the beginning. I got so used to it I didn't even hear it after a while..." She picked up her fork, but then set it down, unable to eat. Years of locked-up anger filled her belly. "He was a master at making me feel stupid." She brushed her hair behind her ear, wondering if Charlie thought she was a fool. What woman stayed in a marriage like hers? She was positive Charlie wouldn't have. "It's hard to admit I allowed someone to treat me the way he did for so many years."

"I wish I wasn't flying out tonight." Charlie squeezed Rory's hand again.

Rory smiled. "Me too."

They ate in silence for a few minutes. Rory wanted to tell Charlie how she felt as if she'd been frozen and was waking up to this new universe that she wasn't a part of. Like she'd been on the sidelines, watching a game she didn't know how to play but desperately wanted to learn. But she didn't know if Charlie, who was as independent as they came, would understand. Instead she said, "I feel like I missed out on being something."

Her eyes drifted to the trailing bougainvillea along the archway, reminding her of her mother's greenhouse, which had always been full of blooming plants. Her mother had been strong. She told Charlie about her mother's cancer coming back and how she'd stayed with Rory the last year and a half of her life. She didn't want to talk about Derek anymore. "We got so close during that period. My mom and I were never close when I was growing up. I just wish we could've had more time together."

Her mother had adored three things in her life: working with plants, politics, and Rory's father, Billy. Rory's mother had worked at a nursery and at night dabbled in local politics, eventually becoming a state representative. Billy had stayed home with the two kids and had converted the basement of their small house into a woodshop, where he would create works of art, like the intricately carved jewelry box he'd made for Rory on her tenth birthday, one of the few things she'd brought with her on her journey. "When I was a kid, I used to resent my mom's ambition, wishing she spent more time with us, but she had passion. She's a big reason I got up the courage to leave." Rory's gaze traveled back to Charlie. "She lived for her causes."

Glancing around the restaurant at the other patrons, Rory gathered strength as she thought out her words. "I used to have passion. I think I told you about my dance. I took ballet for years and then modern dance, and then…" She pushed her salad around with her fork, not wanting to bring up the darkness from the past. She thought about something her mother had said while she was staying with Rory in Phoenix: "You need to have light in your life. Just like a plant, without light, you will wither and die." She looked at Charlie. "Anyway, I guess what I'm trying to say is that I want to get that desire back that I used to have. Not the dancer part. I know I'm too old for that—but the passion about life." She smiled and straightened her shoulders. "When my mom died, I inherited some money—not a lot, but enough to help me get started on my own. I hate to say it, but I think one of the reasons I stayed was because of money. I worried about being a single parent and what that would do to Jillian."

"It sounds like you've made up your mind to end it."

"I don't know. Maybe I just need a break. Maybe things really aren't as bad as I've made them out to be. It's weird. I remember years ago, I used to wish Derek would hit me or cheat on me, something to justify me leaving. I kept telling myself things weren't as bad as they seemed." She remembered the voices in her head as she pushed the grocery cart through the aisles, telling her life was normal; life was good. She sometimes wished she would contract a serious illness because then Derek would be nice to her.

"Don't beat yourself up." Charlie reached over and touched Rory's arm.

The second glass of wine was having an effect on Rory. She felt her body relaxing, the tension slipping away along with her reticence. She heard herself saying, "I had an affair."

Charlie did a double take and dropped her fork onto her plate. She then gave Rory a devilish grin. "You really are full of surprises."

Rory felt her face redden.

"When?"

"It started about a year ago, right after my mom died. It was crazy." She wiped her mouth with the cloth napkin as she shook her head. It had been her secret, something she had loved and hated at the same time. "My brother, Nick, was in town helping me sort out my mother's things. Anyway, I took Nick to this club that played live music, and Derek stayed home." She smiled as she thought of that night. "I'll never forget the feeling I had when Ben walked onto the stage."

"A musician?" Charlie's eyes lit up.

"He was the lead guitarist in the band, and he had the most soulful blue eyes. I remember when he was singing, I felt as if he was looking straight inside my heart. I know it sounds silly, like some kind of schoolgirl with a crush, but I'm telling you something was there from the minute I saw him. I swear I thought I'd lost my mind. While the band was on break, I couldn't stop watching him from across the room. He was with a group of people at the bar, and it was like I was in a trance. I completely forgot about Nick."

"So what happened?" Charlie asked.

A breeze blew by, ruffling Rory's skirt. She adjusted her position in her seat, thinking about Charlie's question. It felt strange talking about the affair. She hadn't shared it with anyone before. "He gave me his number."

"And you called him."

"I hadn't planned on it. But I couldn't get him out of my head."

She told Charlie how a week later she had come across the piece of paper stuck in her dresser drawer. Derek had been away at a police convention, and on a whim she had gone over to the phone on the nightstand. Her heart had raced as she watched her fingers punch in the numbers. She had felt alive for the first time in a long time, but she was still ready to hang up, knowing it was wrong. Then she heard his voice, that deep, soulful drawl, and she had sat silent on the line, temporarily frozen.

They had talked for an hour, and he asked her to come to his show that night. She'd never planned on having the affair, never consciously pursued it—it had just happened. Like rising floodwaters, she had gotten swept away before realizing it was too late to turn back.

"So why did you break it off?" Charlie refilled their wineglasses.

Rory brushed her hair behind her ear. "We'd been seeing each other for six months, and each time I told myself it would be the last. I didn't want to believe I was actually having an affair. I had become one of the people I used to hate. I never understood how someone could cheat. Why not just leave if you're that unhappy?" She felt her cheeks burn. "Derek was the only man I'd ever been with. I never dated in high school. I was too engrossed in dance and..." Her voice trailed off, pushing back the dark thoughts from the past and envisioning the day she had left Ben.

She had replayed the day so many times, like rewinding a scene in a movie over and over until it was indelibly etched in her mind. Sometimes she would change the ending: Ben wouldn't walk away, or she went off with him, or they continued with what they'd had, but she knew that wouldn't have lasted. They both had wanted more. She would never forget the date: March 16, her forty-second birthday and the anniversary of her father's death. They were meeting for lunch at a restaurant. She'd told Derek she was treating herself to a day at the spa. She'd gotten good at lying to him, and she hated herself each time she did it, but Ben was like a powerful drug that she couldn't let go.

Ben had already been seated at the small table on the high balcony of their favorite restaurant that overlooked the city with Camelback Mountain in the distance. Her doubts and fears about the affair had slipped away the minute she had seen him. He had stood up and kissed her as she approached, and she had been filled with the familiar rush of ecstasy, but it was overshadowed by her sense that Ben had something on his mind. He'd sounded cryptic on the phone, and she'd been unable to shake the nagging feeling that there was something he wanted to tell her.

"Happy birthday." His blue eyes had a glint of something, like a schoolboy ready to pull a prank.

"Now I know something's up. I can see it in your eyes." She had given him an inquisitive squint.

The waiter had come over with a bottle of champagne and showed it to Ben, who nodded with approval. Rory watched as he popped the cork and filled the tall glasses with the pale-golden liquid that fizzled and smoked. Ben held his glass up. "To the most beautiful woman I've ever known."

Rory had felt her cheeks burn. She loved the way Ben talked to her, but at the same time, she had wondered if he really meant what he said. She hated that she couldn't shake the cynical side of her. Was it because she'd been around Derek too long? And then he had said it: the sentence that had brought their whole relationship to a screeching halt. The words that had ripped open the box of the safe cocoon where just the two of them existed.

"I want you to go with me on tour."

Rory had felt her shoulders sag with the weight of his words, and she didn't know how to respond.

"I know it's sudden. But I want you in my life. All the time."

She had sat stunned. She'd known about the tour. He was going to be gone for six weeks. But she hadn't wanted to think about it.

Each time she was with Ben, it had been like an encapsulated moment in time with no past and no future. But now he was asking her to go with him. To step out of the box. Make what they were doing real. She was having difficulty breathing. She had looked out at the distant mountain, searching for an answer. She wasn't ready for this. What would Jillian think? And Derek? Her house, her life—was she ready to leave it all?

Now shifting her gaze from the vineyard, she glanced over at Charlie, wanting to tell her that she had broken it off because she had been scared. "You probably think this sounds stupid, but all I could think about was that I was a mother, a wife. I wasn't someone who just took off with a guy in a band and traveled around."

"Have you thought about looking him up now?"

Rory gave a sheepish grin. "You don't know how many times I picked up my phone. Ben awakened something in me. I used to tell him about my dreams of becoming a member of the Alvin Ailey Dance Theatre, and he didn't laugh at me. Instead he encouraged me, told me never to give up on my dreams. He gave me hope to dream again, to find something that brings me joy."

"Where do you think he is now?"

"I don't have a clue." Rory pushed her empty salad bowl away and leaned back in her chair. "But that's not what I need. Right now I want to figure out if I can be on my own without Derek, without any man." She gazed across the restaurant, her eyes settling on a woman seated alone. "I guess I'm just afraid."

"Of what?"

"Not ever finding out who I am."

3

Driving north on the 101 with Temecula in her rearview mirror, she remembered a trip she, Derek, and Jillian had taken years before to Yosemite National Park. She had been in awe of the scenery: the giant sequoias, the spectacular waterfalls, and the rock formations. Derek had gotten her a Nikon camera with a wide-angle and telephoto lens for her birthday that year, knowing how much she loved taking pictures.

She thought about their den filled with photos, Jillian as a small child, pictures of mesas striated in reds and browns. Giant cacti. She had left them all behind except one that Derek had taken. A close-up of her and Jillian hugging each other on Mother's Day—their cheeks pressed together with smiles on their faces. Every time she saw Jillian's effervescent blue eyes and long platinum-blond hair it filled her with joy.

The wind whipped into the car window, and Rory felt a bubble of excitement swell inside, loving the spontaneity of being able to go anywhere without a schedule. Derek was schedule oriented. Even if they were just taking a weekend drive to the mountains, he had the whole trip planned to the minute. Her old adventurous spirit was rising to the surface; it reminded her of the feeling she used to have with her dad, who had been an eternal child at heart. Like the time when she was seven and her dad had woken her before dawn so they could climb out her dormer bedroom window onto the roof to fly their homemade wooden airplanes just as the sun was rising. Or the time he'd told Nick and her that they had ten minutes to pack a bag with some clothes, not telling them where they were going. She remembered the three of them riding in the front seat of his pickup with the cassette player turned up full blast, singing at the top of their lungs. They had driven for hours and ended up in the Appalachian Mountains. After driving up a steep, winding road, he had pulled the truck over, and led them to a spot that overlooked a magnificent view of the valley. Rory remembered feeling in awe as she gazed at the blanket of speckled gold, red, and amber foliage.

Now she heard something. A knocking sound. Was it coming from the engine? Her stomach clenched, and her first thought was Derek—he could fix anything. She knew nothing about cars. Why hadn't she paid attention as a kid when her brother was tinkering with the cars in their garage? She leaned her head out the window. The knocking had stopped. Maybe it hadn't been her car after all.

The white pavement flew by under the tires as she kept pace in the fast lane, passing cars that went too slowly, always on the lookout for radar traps. She didn't have to drive fast; she wasn't in a hurry. But it kept her alert and focused. Her hair, blown loose from the large clip, fanned around her face, and she cranked the handle to roll up the window.

Music from the seventies and eighties blasted through the speakers, with songs like "Lyin' Eyes," by the Eagles, and Dire Straits' "Money for Nothing."

Rory sang along slightly off key while she rocked her head with her fingers drumming the steering wheel.

The song ended, and then she heard the unmistakable beat pump out of the car's speakers: the song that she'd tried to erase from her mind. She reached for the dial to change the station, but it was too late; she was already there.

———◇◈◇———

March 9, 1989, a week before her eighteenth birthday. "The Heat Is On" sliced through the silence as she hit the play button again on the tape deck. The pounding rhythm filled the living room. This was her fifth rundown of the dance. Sweat had broken out on her forehead, and more trickled down the front of her tank top, settling between her breasts, but she wasn't giving up—she wanted it to be perfect. Her modern dance solo performance was only a week away.

There was a knock at the door. Lifting the curtain behind the couch, she spied a man with his hands pressed into his jean pockets. He stomped his heavy motorcycle boots on the porch, wearing a thin black jacket over a wife-beater undershirt, not enough clothing for the cutting March air, where the clouds were so thick it seemed as if the sun was gone forever.

There was another sharp rap on the door.

Rory had seen him once before. He had been outside talking with her dad. She tried to remember his name. Kyle? She opened the front door a crack.

"Hey, is Billy around?" His shoulders were hunched up against the cold.

"No, I'm not sure where he went." A gust of frigid air blew into the room.

"I don't really need to see him. Just came by to pick up a box he made for me. It's probably in the shop." He smiled. "Kirk Lucas. You probably don't remember me. You're Rory, right?" He shifted his weight from side to side.

"Yeah." She hesitated, and then opened the door wider, feeling bad about leaving him in the cold. "Come on in. I'll get it."

He stepped into the warm room lit by a small lamp beside the couch. "Good music."

"I was practicing my dance."

"Your dad says you're really good."

She flashed a quick smile. "Wait here; I'll be right back."

She padded barefoot down the wooden steps and looked around the cluttered workshop, sorting through various wood pieces sitting on a long table. She heard footsteps on the stairs.

"Thought I'd come down and help. I know Billy's not the most organized person. Forgot to tell you what it looked like anyway."

"I can find it." She felt suddenly uncomfortable dressed in her thin tank top and tight leggings. The basement was lit by a single bulb hanging from a wire, leaving the corners in darkness. She hit the switch on the long fluorescent light over her father's work area. It flickered on with a buzzing sound. Kirk walked over to another table along the far wall, his heavy boots clunking across the concrete floor. He rooted through an assortment of wood scraps lying about. "I guess I should've called first."

She heard his boots clunk back toward her against the muffled beat of the music from upstairs.

"Maybe it's on this shelf." He reached up right beside her. His jacket brushed her bare arm, and she flinched. She smelled his heavy musk-scented cologne. "I don't see it. Hate to have wasted a trip…" The bright florescent light cast a shadow across his face, only inches from hers. He had a glazed look in his eyes, and Rory wondered if he was high on something.

She didn't like the smile on his face and the way he was looking at her. "You should come back when my dad is home." Rory waited for him to move.

"After you." He gestured for her to pass.

She headed toward the stairs, wanting to break into a run, not

28

liking the trapped feeling of the basement. Once she was back in the living room, the blood that had been pumping in her neck settled back down.

"Tell Billy I'll be back." Kirk headed over to the front door.

When it closed behind him, she restarted the song, but didn't feel like practicing anymore. She headed down the hall to her bedroom instead. Standing in front of the large round mirror above the vanity, she studied her reflection. At five feet seven, she wished she still had her willowy frame from childhood. She hated her breasts and wore flattening sports bras, trying to cover them up, feeling they just got in the way when she danced.

She was in her senior year in high school, and her mother had been hounding her to look at colleges, but all she wanted to do when she graduated was head off to New York. Her dance instructor, Ms. Petrova, had been encouraging her, telling her she had a gift, a natural talent that no amount of instruction could teach.

The music from the living room drifted down the hall. She knew she needed to practice, but her eyes settled on the photo taped to the mirror of her father and her after her last performance. With a bouquet of yellow roses in one arm and the other one around her dad, she smiled into the camera. She traced her finger over the huge grin on her father's face, his blond hair pulled back in a ponytail, his chest puffed out with pride. At her performances, she always knew where her father was seated in the audience because she could hear his distinctive whistle after her dance, and she would look out into the crowd to see him giving her a standing ovation. Her dad was her biggest fan, telling her she would be a star someday.

He had filled her with dreams since she was a small child, like telling her he'd take her to Mount Rushmore, where she could climb the rocks and sit on Teddy Roosevelt's nose. And then her mother would bring reality to the situation, telling her father he shouldn't get Rory's hopes up when he knew full well that it wasn't true. But Rory adored her dad. He sparked something magical inside her.

Fiddling with a necklace on her vanity, trying to get a knot out of the chain, she felt a movement behind her and looked up.

Kirk Lucas's reflection was in the mirror.

She screamed and jumped out of her seat, knocking over the small vanity chair. She tried to run from the room, but Kirk grabbed her arm and pulled her back with a guttural laugh. "I told you I didn't want to waste a trip. Couldn't stop thinking about you all sweaty in here, dancing." She turned her face away, struggling to break free from his grasp. "I saw the way you were looking at me. I know what you want." His fingers dug into her flesh, and he grabbed her face with his other hand and kissed her hard on the mouth. His saliva against her lips and the smell of stale cigarettes made her stomach turn, and she tried to push him away, but he overpowered her.

She kicked at him, which just pumped him up even more. He made a noise that didn't sound human. His dilated pupils made him look crazed as he swung her around like a rag doll and threw her against the vanity, knocking perfume bottles and pictures across the room. He bent her backward, groping at her breasts. She grabbed his hair, yanking out a handful, her legs still kicking wildly.

"You like it rough, huh?" Spittle flew out of his mouth and landed on her cheek.

He ripped her tank top off and then her bra. She tried to cover her chest, but he grabbed her arm and bit her nipple. She screamed as he slammed her against the closet door, her forehead hitting the doorjamb. A shooting pain sliced through her head.

Reaching with one hand, he tore her leggings away as if they were made of tissue paper. A warm liquid ran down her face and mixed with her tears; she knew she was bleeding. He pushed her back at arm's length and stared at her body. Wearing only a pair of white lace underpants, she stared up at the crystal light fixture, concentrating on the geometric patterns cast on the ceiling by the delicate etchings in the glass, unable to witness what was happening. She felt him rip the last of her clothing off as fear filled every pore of her body.

He let go of her for an instant. That second of freedom, when she realized his hands were not holding her, she lunged forward, striking out with her arms and legs, trying to get past him, but he quickly slammed her back against the wall and then slapped her hard across her face. Her cheek stung like it was on fire, and she let out a scream that echoed from the core of her body, cutting through the air like a machete.

Then from nowhere she saw Nick, leaping like a cougar onto Kirk's back, yanking him away. Thrown off guard temporarily, Kirk came back fighting. He swung at Nick, his fist connecting with Nick's jaw. Nick staggered backward but then lunged forward again, grabbing Kirk's shoulders and throwing him to the ground. But Kirk immediately sprang up and began pummeling Nick in the head. Grunting, animalistic sounds came from both men.

Rory screamed and ran over to the bed, hunched up in a ball.

Nick got in a few punches of his own, as the two of them slammed backward into the vanity, which gave way under the impact and came crashing to the floor. The two scrambled to their feet, and Kirk grabbed hold of Nick's throat. Rory saw the veins popping on the side of Nick's temple. Kirk was going to kill him. Her body convulsed with fear as she frantically searched the room for some kind of weapon. Then something whipped through the air, smashing against the back of Kirk's head, and his body slumped to the floor.

It was her father, winter coat still on, a lacrosse stick in his hand, breathing heavily over Kirk's motionless body.

Nick stood by the broken vanity with blood streaming from his lip. He wiped it away and said, "Is he dead?" His words cracked the silence. Her dad nudged Kirk with his boot, and a slight moan seeped out of Kirk's mouth.

"No." Her father turned toward her, picked up the blanket that lay at the foot of the bed, and wrapped it around her. Her body shook with spasms as he brushed her face, wiping away the blood with his fingers. He asked her if she was OK, and she nodded with heaving sobs. He whispered, "Did he?" Rory shook her head.

Her father turned to Nick but was looking down at Kirk's body. "You've got to help me get him out of here."

"Shouldn't we call the police?"

"No!" He then added in a calmer tone, "Not right now. I don't want to put Rory through anything else. Right, Rory?" He looked over at her, and she nodded.

"What are you going to do with him?" Nick asked.

"Don't worry about that. Just help me get him in his car." Her father rooted through Kirk's pockets and pulled out his keys. "I want you to stay with Rory after I leave."

The two lifted the body up. Her father grabbed him under the arms, and Nick took his legs. Kirk moaned in protest but was too weak to resist. The two lumbered out of the bedroom, Kirk's body swaying as they turned the corner out of sight.

The week after the attack, tensions in the house were mounting. Her mother wanted to press charges against Kirk. She remembered her parents arguing in the kitchen, their voices hushed but angered, her mother insisting they contact the police and her father begging her to let it go. She never got to ask her father why he was so insistent on not going after Kirk.

It was March 16, her eighteenth birthday. Canned laughter... gunshots and tires screeching...more laughter...the low, resonant sound of a newscaster's voice. Rory lay cocooned in the afghan on the couch, while Nick sat in the recliner, flicking through channels with the remote. Nick was supposed to be back in North Carolina, where he was in mechanic's school. He'd been home for a week on break and was supposed to head back the day before, but he'd decided to stay an extra day for her birthday. Rory knew he was having a hard time dealing with the attack. They all were.

The black sky outside the window looked ominous against the warm glow of the living room lamp. Rory stared blankly at the television screen. Her English essay lay on the coffee table with only two words written on the page. She couldn't concentrate. Her mind kept replaying the nightmare from last week in her head.

How had it happened? Had she given off some kind of vibe that made Kirk come back inside? She squeezed her eyes shut, trying to shut out the image of what had almost happened. Physically she hadn't lost her virginity, but emotionally she'd lost so much more. It was as if he'd reached inside her and stripped away the lightness, the joy of life, and opened her eyes to the darkness.

And then the phone rang.

Nick got up from the recliner and headed into the kitchen. His voice was muffled, so she couldn't hear his words, but when he came back in the room, the look on his face told her the news was not good. She remembered thinking whatever it was it couldn't be worse than what she'd gone through.

But it was.

The call had been from Uncle Jimmy, her father's younger brother. Her father had fatally crashed his motorcycle into a telephone pole. None of it made sense. Her father was supposed to be on his way home; they were going to dinner for her birthday. It had to be a mistake; his motorcycle was in the garage, wasn't it? The days that followed flipped by in her mind like an old newsreel, coming through jagged and out of focus.

Now Rory pulled off the highway somewhere north of Santa Barbara, stopping for gas. Taking out her anger on the gas nozzle, she jammed it into the tank. She hadn't allowed herself to think of that day for years. She stared at the gas pump as she watched the numbers flip by quickly, wishing she could turn back the clock, wishing she had never opened the door. Leaving the gas station, she pulled back out onto the road, remembering how shattered her life had become after that phone call. Her hands gripped the steering wheel, her breathing shallow as the gray ribbon of asphalt snaked its way around the curve of the road. The fresh, salty smell of the ocean rolled in through the open car window. She needed to stop soon for the night. The next town she came to she'd find a hotel. The sun shimmered on the dark Pacific, turning the rocky hills a deep coral. She thought about pulling over to savor the view, but she'd stopped enough times already.

Images of her father's funeral flashed in her head—the claustrophobic feeling as she walked through the throng of people in the house, sitting on the bed staring at the picture of her father and her still taped to the mirror above the space where her broken vanity had once stood.

She remembered escaping to the backyard, the cold metal of the glider stinging the backs of her stockinged legs and thinking how cruel God was that her father had to die and a man like Kirk got to live.

Her family became fractured, like shards of glass that had once been whole. Her mother spent most of her time locked in her bedroom, Nick went back to North Carolina, and Rory tried to immerse herself back into her dance.

She tried for two months, pretending life was normal, but then one day in dance class, the facade cracked. She went into the empty dressing room of the studio and sat on the bench, needing a break.

She couldn't connect with the music. She had watched herself in the mirror, moving with grace, following all the steps, but it was as if her soul was a million miles away. The joy was gone.

The outward signs from her attack had disappeared, except for the scar along her hairline, but buried deep, a small voice whispered that maybe the dance was to blame for all of it. Was it the music and the way she was dressed that had made Kirk come back inside? And if she hadn't been attacked, her father would still be alive.

The police reported that her father had had a blood alcohol level over four times the limit when he crashed. He never drank like that. She knew he smoked pot, something her mother was constantly nagging him about, but he rarely drank. But after the attack, her father had changed; he had barely spoken two words to Rory that week, and she felt that just looking at her pained him so much he had to walk away. She believed he blamed himself for the attack. But it hadn't been his fault; if anything, it had been hers.

The music filtered into the dressing room, and she could hear Ms. Petrova's stern voice: "And one and two and one and…" She rose from the bench and left the World of Dance Studio, never to return.

4

Her suitcase banged along the concrete steps as she climbed her way to the second floor. She unlocked the door with her key card, maneuvering the luggage into the efficiency decorated in a red, white, and blue nautical theme, then dropped her purse on the bed, crossed the carpet, and slid open the glass door that faced the ocean, letting the sea air remove the stuffiness.

She stepped onto the balcony with the hotel menu in her hand and ordered a bottle of wine and a pizza and then sat back, ready to watch the sun set. The sky was streaked with shades of pink along the horizon, the sun partially hidden behind some low clouds. She set her cell phone on the small table, checking it one more time to see if there were any missed calls. Nothing. No calls from Derek.

She'd been gone for two days—didn't he wonder where she was? Maybe he didn't care anymore. Maybe there really was nothing left between them. A wave of sorrow washed over her. She had tried having talks with Derek about their relationship, but every time she brought up the topic, he would roll his eyes and say, "Here we go again." She had eventually given up.

The amber sun peeked out from under the cloud as it sank closer to the horizon. Seagulls dipped and soared along the beach, cawing to each other as they fought over bits of food being thrown by some children, whose parents looked on from a distance.

The scene reminded Rory of the childhood summer when her family had rented a small cottage on the beach in Ocean City, Maryland, about two and a half hours from the house where she had grown up. It was the only time she could remember a real family vacation. Two whole weeks, and the memories remained strong. She could still picture her mother and father running on the beach, laughing and splashing water on each other as she and Nick watched.

Her parents had been a unique couple. Rory loved hearing the story of how they'd eloped after graduating high school and rode cross-country from Maryland all the way to California in her mother's VW Beetle so she could start school at Berkeley. Her mother had been an only child of an affluent family, and her father had been the oldest of three from a blue-collar background. Carole's parents hadn't wanted her to marry Billy, but as her father used to put it, wild horses couldn't have kept him from her mom. Rory used to think it was the most romantic thing she'd ever heard. She loved the stories he would tell of those days in San Francisco in the midsixties. While her father did odd carpentry jobs, her mother got a degree in political science. They were like split bookends becoming one when put together. She used to picture meeting someone someday and falling in love just like her parents had: a palpable love that would withstand anything.

Her parents rarely argued, except for little things, like when her mother would come home to find the house destroyed by Nick and Rory while her father was down in the basement. But her mother never stayed mad, because her father had a way of making her smile. Rory for years had pretended her marriage was like that, but deep down she knew it never would be.

The half-eaten pizza lay on the small table, and the sun had slipped below the surface of the sea, leaving a sprinkling of stars in its place. Her eyes drifted to a couple walking hand in hand along the now quiet beach, their silhouettes lit by the sliver of moon high in the sky. Music from another balcony played softly in the background, and she found herself humming to the haunting melody of

Peter Gabriel's "In Your Eyes." She thought of Derek, of holding his hand for the first time.

The dark waters of the Pacific faded from sight, and she was standing in a kitchen searching for a glass. Whose kitchen she had no idea, just another house where the parents were out of town, a hangout for a Saturday night. It was early September 1989, six months after the attack and the death of her father. Nick was still in school in North Carolina, and her mother had been nagging her to enroll in community college or get a job. She'd barely graduated high school and had spent the summer getting high with a new group of friends, experimenting with different drugs, hoping something would take away her pain for good.

The first time she'd smoked pot had been the afternoon she'd left the dance studio. She'd run into some kids from school, and they'd asked her if she wanted to hang out. After that, everything else slipped away, and she felt she'd found the answer to her problem. But as the months passed and she sank deeper into her own personal abyss, a tiny voice had been crying out inside.

She had wandered upstairs, leaving the crowded basement full of partying teens, needing to get away. Heavy metal music blared through the speakers so loudly she could feel it reverberating in her chest. The music had stopped, but even in its absence, she could still hear the bass, pounding in her ears. And then the song "In Your Eyes" had resonated through the house. She hummed it aloud as she opened the white painted cupboard.

Feeling someone's breath on her back, she turned quickly and jumped. Not six inches from her face were two thin slits of eyes that made Rory wonder how he could even see. He teetered back and forth on his sneakers with a shit-eating grin plastered across his face.

She instinctively backed away, but he just moved closer, forcing her against the Formica counter. He touched her cheek, and fear mixed with anger swelled inside her. This wasn't happening, not again.

"You sure are pretty," he slurred.

She glanced beside her on the counter, looking for some kind of defense, anything, but her hand futilely slid along the smooth surface.

He leaned in closer, and she could smell his alcohol-laden breath, blowing hot against her face. She screamed, shoving him with all her strength, knocking him backward. A rage she hadn't even known existed had spilled out onto the hapless stranger. She began beating his chest with her fists.

"What the fuck! What's your problem?" the guy said, his hands covering his face. "Are you crazy, bitch? I just wanted to say hi." He stumbled out of the room.

That night, standing alone in the middle of the empty kitchen, she had stared down at the brightly lit checkered linoleum floor, thinking it looked surreal. A strange sensation had swept over her. Goosebumps had risen on her skin. What had just happened?

She walked back to the counter and grabbed the edge to steady herself. Looking out into the darkness through the open window over the sink, she had seen the fleeting glow of fireflies, and she was a little girl, catching fireflies in the backyard with her dad. She heard a siren off in the distance. Was that the last sound her father had heard on the side of the road?

The adrenaline that, seconds before, had been pumping through her veins drained away, and she crumbled to the floor, her knees curled to her chest. She buried her head in her hands and sobbed. She had been fighting off a feeling of despair all day, and the memory of her father was the proverbial last card that toppled down the house.

She rocked back and forth as a voice from the deep recesses

of her mind silently chanted in her head, *Please, dear Lord, help me…
please, dear Lord, help me,* over and over again.

"Are you OK?"

She glanced up, swiping away her tears, to see a guy dressed in
jeans and a button-down shirt with short, cropped blond hair. His
military-style black boots loomed before her.

"You need help?" His voice sounded concerned.

She shook her head, but then it dawned on her—hadn't she just
been begging for help? An unexpected smile came to her lips. "I'm
OK."

He extended his hand to help her up, and without knowing why,
she grabbed hold, noticing how the blond hairs on the back of his
hand contrasted sharply with his tanned skin. His palm was slightly
rough but warm and dry, reminding her of her father's hands.

"You sure you're all right?" he asked, once she was standing.

"I don't know."

He pulled a chair out from the bleached oak table in the center
of the room and got her a glass of water. He introduced himself as
Derek Jensen and asked what her name was.

"You wanna talk about it?" he said after setting her drink on the
table.

She turned the glass around in her hand, staring at the blue flowers etched on the sides, and thought, yeah, she did want to talk about
it, but she wouldn't know where to start. Her thoughts were jumbled
in her head. She hated her life but didn't know how to change it. She
had been on a destructive path for the past few months, and she
wanted off.

Her eyes drifted to the magnetic frames on the white refrigerator across the room. Smiling faces. A happy family. Something she
no longer had. In just a few months, her family had become splin-
tered, her brother rarely came home and her mother, even though

she tried connecting with Rory, and begged her to go to counseling, spent most of her time at work. She stared at the blond stranger sitting across the table; she liked his smile, his strong build.

She wanted to tell him how she'd had dreams of dancing in New York. She had been the star pupil in Ms. Petrova's dance studio. She wanted to scream out that it had all been ripped away—dance no longer filled her with passion. She felt her heart was just an empty shell beating in her chest.

But instead she had asked him questions. Why was he at the party? Where was he from? How old was he? She liked listening to him talk. He was originally from Maryland. He was twenty-three, and he'd stopped by looking for an old friend who lived here. She discovered he'd spent two years in the marines before working as a police officer with the Phoenix Police Department. And then he had taken a leave of absence to help his father, who was recovering from heart surgery. He had been a man in her eyes, so different from the boys her own age. And there was something about him that had made her feel safe, like a sturdy rock in a sea of quicksand.

Now sitting on the balcony of the Avila hotel, she realized that the music had stopped. The only sound was the rhythmic ebb and flow of the ocean tide. Her limbs felt as heavy as the wet sand below. Why was sitting in a car all day so tiring? But it wasn't just tiredness; part of it was the melancholy that had settled in her chest. She owed Derek a lot—he'd pulled her out of her emotional wreckage. He'd gotten her off drugs, made her laugh again. Then after three months of dating, she'd gotten pregnant. Her mother had wanted her to give the baby up for adoption, but Rory wouldn't listen. She had felt the baby would bring her happiness again.

She took a deep breath of the salty, kelp-laden air, wondering if she would have stayed with Derek if she hadn't gotten pregnant. But Jillian had been the thread that kept them together. She knew

Derek adored Jillian as much as she did. And then, in what seemed like a heartbeat, Jillian had left for college, and it was just the two of them. And before she'd even had a chance to adjust, her mother had been diagnosed with breast cancer.

She'd flown to Maryland to be with her mother when she had the mastectomy. She'd stayed with Nick and his wife, Cass. And that was when it hit her that her marriage wasn't working. Sitting in Nick and Cass's kitchen and watching the two of them together made Rory realize what a relationship should really be like. They idolized each other, respected each other, finished each other's sentences.

When she'd flown back home after staying for two weeks, she thought about each little barb that Derek had thrown at her. She remembered the first one that had stung the worst. They had been married for about two years, and they'd gone out and had too much to drink. When they got home, Rory had felt nauseous and wanted to go to bed, but Derek had been feeling amorous and wasn't taking no for an answer, thinking he could change her mind. He kept groping her until eventually Rory had sat up in bed and screamed at him to stop. He looked shocked, not realizing how serious her words had been. She had never told him about the attack with Kirk Lucas. In the beginning, she hadn't told him because she couldn't bring herself to even form the words—it was too painful—and as time passed, there never seemed to be the right time. But that night she felt she needed to explain why his advances had upset her so much. His reaction wasn't what she'd expected, though. His only words were, "It takes two to tango," and he had stormed out of the room. She remembered the pain she had felt, like a knife in her heart.

For several days, the words festered, even though he had apologized the next morning and told her that if she ever wanted to talk about it, he'd listen. But it was too late. She tried convincing herself he hadn't said anything worse than what she had thought years ago right after the attack. That she had somehow brought it on. But she knew that wasn't true, and to hear it from Derek was like he'd pitted her heart with rust, and no matter how hard she tried to paint over the words, they slowly ate away at her love for him and, strangely, they ate away at her self-esteem as well.

Over the years, the barbs kept coming, each one another pit to her heart. She told him she wanted the two of them to go to counseling, but he told her that seeing a shrink could jeopardize his career. She argued that a marriage counselor wasn't a shrink, but he wouldn't listen.

And then her mother's cancer came back and spread to her liver; the doctors said it was inoperable. And to Rory's surprise, her mother called her saying she wanted to come to Phoenix and live with Rory. It filled Rory's heart with love that her mother wanted to be with her. For two years, Rory devoted her life to caring for her mother. During that time, Derek was rarely around, leaving early and getting breakfast on his way into the station and coming home late, sometimes after Rory was in bed. And then the cancer finally won.

Now she stood up from the plastic chair on the balcony feeling her brain shutting down. She hesitated with her hand on the glass door. She wanted to leave it open to hear the waves, but leaving it open made her feel exposed. If Derek had been with her, she wouldn't have given it a thought. The heavy glass door swooshed along the track, silencing the room.

5

She had the beach to herself. The temperature was slightly chilly, but it felt good as she ran along the sand, the fresh air clearing her head. Having woken early, she had made coffee in her room and then headed out for a run. Normally she would have lingered in bed, never having been an early riser, but her muscles were craving exercise. She thought how opposite she and Derek were in so many things. Even on his days off, he'd jump out of bed at first light ready to face the day with gusto. He always washed and dressed before leaving the bedroom; she could stay in her pajamas all day if she wasn't going out. She used to beg him to stay in bed on Sunday mornings and listen to the birds sing outside the open window, but even when he did, she could feel his energy pulling away.

She ran along the water's edge where the sand was hard packed, jumping over large strands of washed-up seaweed that looked like octopus legs. Dodging the tide as it rolled up onto the beach, she felt her tank top clinging to the sweat between her shoulder blades. She loved to run; it was like therapy to her. It helped her think.

As she was finishing, a dog scurried up to her, jumping by her side. Rory stopped running and sucked in air, laughing as the little dog did back flips, trying to get her attention.

About twenty yards away, she spied an elderly man sitting on a bench facing the ocean near the small boardwalk that divided the beach from the shops. He waved to her with a leash in his hand.

As she approached, the old man called out, "She's a fickle little thing. I think she would leave me in a heartbeat if she could find a woman to take her."

"A woman?"

"My wife's dog. She passed away last year, and Mixie here has been searching for her replacement. She's just biding her time with me until she finds the right one."

"She's adorable." Rory brushed strands of hair from her face, cupping her hands over her eyes to block out the sun that had risen over the buildings along the boardwalk. "What kind of dog is she?"

"God only knows—hence the name Mixie. My wife got her from a rescue about ten years ago."

Rory dance-stepped around Mixie as the dog ran between her legs, almost knocking her off balance.

"I think you better sit." The man motioned toward the other end of the bench. "Mixie won't settle until she thinks you're going to stay."

She wiped the sweat off her brow with the back of her hand and inhaled the sea air, looking out toward the white foam of the crashing waves. "It's so beautiful. Do you live here?"

"My wife and I moved to Avila about eight years ago. She always wanted to live by the ocean."

His wistful tone told Rory he was still grieving. "Was your wife sick for long?" Her thoughts were of her mother toward the end, lying under multiple covers that never seemed to make her warm enough.

"One minute she was playing canasta, and the next her heart gave out." He paused.

"That must've been a shock."

"The hardest thing I've ever experienced." His eyes began to water. He looked kind, Rory thought, with thinning white hair and laugh lines deeply etched around his eyes.

"I lost my mother a little over a year ago, but she'd been sick for quite a while…" Her words drifted off as she glanced down at Mixie lying by her feet, the way Daphne used to.

"Dying is dying; no matter how someone goes, they're still gone forever," the man said. He looked out at the sea, and Rory followed his gaze to two pelicans flying just above the water. He continued, "Life isn't the same without her. I'm just going through the motions now."

Rory nodded. She heard the love in the old man's voice. She felt as if his wife was still with him, sitting beside him on the bench.

"How long have you been married?" the man asked.

She looked quizzically at him.

He pointed to her finger.

"Oh." She glanced at her hand. "Twenty-four years." More than half her life, she thought. She looked over at his hand with a gold band still on his finger. "How about you?"

"We would have celebrated our sixtieth this year."

"Wow, that's amazing. That's what I call true love."

"It was more than love."

Rory glanced at him, curious.

"You have to have respect. Young people nowadays seem to have lost all respect for one another."

Rory watched his hands as they sliced through the air.

"I'm a simple man; I don't claim to be a wise sage of any sort, but I say, if you respect each other, you can make it work."

She nodded. He made it sound so easy. She had hoped he was going to reveal the secret to a perfect marriage. She didn't know why she had expected him to have the answers; *she* surely didn't. Rory wondered why some marriages worked and some didn't. Like Nick and Cass—they'd had their ups and downs, but Rory knew they still loved each other as much as if not more than when they were first married.

"How about you and your husband?" he asked. "Are you still madly in love?"

Rory's eyes drifted down to the cigarette butts scattered in the sand by the bench, and then she watched a plastic bag blow along the beach with images of her life with Derek: the excitement of moving out west years ago; camping trips in Santa Fe; exploring the Grand Canyon; Derek teaching her to rock climb and ride horses. But then in a flash, the images flipped, and she pictured Derek yelling at her for coming home late from a book club, criticizing her because she'd forgotten to run one of his errands, or belittling her for no reason. She wondered if it brought him pleasure to knock her down.

"We're separated." She needed to say the words.

"I'm sorry to hear that."

Rory glanced behind her at the sounds of the shopkeepers setting up for the day, watching a man stack brightly colored buckets out in front of his shop. They sat for a minute in silence. And then her gaze drifted to the ocean. Specks of sunlight glistened on the water like tiny silver fish jumping about. She searched for answers. Why hadn't things worked out between her and Derek? "We had too many differences," she said, thinking out loud. She ran through the list in her head. He was organized, his sock drawer arranged by colors. His shirts hung to the right in the closet, his shoes neatly in a row. She was the opposite: shoving her clothes in the dresser, giving in to the natural order of chaos. They both loved the outdoors, but while she was content to observe it sitting on the screened porch, marveling at the intricate detail of the newly blossomed rose, he *became* the outdoors, conquering it as if it were a force to be reckoned with—riding his bike sixty miles, rock climbing to the highest summit—but if someone asked him what color the rock was he had just climbed or what kind of clouds were in the sky, he wouldn't know the answer. She cried easily, tearing up while watching a parade, at weddings, even when she sang hymns in church, especially the hymn "I Come to the Garden Alone." She had cried for almost an hour after watching the movie *Love Story.* She would even cry when she laughed. Derek rarely cried. She had caught him crying at the movie *Beaches,* although he would never admit it. It was a stifled cry where he had to get up and leave the room, clearing his throat and saying he needed a drink. He didn't like weakness, wearing his strength like armor, shielding himself from his emotions. She wore her emotions on her sleeve, displaying them like a colorful silk scarf, loose and fluid.

She was a worrier about things that might never happen, like what if her car broke down, or what if she ended up alone? He was a warrior, facing obstacles head on. If the water heater broke, he'd take it apart and fix it. He didn't dwell on problems—he solved them, and if he couldn't, he moved on. Like when the car kept cutting off for no reason. He gave it a tune-up, and when it still cut off, he took it to a mechanic, and when it still cut off, he sold it and bought a new one. She dug her running shoe into the sand. Had it bothered him that he wasn't able to fix their marriage?

She glanced over at the old man. "I guess you think I'm one of those people who didn't really try to make it work." She wondered why it mattered to her what he thought.

"Who am I to judge? I was fortunate in who I married." He smiled at Rory, his eyes crinkling at the corners. "Miriam and I were simpatico."

She watched a man jogging along the beach, the defined muscles of his back reminding her of Derek. "I wonder if you can fall out of love with someone, or is it that you never really loved them in the first place?"

"I'm afraid I don't have the answer to that one."

6

She had showered after her run and then eaten a huge breakfast of scrambled eggs, bacon, and hash browns in a small restaurant along the boardwalk, and now she had her feet up on the railing of the balcony, feeling blissfully sated. Gazing at the beach filled with people enjoying the Labor Day weekend, she pictured Derek finishing up his bike tournament in Phoenix. She wondered if he was thinking about what she was doing. Her eyes drifted to a young girl with long blond hair, twirling in the sand with her arms spread wide as the water lapped around her ankles. Her head was thrown back, and she appeared lost in her own world. Rory was reminded of herself at that age, especially when she was dancing. Everything else had faded into the background.

But now instead of being lost in her own world, she just felt lost, and the thought of living on her own scared the hell out of her. She would need to get a job and find a place to live if she was really going to do this.

A little dog yapped along the boardwalk, and Rory recognized Mixie and Gerald, the old man from the bench. Respect—that's what Gerald had said was the key. Derek didn't respect her. She'd allowed him to erode her confidence like the shifting sands of the tide until she was no longer the person she had once been.

She used to think that *her* marriage was the only one that wasn't working. When Derek and she were out with friends or at a PTA meeting for school, she would look around at the other couples and think how happy their lives were.

Now she wondered how many of them had just appeared that way. On the outside, her life had probably appeared perfect—beautiful daughter, stucco rancher with the red-tiled roof in a neighborhood filled with families. But living with Derek had been like living with Dr. Jekyll and Mr. Hyde. Was it possible to love someone and hate him at the same time?

Now, Rory jerked, startled by the ring of her cell phone, which was lying facedown on the balcony table beside her. Her pulse quickened. Was Derek finally calling her? And if so, what was she going to say? But a smile spread across her face when she checked the screen; it was Jillian.

Rory had called Jillian when she'd first left Phoenix and told her she was taking a little vacation. She hadn't told her she'd packed all her belongings in the car. She hadn't wanted to upset Jillian, and a part of her hadn't wanted to let go of the family dream she'd held on to for so many years...the dream where Jillian moved back to Phoenix after college, got married, and had children, and they would all get together for big Sunday dinners. Derek's two sisters and his parents had moved to Phoenix years ago. And now his sisters were both married with families of their own. Over the years Rory's house had become the holiday house where everyone gathered to celebrate, and she had always pictured it would continue. But she couldn't lie to her daughter. Before the call had ended, she'd told Jillian the truth.

Now she stared out at the dark water that foamed up and crashed onto the shore, telling Jillian that she was halfway up the California coast in a town called Avila still figuring out what she was going to do. She then asked Jillian about her boyfriend, Joe. Jillian and Joe had recently gotten an apartment together. "Anything exciting going on?"

"*Well*...I wasn't going to tell you right away, but I can't keep it from you." Jillian's tone was bubbling with glee.

Rory dropped her feet from the railing in anticipation, knowing it was something big.

There was a pause on the other end of the line.

"What? *Tell me*," Rory said. She gripped the phone harder. Jillian's pregnant…she's getting married…she was transferring schools and moving back to the West Coast!

"We're moving to London in the spring."

"What?" Rory shot up out of her chair. She felt the blood draining from her head and slowly sat back down. She pictured Jillian—the dimple she'd get on the right side of her cheek when she smiled, her blond curls that hung down to her waist, her porcelain skin that revealed her emotions, turning pink when she was excited, crimson when she was embarrassed.

"A friend of mine from school has an uncle that runs a gallery over there, and he's losing his assistant administrator this spring…"

Rory's joy faded as quickly as it had come. She felt as if she'd just been tackled to the ground. She could hear Jillian's excited voice, but the words were distant, her mind focused on the word *London*. The East Coast had been hard enough to adjust to, but England! It might as well be another planet. Just seconds ago, Jillian was in high school, and the two of them were huddled together on the couch in the den, eating popcorn sprinkled with parmesan cheese while they made fun of the contestants on *The Bachelor*.

There was silence on the line. "Mom? Are you there?"

"What about school?"

"I'll continue my studies over there, at night. Mom, this is like a dream job!"

"What about Joe? *His* job?" Joe was an editor at a small publishing house.

Jillian laughed. "They have jobs in England too. He doesn't

BENDING TOWARD THE LIGHT

want me to miss this opportunity. He's incredibly supportive. Look, Mom—"

"I think it's wonderful," Rory said with forced cheerfulness. She knew how much this meant to Jillian, but she felt ripped apart inside. Her love for her daughter was so great that sometimes it hurt. She was having trouble breathing but didn't want Jillian to hear the pain in her voice. "I'm so excited for you," she said, which wasn't a lie because in a way Jillian's feelings had always felt like an extension of her own. If Jillian was sad, she was sad. When Jillian was little and would come home from school upset that another child had made fun of her, it had felt like a blow to Rory's gut as if she'd been made fun of as well. "I know this is what you've always wanted. I just never imagined it would be halfway across the world." She forced a laugh as her eyes focused on the concrete floor of the balcony, marred with black stains.

"Just think of it as a little longer plane ride," Jillian said.

Tears filled Rory's eyes. The life she'd always imagined was slipping further away. Now her future appeared before her like a blank slate.

After a few seconds, Jillian said, "I talked to Dad yesterday."

"Yeah?" Rory swiped her eye with the back of her hand.

"He's worried about you. He doesn't think you're going to make it by yourself. He says you'll be back in a couple of weeks."

"Oh, really?" She stiffened in her chair. "Is that what you think too?"

"No! I think you're a lot stronger than even you realize. I just thought you should know how he feels."

"Thanks for telling me." She had been battling in her head whether to go back, but now she felt something stir inside, a determination to prove him wrong.

"Maybe I shouldn't have said anything."

"No, I'm glad you did." So Derek didn't think she could make it on her own. No wonder he hadn't called. Her sadness morphed into anger.

———⊰●⊱———

She brushed past the meandering shoppers as she marched along the boardwalk. This was just the prod she'd needed to push her in the right direction. She pictured Derek's smug expression, waiting for her to return like a child who had threatened to run away. Not this time.

As she entered the small bookstore, a bell jingled overhead. The young clerk looked up from the book he was reading and smiled, asking if she needed help. She told him, "No, thanks," and then glanced down the aisles of books until she spotted a sign that read Travel Section. She made a beeline to the aisle.

Scanning the shelves, she picked up a book on Italy and flipped through the pages filled with beautiful pictures of the Italian countryside: old stone buildings with narrow cobblestone streets, window boxes filled with flowers. She imagined herself living in a small villa, sitting at a sidewalk café, sipping lattes with a gorgeous Italian man, but then reality set in. Who was she kidding? She'd never even gone on a vacation by herself.

She picked up another book on Northern California. Giant redwoods, jagged coastline, and pine-covered mountains stared back at her. She liked the rugged, untamed quality, so different from the desert landscape of Phoenix, but different was what she wanted.

She set the book and a map of Northern California down on the counter. The male clerk, with his spiked blond hair, tanned skin, and metal-studded lip, said, "Doing some traveling?"

"I'm going to start a new life." Her words spilled out with excitement.

Willow Bend. Her bare feet sank into the cool, wet sand as she walked along the shoreline with her sandals dangling in her hand. She thought about the town and what it would be like. After leaving the bookstore yesterday, she'd gone back to her hotel room and spread the map out on the bed. She then picked promising places from the book on Northern California and located them on the map, circling them with a pen. The first was Healdsburg, a town about an hour north of San Francisco known for its wineries; the second was Mariposa, a town near Yosemite that she remembered driving through on their trip years ago; and the third was called Willow Bend, the farthest north and about an hour from the coast.

She had stared at the circles on the map and felt they were daring her to continue with the journey, and then a sinking dread had crept over her like a fog silently floating over the water. Could she really do this? Find the person she had once been?

"Finding myself...what a cliché," she had said out loud to the empty room. Wasn't that what selfish people did—used that line as an excuse to just do whatever they wanted to do? She had tossed the map across the room and had gone out for another run on the beach, wanting to rid her mind of the uneasiness that loomed inside.

Later that night, she'd poured herself a glass of wine, picked up the map off the floor where she had thrown it along with the book, and headed out to the balcony. *No more fears*, she told herself. By the time she finished her wine, she had chosen Willow Bend. She read the description for the third time out loud from the book. "Located in redwood country, Willow Bend is a unique and diverse town, from the co-op of organic farmers that sell their produce locally and around the state to the Willow Bend Arts Council, which boasts some of the area's most talented artists. Several top-shelf wineries surround Willow Bend, which is bordered by Six Rivers National Forest, attracting hikers, campers, and tourists wanting to enjoy fishing or kayaking along the Trinity River." It had a population of less than three thousand, and Rory liked that too: a small town as opposed to a big city, where it might be too easy to remain anonymous and not meet new people. She was filled with an eagerness to start her new life.

Now the waves slowly buried her feet deeper in the sand with each pass as she stood facing the ocean, until they finally disappeared, anchoring her to the ground. She glanced down the beach at a group of teenage girls huddled in a circle, their laughter drifting with the ocean breeze. She'd never had a close-knit group of girlfriends, as Jillian had. Her life had been spent in the dance studio or with her dad in his workshop. She hadn't regretted it, but looking back, she wondered if having a close group of friends like that might have helped keep her from falling apart after the death of her father.

A wave splashed up, getting her shorts wet, and she pushed back the wistful feeling. She was starting fresh—a new town, a new life! Exhilaration washed over her. She wanted to call Derek and tell him what she was doing, but then changed her mind. She was afraid he would manipulate her into coming back. She would write him a letter instead, once she got to Willow Bend. She pulled her feet free from the heavy sand and headed back to the hotel to pack up her things.

7

A slight mist blew across the road as she passed by jagged cliffs and rocky shoreline about two hours from her destination. She had contacted a real estate agent in Willow Bend who was meeting with her the next day to look for a place to rent. She pictured herself in her own space, wondering what it would be like. Would she find an apartment or a cabin in the woods? She frowned—maybe not a cabin in the woods. She remembered the picture in the travel book of the eighteen-foot statue of Bigfoot that stood by the highway into town with the inscription that read Willow Bend, Bigfoot Capital of the Country. A chill went up her spine as she thought of being alone in a cabin late at night peering out the darkened window to spy an enormous giant standing on the other side.

OK, she told herself, *no cabins*, but she needed to feel permanence to her separation. She wasn't getting that staying in a hotel.

The almost-full moon cast a glow as she drove past the tall pines and giant redwoods that lined the main road into town. A wooden sign on the side of the road read Welcome to Willow Bend Pop. 2846, and then she saw the giant beast, looming beside the road. Rory pulled over past the statue of Bigfoot and turned on the overhead light. She grabbed the directions to the hotel she'd copied from the Internet. The pictures from the travel book of sparkling rivers and flower-filled meadows were hard to imagine in the darkness of the dense, looming pines. Things would look better in daylight, she reassured herself.

The hotel was a rustic-looking building with a few motorcycles, SUVs, and pickup trucks parked out front. A large neon sign hung on a pole by the road with a picture of the hairy monster, the red letters *Bigfoot Inn* blinking off and on. As she crossed the gravel parking lot, she kept looking over her shoulder, imagining something stepping out of the woods that surrounded the hotel.

Opening the rough-hewn oak door, she heard country music drifting from the bar next to the lobby, along with the smell of barbeque. She crossed the large braided rug and stood before the smiling desk clerk at the rustic pine counter. He told her about the accommodations and interesting things to do in Willow Bend, making her feel welcome. He then said they were serving dinner in the pub for another half hour.

She entered the dimly lit room, which smelled of wood. It was scattered with a few customers, but she felt something familiar about the place. She liked the cozy atmosphere. The warm light reflected off the reddish-stained log cabin walls lined with pictures of Bigfoot along with a large plaque titled THE LEGEND OF BIG-FOOT. Rory walked over and read about the elusive hairy beast.

Bigfoot, or Sasquatch, is a bipedal apelike creature that ranges between six to ten feet in height and weighs over five hundred pounds. Humboldt County boasts more sightings than any other county in California…

She read about the famous footage shot in 1967 by Gimlin and Patterson that captured the beast on film and how Bigfoot had remained a mystery for centuries. Was the monster real?

Her eye caught sight of a small kayak hanging from the ceiling, and then she glanced at the diverse mix of patrons around the room. A couple of middle-aged bikers were seated at a table, one bearded with an American flag do-rag on his head and the other one dressed in leather riding pants. She thought of her dad and his prized Norton motorcycle. Another table had three couples that looked to be in their late twenties, laughing and animatedly talking.

She sat down at an empty table, feeling oddly at home here. Maybe it was because there was such a varied mix of people—she felt she didn't stand out, as if she was automatically accepted to the unique group.

She spotted a man with a long blond ponytail seated at the bar, his back to her. He wore a flannel shirt with the sleeves rolled up, and he reminded Rory of her dad. He had the same sinewy build. It was uncanny how much he resembled her father. She was tempted to walk over and check out his face. She had been reminiscing about her father so much on the ride up that she thought maybe her mind was playing tricks on her.

A waitress came and took her order. While she waited for her meal, Rory's eyes kept drifting back to the man at the bar. She took out the folded photo from her wallet. The paper was worn and frayed. White creases had formed across the middle from years of folding and unfolding. She had other pictures of her father in an album, but ever since he died, she had kept this one close. The one that had been pinned to her bedroom mirror.

She ran her finger over his smiling face. After all these years, she still hadn't reconciled with feeling partly responsible for his death. She glanced back at the pony-tailed stranger, wanting to run up to him and tell him how she wished she could've turned back time and never let Kirk Lucas into the house. Men like Kirk Lucas were monsters. Her eyes wandered to the pictures of Bigfoot on the wall. Maybe she had picked Willow Bend for a reason. Maybe it was time to face the demons of her past.

She spent the next day and a half looking at possible places to stay. One place smelled like the previous owner had a cat obsession. Another would have been perfect—beautiful polished wood beams and a giant stone fireplace—but it had a price tag to match. Money had never been a worry before. When Derek's father had sold his business ten years ago, he had given each of his children a considerable sum of money. Derek had invested wisely, and along with his detective salary, they had lived comfortably. Rory knew her lifestyle would change dramatically once she was on her own because she wasn't about to ask Derek for money. She didn't want him to have any hold on her.

A year ago she had opened a savings account at a new bank and deposited her inheritance from her mother. She had told herself at the time that she was putting it there temporarily until she figured out how she wanted to invest it. But then she began to add more money into the account—fifty dollars here, twenty dollars there—telling herself it was an emergency fund. Rory had always been the one to pay the bills. Derek said he didn't have the time, but Rory felt that he saw it as one more thing he could lord over her. Periodically, he would want to see the accounts, and then he would question her about every purchase or expense. And when she suggested that he take over the bill paying, he would come back with his usual line—"I guess I have to do everything around here"—which Rory never quite understood, considering she did the shopping, the cleaning, the errands, the laundry; she even did the yard work.

Her savings had grown, but she knew how quickly it could disappear. Each place she looked at that was realistically in her budget made her miss her comfy furniture and state-of-the-art kitchen, but she assured herself she didn't need those things. This was a lesson to see how little she really did need.

She finally decided on Willow Grove Resort, a cluster of

one-, two-, and three-bedroom cottages set around a pond about five miles out of town. She chose a sparsely furnished efficiency and signed a month-to-month lease. She didn't want to be tied down.

The next day she packed her suitcase from the hotel, feeling excited that she could finally unload her belongings from the back of the Falcon, and then spent the morning shopping in town for things to make her new place livable.

Hurriedly unlocking the door with the set of keys the agent had given her, she dropped the shopping bags on the floor next to the small, scratched wooden table, the surface a roadmap of all the past residents—splotches of dark-red fingernail polish, the initials J. K. carved in one corner, dots of cream-colored paint. She rooted through the bags until she came to what she was looking for. Removing the cellophane wrapper, she shook the brightly colored tablecloth, spread it smoothly over the marks and scratches, and stood back, smiling at the transformation.

She searched for a vase in the pine cupboards but couldn't find one; improvising with a glass, she removed the tissue-wrapped bouquet of wildflowers from one of the bags and placed it in the water-filled glass. She set the makeshift vase in the center of the table. The scent of the flowers transported her to her backyard as a child—her mother's garden in full bloom, lying on the glider, looking up at the sky. *Things are going to be OK*, she thought.

Ever since she had left Phoenix, she'd had to think about where she was when she woke and reorient herself with her surroundings. She wanted so badly for this place to feel like home. She had lived in only two houses her whole life.

The memory of the old craftsman-style bungalow with the stone steps and porch on Sycamore Avenue where she had grown up brought a warm feeling. She remembered how as a child she had envied her cousin Melissa's big split-foyer home in a brand-new development, wishing she could live in a new house, but now the charm of the Sycamore house, with its curved archways and worn wood floors, brought back a nostalgic feeling.

As she threw her jacket on the single bed with the old metal frame, a pang of yearning shot through her. No longer would she be curling up with one of her books in her king-sized bed in Phoenix with the white embroidered comforter and matching shams that she had spent days picking out.

Her eyes scanned the room of the tiny cottage: a small desk and lamp, a couch that had seen better days, a nondescript coffee table, and the kitchen table, now standing out like a brightly colored daffodil in a desert landscape.

She removed a thin quilt from one of the shopping bags and unfolded it, running her hands over the intricately stitched pattern—it reminded her of Grandma Harper's house, which had been filled with her grandmother's hand-stitched quilts. She had loved staying with her grandmother, summer nights drinking iced tea in the backyard. Bedtime was the best part; her grandmother would tuck down the edges of the quilt, telling her she was snug as a bug in a rug, and then read her the Reddy Fox books.

Now she spread the quilt over the ratty plaid fabric of the sofa and tucked the edges in tightly, covering up the stains and tears along with her trepidation of living alone.

She opened the last bag and removed the two eight-by-ten framed prints she had found at a small gallery. They had caught her eye immediately; both were impressionistic landscapes with a house in the background. She loved pictures of houses, because they would conjure up stories of what was inside. They were always happy stories.

Sometimes when she was stopped at a traffic light at night, she would peer into the windows of the houses along the street, their lights on, imagining a family seated around the dinner table, laughing and recounting stories of their day. Other times, usually after she and Derek had fought, she would get in the car and drive out of town to a small house in the desert that she had unexpectedly come across one day. Something about the house had captured her heart. It wasn't fancy, but it had charm. The yard was just a brown patch of dirt, but the porch was decorated with red, yellow, and blue pots filled with succulents of all sizes, from tiny pots of silvery-leafed senecio to giant agave that almost reached the ceiling. But there was one plant that always caught her eye. It was stuck behind several other pots, and it had a long, thin trunk that curved and angled until it had made its way above the others, where it was topped with long green leaves that leaned over the porch, reaching for the sun. She loved the tenacity of that plant and she would sit in her car and picture Jillian and her living in the house, just the two of them, Jillian running in the yard with laughter.

Now she set the prints on the back of the couch, realizing she had forgotten to buy nails. She went over to the kitchen area and rummaged through the drawers. Derek's voice played in the back of her head, telling her how she was never prepared.

Anger rose up inside as she pulled things out of the drawer, throwing them on the counter in frustration, and then eventually gave up, sinking down into one of the kitchen chairs. Maybe he was right; she didn't think things through. She couldn't even hang a picture—how could she expect to live on her own? She rested her forehead in her hands. She needed to get a grip. She needed to get a job.

Yesterday when the real estate agent had taken her to see Willow Grove, the agent had asked her what kind of work she did. When Jillian was young, Rory had felt justified in saying she was a stay-at-home mom. But ever since Jillian had gone off to college, Rory had watched the other women on her street head out to work, dressed in smart business suits, and she would wish she was one of them. They had purpose, but each time she thought about stepping out into the world, she would be overtaken with fear, and she would retreat back into the security of her role as housewife. She had used Derek as an excuse, but she knew it was mostly because she doubted herself. The look on the real estate agent's face reinforced her feeling of inadequacy, when Rory had told her that, other than the brief stint as a dance teacher, she hadn't worked outside the home for more than twenty years.

Her cell phone rang from her purse, and she rooted through the large sack-like bag, filled with everything imaginable. She finally spied the phone and read the letters BRO on the caller ID.

She smiled, happy to hear from her brother. She hadn't spoken to Nick since leaving.

"Did Jillian call you?" She walked out front to the small porch and sat down on the green-painted rocker, staring out at the meadow filled with California poppy and lupine that surrounded the pond, and breathed in the rich scent of pine that permeated the air.

"What makes you think that?" Nick replied.

"Because I haven't heard from you in over a month."

"She's just worried about you." There was a pause on the line, and then Nick said, "So you finally did it."

"You don't have to sound so happy about it. Be a little more sympathetic," she mocked as she rocked slowly back and forth.

"You're just twenty-four years too late."

She laughed. "Thanks for being so supportive."

"I am! I support you completely. Where're you staying?"

"Right now I'm sitting in a rocker overlooking Six Rivers National Forest. I got a monthly lease on this place. I think I'm gonna like it here." She felt a sense of pride for having made it all the way up the coast of California on her own and finding a place to live.

These were things that most people took for granted, but in her sheltered world, they were monumental steps.

"So what's Derek have to say about all this?" Nick asked.

"I haven't heard from him."

"What?"

"I know. It's weird. Maybe he's glad. Maybe—"

"No way. Not Derek."

"I know, I know. but whatever the reason, I'm glad he hasn't. I needed time to figure things out."

"So you finally realized you're better off without him."

"Nick, stop. I know you think my marital problems were all Derek's fault, but I was as much to blame."

"Oh, come on—"

"Wait—hear me out. You've got to admit I was a mess when I met Derek." Rory wrapped a strand of hair around her finger, a nervous habit she'd had since childhood.

"I saw the way he treated you. I remember when I came home from North Carolina, he was practically living in our house, and he acted like he owned the place...like he owned you."

"Don't you think part of that was because you'd been away at school, and you weren't used to having another guy around? Anyway, my point is that my marriage wasn't as black and white as you make it out to be. This is as much about me as it is about Derek. I never allowed myself to grow."

"Because you were living with a tyrant."

"Wow, you really hate him." She knew Nick was being protective of her, and she loved that about him, but she hadn't liked feeling torn between her brother and her husband. She wished Nick had noticed the good qualities in Derek as well. Like when he used to take Jillian and her for a surprise weekend away. Derek would plan the whole trip in advance but not let them know where they were going, just what to pack. Once it had been to the Grand Canyon, where they'd rafted down the river, camping along the way.

"I'm sorry, Rory, but I think you're rationalizing Derek's behavior."

"Maybe you're right." Rory wanted to get off the subject of Derek. She knew Nick meant well, but she didn't feel like discussing it anymore. She changed the subject. "Dad's been on my mind a lot lately. The other night when I first got here, I could've sworn Dad's double was at the bar in the hotel."

"Talk about Freudian." Nick laughed.

"Very funny." She smiled as she pictured Nick's face on the other end—his curly dark-blond hair that was now mostly gray, his hands that always had a trace of motor grease on them, his smile that made Rory feel like she was a child again. She missed her big brother. He had never moved from Maryland, still living within fifteen minutes of where they had grown up. "Dad was like a kid himself," she continued. "I can't believe Mom trusted him with us. I mean, do you remember some of the things we got into, like the time we tried to wallpaper the bathroom with toothpaste and comic books, and Dad told us we were little Picassos?"

Nick laughed on the other end.

"When Mom was out here, toward the end, she did a lot of talking about Dad. I think she still missed him after all those years."

She stared out at the meadow, watching a circle of white butterflies dancing above the tall grass. Birds chattered in the pines, but all she heard was her dad's infectious laugh, remembering how he'd laugh so hard when he told a joke he could barely get to the punch line. "He was such a great guy."

"I think you put Dad on a pedestal."

"On a–?"

"Dad adored you and would've done anything for you. But he

wasn't perfect." Nick's voice had a caustic tone. "Uncle Jimmy said something the other day." Nick paused.

"What?"

"Kirk Lucas came up." There was another silence on the line before Nick continued. Rory knew he was waiting for her approval. They never talked about that day. "The reason Kirk Lucas came to the house that day was because Dad owed him money for some pot."

"I thought—"

"Why do you think Dad took it so hard? Uncle Jimmy said it ate him up, thinking he was the reason you were attacked."

"But he wasn't...I shouldn't—"

"Don't even go there. No way was it your fault. He also said..." Nick stopped.

Rory waited. "Said what?" She leaned forward, silencing the creaking rungs of the rocker. She heard Nick breathing. "Nick?"

"Forget it."

"You gotta tell me now," she said. "C'mon."

There was a pause, and she heard him inhale. "Kirk Lucas died around the same time as Dad."

"Died? How?" Rory said the words slowly. She pictured Kirk's face next to hers, his foul breath. A swell of nausea rose inside. She remembered whispered conversations between Uncle Jimmy and her mom a few weeks after her father's death. Had they known?

"He'd been beaten to death. Cops thought it was a drug deal gone bad. Uncle Jimmy kind of hinted that maybe it wasn't such a coincidence."

"What? You don't think—" An unease crept over her.

"C'mon, Rory."

"You think Dad had something to do with it?" She wrapped her arm around her middle. "What did Uncle Jimmy say?" The bright, afternoon sun shimmered on the pond with flecks of silver but an ominous feeling like a thick gray cloud had settled in her stomach.

"Nothing specific. I just got the feeling he knew something he wasn't telling me."

"Dad could never kill someone." But even as she said the words, she wondered if that was true. Had her father murdered the man who had attacked her? She suddenly felt lightheaded. Her brain didn't even know how to process it.

"Well, if he did do it, it was Dad's decision. Don't start feeling guilty about it now."

"I still don't believe Dad had it in him; he couldn't kill someone."

"I think anyone can kill if the circumstance is right," Nick replied.

She didn't agree with Nick, but then she pictured Jillian. What if someone had tried to rape her daughter—what would she do? She would want to kill him, but would she actually be able to do it? She rose from the rocker and began pacing along the wooden porch, trying to process the idea that her father had possibly beaten a man to death.

She remembered a conversation she'd had with Grandma Harper. Her grandmother had told her that her dad had showed up at her grandmother's house the night he died. She said he had looked bad and kept staring at the wall of family pictures in the kitchen. She asked him what was wrong, but he wouldn't say. He kept rubbing his hands on his pants and acting weird. She had tried to cheer him up, telling him he'd been her favorite, that he had a way of making people laugh that was special, but he had remained silent. Her grandmother said she never imagined that would be the last time she would ever see him. Now Rory wondered if his odd behavior had anything to do with Kirk's death. She stared out at the meadow, feeling a rush of emotions, remembering the pain she'd endured after her father died.

"Rory—are you—listen, I shouldn't have—"

"Grandma said she blamed herself for Dad's death. She said she wished she'd done more to make sure he was all right. And Mom said she felt *she* was to blame because she'd been so busy with her council job. Do you think maybe we all had a part in it?"

"*No*," Nick replied a little too forcefully. "No one put the pot and the alcohol in Dad's hands." Rory heard the anger and frustration in Nick's voice.

She watched a car ride by along the gravel drive that connected the cottages. It was the woman with the young boy she had met yesterday when she had come to look at the place—Marlena and her eight-year-old son, Ethan. They lived in the cottage next door. Her brain tried to focus on something normal, something concrete. She brushed away strands of hair that blew across her face, thinking it now seemed a millennium ago when she'd met them.

"Rory." She heard the concern in Nick's voice.

"Yeah?"

"You OK?"

"I don't know."

"Look. It wasn't your fault. I know you, and I know what you're thinking right now, but you've gotta stop. Dad was the one who chose to get drunk and ride his motorcycle. End of story." Nick paused before continuing, "Look, if you want to come back to Maryland for a little R&R, just say the word. I know Cass would love to have you, and now that Michael's moved out, we have an empty room just waiting for you."

Then she heard Cass's voice on the line. "We love you and miss you. And we mean it—our door is always open."

"Thanks, Cass. I'd love to, sometime." She loved her sister-in-law and wished they lived closer. Nick was right; she couldn't change the past, any of it, not her marriage and not what had happened to her father.

"Seriously, you have an open invitation, and if you want any company sitting on that porch, we can be out there in a heartbeat," Nick added.

"Thanks, Nick. I love you both." Tears welled in Rory's eyes as she realized how much they cared for her. "I'll call you next week and keep you updated on my progress." She brushed the tears away. Traveling up the coast, she had thought that she was leaving her troubles behind. The farther she'd wound around the tight mountain roads, she had hoped she was losing whatever had been dragging her down, but she had been wrong. Derek wasn't her only problem. Until she accepted the past, she would never heal.

After hanging up, she watched Marlena take groceries out of her car. She was dressed in a flowered cotton sundress and sandals, with thick black hair that hung down below the middle of her back; Rory thought she was pretty. Marlena's dark eyes, ruddy complexion, and wide cheekbones made Rory think she might be Native American. She watched her go inside, wondering what the woman's story was. Was she married? She hadn't seen a man around.

She opened the wood-framed screen door, repeating Nick's words in her head. It wasn't her fault. She needed to forgive herself and move forward. She glanced at the two framed prints propped on the couch. Nails. She'd forgotten what she had been doing when the phone rang. The kitchen counter was piled with things she had pulled from the drawers. She carefully put everything back and then pulled one drawer out a little farther as her eye caught sight of something. She laughed. Stuck in the back were several nails.

———

Later that evening at the kitchen table, she poured a glass of wine and then stared at the blank page before her. Picking up the pen, she wondered how to begin. She wrote, *Dear Derek*, and then scratched it out. It didn't feel right starting with *dear*; it felt phony. She ripped the sheet off the pad and started again. This time she wrote, *Derek*.

She tapped the pen on the paper; she had wanted to write to him ever since she'd decided to come to Willow Bend, but now she hadn't a clue what to write. She set the pen down and stared out the open window, framed by white tied-back curtains, to the meadow, the tall grasses swaying in the breeze. She watched a small fox cavort down to the edge of the pond. The scene was so different from Phoenix; she felt as if she was in another world, in limbo, not really belonging anywhere. She picked up the pen again, and this time her thoughts came spilling out onto the paper.

She finished the three-page letter and studied her erratic handwriting. She'd never had good penmanship. She remembered her high school shorthand teacher had told her she would never make it as a secretary, which at the time made her laugh, because she knew she was going to be a dancer. For most people, her handwriting was close to illegible, but she knew Derek had learned to decipher it over the years. She read it back several times, feeling that she had accomplished what she had wanted to say. She had kept the tone from sounding accusatory; she hadn't placed the blame on Derek for her decision to leave. She wanted Derek to know that she felt they were both equally at fault. Most importantly, she wanted him to know that she wasn't coming back.

Before writing the words, she hadn't consciously thought that this was the end, but seeing her thoughts on paper she realized that it was over and had been for a long time. There was no going back. She thought it strange that she didn't feel sad or upset, that she didn't miss Derek, not in the way she should. She missed her house and the familiarity of her life—working in the garden, discovering new recipes and trying them out on Derek, curling up in her favorite chair out back on the brick patio surrounded by her colorful flowers—but she didn't miss *him*. She didn't have that warm feeling deep down in her belly, like she did every time she pictured Ben Colter.

Ben. Had it been a mistake not to have gone with him on tour? Would Jillian really have thought badly of her, or was the real reason she hadn't gone with him the fear that things might not work out, and then what would she be left with? She smiled thinking of the time she and Ben had ridden a bicycle built for two. They'd driven to a small town about an hour outside of Phoenix, and Ben had spotted the bike leaning against a brick wall of an old building. He pulled the car over and jumped out. Rory had no idea what he was doing while she watched him disappear into the building. A few minutes later, he had come back out with a grin on his face and motioned for her to join him. He told her he'd asked the old man inside if he would let him borrow his bike for twenty bucks, and the man had said sure but that he would've let him ride it for free.

The two rode all around the small town, ending up on a dirt road where they pulled off and sat in the shade of a sissoo tree. The musical sound of a curve-billed thrasher high up in the tree serenaded them. The dry desert breeze blew through her hair, and Rory had wanted to capture the moment—the smells, the sounds, the feel of Ben's shoulder against her cheek.

Now she set the pen down beside her letter to Derek and wondered what town Ben was in; but then she pushed the thought aside, not wanting to go down that road.

She realized now that it hadn't been love that had been keeping her in Phoenix for so long; it had been fear. She folded the letter up, put it in an envelope, and sealed it. She wrote the address—3915 Corral Canyon Road, Phoenix, Arizona 85018—on the front, feeling strange to think that it would no longer be her address.

She pictured her garden: her roses, the terra cotta pots filled with a rainbow of colors...bright-orange, purple, and red flowers. Would Derek tend to them now? She doubted it. She stared at the address again and then looked at her hand resting on the envelope. Gazing at the ring on her finger, she slowly reached over and, with her other hand, slid the gold band off, tugging to get it over her knuckle. It felt odd; she never took the ring off, not even when she worked in the garden.

She placed the ring on the table next to the envelope, feeling lighter, as if an anchor had been lifted and she was free to sail.

She took a sip of wine and stared out the window. The sky was getting darker. She loved that dusky time of night in late summer, where everything slowed down and a cozy feeling took over, as if the world was getting tucked into bed. A firefly glowed for an instant outside the window. She smiled, feeling it was another sign, her father telling her she was on the right path.

Rory nervously wiped the granite countertop, awaiting the lunchtime crowd. The smell of cinnamon-raisin cookies, fresh out of the oven, filtered through the air. It was her second day on the job at the Willow Bend Luncheonette.

Two days before, after seeing a Help Wanted sign in the window of the small restaurant, she had told the owner, Casey, that she'd waitressed before; she just left off the fact that it had only been for a few weeks over twenty years ago—the summer after graduation, she'd worked at a small restaurant but had gotten fired when her boss caught her out back by the dumpster smoking a joint with one of the busboys. At the time, she had thought it was funny, her boss an idiot.

But Casey hired her right on the spot and told her she could start the next day. She didn't sleep well the night before, tossing and turning with apprehension mixed with excitement. And then sometime in the night, she woke from a nightmare—the vivid kind that stayed around the next day. She was hiding in a darkened, unfamiliar room as footsteps grew closer. The door opened slowly, yellow light illuminating the room, and her father, his hands covered in blood, stood in the doorway. She awoke at four thirty, drenched in sweat and unable to fall back asleep.

The next night, though, she'd slept like a log. She had been exhausted. Her work hours were six thirty in the morning to three o'clock in the afternoon. By eight o'clock, the place was packed with tourists and locals eating breakfast. She felt like she was running around in three different directions, refilling coffees, retrieving an extra toast order, and replacing a missing ketchup bottle from someone's table, in between delivering trays of food. Her station consisted of four tables, and she took turns with the other waitresses on carryout orders. The sounds of clinking silverware, plates clanging together, and the loud drone of voices had died down by ten, but by noon it had picked back up. She had only messed up two orders, forgetting to hold the bacon on one person's BLT, which hadn't seemed like much of a sandwich to her, and giving someone else the wrong side with a breakfast platter. She felt it wasn't too bad for her first day.

The luncheonette was on the corner of Pine and Poplar, the main streets in town. Willow Bend still had the charm of the old gold rush town it had once been. The downtown section consisted of five square blocks of shops and homes. And past that were two interstate highways that intersected, each bordered by pine-covered hills scattered with cabins, organic farms, wineries, and the forest.

Jam-packed with all sorts of things, from old road signs hanging on the walls to disposable rain gear that had Go Green written across the front, the Willow Bend Luncheonette was a bustling place. A chalkboard on an easel listing the day's specials stood at the entrance, and past that was a small counter area with stools and a large glass cabinet holding a variety of muffins, cookies, and scones. The rest of the space was filled with tables, a sofa, and two large overstuffed chairs for sipping organic lattes or chai tea.

Two other waitresses worked there, Astral and Mariana, both in their early twenties. Astral told Rory she was also a Reiki master and did auric readings. She offered to do one on Rory if she wanted. She then went on, telling Rory how dedicated Casey was to bettering the environment. The luncheonette boasted that it was eco-friendly; Rory wasn't quite sure what that meant.

The girls were nice, helping her out when she didn't know what to do—like how to work the temperamental espresso machine and how to mix the right amount of tinctures into the special teas. There were tinctures for indigestion and sluggishness, and even ones that boosted the blood. Rory had been afraid of accidentally putting too many drops in someone's tea, making their blood boost so much that they had a heart attack, but Mariana had assured her that they were all safe, even if someone drank the whole bottle.

At the end of the day, Astral, in her tie-dyed shirt and long skirt with dread-locked red hair, had asked Rory how long she had been waiting, and Rory gave her a puzzled look and replied, "Waiting for what?" Astral had answered, "Waiting *tables*." Rory had felt her face redden. She wondered if the girls knew that she hadn't a clue what she was doing.

Now she finished wiping the counter as the tables began filling up. "Here we go again," she mumbled to herself. "Round two." Her breath became shallow as she walked over to a group of five men recounting events from their kayak run on the river. She recited the specials to them, surprised at how normal her voice sounded, because it was quivering on the inside. She carefully wrote down their orders on the little green pad, wanting to make sure her words were legible. She wanted to do well and couldn't wait until it became routine to her. She could do this, she kept repeating in her head.

By two o'clock, it had quieted down again. She had survived another day. She was filling the salt shakers with sea salt when she saw her neighbor, Marlena, come through the door. Marlena spotted her, looking surprised. "I didn't know you worked here."

"Just started yesterday."

Marlena slid onto a stool with a smile that didn't reach her eyes. They were nearly black and had a soulful quality that was hard to read. Rory couldn't tell if it was shyness or if Marlena was just aloof, but Rory felt she was holding back. She wondered if she herself appeared that way when she first met someone. In high school, the other girls had mistaken Rory's reserved behavior for snobbery. She still had to work at it—not like Derek, who could walk into a crowded room and strike up a conversation with the first person he met.

"What can I get you?" She smiled at Marlena from behind the counter.

"An iced chai."

Rory fixed her drink and then, without really thinking, asked Marlena if she and Ethan would like to come to dinner the next night. It surprised her. Inviting people she barely knew to her house wasn't like her—that had been Derek's expertise—but being in a town alone with no family to rely on had her doing things she wouldn't normally do. There was a change in Marlena after she accepted; she looked happier. Rory was glad she had asked her.

She raced around the tiny kitchen, her eyes darting to the small round clock on the wall above the cupboard. The hands read 6:25 p.m.: five more minutes. The dinner had taken longer to prepare than she had expected, even though she had chosen a simple penne pasta with zucchini dish. In Phoenix, she would pore over cookbooks, coming up with new dishes, or sometimes she would create something of her own, but she always knew where everything was in her kitchen with the new stainless steel Thermador range and Sub-Zero fridge, and she didn't have to search for a peeler, a grater, or a colander.

The aroma of the garlic bread told her it was ready to come out of the oven. She hurriedly grabbed the hot pad, almost knocking the pasta bowl on the floor in the process.

This was more than just a dinner; this was a celebratory ritual marking her independence. She could feel pride spilling across her face as her eyes feasted on the brightly decorated table, the flames of the lit candles dancing with the pine-scented breeze. A sudden wave of nerves washed over her. Had she remembered to add the oregano? Would Marlena and Ethan like the food? Would they like her? She knew from their last conversation that Marlena was a widow who worked at a local winery and had been living here for only a month. They'd moved from Eureka, a town about an hour away on the coast.

She swiped an errant strand of hair from her face with the back of her hand. There was a knock on the door. "Come on in!" Her singsong tone masked her worries as she called out over the Jack Johnson CD playing in the background.

The wood-framed screen door squeaked on its hinges and then slammed shut. A golden light from the evening sun bathed the room as Marlena, Ethan, and his dog, Shiloh, entered. Rory's smile covered the swell of anxiety as she placed the bowl of pasta on the already set table and then wiped her sweating palms across the back of her jeans. "Have a seat." She stepped back and gestured toward the table as her words exhaled the tension building in her chest. Ethan shyly looked down at the floor, standing partially behind Marlena. He had dark hair like his mother.

"I hope you don't mind that we brought the dog. Ethan doesn't like to go anywhere without him."

"No, not at all." Rory reached down and ruffled Shiloh's fur. "My grandmother had a Border collie when I was young. They're great dogs—really smart."

"My dad says dogs shouldn't live in the house, but I think he's wrong," Ethan said softly.

Rory gave Marlena a puzzled look: Hadn't she said her husband had died?

Marlena looked over at Ethan, ignoring Rory's glance. "Ethan, I forgot the wine. Can you run back over to the cottage and get it off the table?" Ethan nodded, and then he and Shiloh ran back out, the screen door slamming behind them.

"I thought you said his father died," Rory said.

"Ethan just has trouble with his tenses; he still refers to him sometimes in the present."

"I lost my father a long time ago," Rory said. "I remember it was several years before I stopped thinking of him in the present. How old was he when his father died?"

Marlena's long, thick black hair shielded her face as she walked over toward the window that faced her cottage. "Young." Marlena paused. "He was four."

Ethan returned minutes later with the wine, and they all sat down with Shiloh curled up under the table. Rory dished up the pasta, happy to be doing something with her hands. This was the part she dreaded—small talk.

The conversation sputtered slowly into gear, with Ethan not making eye contact and Marlena responding to Rory's questions with one-word answers.

About halfway through the meal, Rory's cell rang. She excused herself and went over to her phone on the kitchen counter. Seeing the name Derek, her pulse quickened. She let it go to voice mail.

"I'm sorry; you were saying?" Rory sat back down at the table and stabbed a forkful of salad.

Marlena had been talking about her grandmother, who lived on a reservation nearby, but before she could continue, Rory's phone went off again.

"Excuse me." She went back to the counter and checked her phone. Derek again. She hadn't heard from him since she had left over a week ago. Her thumb hovered over the answer button. What if something had happened to Jillian? She punched the green square. The word "hello" pushed past the lump stuck in her throat.

"It's about *time*. I got your letter."

Her knees weakened with the force of his words. He wasn't calling about Jillian. "Can we talk about this later? This isn't really a good time."

"No, we can't talk about it later! You send me this *letter* and expect me to just accept this?"

"Derek, I'm sorry, but I can't talk right now." Her heart pounded like a warning drum, telling her to flee. Why didn't she just hang up?

"I don't give a shit! We need to talk!" He shouted so loudly into the phone that she was sure Marlena could hear him. Her whitened knuckles gripped the phone tightly against her ear with her back to the table. "Derek, I'm hanging up."

"*Don't hang up on—*" She hit the end button and then pressed the power button, shutting down her phone. Her eyes settled on the dingy-white, chipped Formica counter piled with pots and pans. Her embarrassment wrapped around her as she turned slowly back to the table. She bit her lip, trying to regain her composure. She wasn't going to allow him to talk to her like that anymore.

"I'm sorry." Rory slumped into her chair. Marlena gently touched the back of Rory's hand, which triggered tears and bottled-up emotions. Anger rose up like a cresting wave. Why did she allow Derek's words to knock her down so easily? She shook her head. "I'm sorry," she repeated. They were the only words that would come out.

Marlena handed Rory the napkin sitting by her plate, not saying anything as her hand stroked Rory's back. Rory wiped away the tears and pushed back her shoulders, sitting erect. She forced a smile, not allowing the phone call to ruin the evening.

"Well, aren't I the perfect hostess?" she said, trying to make light of it. She glanced over at Ethan, who was on to his second helping of pasta, unperturbed by it all. Rory chuckled—at least her food was a hit.

9

It was Saturday, just before nine o'clock, and Rory had the day off. The sun felt warm streaming through the car window, with not a cloud in the sky. She pulled the Falcon into the graveled lot past the brown sign that read Six Rivers National Forest—Trail Entrance. A large arrow pointed toward the parking area. Her Nikon sat on the seat next to her. Her plan was to jog for about a half hour and then come back, get her camera, and take some pictures.

Dressed in nylon running shorts and a T-shirt with the faded letters ARIZONA printed across the front, she locked her car, slipped the key into the zippered pocket on the inside of her shorts, and then headed off toward the trail, her running shoes crunching on the wood-chipped path.

It was about ten degrees cooler in the forest, with the thick canopy of pines blocking out the sun. The air smelled clean, pristine, but she could feel the effects of the higher elevation on her breathing and slowed her pace to adjust for it.

She smiled thinking of yesterday, getting her paycheck after completing her first whole week. The tip jar she'd set on the kitchen counter at the cottage was quickly filling up, and seeing her name printed across the front of the check had filled her with an overwhelming sense of accomplishment.

She followed the wide trail, studying the scenery along the way and snapping images in her mind of pictures she could take when she returned with her camera. Water trickling off moss-covered rocks, tiny purple flowers nestled at the base of a giant pine; she even spotted an eagle sitting high in a tree.

Her mind drifted as it did when she jogged, with a montage of thoughts, from buying a new pair of running shoes for work to the dream she'd had of her father's blood-stained hands to the text she had sent Derek the morning after his phone call telling him not to call again unless he could talk civilly. She reiterated that she wasn't going to change her mind about not coming back no matter how much he yelled.

She had expected a phone call right after the text, and when she didn't hear from him, she thought perhaps he'd accepted what she had written, but she didn't really believe it. She knew eventually they would have to talk, but every time she thought about it, a knot formed in her stomach. She hated confrontations. She wished they could just end it, amicably. She liked her new life and wondered why she'd been so afraid of making the move for so many years.

Her mother-in-law had called her a couple of days ago, saying she was worried about Rory, living alone. Bad things could happen when you were all alone, she'd said, in her faded German accent. She had wanted to know when Rory was coming back, assuring Rory that she and Derek could patch things up. Rory had wanted to tell her that the hole in their marriage was too big for a patch, but instead she'd said she was doing fine on her own for now and needed time to think.

She had told Marlena about the phone call last night when she'd gone there for dinner. And Marlena had laughed, saying Derek's mother was a mother bear. When Rory had given her a puzzled look, Marlena replied, "They'd do anything to protect their cub." She liked Marlena, liked her strength, her courage—seeing Marlena help Ethan with his homework and glancing around the cottage at Marlena's touches throughout the room—striped hand-woven throws in bright reds, yellows, and blues draped over the living room furniture; a large tapestry with the profile of a Native American woman hung on the wall. Turquoise, coral, and other colorful stones along with silver beads of various shapes in compartmentalized trays covered the coffee table. Marlena had told Rory that her dream was to have her own jewelry shop one day, and Rory had felt a twinge of jealousy, wishing she had something she was fervent about like that. She admired Marlena's independence, raising her son all on her own.

She had no idea how long she'd been jogging, but she guessed it had been at least a half hour, so she turned around and retraced her path back to the car. Her body felt in sync with the forest; each rhythmic beat of her sneakered foot against the cushiony pine needles made her feel as if she were one of the woodland creatures, her breath in harmony with the sounds of the forest like she belonged here.

She glanced down at her hands and was reminded of last night, when she'd slipped on one of Marlena's rings. She'd held her slender, double-jointed fingers out in front of her, comparing them to Marlena's sturdy, calloused ones. Rory had watched Marlena's hands deftly string a necklace. The slightly rough, ruddy skin of her fingers moved with precision. She had strong, capable hands, and Rory thought she was a remarkable woman, unflappable, her hands an emblem of her strength.

Now Rory held one hand out in front of her as she jogged, noticing how her fingers bent backward, and wondered what Marlena thought of *her*. She'd confessed to Marlena how she'd wanted to leave Derek when Jillian was young, but the thought of being a single parent had scared her. She had told Marlena that not being happy had never been enough of a reason to leave.

Rory smiled, thinking of Marlena's words in response: *Now is your time to find happiness.* Marlena's soft-spoken voice made Rory feel at ease, giving her a sense of hope for the future.

She'd had very few friends over the years. A wall had gone up around her, isolating her from the outside world. She had retreated into her house and immersed herself in cookbooks, gardening, and taking care of Jillian.

"Exuding love," she whispered as she jogged past the tall pines lining the path. Those had been Marlena's words to her last night when Rory had said she felt like she had nothing to offer. Marlena had told her how she had seen Rory bring Ethan out of his shell and get him to laugh, something he hadn't done in a long time. Marlena had said that Rory exuded love, and that was her gift.

Rory smiled, but inside she thought, *Exude love?* What good did that do her? Anybody could exude love. She wanted to be able to be *good* at something, to say, "I'm an artist" or "I'm a jewelry maker"— something that made her unique.

She grabbed her camera case and a water bottle off the seat and noticed that several other cars were now parked in the lot. She checked her watch—10:30 a.m. Not bad, she thought—and then re-locked her car and headed back into the forest, hoping to get some great shots, as she had done at Yosemite years ago.

With her camera case slung over her back, she breathed in the rich pine smell that seemed to emanate from everywhere. Shafts of light streamed onto the path from the break in the trees. She heard a rustling sound somewhere off the path, stopped, and looked through the tall trees. About fifteen yards in was a buck, its head down, grazing on a plant.

Rory slowly brought her camera around and focused in on the deer. Just as she got the deer sighted into her lens, he picked up his head, staring straight into the camera, his large antlers branching out wide and his dark eyes looking wary. She clicked several shots before he took off.

She continued down the trail, hoping she would catch up with the bald eagle she had spotted earlier. Finding the moss-covered rock, she took several shots, and then she followed another narrower trail she hadn't taken before, shooting hundreds of pictures, winding her way from trail to trail.

Something in the path farther down grabbed her eye: a small, furry creature with a bushy tail. She crouched down and zoomed in with her lens. She wasn't sure what it was. Larger than a squirrel but smaller than a raccoon, it had pointy ears and a cute face with black eyes that stared back at her in the lens. But just as she was about to take the shot, the creature took off down the path.

She chased after the animal, knowing she'd probably lose it but determined to get a shot. And then it stopped, glanced back at her, and took off down another path, as if beckoning her to follow. She continued running until her breath became labored, and she realized she wasn't going to catch up.

She stopped on the path with her hands on her thighs, sucking in air. Her stomach growled loudly. Sweat trickled down her sides, and her T-shirt clung to her back. The temperature had soared; it had to be in the nineties, she thought, much warmer than the travel book had said for September.

Checking her watch, she saw it was 1:05 p.m. She'd had no idea she'd been in the forest that long. It was time to head back.

She followed the small brown markers posted sporadically along the path, and after walking for what seemed forever, she realized she had no idea where she was. The markers were not very descriptive—just the name of the path was written on them. Black Arrow Trail—hadn't she been on that before? She glanced at a large boulder along the path. Wasn't that the same rock she had already passed? Her heart beat a little faster as she wiped the sweat from her forehead. She told herself to remain calm; there was no need to panic. If she just stayed on the path, she would eventually get to where she had started. Or would she?

Was this the path she'd come in on? She walked for another quarter mile and came to a fork. She hadn't a clue which way to go. Her legs were getting shaky, and now her stomach was screaming from hunger.

She sat down on a large rock and opened her water bottle, gulping down the last few swallows. The angle of sunlight that filtered through the trees cast long shadows across the path. She checked her watch—1:50 p.m.; she'd been walking for almost an hour and had no idea if she was closer to the parking lot or not. She realized she had left her cell in the car. Great.

She pulled the small pamphlet that she had picked up in town out of her pocket. It had a trail map that wasn't very detailed, and since she didn't know where she was, it was impossible to tell how to get back to where she had started. She read the blurb on the front that described the Six Rivers National Forest as having almost a million acres of land. A million acres! She made a snorting sound. "Lovely," she said out loud.

She heard a crunching sound behind her in the trees and swung around on the rock, feeling as if someone was behind her, but all she saw were trees. The dark pines suddenly took on a more sinister look. An image of Bigfoot flashed through her mind. Was it just a legend? She shook her head, chuckling. Of course it was a hoax, someone dressed in a hairy costume to fool people, but at the same time, a little chill ran up her back.

She took slow breaths in and out. There was no need to panic, she repeated in her head. She stood up and brushed off the seat of her shorts.

After another half hour and still no sight of a parking lot, she wanted to scream. She pulled at her hair in frustration, loosening strands from the band that held it back. The shadows were getting longer. What if she was out here in the dark? No one knew where she was. There was no one who would even wonder about her if she didn't come home tonight. Her legs ached, and her hands were shaking as fear replaced the hunger in her belly. She wanted to cry.

Derek was right; she was an idiot. Who would go off hiking alone in a forest and not pay attention to where they were going? Where were the other people in the cars she'd seen in the parking lot? Had they already left? The town was filled with vacationers, here to explore the area. Why weren't any of them hiking? Was this some section that everyone knew was off limits for some reason? Had she missed some sign that said CLOSED, NO WAY OUT? But she had gone in, so there had to be a way out. She wasn't making any sense.

She envisioned reporters standing in the woods, reciting to a camera, "Still no sight of the woman. Only her car…" Pulling the crumpled pamphlet out of her pocket again, she thought, maybe if she studied the angle of the sun, she could tell which way was east and west and compare it to the map, but the sky was clouding up, and a few heavy drops of rain splattered onto the path. A cool breeze blew through the trees, making her shiver. Her shoulders slumped with defeat as more drops of rain made a pattering sound onto the pamphlet.

A motor rumbled in the distance. A car? Was she getting close? Her heart pumped in her chest. She jumped up, running in the direction of the sound, and tripped her toe on a root. She hit the ground hard, and her camera case fell beside her. She dragged herself up, wiping off the wet pine needles stuck to her palms, and then quickly checked her camera. No damage. The engine sound had faded. She sank onto her haunches with fatigue. The burst of adrenaline was gone. As she put her head in her hands, the steady rain soaked through her thin T-shirt and made loud splattering sounds as it hit the dirt.

Derek flashed in her mind again. Maybe this was a sign that she shouldn't have left him. Derek never would've gotten lost in the woods. He would've paid attention or brought a GPS. All his preparations that used to drive her crazy, wishing he could be less rigid and go with the flow, didn't seem so stupid now.

She wished she was back in Arizona, sitting on her patio, admiring her garden, safe and secure. If she got out of this unscathed, she would call Derek and at least talk to him. Why had she had such a strong desire to be on her own? Birds fluttered in the trees, and something rustled and crackled in the brush, but she didn't respond.

She stared hopelessly down at her shoes, now covered in mud. She felt the weight of the enormous trees above her, making her feel like a Lilliputian in the land of the giants. Some of the trees had lived in this forest for thousands of years, and she wasn't even going to survive one day. But as the cold rain trickled down her neck, seeping inside her bra, something changed. She thought, *No I'm not going to give up. The first sign of trouble, and what do I want to do? Run back to Derek. No.* A determined feeling swelled inside her, and she thought of Marlena. Surviving on her own. She could find her way out of the woods. She tilted her head back, craning to see the tops of the trees. What would Marlena do?

She needed to think logically. There had to be a way out. She listened to the sounds of the forest. Water was running to her left. She remembered crossing a stream, so she headed toward the sound.

After crossing back over the stream, she came to another path, but before she took it, she closed her eyes and tried to visualize coming to the stream the first time. She'd come from the right. She followed that trail, checking the numerous pictures she'd taken on her camera to see if anything looked familiar. She stopped at a photo of a partially fallen pine resting against another; up ahead on the trail was a tree just like that. She flipped back through the pictures and realized she was getting close to the trailhead. Her pace quickened, and she felt a bubble of laughter rise inside. She'd done it!

She was completely drenched, but she was too elated to even notice. Half her hair had fallen out of the band, and it clung to her neck and back as she passed by the moss-covered rock. She knew where she was now.

The rain stopped as quickly as it had come, and there were glimpses of sunlight peeking through the pines. The pungent aroma of peat filled her nostrils. A motor sound roared in the distance, getting louder, and then from around the bend, a four-wheeler appeared with a green emblem on the side. A park ranger. The man slowed the vehicle down and came to a stop beside her.

"Need help?" Dressed in a gray-and-green uniform, the ranger removed his helmet and ran his fingers through his sandy-blond hair.

"No," she said with a smile. She didn't need help.

10

Rory headed back to work from the one-hour photo lab where she'd had several of her pictures printed out to hang in the cottage. She needed to get a new printer, having left the one in Phoenix behind. All she'd taken was her laptop. Passing a shop window, she noticed a flyer that read, A Night of Wine and Music—Featuring the Starlighters. Rory thought of Ben and wondered where he was now. It was around this time last year that she'd started seeing him. September 6—the date was etched in her mind. The past few nights, lying alone in bed, she had thought about him, remembering the touch of his long fingers and how they had sparked a flame in her.

She thought of their trip to Sedona, one of the only times she'd stayed overnight with Ben. Derek had gone on a weekend skeet-shooting trip with some friends. Ben and Rory had sat on Bell Rock, waiting for the sunset. The warm desert air had brushed over them as the sky turned to fire, lighting up the rocks and intensifying their deep coral color. She remembered lying back against the warm stone, listening to Ben play the guitar, his voice resonating deep into her soul.

They'd joked about the vortexes that were advertised around Sedona—a place where forces had collided not by wind or water but by a spiritual energy. Being near one supposedly strengthened a person's inner being. Ben had laughed, saying it was just a myth made up by a bunch of old hippies. But she remembered how at that moment, listening to Ben's voice along with the delicate sound of the guitar strings, she'd experienced an electrifying feeling, as if her body had been lit up from within. She hadn't told Ben, but the feeling had remained with her for the rest of the night.

Now, she thought about calling him so she could hear his voice again, but she knew she couldn't, at least not until she figured out what she was doing. Holding the pack of pictures, she thought of the photograph of Ben and his parents that hung on the wall by her bed along with a collection of other photos she'd brought with her, the close-up of her and Jillian, one of her and Nick with their arms wrapped around each other's necks when she was seven and Nick was nine, and one of Daphne as a puppy.

When she'd gotten a frame for Ben's picture and hung it next to the others, she told herself she was doing it because she liked the picture; it had an artistic charm. She'd found it on the seat of her car the day after she'd broken off their relationship. It was a picture of Ben and his parents standing in front of their family store in Arcadia, the small town in Louisiana where Ben had grown up. His parents smiled as they stood arm in arm with a twelve-year-old Ben, tall and lanky, dressed in a pair of jeans and a T-shirt.

She'd seen the photo over at Ben's apartment one afternoon and told him how cute she thought he looked and how beautiful his mother was. He'd told her about the day the photo was taken. They were moving to Shreveport, leaving the family store, which had been in the family since the early 1900s, to be run by his uncle. She was drawn to the photo, the way his smile warmed her heart, the yearning look in his eyes…she wasn't quite sure what it was. She'd asked him what it had been like, growing up in a small town.

She remembered the look on his face when he thought about the question. A melancholy smile had appeared. He told her he'd loved the freedom of being able to walk out the door on a summer's morning and not come back until dusk. He loved sneaking out onto the sofa after having been sent to bed for the night and listening through the open window to his dad playing the mandolin on the front porch; their next door neighbor playing the banjo; and his mother, Marie, singing a soft tune in her lilting soprano.

Marie Boudreaux Colter. Five months into their relationship, Ben's mother had come to Phoenix. Ben had called Rory one morning and told her he had a surprise for her. They met at a small Thai restaurant the two frequented often, partly because she loved Thai food but also because she knew Derek hated it. When she walked in, she saw an elderly woman seated next to Ben. She recognized her from the photo; she was older and grayer, but there was no mistaking her. She had the same blue eyes as Ben.

Rory had stopped at the entrance by the koi pond, the trickling waterfall making soft, splashing sounds, afraid to go any closer. Ben had jumped up and run over, leading her by the arm to introduce her to his mother. She had been furious with Ben. Why would he do this without warning her? Confusion mixed with embarrassment stirred inside her as she sat down next to Marie, wondering if Ben had mentioned to his mother that she was married. Her right index finger rubbed at the ring on her left hand from under the table. Thoughts raced in her head, imagining what the woman must think of her. Did she see her as an adulteress? Did she think she was using her son? What was Ben thinking? But after minutes of talking with Marie, listening to her singsong voice with its Cajun accent, she had forgotten why she was there.

She had learned more about Ben from that encounter than she had the whole time they'd been together. She found out he had played Little League for six years, right fielder, like Hank Aaron, his hero. His mother told her Ben knew all of Hank's stats, like breaking Babe Ruth's home run record. Rory had no idea he'd been that passionate about baseball until she heard the fervor in his voice when he defended Hank's record. She was mesmerized listening to Marie, and she barely touched her chicken satay, not even noticing the other patrons who passed by their table.

She had studied Marie, who was now a widow: her slightly arthritic fingers at one time, Rory imagined, had been beautiful. Her only adornments were the matching platinum and diamond rings she wore on her left hand, hanging loosely, held on by her enlarged knuckle. Rory fingered her gold band under the table again, wanting to slip it off.

She saw the love in Marie's eyes for her son when she told Rory how, at four, Ben knew all the words to "Blue Moon of Kentucky," a song by Bill Monroe, and had sung it in church.

Watching Marie pat Ben's arm when she talked about the first time he played the guitar, Rory thought of her own mom, wishing she'd had as close a relationship growing up as Ben had with his mother.

By the end of the lunch, Marie had invited Rory back to Louisiana, telling her she would fix her Ben's favorite dish, crawfish étouffée. Leaving the restaurant, Rory had felt happy, forgetting that she and Ben were not really a couple, but as she drove back home, depression had set in. What was she doing? Being with Marie had changed things; no longer was her relationship with Ben a secret. Before, it had been like a box of chocolates stashed under the bed that no one knew about, something that was forbidden and exciting every time she went to get more, but now it just seemed wrong, seedy. The smell of Marie's jasmine-scented perfume lingered on Rory after Marie had hugged her outside the restaurant, again urging her to come to Louisiana. She had felt like a fraud.

That night, she had sat across from Derek at their small kitchen table. They rarely used the formal dining room anymore, usually eating in the den in front of the television with Derek in his leather recliner and Rory curled up in her favorite overstuffed corduroy chair, but this night she'd set the table, even laying out the blue-and-white tablecloth her mother had given her years ago. She had dished out leftover spaghetti from the rust-colored earthenware bowl. The smell of garlic permeated the air. She had sat in silence, watching Derek chew his food and tear off a hunk of bread from the loaf in the basket, as he told her about the hundred-mile bike race he would be competing in in two weeks. She studied the lines on his face, the way his jaw muscles moved when he ate, knowing he hadn't a clue as to how she'd spent her afternoon. She listened to him talk about the new spokes he'd ordered for his bike, her mind taking in his words, but her heart was in the Thai restaurant. She had felt so alone. How had things gotten so messed up? She wished she'd never met Ben. She wished that Derek *was* Ben.

Now she flipped through the pack of pictures, not looking where she was walking, and collided with someone at the door to the luncheonette. "Sorry," she said and then noticed it was the park ranger from last Saturday. "Oh, hi…"

He tilted his head with a puzzled look. "You look…"

"The forest, after the rain."

"Ah, right. Much drier now."

Rory chuckled and then introduced herself.

He told her his name was Will.

Rory glanced at the thin gold nameplate pinned to his shirt and read the words Deputy Ranger Powers. She thought for a second and then said, "Wait a minute. Your name is Will *Powers*?"

"My parents were comedians."

"Seriously?"

He laughed as he held the door open for her. "No, but I think they got a kick out of it." He followed her into the restaurant. "They thought it would give me some kind of strength or something, but I just got ribbed in school."

Rory laughed and then went behind the counter, setting down her pack of pictures. Astral scooted past her, ringing up an order on the cash register. The sizzling sound of the food cooking on the grill mixed with the hum of voices as the lunchtime crowd filed in didn't faze Rory. She wasn't nervous anymore.

She tied her short green apron, the words Eat Local, Think Global stenciled on the pocket, around her waist.

Will slid onto a stool at the counter.

"My dad's name was William," Rory said.

"Must've been a good man. Are those from the forest?" He motioned with his head at the envelope of pictures sitting on the counter.

She nodded.

"Mind if I take a look?"

"Go ahead." She handed him the pack and then headed over to Jeremiah Danvers, her landlord at Willow Grove, a man in his early seventies with a salt-and-pepper beard that hung down to his chest. He had lived in the area his whole life. He ate at the luncheonette every day at noon, ordering the same thing, tuna salad on rye, no tomato. He had taken to sitting in Rory's section and would fill her in on the town gossip and history in between her runs back and forth from the kitchen. He loved to complain about the hippies—as he called them—that were taking over the town. Rory had figured out he was referring to the organic farmers that had moved to the area. She wondered if he knew that Casey, the owner, was one of them.

"These are good," Will said to her, holding up the thick pack of pictures as she headed past the counter with a tray of sandwiches.

"Thanks." She smiled as she delivered her tray of food to a table and then returned, set the empty tray on the counter, and wiped her hands on the apron. "I haven't had a chance to really look at them."

"You've got talent."

"I don't know about that." Rory looked down at the counter and wiped away some crumbs, surprised by the compliment. The last time anyone had told her she had talent was years ago in dance class. She'd always liked the pictures she took, but she didn't feel that they were anything special. "I think the subject matter has a lot to do with it. It's hard not to take a good picture around here."

"But you've got an eye. The arts festival is next weekend. If you go, I'll probably see you there."

Did she have an eye, or was he just flirting with her?

11

She lay in bed with her arm folded behind her head and stared at the darkened ceiling, her thoughts sifting through the day at the Willow Bend Arts Festival and her dinner with Will. Getting dressed that morning, she'd put on a touch of makeup, thinking about Will as she applied her mascara, telling herself she *wasn't* doing it because of him—she just felt like wearing makeup. He seemed like a nice guy, down to earth with a boyish charm that made her laugh.

They'd run into each other a couple of times since the day at the luncheonette, once at the drugstore in town and then again at the market. Each time, they had talked for several minutes. She found out he was eight years younger than she, but she told herself they were just friends, so what did it matter? The last thing she wanted right now was a relationship.

She'd had a good time at the festival. He'd introduced her to Carter Bennett, a local photographer. She had felt her cheeks burning when he told Carter that she had a lot of talent for taking pictures. Rory thought her work was nothing compared to the photos that hung on the burlap-covered walls of Carter's booth—a wide-angle shot of a flower, the brilliant red color jumping off the paper, and black-and-white photos of misty giant redwoods that had an Ansel Adams quality to them. He was a true artist, she thought, like her father, who'd had a way of making his wood pieces come to life, capturing the beauty of the wood and enhancing it into a work of art. She saw the same thing in Carter's work, taking the natural beauty of a flower and expanding it to another level. She felt her photos looked childish in comparison, but then she thought maybe she could improve. She had picked up a flyer about a digital photography class Carter was giving in a couple of weeks.

Now she rolled onto her side and curled her legs up as she remembered the back of Will's flannel shirt, his broad shoulders inches from her as he had studied a painting in one of the booths. Instead of admiring the scene of the ocean waves crashing on the rocky shores with thick globs of paint jutting out from the canvas, Rory had smelled the scent of Will's cologne. And it reminded her of autumn as a child, breathing in the crisp smell of dried leaves mixed with cider—then a sudden image of him in bed without a shirt flashed through her head. And it was at that instant he turned from the painting and faced her. She had quickly averted her eyes to another painting, feeling as if he'd read her thoughts. What was the matter with her? But then he'd walked her to her car and asked her if she'd like to get dinner.

He'd kept her in stitches at the restaurant, telling her amusing stories of his ranger experiences. Like the time he'd stumbled upon a group of nudists on a retreat who had picked some wild berries and broken out in hives all over their bodies. He said he couldn't get that image out of his head for days afterward. She found out he had been a forest ranger for the past ten years after graduating from Utah State University with a degree in forest management. He was raised in Utah and was from a Mormon family, but since getting the job with the Forest Service, he had been stationed in Wyoming, Montana, and California.

She said his life sounded like one big adventure, and he told her that it wasn't as glamorous as he had made it sound. Most of the time, he just drove around picking up trash tourists had left behind. She didn't think that was true. She asked him about the whole Bigfoot thing and what he thought of it. He laughed and told her how most of the sightings had been discounted, but if she wanted, he'd take her to the Bigfoot Museum just outside of town so she could decide for herself.

She pictured his green eyes as they lit up when he talked about the wildlife in the area. He could also name every kind of plant native to the region as well, with excitement in his voice. She thought how lucky he was to be, like Ben, doing something he loved. She found out he'd been married once right out of school to his college sweetheart, but it hadn't lasted long. He told her his wife didn't like living in the remote areas he was assigned to. She eventually left him and moved to Denver. He said now he was married to his job and his dog, a large black Labrador mix named Jasper that he had trained in search and rescue.

Rory liked that he hadn't pushed her into taking things any further. He hadn't tried to kiss her good night or suggest they go to his place when they left the restaurant. He had just said good night.

Now she heard tires on the gravel outside her cottage, and a headlight beam shone through her window across the darkened room. She wondered who was driving down the lane so late at night. It was after eleven, and usually things were dead quiet at this time. She couldn't fall asleep, so she turned on the small lamp beside her bed and padded over to the refrigerator to get something to drink.

She sat down at the kitchen table with a glass of milk and glanced at the mail scattered in front of her. Pushing aside the junk mail, she touched the large manila envelope lying in front of her. She flipped it over and read the return Phoenix address of Harmon, Whitley, and Feldman, Attorneys at Law. She knew when she had picked it up from her post office box what it was, but she hadn't been able to open it. Every time she looked at it, something gripped her stomach, and a swell of anxiety rode through her, telling her to wait until later.

Several days ago, when she had contacted the attorneys, she had been sure of what she wanted. It had come to her one night at Marlena's as she thought about how Marlena and Ethan didn't have much, but they were happy, and she realized that she had been happier over the past few weeks than she had been for years.

The paralegal she spoke with on the phone told her he could send her a packet that would list the details. He said if it was a no-fault divorce and both parties were in agreement, it would be pretty cut and dry. Arizona was a community property state. All she'd have to do was send them an initial fee, and most of the work could be done through the mail. She wondered if Derek would try to make things difficult. *Could* they both be in agreement? Would he be willing to sell the house?

Her hand hesitated for a second over the envelope before tearing it open. A voice inside told her there was nothing to fear; this was what she wanted. She read the words Petition for Dissolution of Marriage in bold black across the top of the page and thought they sounded so final.

She set the papers back down and took a sip of milk, trying to get rid of the empty feeling that filled her gut. Why was this so hard? She was adjusting to her life at Willow Bend, but it still wasn't home. She missed her cozy den with her collection of pottery and wall of photographs. She missed the comfort of a warm body next to her in bed. Glancing at the pile of papers, she felt it was more than divorcing her husband; she was divorcing the life she'd known for over twenty years—so many memories.

Often after one of Derek's verbal blowups, she would tell herself that was it, she wasn't taking it anymore, she was leaving. But then things would change—he would be nice and solicitous to her, that feeling of eternal hope would rise, and she would think this time things would be different. But she knew now that they would never change. She and Derek were not meant to be together.

She glanced around the dimly lit room; the only sound was the humming of the refrigerator. Her eyes watered as she pictured Daphne, who had always been there to cheer her up when she was feeling down and showered her with unconditional love. Maybe she would get a dog.

She finished her milk, and as she made her way back to bed, she heard the sound of a car engine again. She stood beside the window out of view, watching it slowly drive down, turn out of the entrance to Willow Grove, and then accelerate onto the two-lane road. Only half the cottages were occupied right now, and again she wondered who it had been this late at night. As she headed across the room, an uneasy feeling crept over her. She turned and walked over to the door, jiggling the knob to make sure it was locked.

12

The aroma of sizzling steaks wafted through the California Roadhouse restaurant, making Rory salivate as she realized all she'd eaten was a yogurt that morning. It was one of her eat-out nights. Every Tuesday and Thursday, in an effort to get to know the town better, she would go out for dinner. California Roadhouse sat on the outskirts of town along Highway 299. Sitting at a table, waiting for her burger and fries, she observed the bustling atmosphere: families engaged in conversations and servers dressed in red-and-white-checked shirts and cowboy hats, carrying large trays laden with heaping plates of food. Several tables away, she recognized, Muriel, the manager of the bookstore, one of Rory's new favorite hangouts. Muriel was with a man and Rory wondered if it was Muriel's husband. She assumed it was by the comfortable, nonchalant way they dined.

It had been over a month since she had arrived in Willow Bend, and she remembered how much she had hated eating alone in the beginning, feeling conspicuous. She would usually get out her cell phone and play a game or bring a book, trying to appear at ease. But now she was used to eating alone and enjoyed observing other people.

A family of five was seated at a table across from her. She watched as the mother wiped ketchup from her young son's face while the father jiggled their infant daughter on his lap. Even through the chaos of their meal, she saw the looks the parents gave each other. They were happy, or maybe she wanted to believe that. Had she looked happy with Derek long ago?

The waitress brought her food and refilled her Coke. The smell of the cheeseburger made her stomach rumble, and she quickly bit in, savoring the smoky flavor and thinking it was one of the best burgers she'd ever tasted.

She swirled her straw in her glass and glanced out the window to the darkened parking lot, thinking how much her life had changed from the minute her alarm went off at 5:15 a.m. to the time her head hit the pillow at night.

She no longer lingered in bed in the morning, and even though it was hard dragging her body out from under the warmth of her down comforter, once she was up, she had the routine down to a science: ten steps to the kitchen counter, where she'd flip the switch on the already filled four-cup coffee pot. Six steps to the bathroom. In and out of the shower in less than five minutes.

Her daily uniform of jeans, T-shirt, and Nikes was laid out the night before on the chair. Instead of lingering in her pajamas until ten or eleven—in Phoenix there had been days she had cleaned the house, taken out the trash, and worked in the garden without getting dressed—she was out the door now in twenty minutes flat. The cottage was neat and tidy by the time she left—her pajamas in the hamper, the bed made, and the dishes in the dish rack. The irony of it struck her—for years she had rebelled against Derek's fastidious habits, purposefully leaving her clothes scattered about, odds and ends cluttered on the counters. She told herself she kept things neat now because there was so little room. Or was it that there was no need to rebel anymore?

Now she waited for the waitress to bring her the check, feeling sated. She rubbed the back of her calf, which still ached from the ballet class the night before. It had been her second week of taking dance. During one of their nightly ritual phone calls, Jillian had suggested she take a dance class. Jillian had started calling her every night since Rory had arrived in Willow Bend. They'd chat sometimes for just a few minutes and sometimes for an hour. Jillian would fill Rory in on the drama in the art department at school, and Rory would tell Jillian about the unique customers she had dealt with or Astral's latest rant about GMOs and how they were going to end the world. Rory loved their conversations and looked forward to them each night. And she was glad Jillian had talked her into the dance class.

When she had called the only dance studio in Willow Bend to inquire about taking a class, the instructor had told her she could join even though the session had already started. She told Rory that several of the women were former dancers or dance teachers but that most of the class consisted of adults who just loved to dance. She said it was very informal, and with her background, she should not have a problem fitting in.

She had been nervous the first night, worrying that she had forgotten all her training. Standing at the barre, she had studied her reflection in the floor-to-ceiling mirrors that lined one wall, comparing herself to the other women, wondering how good everyone else was. She was no longer the star pupil, like she had been years ago. The tall brunette doing stretches a few feet away looked to be no more than twenty-five. She was probably the best in the class. A slightly plump woman, maybe Rory's age, was talking to a woman next to her who appeared to be in her sixties. Rory felt some relief that she wasn't the oldest in the class.

The bright fluorescent lights filled every corner of the large, windowless room, shining on the pale oak flooring that gleamed in the mirrors, leaving nothing in shadow. Dressed in a black sleeveless leotard and black tights, feeling the newness of her outfit, she pushed back her shoulders, elongating her body and erasing the slight pouch of skin where the front of her arm pressed against her bra.

She'd been one of the first to arrive, liking to be early, especially for something new, and while she had waited for the rest of the class to file in, she had gotten out her ballet shoes that she had purchased the day before and held one up to her nose, remembering how much she had loved the warm smell of the leather. She used to eat, sleep, and breathe dance.

She smiled at the woman standing next to her at the barre, hoping her insecurities weren't showing through. The woman, who looked to be in her late fifties, with perfect posture and gray hair pulled tightly in a bun, didn't smile back, her eyes focused straight ahead, making Rory feel snubbed.

The instructor entered the studio talking with another student while Rory summed up the woman next to her. Probably a former dancer, a typical prima ballerina, still thinking she was in her prime—better than everyone else.

The instructor caught sight of Rory and introduced her to the class. The other women nodded acknowledgments to her, and she felt her cheeks getting hot—she didn't want the spotlight. She glanced back at the woman next to her and was surprised when the woman smiled and introduced herself as Caroline, patting Rory's arm with a welcoming gesture. Maybe she'd been wrong about her. She felt the tension that had built up in her shoulders slipping away.

The music started, a slow classical piece, as the instructor led them through their warm-up stretches. Simple moves like *ronde de jambes* and *tendus* that had been second nature to her in the past were now taking her total concentration.

At the end of class, she packed her ballet slippers away in her bag; even though she was sweating and slightly out of breath, she thought how good she felt to be accepted in the group. She laughed, hearing another woman complain of her aching feet. It hadn't been easy, and there had been a few times when she had completely lost it, like when she started off on the wrong foot for her *pas de basque* and bumped into the woman next to her, practically knocking her over, but she could feel it coming back, and she loved it.

After class, Caroline asked Rory if she'd like to join a few of the others at a pub down the road. Rory accepted and was glad she had. She liked the group, who all shared a common love of dance—especially Caroline, who was divorced, had two married children, and owned one of the clothing boutiques in town. As they were leaving the pub, the group of women hugged each other, making jokes about how their instructor was secretly a sadist.

"Soak your feet tonight!" Caroline had shouted to Rory on her way to her car.

Now as she rubbed the cramp from her calf, she spotted an attractive woman with long brown hair, tall leather boots, and a suede jacket walk through the door to the California Roadhouse followed by three men. Rory did a double take. It couldn't be. Maybe the man just looked like Ben. But then she heard his laugh and felt her heart racing in her chest. She squeezed the straw between her fingers. What was he doing here?

She wiped her face with her napkin and looked down at the ketchup stain on her T-shirt. She wondered if she could somehow slip out the back, unnoticed, but at the same time, she wanted to run up and jump in his arms. Pulling the band out of her ponytail, she fingered her hair around her face to conceal her profile and slipped down in her chair, trying to make herself invisible. She wasn't wearing any makeup. Usually she'd change before going out to dinner, but tonight she'd been running errands and hadn't gone home after work.

She watched the group head to their table on the far side of the restaurant. He sat down, facing her right side, but he was too engrossed in whatever the brown-haired woman seated next to him was saying to notice her. Rory wondered if he hated her for rejecting him.

She glanced around anxiously; she hadn't paid yet. Where was the waitress? She kept her head averted, taking quick peeks in his direction every few seconds. Was he with that woman? She could see the waitress out of the corner of her eye making her way to her table.

She did another quick peek and almost jumped out of her seat. He was staring straight at her. A wave of excitement washed over her. She quickly looked away but then glanced back. He had stood up and was leaning down, saying something to the group. The other patrons faded into the background as she saw him stride toward her as if in slow motion. She reflexively ran her tongue over her teeth, making sure no food was stuck. She felt like a schoolgirl, watching the cute guy walk up to her in the cafeteria; she wished she hadn't eaten the whole burger.

He stood beside her table, all six feet, three inches of him, dressed in a pair of jeans, faded black T-shirt, and cowboy boots. He brushed his dark hair back from his face, a habit she remembered.

"Aurora June, as I live and breathe." He was the only one who called her by her given name. He liked the story of how she'd gotten her name. Her father had chosen it because she was born exactly at dawn, and she'd been conceived in June. "What are you doing here?" His blue eyes bore into her, and his melodious southern drawl was like warm fingers caressing her body. She'd dreamed of that voice for months after he had left.

"I live here now." She laughed nervously, thinking she sounded like an idiot. "What are you doing here?"

"We're playing in Eureka. Just stopping here for the night. Gary's brother lives here."

"That's great." She couldn't believe she was making small talk with him; she was having a hard time even breathing, let alone making words come out of her mouth.

"Are you alone?" He looked around the restaurant at the thinning crowd. She knew he was searching for Derek.

"All by myself." Her words came out a few decibels louder than she had expected. She let out another short laugh as she felt her cheeks burning.

"Mind if I sit?"

"Sure." This was a dream; it had to be.

They sat across the table from each other, neither one speaking for several minutes. Rory wound her hair around her finger as she tried to think of something to say.

"When'd you move here?" Ben's eyes had not broken their hold on her.

"About a month and a half ago." She unwound her hair and placed her hands in her lap. The green pendant light that hung over the table cast a glow on Ben's face: his day-old growth of beard, his deep-blue eyes and angular jaw, his dark wavy hair that brushed against the neck of his faded T-shirt. Did she want him to know she had left Derek? If she told Ben about leaving Derek, would that make him think she was available, that she wanted to start up again? She averted her eyes.

"I thought about you a lot," Ben said.

She wanted to say, "I thought about you too. I dreamed about your voice, and sometimes I ached for you," but she didn't. Without Derek, she felt she was hanging off a cliff with no safety net, nothing to stop her now. Their relationship had been intense, but she had told herself it had just been an infatuation. She picked at the paper napkin beside her empty plate, still not making eye contact. "It's been a while," was all she said.

"So why'd you leave Phoenix?"

She looked across the restaurant at the attractive woman that had been seated next to Ben. "Are you with her?"

"What?"

"That woman—are you with her?" She nodded in the direction of the table.

He followed her gaze. "Sherry? No, that's Gary's fiancée."

"Oh." A part of her had wanted him to say that yes, he was with the woman; then it would be settled for her.

"I told you why I was here, but you still haven't—"

"I left Derek."

Ben's eyebrows shot up.

"I'm still trying to figure out what I'm doing." She looked away, feeling tears welling and not knowing why.

"Hey." Ben reached out and took her hand in his. His hand felt warm. She loved his hands. A smile came but quickly faded. Was Ben the reason she had left?

She slipped her hand out of his, afraid to fall back into what they'd had. She needed time to think.

"I'm sorry…" She swiped the tears with the back of her hand. "This is so unexpected."

Ben gave her a heartfelt look. "You look just as beautiful as I remember."

She laughed. "I'm a mess. I haven't changed since work." She told him about her job at the luncheonette.

He sat silent for several minutes, staring at her, and then said, "I wish you'd gone with me."

"Things got so complicated and crazy," Rory whispered as she tore off little pieces of the napkin.

"Complicated, yeah." Ben sighed and leaned back in his chair, looking around the restaurant.

Rory felt like she was in the twilight zone. Minutes ago, she'd been debating whether to do a load of laundry tonight or wait until tomorrow, and now she was sitting across from Ben.

The waitress arrived with the check. "Wanna get a drink?" Ben said.

Rory glanced over at the table where Ben had been sitting earlier. "What about your food?"

"I'm not hungry. I heard there's a place down the street that plays good music."

Rory set the torn napkin back on the table. A part of her wanted to so badly, but a voice in her head told her no. She was afraid to open that door again. And she wasn't prepared. She felt dirty and exhausted from work. She needed time to think. "I'm beat, and I have to get up really early."

"Come to my show tomorrow night." Ben's eyes were fixed on her. "I'll text you the details."

13

At a few minutes past eight, she walked into the crowded club dressed in a pair of faded boot-cut jeans that hugged her body, a white blouse, the turquoise earrings she'd bought from Marlena, and a pair of custom-made J. B. Hill cowboy boots she had gotten several years ago in Texas. She had spent an hour choosing what to wear. The band wasn't onstage, and she searched the crowd to see if Ben was anywhere in sight.

The noisy room was filled with people laughing and talking over the recorded music that played in the background. She snaked her way to the bar and looked around the large room through the sea of people to the tables surrounding the stage. They were already filled, so she took an empty stool and waited for the bartender's attention. When he finally glanced in her direction, she ordered a Corona.

She tapped her foot against the rung of the stool with her hands clasped together in her lap. The bartender slid the beer over to her. She smiled and took a long swallow, glad to have something to hold on to, and hoped the alcohol would ease her nerves.

On the hour drive to Eureka, she'd thought about the past twenty-four hours. When she had gotten home last night, she'd tossed in bed, unable to get Ben out of her mind, wondering if fate had brought them together again. But why now?

She was making a life for herself—weekends with Will, Marlena, and Ethan hiking, kayaking, and picnicking in the meadow, even visiting the Bigfoot Museum. She loved her dance class and was looking forward to starting a photography class next week with Carter

Bennett. And she loved her job, even though it was exhausting. She also loved the unique and eccentric people of the town—like Pops, the owner of Popeye's Auto Repair, who had a tattoo of the cartoon character on his forearm. He had helped her once when her Falcon had broken down on the side of the road, giving her a ride in his tow truck. He had admired her restored car, and she told him how her brother and uncle were both mechanics. Now he was one of her lunchtime regulars, reciting poetry to her and telling her she was his muse. So how would Ben fit into the picture?

Now the lights dimmed as the band walked on stage, and she told herself she wasn't going to overthink tonight. She was just going to have fun. Ben made his way to the center with his guitar slung over his shoulder. "Good evening. How is everyone tonight?" he said into the microphone. His deep Louisiana drawl resonated through the room, and the crowd responded with whoops and hollers.

Their first song was an up-tempo tune that Rory had heard them play before. She watched Ben, the spotlight shining on him as he sang into the microphone, and she knew he was where he belonged. He was a natural on stage. Dressed in jeans and a faded denim shirt with the sleeves rolled up, he moved his fingers rapidly across the frets of the guitar. She closed her eyes and let the music fill her, thinking he sounded even better than she had remembered.

The song ended, and Ben introduced the members of the band. "And now we're going to do a little song that I wrote a while back about someone very special to me, someone I thought I would never see again, but miracles can happen, and I would like to dedicate this to her tonight." Rory's heart hammered against her chest. He was looking directly at her when he said it, and several of the patrons turned their heads, following his gaze. She felt embarrassed, realizing she was in the spotlight, and averted her eyes, feeling her face get hot.

The song was a slow ballad with lines about losing love and watching your soul walk out the door. Rory adjusted herself on the barstool, feeling uncomfortable. She felt the occasional glance in her direction from the other patrons. Had he really been that hurt, or was it just a song?

When she had broken it off, she had told herself he was a musician and probably picked up women all the time. She had pictured him moving on to another town and forgetting all about her. At forty-three, he had never been married, and she assumed that was the way he liked it. He was a wanderer, moving away from Louisiana at eighteen and living in Austin, Biloxi, Nashville, Los Angeles, and Phoenix.

The band finished their set and left the stage. Minutes later, Rory saw Ben heading in her direction. He walked up to her and gave her a soft kiss on the lips. Warmth rushed through her body.

"What'd you think?" He slid onto the stool next to her.

"You sounded fantastic."

"I meant the song." Ben motioned to the bartender and asked for a Coke, and then he turned back to her.

Rory smiled and looked down at her beer. "It was beautiful." She gave a nervous laugh. She felt his eyes on her as she turned the beer bottle around in her hands.

"It took me a long time to get over you not coming with me."

Rory looked up at him with a furrowed brow and a slight smile. "Things were—"

Ben put up his hands to stop her. "I know, I know—complicated. We don't have to go into all that. I'm just glad you're here."

A fan came up to Ben, shaking his hand and telling him that he loved the new CD. Ben's gaze left Rory, and he smiled at the man. The guy continued praising Ben and then went on to tell him how he played the guitar too. Rory observed Ben as he listened intently, nodding to the fan as if they were friends.

The song lyrics kept repeating in her head: "I thought we'd never be apart, and then she broke my heart when she left me." Had she really broken his heart? Was what she was searching for right here?

Ben finished talking to the man and turned to her, a smile on his face. Rory felt a tight band around her chest that made it hard for her to breathe. The thought of him in love with her was more than she could handle right now. She wasn't ready for a relationship. She wanted to try to make it on her own and prove to herself she could be independent.

"I'm meeting a producer tomorrow about another tour. He heard us play in Fresno and thinks he can build a cross-country show for us," Ben said. Rory could see the excitement in his face. He was so passionate about his music. "We're going to San Diego after this. Have you ever been there?"

She shook her head.

"You'd love it."

There was a lump in her throat that kept any words from coming out. She took a sip of beer, trying to swallow it away.

"You should come. It's just for two nights."

Her first instinct was to say yes. She could probably get off from work. But would it just be a couple of nights? Would he want her to go to the next town…and then what? "So when did your new CD come out?" Rory asked with her head tilted down, her hair partially covering her face as she turned her beer bottle in her hands. She was trying hard to be strong, because a part of her wanted to say, *I'll go to San Diego with you. I'll spend the rest of my life with you.* That would be crazy, though, impulsive. But hadn't it been impulsive to just pack up her car and leave a twenty-four-year marriage in one afternoon?

"I gotta get back on stage." He touched her cheek and pushed her hair back from her face as he got off the stool.

By the end of the evening, after the band had packed up, the patrons had all left, and the barstools rested on top of the bar, the staff swept the floor while Rory waited for Ben. The lights were turned up, and the scuffling of chairs being moved around filled the room. After two beers, her nerves had settled back down. She'd gotten lost in the music and was glad she had come.

Ben came walking out, his guitar in a soft case slung over his back. Watching him slowly stride across the room, she felt that fire she used to feel stirring inside her.

They headed down the street, and Ben put his arm around her. It felt good. She tilted her head back against his shoulder and looked up at the clear night sky, sprinkled with myriad stars. A cool breeze blew strands of hair across her face. She brushed them back with her fingers, listening to the sound of their boots clicking in unison on the pavement.

"Do you ever feel insignificant when you look at the sky?" Rory asked.

"You mean because we're just a speck on the screen?"

"It's so easy to think the world revolves around us. And then you look up in the sky and you realize how arrogant we can be."

Ben stopped and turned to face her. He cupped her chin in his hand. "All I know is that when I look at you, I see the stars, I see the sky—nothing else matters." He leaned down and kissed her.

They walked in silence to her car. "Come back to my hotel." He ran his fingers through her hair and then leaned down, softly kissing her lips.

———

Standing beside the bed, Ben drew her to him and they kissed, exploring with their tongues. He pulled back. "Come to San Diego with me," he whispered. Rory placed her finger to his lips and began to unbutton her blouse, but he stopped her and did it himself. He gently pulled her blouse off and undid her bra, letting it fall to the ground. He cupped her breast in his hand, leaned down, and brushed his lips across her nipple, sending shivers up her spine. He had her sit on the edge of the bed while he slipped off her boots one at a time and then her jeans. He took her hand, pulling her back up.

She closed her eyes while his fingers gently stroked her face, her arms, and her breasts. Her body ached with his touch.

They woke the next morning in a tangle of sheets. Rory stretched her arms over her head, and Ben rolled over in her direction. It felt luxurious waking up with him, to lie next to him without having to rush out the door. In Phoenix, their meetings had been brief and clandestine, and there had always been a hint of regret in the back of her mind, knowing she was betraying Derek.

Now she turned toward him and studied his face—his hooded blue eyes that she felt looked straight into her soul, the faint lines etched across his forehead. She touched the rough, unshaven skin of his cheek. Last night had been exquisite. She had let go and been filled with ecstasy, but now the voice of reason was whispering in the back of her head.

Ben brushed her hair back off her face, exposing the tiny scar up at her hairline. He ran his finger across it. "You never told me how you got that."

She kissed him and mumbled something about a fall. "Let's get breakfast. I'm starving!"

The smell of bacon filled the crowded diner, making her stomach growl. She heard the sound of the waitress calling back an order over the din of voices. They squeezed their way down to an empty booth.

After they ordered from the plastic-coated menus, the waitress brought them their coffee. Ben poured four sugar packets into the mug. Rory used to tease him that he would become a diabetic if he didn't cut back on his sugar. Once she had seen him put Coke on his corn flakes because he was out of milk.

Within minutes, the waitress brought their orders, hurriedly setting the thick white plates on the table and then rushing away. Ben began playing the restaurant game he loved to play, making up stories about the patrons—silly stories, like the woman with the giant nose seated several tables away was actually a Russian spy and the man she was with was a CIA operative, but they'd fallen in love and were now in hiding. Rory couldn't help but laugh at his ridiculous scenarios.

Ben took a bite of his egg sandwich. He chewed slowly, and Rory watched his jaw muscle moving back and forth. God, he was good looking. That tingling warmth stirred inside her again, and she had to look away. She needed strength for what she knew she had to say. She looked down at her plate, afraid to make eye contact. Pushing her fork around her syrupy pancakes, unable to take another bite, she stalled.

Ben spoke up. "I was thinking that after I get out of my meeting with the producer this afternoon, we could get together for an early dinner before—"

"I won't be here for dinner. I've decided to leave after breakfast."

"*What?* I thought…after last night…I thought you—"

She shook her head back and forth slowly, still not looking up. "I might be making the biggest mistake of my life, but I've got to do what my gut's telling me." She glanced across the diner at the flurry of activity, the waitresses hustling with their orders, but it all seemed to be passing by in slow motion. "I've been carrying a lot of baggage for years, Ben. Being dependent on someone else. I need this time to be alone, to figure out who I am." She felt as if she was reciting lines from a script. She knew it sounded rehearsed, because it was. All morning she had played over in her head how she was going to tell him. She looked up from her plate. Ben was silent. "The timing is just off, and I don't expect you to wait for me, but this is something I have to do." Tears filled her eyes. "Please don't hate me."

"I could never hate you." He placed his napkin down on the table and sat back against the booth. He sighed. "Is it because of my traveling?"

She shook her head. "It has nothing to do with you."

"I'm not gonna beg."

"I don't expect you to." They waited for the check in silence.

Outside, the sunlight streamed down on Ben's face as he looked at her. "Well, Aurora June, I wish you the best. I hope you find what you're looking for." He touched her cheek. "Maybe one day you'll realize it was standing right in front of you."

14

Her headlights cast a beam along the two-lane road on her morning commute into work. The double yellow line along the gray asphalt wound its way, like a ribbon, toward town. She had the road to herself, except for the occasional tractor-trailer passing through on its way to another town. Her senses were heightened along this stretch of road bordered by a thick forest of pines and giant sequoias, never knowing when they would release a deer into her path.

She'd begun to love this time of day, just before dawn, where she could reflect on her life. She felt like they were stolen minutes just for her, something extra.

It had been two weeks since she'd seen Ben. Several times she had picked up her phone to call him, but then a voice in her head told her to stop. She had made her decision and needed to stick with it. She was making a life here. And it was a busy life, so busy she didn't have time to think about Ben—at least not in the daytime.

When she was asleep was a different story. She had one dream where she was living with Ben in a small cottage on the bayou. She'd never been to Louisiana, but Ben's stories had been so vivid, her imagination knew exactly what it looked like. She remembered every room in the house even though it was a house she'd never seen before. It was a typical dream that made sense while she was dreaming but in the light of day seemed bizarre. She was struggling to open a jar of marbles when Ben walked up behind her, took the jar, and opened it for her. Her mother was seated at the kitchen table, smiling and looking like she did before she got sick—the way she did when Rory was a child. That was all Rory could remember, but it had left her with a gnawing feeling, wondering if she had made the right choice.

Now she slowed down at the blinking yellow light at the crossroads. No need to stop: the town was still tucked safely in bed. She turned right onto Poplar Street, passing the Bigfoot Inn, the bright-red neon letters lit up along the side of the road. Across from the inn was the town's lone church, a white clapboard building with a tall steeple, dwarfed by the giant trees that loomed behind. The sign outside read The Church of God. No Catholic church, no synagogues, no specific denomination. She liked that—one God for everyone.

She passed by Willow Market, the only grocery store in town. You could probably fit three Willow Markets in one of her supermarkets back in Phoenix, but they somehow had everything she needed.

Making sure she stayed within the twenty-five-miles-per-hour speed limit, she hovered her foot over the pedal. When she'd first started at the luncheonette, she used to speed through town, always on the lookout for hidden radar, but now she enjoyed the slow pace. Passing the residential block of cabin-style homes with the occasional light on in the window, she would imagine someone stirring, about to start their day.

Farther down was the row of shops and the old-fashioned lampposts that lined both sides, casting circles of light below as she passed the Native American Arts Shop and Caroline's Dress Boutique.

Last week after dance class, Caroline had asked if she'd like to go to the movies on Friday. They had seen a romantic comedy, a chick flick, one that she and Jillian would have seen together, and afterward they'd eaten at the Grove, a small bistro in town.

At the restaurant, Rory laughed, thinking of a scene from the movie. "I loved the part when she dumps the bucket of ice on them," she said, referring to the main character's actions when she found her husband in bed with another woman.

"I wish I'd thought of that," Caroline replied.

"You mean—"

"Yep. Walked in to find the bastard and his latest twenty-year-old on my brand-new six-hundred-count Egyptian-cotton sheets."

"I didn't know." Rory felt bad for having laughed and wished she could take back her words. "I'm sure that must've been horrible."

"I survived," Caroline replied, holding up her wineglass.

Rory knew Caroline had been a dancer years ago with the Portland Ballet, and that's where she had met her husband, who had been the director. But she didn't know why their marriage had ended.

"I would've liked to have broken his legs back then," Caroline continued, "but now it doesn't bother me."

Rory nodded, feeling awkward. The movie didn't seem as funny anymore. She wanted to change the subject. "How long were you with the company?"

"Not long—about two years. I got pregnant with the twins a year after we were married. I lost my job and raised two kids while he got to continue with his career." Caroline had a wistful smile. "But what I didn't know was that he'd been cheating on me the whole time. He'd pick a different ballerina every year."

"What did you do?"

"I took him for everything he had and moved here. The boys were away at college, and I wanted to get as far away from the dance world as possible. So I got a job at the dress boutique and eventually bought it."

Now Rory drove past the drugstore that also sold wine, wondering how someone knew what the right decision was. She wondered if Caroline was happy now. A sliver of guilt pressed on her chest as she thought of her affair with Ben. Caroline's husband had been a creep, but how was it any different from what she had done? At least she hadn't had multiple affairs. Ben had been special. A one-time aberration. And her marriage had already disintegrated. The list of justifications kept coming.

She slowed down as she glanced in the picture window with the semicircular gold lettering of Tanoak Records and Books. Her favorite shop. If Ben was so special, why didn't she go with him to San Diego? Was she purposely punishing herself for having cheated? But she knew that wasn't it. There was a defiance inside that she couldn't explain. A feeling that she had to prove to herself, if no one else, that she was independent. She didn't need anyone.

She drove past the luncheonette, seeing a light on in the back. Probably Jesus, the cook—the third cook they'd been through since she'd started. After parking in the gravel lot on the corner, she opened the car door and inhaled the ubiquitous smell of pine; then she stepped onto the sidewalk, feeling her adrenaline pump, as if a director was shouting, "Action!" She pushed the thoughts of Ben out of her mind, ready to face the bustling day—her quiet, stolen minutes gone.

"So Earl gets a hunting dog from this breeder and sends the dog out to search for ducks, but the dog comes back with a stick in his mouth and starts humping Earl's leg. Earl takes the dog back to the breeder and tells him what he did, saying the dog's no good. The breeder says, 'Hell, he's just trying to tell you there are more freaking ducks out there than you can shake a stick at,'" Will said, laughing so hard at his own joke it made Rory laugh, reminding her of her dad when he told jokes.

Will sat across the counter of the luncheonette, a slice of apple pie in front of him. It was ten minutes to three, and Will was the only customer left. He had become a regular, usually showing up a little before closing, amusing Rory with his repertoire of anecdotes.

Her doubts about not going with Ben were nestled in the far recesses of her brain now. Earlier, during the rush of the lunch crowd, Mr. Danvers, her grizzled-looking landlord, had stopped her on one of her trips past his table and said that she was the best addition to the town in years. And as she walked back toward the kitchen, she realized she was happy. And she'd accomplished what she'd set out to do: she had her own place, a job, friends. She found she laughed more now, and the feeling that the other shoe was about to drop had ceased. She was shedding the shell of protection she'd built up over the years.

Will had just finished another joke about a man and a zebra at a nun's convention. Even though most of his jokes were corny, it was his delivery that made Rory laugh so hard she had tears in her eyes. Her elbows were leaning on the counter as she faced him when the door to the restaurant opened. Rory glanced over, still laughing, even as she felt the smile vanish from her face.

Derek's muscular, six-foot frame filled the entranceway. Her breath hitched in her throat. What was he doing here? How did he know where she was? She felt the blood drain from her face. He walked deliberately over to the counter, dressed in a suit jacket, polo shirt, and neatly pressed slacks that now showed a few wrinkles from their travels. His blond hair seemed to be flecked more with gray, and Rory felt he looked older than he had two months ago. His eyes locked on to Rory's, and she slowly removed her elbows from the counter and stood up straight.

Derek glanced over at Will and then back to Rory and said, "So this is why you're not coming back?"

Rory's stomach tightened, and her heart pounded. She gave a quick smile to Will. "Derek, what are you doing here?"

"I came to see my wife."

She wanted to ask him how he had found her, but she didn't want to talk here. Her shift only had a few minutes left. "Wait here." She went into the back and asked Astral if she could leave a few minutes early, and Astral said to go ahead. She removed her apron and grabbed her purse, her palms sweating. She stood there for a few seconds, taking deep breaths, telling herself to remain calm.

Walking around the counter, she said, "Let's go."

Will mouthed to her, "You OK?"

She responded with a nod, trying to appear composed, but inside she was trembling with apprehension. She had known she was eventually going to have to face Derek; she just hadn't expected it to be today.

15

O ut on the street, Rory squinted from the afternoon sun and asked Derek how he had found her.

"I *am* a detective." He gave her a slight grin, his blue eyes crinkling at the corners. He looked good, she thought, and she was taken back to that first night in that kitchen when he had helped her off the floor. A tiny swirl of emotion fluttered in her stomach. He continued, "It wasn't hard to find you. You sent me that letter postmarked Willow Bend, California. Once I got to town, all I had to do was show your picture to a couple of people, and they pointed me straight to the luncheonette."

"When'd you get here?" She was stalling for time, trying to collect her thoughts, her mind still reeling from seeing him in the doorway.

"About an hour ago. I flew into Sacramento this morning and rented a car."

"Why didn't you just call?"

"I wanted to see you in person, and I had some vacation time coming, so I thought maybe a trip to California would be nice. Maybe I could get in some fishing."

She could tell he was trying to be funny, but her nerves were too jittery to laugh. He was being Dr. Jekyll right now…or was it Mr. Hyde? She never could remember which one was the nice guy, but she was worried that the other half was lingering just below the surface. "I guess we could go somewhere and talk," she said.

"Why not your place?"

Taking him to the cottage would be a mistake. She knew what would happen. He had done it so many times before: pour on the charm, tell her how much he loved her, and then came the touch, his hand on her face and hair, but that had been in the past. She couldn't remember a time in the last two years when he'd tried to seduce her. No matter, she thought; she wanted to talk someplace public. "Let's go to the pub at the Bigfoot Inn. You can follow me."

"Why don't we ride together?" He stood on the curb, the keys to his rental in his hand.

"I want to drive. It's not far. Just follow me." She headed toward her car.

"Afraid to be in a car with me?" He called after her, and she could hear the hurt tone masked by his sarcasm, but she didn't answer. She just kept on walking and thinking, *Yes, I'm afraid to be in the car with you,* knowing she would be a trapped audience. Ever since she had left him, she had been able to distance herself from his energy, the power he had that bowled her over, making her unable to think clearly. She wasn't going to back down this time. She needed time alone in the car to sort things out in her head about what she wanted to say.

She pulled into the parking lot of the Bigfoot Inn with Derek right behind her. The red neon sign blinked out front. She remembered how nervous she'd felt that first night in town and how much things had changed since then. She had come here a few nights ago with Will and a group of his friends, playing darts and drinking beer. Walking up the stone steps with Derek felt completely different; her lightheartedness from the other night was replaced with a lead weight of dismay.

The place was almost empty, just a couple of men at the bar. Garth Brooks's voice resonated from the speakers in the background. A television behind the bar was tuned to a sports channel, the sound turned down. They sat at a table, and a waitress came over. Derek ordered a beer, and Rory decided to order one too. She needed something to calm her anxiety.

She felt Derek staring at her while she dug at a hangnail on her thumb, her eyes locked on her hand. She didn't know where to start. She felt like she was sitting across from a stranger. How could things change so much in two months? But it had been longer than that— they'd been becoming strangers for years. The waitress brought the beers over. Rory grabbed hers and took a long gulp, and then she hung on to the bottle with both hands.

She stared down at the drops of water on the outside of the brown glass. Without looking up, she said, "I haven't changed my mind. I'm not coming back."

"You fucking him?"

She looked up. Even though it was broad daylight outside, the windowless room was dimly lit, casting a shadow across the side of Derek's face. His words were like a blow to her gut. It had been so long since someone had talked to her like that. She shook her head. "Don't even go there."

"What do you mean, 'Don't go there'? You tell me you're leaving, out of the blue, and then I find you with that *guy*. I saw the way he was looking at you and the way you looked at him."

Had she been looking at Will a certain way? But that was beside the point. "Derek, you knew we were having problems. I tried to talk to you about it, but you'd never listen. It has nothing to do with anyone else."

Derek sat back in his chair with his shoulders slumped and glanced around the room.

"What is it you want, Rory? You want to go to counseling or some kind of couple's retreat? I'll go. I know I haven't tried working at it before." She saw the anger recede in his face. He looked tired.

"It's too late. I want to be on my own." She steeled herself to look in his eyes, knowing if she did, she might lose her resolve.

"I guess you don't care about what *I* want."

"No, I don't." She inhaled deeply, gathering strength. "I know it's selfish, but I've spent my whole adult life doing what *you* wanted me to. I'm forty-two; I only get one chance, and this is what I've decided."

"So being a mother to Jillian wasn't what you wanted to do? I'm sure your daughter would love to hear that."

Another zing to her gut. "That's not what I meant, and you know it. I loved taking care of Jillian, but Jillian's an adult." She watched the muscles of Derek's jaw twitch. She knew he was doing all he could to control himself.

A part of her felt that the main reason he wanted her back was because she had upset his routine—he no longer had her there to run his errands, fix his meals, and wash his clothes. But as those thoughts ran through her mind, she saw a hint of sadness in his eyes. Had he really missed her? Did she mean more to him than just someone who kept his life running smoothly? She felt her resolve slipping a bit, but she hung on tightly. "I guess you know about Jillian moving to England."

"You know, ever since your mother came to live with us—that's when things started to change," Derek said.

Rory shook her head. "Things had changed before that; I just never had the courage to do anything about it. You have to admit our marriage has had problems for a long time. Way before my mother came to Phoenix." She stared at the game on the television, the players running across the field, her eyes fixed mindlessly to the screen. "I contacted an attorney. I want a divorce." She felt a release as soon as the words spilled out. She waited for his answer, expecting him to spit out some vicious remark. Her eyes went from the screen to his face. He turned his beer bottle around in his hands. "So that's how it's going to be." He shook his head. He suddenly had a defeated look, something she'd never seen on him before. A part of her felt sorry for him. He really didn't have a clue why she was leaving.

"If we'd gotten help years ago, maybe things could've been different, but maybe not. Maybe we just weren't meant to be together." She paused for a second and nervously played with a strand of hair. "I don't think you're really happy with me either."

The waitress came back to see if they needed anything else, and Derek ordered another beer for both of them. He nodded slowly a couple of times as he held on to his beer. She noticed his strong hands that were tanned and rough, the blond hairs bleached from the Arizona sun, and remembered years ago how secure they had made her feel when they touched her.

His eyes went from his beer to Rory. He smiled. "You remember that time when Jillian was a baby? We went to that fancy restaurant where they seated us in that room of couples." Rory nodded and smiled. He continued, "Jillian was making such a fuss, and everyone was giving us dirty looks. And then I had to feed you your dinner."

"I remember," Rory said. She thought back to that night. It had been one of the few times they had gone out when Jillian was a baby. Jillian had only been ten months old and had just learned to walk, and she wanted to toddle around the room going up to the intimate tables of two. Every time Rory tried to pick her up and take her back to their table, she would scream. So finally Rory, out of desperation, had to nurse her to keep her quiet, but when Jillian nursed, she also liked to hold Rory's free hand, and it was right then that the waitress had brought them their food. "We drew a lot of attention that night." She remembered how they had joked about it the next day. She smiled, the memory triggering a happy feeling.

Things had been good at one time.

Derek recalled other good times like the camping trip they had gone on where he had taught Jillian how to fish and skim rocks across the water. Rory knew what he was doing, but she wasn't going to let it work. She wasn't going to be lured back with fond memories of the past. For each of those happy moments, she could bring up three bad ones, but she didn't. She was surprised at how strong she felt. Maybe it was the beer, but the knot in her stomach was gone. She thought part of it was that the anticipation was over. She had faced Derek and told him she wanted a divorce, and her world hadn't ended.

The pub began filling up with the after-work crowd, coming in for a quick drink or an early dinner. Derek flagged the waitress and asked her for some menus.

They talked about Jillian. Talking about Jillian was safe territory. She said how hard it was going to be having Jillian live in England, but she was glad Jillian was living out her dreams.

Derek jokingly asked if that was what *she* was doing: living her dreams as a waitress in a small town. She knew he thought it was funny, but Rory didn't laugh, partly because she realized she didn't have any dreams. She had thrown away her dreams of being a dancer after her father had died and had never replaced them with anything else. But this had been a huge step for her, and she felt that he had trivialized what she was doing. He was doing it again, making her feel insignificant.

Rory set down her pork barbeque sandwich and roughly wiped her face with her napkin. She'd been listening to Derek talk about the past while she ate, not saying much in response. She studied his mannerisms, the way his hands moved when he talked, how they emphasized his words. He exuded confidence. At forty-eight, he was still in great physical condition. He had removed his jacket, and she noticed the defined muscles of his biceps. *Indomitable*: that was the word she thought of when she thought of him. She had once loved that about him, but now she felt trapped under his strength.

He was in the middle of telling her about a case he was working on when she interjected, "My life matters."

Derek looked at her with a confused expression. "What?"

"My life is important too." She glanced around the pub, gathering up her thoughts. "I feel like you think I'm just being childish, like a rebellious teenager that needs to come to her senses. I don't think you really understand why I left. You've never asked me what I was thinking or feeling or what I wanted. It's always been about you." She felt the thumping of her heart against her ribs. "I think you thought I was there to serve you." She saw the look of bewilderment on Derek's face, but she kept on going, unable to stop as the stream of words poured out. "You never wanted me to do anything on my own, and for years I believed what you said about how I was needed at home and that was more important, but I think the real reason you didn't want me to work or go back to school was because you were afraid I might find something else and not need you. You liked me being vulnerable."

"So it's all *my* fault?" Derek threw up his hands defensively.

"I'm not saying that. I'm as much to blame. I allowed it to happen, and I think over the years I lost who I was. I'd always defined myself as a wife and mother, but that's like saying I was a daughter or a sister. They're just labels, but they don't define me as a person."

"I think you've read too many psychology books."

"Don't you see? You're a detective. You have a purpose in your life, and you love your work. Jillian has her love of art, and she's pursuing that."

"Well, then go back to school, if that's what you want, or get a job as a waitress, but you can do that in Phoenix."

She inhaled her frustration, making it hard for her to breathe. He didn't understand that she *couldn't* do it in Phoenix; things would never change between them. She felt that familiar feeling rising inside like the fluttering wings of bird in a cage. He could say all the right things now, but she knew as soon as she got back there, they would fall back into the same old pattern. He would suck the energy out of her, and she would never be able to find her way.

Their plates had been cleared away, and the waitress asked if she could get them anything else. Derek started to say something, but Rory interrupted him and said they would take the check. Derek looked at her, a little surprised. She could tell her assertiveness baffled him.

"Derek, all the talking in the world isn't going to change how I feel. You're going to have to accept the fact that it's over. I'm sorry you came all the way up here. You should've called."

"It's a long drive back to Sacramento. I thought maybe I could spend the night."

She looked at him in disbelief. He wasn't hearing her, she thought, or he didn't want to hear her, thinking he could still persuade her to go back with him. She pursed her lips as she collected her words. "I have to work tomorrow, and it's getting late. You should probably get on the road now."

Before he could respond, Rory grabbed the check as the waitress set the tab in front of Derek. She glanced at the amount, set the cash on the table, and stood.

Out in the parking lot, he leaned against her car. "So what's next?"

Rory stared at the blinking neon Bigfoot and then back to Derek. "I'm not sure. I'm hoping we can do this whole thing civilly." He came toward her, reaching forward to kiss her. She turned her face to the side, and he kissed her cheek. "Derek, please don't." That

131

familiar smell of Drakkar Noir. She had bought him a bottle last Christmas.

He backed away, his fists clenched at his sides. Sadness—or was it hurt pride—filled his eyes. Not saying anything, he got in his car and drove off. She stood in the parking lot for several minutes. Tears welled in her eyes and spilled onto her cheeks. She had done it. She had stood firm, but her mind swirled with thoughts. All the good times he'd brought up were spinning in her head.

She thought back to their wedding day: April 14, 1990. The day before Easter. The Catholic church that she'd gone to her whole life had been filled with Easter lilies. She remembered how the smell had made her nauseous. She'd tried to hide her pregnancy under a loose, flowing white dress. No one but her mother and Derek knew. Then August 28—the day Jillian was born. Rushing to the hospital, Derek at her side the whole time. Their early years in Phoenix— buying a house—she'd been so excited the day they moved in, eating pizza on the floor among all the boxes. They had made love on the living room rug after Jillian had fallen asleep, christening the new house, as Derek had put it. Why did things have to go so wrong?

Derek's car was out of sight. He'd finally accepted what she wanted. So why did she feel as if her heart had been pricked by thorns? He had somehow made her feel like *he* was the victim. She got in her car and stared at the dashboard, the white numbers of the speedometer spread out vertically, 5, 10, 15, 20…like the years of her marriage. She sobbed, gulping in air; it was over. Her life for the past twenty-four years had ended. She was able to pursue whatever she wanted, but instead of elation with the new freedom, she felt only sadness. She put the key into the ignition, cranking the engine to life.

The anchor was out of the water; nothing was holding her back now. She swallowed the tiny particles of fear rising to the surface of her gut. *Divorce.* The word itself hurt. She wondered if it was because of her parents' marriage and her grandparents' and her brother's—everyone she was close to had stayed married. They had been able to make things work.

Was she a failure? Did she still love Derek? She searched her soul, remembering Charlie asking her that same question in Temecula, and she thought that if she still loved him, she shouldn't have to search for the answer.

16

Wrapped in a wool plaid blanket on the worn leather couch, Rory drank in the aroma of peppers, onions, and garlic from Will's chili, which filled the A-frame house nestled in the woods. The staccato sound of the rain lashed against the tall windows.

It had been raining for three days straight, and her Arizona body wasn't used to the cooler-than-normal November temperatures and winter rains that had moved in early. She had gone out and bought rain gear, and she had even broken down and bought rubber boots when Will informed her that they could get volumes of rain over the winter months.

Her dog-eared poetry book was sitting on her lap, and she'd just finished reciting a William Carlos Williams poem to Will. Her English teacher senior year in high school, Mr. Chambers, had given her the book. It had been toward the end of the year, and he had called her to his desk as she was leaving class. She had just barely been passing. He had said he knew that she had gone through a lot of trauma over the past several months but that he also knew she had potential and hoped she would read the book over the summer.

Potential.

She could hear her old dance teacher, Ms. Petrova's, heavily Russian-accented voice, shouting over the phone after Rory had dropped out of dance: "Such po*ten*tial! What a waste!"—which came out as "*Vut a vaste!*"

Potential—now the word resonated in her head. A word full of hope and promise. At forty-two, what kind of potential did she have? She glanced over at Will, who was stirring the big pot on the stove. "Why is it when we're young, we think we have all the time in the world—that there will always be tomorrows?"

He looked up from the stove and gave her a quizzical stare.

"I threw so much away when I was young. Do you ever wish you could turn back the clock? Go back to high school…" Her words drifted off.

"High school?" Will wiped his hands on a dish towel. "No way. I was a big geek in high school. I hated it."

She laughed. "I can't picture you as a geek."

"I still have the pocket protector to prove it."

"Now I know you're kidding."

Will left the chili and headed to the fireplace that faced the couch. He squatted down and threw another log on the fire. "OK, so maybe I wasn't a geek, but I still wouldn't want to be back in high school. Being young isn't all it's cracked up to be. A lot of things get better with age."

Uncurling her legs, she stretched them onto the whorled tree-slab coffee table. Will's big black dog, Jasper, lay next to her with his head in her lap. "Sometimes I feel like the world isn't meant to be a happy place." She watched the embers spark and sizzle as Will stoked the fire with a poker. She stroked Jasper's fur as her eyes moved to Will's muscular back that showed through the thin flannel of his shirt. "Derek thought we were sleeping together." Her words came out unexpectedly.

"What?" He stood, brushing his hands on his jeans, and then made his way over to the couch and sat beside her with an inquisitive look.

"He said he could see the way we were looking at each other."

"What'd you tell him?"

"That we were just friends." She searched his face for a reaction. Will nodded and made an *umm* sound in response.

Rory watched the yellow flames dancing, not knowing what Will's "umm" meant, but she told herself it didn't matter—being friends was all she wanted. "I love the smell of a fire—it reminds me of eating s'mores as a kid. We had a fire pit in the backyard, and my dad made the best s'mores. He knew just when to take the marshmallows from the fire…" Rory closed her eyes and clasped her hands together as her mouth savored the memory. "God, they were good!" She turned toward him. "We should make some!"

Will smiled but didn't respond.

"What?"

He continued smiling as he studied her face. "That's one of the things I love about you."

She tilted her head, not sure what he meant.

He got up and headed back to the kitchen area. "You're like a little kid sometimes with your excitement."

She stared back at the fire. Her stomach had done a quick flip when he had said the word "love." But, why? Was she afraid of things going further? She liked their relationship the way it was, purely platonic, no tension of taking it to another level.

"I don't think I have any marshmallows," Will said as he rooted through the cupboards. "I forgot to tell you—I ran into Carter the other day, and he said he really loved your work."

"He did?" She was halfway through the eight-week digital photography session with Carter Bennett. There was that word again: love. People used it all the time, and it didn't mean anything. And she was sure Carter was just being nice. Her work wasn't anything extraordinary.

"He said there's a photography contest in Eureka next month, and he thinks you should enter it."

"I know. He mentioned it in class."

"Are you going to?" Will asked as he tested a spoonful of chili.

Rory shrugged. "I don't know. I'm not a big fan of contests."

A sharp ring sliced through the silence. Rory jumped, and Jasper barked, leaping off the couch. Will's cell phone slid around on the wood coffee table, ringing and vibrating at the same time. "I'm on call; it's probably the station." He left the stove and grabbed the phone.

Rory listened as he responded to whatever information was being given to him on the other end. He finished the call and told her that some kayakers had gotten trapped on the river, and they needed to get a rescue team together. Rory wondered why anyone would want to go kayaking on a day like today. Will apologized profusely, telling her she could stay and have some chili. He would be back as soon as he could. She watched him rush around and pack up a bag. Jasper was waiting at the door.

He started to head out, but then he stopped, came over to her on the couch, and gave her a peck on the cheek. Reflexively, she touched his arm. He hesitated for a second, his eyes catching hers, and then he leaned in and gave her a real kiss, slowly and gently on the lips, before sprinting back to the door.

She watched him dodge the rain as he sprinted to the Jeep and opened the door for Jasper. Her hand went to her lips. What had just happened? The kiss had come out of nowhere, and she wasn't sure what to make of it. She got up and walked over to the window as he got into the driver's seat. He had a focused look on his face. His mind was already at the river. He whipped the Jeep around and took off down the drive.

Rivulets of water ran down the glass onto the ground, forming a narrow stream in the dirt. Bits of leaves and sticks swirled in a miniature whirlpool as they made their way toward the ditch beside the drive. She felt as if she was spinning along with the debris. The kiss had sparked something, but at the same time, it unsettled her because she didn't want to jeopardize their friendship. She also felt a strange feeling of longing, but not for Will—for the passion he had with his job. It was the same passion she had seen in Carter and Ben, even Derek with his detective work and Jillian with her art. When she had first started working at the diner, she had been excited with the newness and wanting to do everything right. She had loved the feeling of earning her own money and the responsibility of being someplace at a certain time. But she wanted more.

17

Sitting on the floor of the cottage, she opened one of the packages that had been delivered earlier that day. She had dipped into her savings account for the purchases, a set of dishes, new wineglasses, two All Clad pots, and a Global eight-inch chef's knife made from "cromova 18" stainless steel with a dimpled metal handle. Removing it from the box, she carefully held the knife in the palm of both hands, feeling its weight and admiring the beauty of its design. She justified the expensive purchases by telling herself that every cook needed a good knife and decent pans, but the real reason was that she wanted everything to turn out right. This was going to be her first Thanksgiving on her own.

Jillian was spending Thanksgiving with Derek. Rory understood Jillian's reasoning. She was going to share Christmas with Rory at Cass and Nick's. It made perfect sense for her to be with her father. That's what she'd told Jillian on the phone, but inside it hurt. She missed Jillian, but she needed to accept the way things were now. She wondered what it would be like at her house this year. Would Jillian do the cooking? Or would Derek's sister Carrie cook? She wondered what his sisters thought of her leaving; neither one had called. After all the years they had shared together, she thought they had been friends, but she knew it was Derek they really cared about—after all, he was their brother. She thought how pleased Nick had been when he heard that she had left Derek. Did Derek's sisters feel the same about her? After getting off the phone with Jillian and feeling sorry for herself for a few minutes, she had changed gears and decided to invite Will, Marlena and Ethan and Mr. Danvers for Thanksgiving dinner. Caroline was spending the holiday with her two sons.

Now she was getting excited about the big day that was less than two weeks away. She had even gone to a small antique shop and found a set of turkey salt and pepper shakers almost identical to the ones her grandmother had given her.

Setting the knife down, she selected a playlist from her songs and cranked up the volume. She sambaed across the room to the rhythmic beat of Paul Simon singing "Late in the Evening," swirling and dipping as she picked up the empty boxes and Styrofoam packing pieces off the floor.

A text came over her phone. It was Charlie, saying she couldn't wait to see her soon. Yesterday she'd gotten a call from Charlie asking if Rory would spend the weekend of December 6th in Carmel with her—for Charlie's birthday, —her fiancé, James, was going to be away on business, and she didn't want to spend her birthday alone.

Rory had said yes immediately but then hesitated—Carmel was over a seven-hour drive, and she wasn't sure how much time she could get off from work. Charlie told her not to worry; she could get the Binghamtons' private jet to come pick her up in Eureka and fly her to Monterey, where they could meet. Charlie was living in San Francisco now to be close to James, having quit her job a month ago. Rory was shocked when she heard that; Charlie had loved her job.

She was excited about Carmel, but she felt like a kid being offered a roller coaster ride, thrilled but also a bit frightened. Flying made her nervous, especially takeoff and landing, when she would close her eyes and silently recite the Lord's Prayer. But a *private jet?* Didn't they crash a lot? She remembered the last flight she'd been on, heading to Maryland for her mother's funeral so her mother could be buried beside Rory's father. How strange that flight had been, with her mother on the same plane as her but riding in the cargo hold in a coffin.

A new song played over the wireless speakers, "I'm Gonna Be (Five Hundred Miles). It was the song Ben had sung to her in Sedona. She felt a clench in her stomach. She clicked on her playlist and changed the song back to Paul Simon, forcing Ben out of her mind.

Her big fuzzy slippers glided over to the kitchen area, where she stuffed the packing material into the trash bin and then pulled the plastic liner out and twirled around toward the door.

She did a pirouette before opening the door on her way to the dumpster, and then jumped back, dropping the trash bag as her hand flew to her chest.

"Oh my God! You scared me."

Nick and Cass were standing in the doorway. Rory's eyebrows rose with bewilderment. "What are you—is everything—"

"Everything's fine," Cass said with a smile as she wrapped her arms around Rory. Cass's thick, curly locks smelled citrusy—a smell Rory always associated with Cass.

"It sounds like you're having a party," Nick added. "I like the outfit." Nick hugged Rory and then stepped back, looking down at her attire of orange and blue polka-dot pajama pants, big fuzzy slippers, and an old sweatshirt of Derek's.

"I haven't gotten dressed yet today." She ran her hand up to her hair, which was piled on top of her head with a chopstick sticking out the side.

She gave Nick a puzzled look, but before she could even ask what they were doing on her doorstep unexpectedly, he answered her question. "Cass had a sociology seminar in Sacramento, and we decided to surprise you. The trip was kind of spur of the moment. Another professor couldn't make it at the last minute, and he asked

Cass to take his place. Anyway, we have to drive back to Sacramento in two days, but we thought we'd stop in and see where you're holed up."

"Come in! It's tiny, but it's home."

"It's charming; I love it!" Cass said.

Cass hadn't changed, Rory thought. Rory had always teased Nick that he had married a clone of his mother. Cass had the same stocky build and massively curly hair like their mother's.

Nick walked around as if he were making sure the place was OK for his sister. He stopped by her bed and studied the framed photos on the wall. "Who are they?" he asked, pointing to the picture of Ben and his parents.

Rory felt her cheeks warm. "A friend—when he was young."

Nick raised his eyebrows. "I guess I don't have to worry about you pining away up here in the wilderness all by yourself."

———◦◦◦———

"You cheated!" Rory playfully slapped Will's arm. He had won three rounds of hearts in a row. Cass, Nick, Marlena, Rory, and Will were seated at the white enamel table in Marlena's cottage. Patchouli-scented candles flickered around the room. Will had just returned from a three-day convention in Denver. Rory had only seen him once since the rainy day at his house and the kiss.

"All right, we're going to get him this time," Rory said to the group. "He's gonna try to bundle, and we can't let him."

Marlena laughed. "It's just a game. I didn't know you were so competitive."

"I'm not," Rory replied defensively.

Will tilted his head, giving her a skeptical look.

Rory stared at him. "What? I'm not!"

"You are *so* competitive! Like every time we play darts, you start freaking out if you're not winning."

"But that—"

"And what about the ringtoss game on the beach that day in Eureka—you wouldn't stop until you were ahead of me."

Rory opened her mouth to protest, but Will cut her off. "And when we played checkers at my house, you—"

"OK! OK! I'm competitive. What's the big deal? I can't help it—I like to win." She laughed with a shrug and a sheepish expression.

"She is the queen of competition. You should've seen her as a kid," Nick interjected. "We used to have weekly game night at our grandmother's house, and Rory was out for blood."

"I was not!" Rory punched Nick in the arm, feigning indignation, but she knew he was right. She had been competitive. She remembered her excitement at beating her cousins and Nick at crazy eights or poker or Monopoly. But somewhere along the way, she had lost it. Along with her adventurous spirit and joy. It was as if the past twenty-odd years, she had become an automaton, doing all the right things but not feeling anything.

Ethan called out from his bedroom, and Marlena got up to see what he wanted, and then Will's cell rang. He excused himself and went outside to take the call. Nick smiled at Rory from across the table.

"What are you grinning about?" Rory asked, even though she thought she knew.

"It's good seeing you happy. You're like a different person—the old Rory." Nick paused and then added, "So what's going on between you and Will?"

"Nothing. We're just friends." She thought about the kiss again. There hadn't been another. It was as if the kiss had never happened.

"Friends? Uh-huh."

"Nick, stop," Cass said. "Rory, ignore your brother; he can't help himself."

"No, I like him," Nick said. "He seems like a nice guy."

"So you're saying you approve. It's OK for me to see him." Rory winked at Cass.

"*No*—geez, what's with you two? All I'm saying is I like the guy. And it makes me happy to know that you're happy."

"Derek was up here a couple of weeks ago." Rory hadn't told Nick or Jillian about Derek's visit, and she wasn't sure why. She also hadn't told Nick that she had mailed the divorce papers back to her attorney to forward to Derek.

"How'd that go?"

"OK. I told him I want a divorce."

She could see the elation in Nick's eyes even though he was trying not to show it, and for some reason it bothered her. Maybe it was because he had been right from the beginning. She never should have married Derek.

"He didn't flip out?"

"Not really. I was expecting it to be a lot worse than it was. My attorney sent him the divorce papers."

"He probably won't sign them. You know he's not going to make this easy for you."

"I don't know. You're prob—" she stopped midsentence when Will opened the front door, and she gave Nick a look that said, "Let's not talk about it anymore." Will hadn't pushed her to find out about Derek's visit, and she had been glad. The only person in Willow Bend with whom she shared details about her past was Marlena. She didn't want to share that part of her life with Will.

Rory picked up her hand, fanning the cards out, as Will sat back down at the table. She glanced over at him, seeing him through

Nick's eyes. The warm light from the lamp on the counter glowed onto his face. He was a nice guy, attractive, funny, intelligent. She could see why Nick would approve. But other than the kiss, Will had never shown signs of wanting to step things up, and neither had she. Maybe it was the age difference, but she had thought of him more like a brother. Now, she wondered if it could be more. Seeing Will holding his cards, her mind flashed to Ben. The first night they'd been together, they'd played gin rummy at the club where he worked, just the two of them, until the club manager had finally kicked them out. She remembered how Ben always kept a pack of cards in his shirt pocket. She wondered where he was now and imagined him sitting in a hotel in some town, playing cards with his band. A twinge of melancholy tugged at her.

<hr />

Will leaned against his Jeep in Marlena's graveled driveway, his hands in his pockets. Rory stood in front of him with her arms wrapped around herself against the night chill. Only a sliver of moon peered out from the clouds that hung in the dark sky, making it hard for Rory to see Will's face. Jasper was already in his usual spot, sitting upright in the passenger seat.

"I like your brother and his wife."

Rory smiled. She liked having Nick and Cass here. It made it feel more like home. She'd been yawning, barely able to keep her eyes open inside Marlena's, but now a second wind of energy swept through her. She didn't want Will to leave; she wanted to be close to him. Nick and Cass had just left for the Bigfoot Inn. Nick had whispered in her ear as he hugged her good night: "I do approve." She had laughed, but it had sparked something. Maybe it was seeing Nick and Cass together and wishing she had what they had, or maybe she just wanted to feel someone's arms around her, because all she could think about right now was hugging Will and burying her face in his chest.

The sound of crickets and cicadas droned in the distance, interrupted by a low *grrummp* sound of a bullfrog near the pond. She reached out and touched Will's arm but didn't get a response. He seemed distant, his mind somewhere else. Had the phone call he'd gotten earlier upset him? A cool breeze blew by, and she slid her arms around him, hoping to draw him in, but his body felt stiff against hers. He patted her back and then released his arms.

"Is everything OK?"

She heard him sigh as he nodded.

"The phone call earlier—was it work?"

His gaze looked past her toward the darkened meadow, and then he smiled and said it was nothing. "I gotta meet some people tomorrow at six on the north side of the park."

Something was different. She wondered what had brought on his sudden change.

"I should probably get home." He gave her a peck on the cheek and then got in his Jeep. She watched him pull away, worrying that he was keeping something from her.

Walking inside her darkened cottage, she thought maybe Will's behavior had something to do with Colorado. Had he met someone there? And what if he had—would that matter?

She fell into her small iron-framed bed with an aching emptiness in her gut. She flipped open her laptop and, without thinking, went to the website she'd been checking periodically, clicking on the box that said Tour Schedule. She scanned the dates and locations of Ben's band. He would be in Monterey the same weekend she was meeting Charlie in Carmel. A flutter rose in her stomach. What was she doing? She shut the laptop, laid it on the floor beside the bed, and then pulled the covers under her chin. Rolling on her side, she curled her legs into her chest. A homesick feeling washed over her. Was it because Nick and Cass were here? Had they somehow made her homesick? But homesick for what? This was her home now.

She stretched her leg out across the cold sheets. Loneliness crept into her bones. She remembered lying next to Derek after she'd broken it off with Ben, his back to her, the sound of his rhythmic snoring like an echo in her head, reinforcing how lonely she felt.

18

The parking lot was empty except for a few cars parked toward the back. Rory leaned against the driver door of the Falcon. Will had called her earlier and asked if she'd like to meet for dinner. It was the first time they had talked since the night at Marlena's four days ago.

During dinner he had been like the old Will, cracking jokes and making her laugh and she forgot about his distant behavior the other night. Now she looked up at the clear black sky sprinkled with stars, feeling the soft breeze against her skin.

Will stood facing her with his hands in his pockets. "Nice night."

She nodded and breathed in the crisp, pine-scented air.

He reached out and brushed a strand of hair that had fallen loose from her clip, his fingers touching her cheek. He then leaned in and kissed her. She kissed him back, reaching her arms around his neck. His hands wrapped around her, drawing her closer. The fatigue she had felt after work, dance class, and two glasses of wine vanished. A swirling desire rose inside. It felt so good to be in his arms.

Headlight beams spotlighted them as an SUV with a kayak strapped to the roof pulled into the parking lot, and three men got out laughing loudly, their voices echoing across the lot. Will released his arms and stepped back. She wanted more, even though there was a tiny voice in the back of her head saying, Slow down; don't complicate things. But she ignored the voice and asked him to follow her to her place. He studied her face, but before he could answer, his phone rang—a tourist camping in the forest had fallen down a rocky slope and possibly broken his leg. The ranger station needed him on the scene. The moment was gone. Before leaving, he kissed her quickly on the lips, and said, "Tomorrow."

The next day she wondered if the universe was purposely keeping them apart. Marlena had to work a double shift at the winery and asked Rory if she could watch Ethan that evening. It seemed the timing was never right. Maybe it was for the best. She didn't need to muddle her life right now with a relationship.

<hr>

Rory's mouth watered as she looked at the eight-by-ten glossy picture of the savory side dish of glazed sweet potatoes. Seated on the couch in an alcove of Tanoak bookstore, she set the magazine in the stack of maybes beside her. Ethan was in front of her on the dark flowered rug surrounded by an array of books, trying to decide which one to get.

She flipped through a *Barefoot Contessa* cookbook with pictures of Ina Garten's house in the Hamptons, a table set outside among the hydrangeas, the white tablecloth blowing in the breeze and a caption that read, "Home is where Jeffrey is." *Oh, please*, Rory thought. Could anyone's life really be that perfect? Her sarcasm masked the envy that simmered inside, wishing her life was like that.

She glanced over at Ethan. She liked their afternoons at the book store. It had gotten to be a ritual. After work, at least once a week they would settle in the cozy nook in the back of the store that was partitioned off by bookshelves. She enjoyed buying Ethan books, remembering how much she'd loved to read at his age.

She felt a connection to Ethan. They had both lost their fathers. As a child, she'd had very few friends. Her world had revolved around dance. She wondered what made Ethan happy.

"I want to get this one," Ethan said, bringing over a *Harry Potter* book.

Rory took the book from him and read the title: *Harry Potter and the Sorcerer's Stone*. The cover pictured a boy flying on a broom. She had never read a *Harry Potter* book. Jillian hadn't been interested in them. She wondered if it might be too old for him.

"It looks a little scary." She furrowed her brow.

"*Please.* My dad and I watched a movie about monsters once, and I didn't get scared." His eyes pleaded with her while he waited for her answer.

The look was wearing her down. She glanced over the reviews on the back of the book. "OK."

"Thanks!" Ethan shouted and then ran over to put the other books back on the shelves.

She had a hard time saying no to him. Something about Ethan pulled at her heartstrings. She wondered what kind of relationship he'd had with his dad. He rarely talked about him. The other day at the cottage, they had been playing a game of crazy eights at the kitchen table, and he said out of the blue, "My dad makes my mom cry. I don't like it when she cries." A twinge of sorrow had filled Rory, seeing the look of sadness in Ethan's eyes, thinking Marlena must've had an intense love for her husband to still be crying over him.

She had asked Ethan if he missed his dad, thinking maybe he wanted to talk about it. She'd been surprised when he said no.

Now, she looked out the window on the side wall to the alley that ran between the shops. It was already getting dark, the days getting shorter. She remembered as a child on fall afternoons walking along Sycamore Avenue back in Takoma Park. The crisp smell that surrounded her as she rustled the scattered leaves lining the sidewalk. Watching the street lamps come on one by one down the steep road. Running up the steps to her house and peeking in the mail slot of the door before opening it, calling to her dad. Like a warm rush of air, a nostalgic feeling brushed over her.

———◦∞◦———

"R-E-S-P-E-C-T," Rory crooned into the wooden spoon microphone she held in her hand. Aretha's soulful voice resonated through the cottage as she and Ethan danced around the tiny kitchen making dinner together. She threw some carrots into the pot for the soup, having let Ethan pick the recipe from the magazine she'd purchased earlier. Stirring the liquid, she dipped her nose toward the steam that rose from the pot and breathed in the aroma of onions and cilantro.

Ethan took the dishes over to the table and then set out the utensils, lining up the spoons evenly with the knives. Rory watched him carefully fold the paper napkins in half and set them beside the soup bowls. He was a good kid, she thought, remembering how some nights, when she was not much older than Ethan, and her mother was working late as usual, she would make the one dish she knew how to fix—spaghetti—and then set the table and call Nick and her dad to come to dinner. She loved the praise her father would give her, telling her what a great cook she was.

Waiting for the soup to finish she sat down at the table with a glass of wine and the stack of mail she had picked up at the post office earlier. Ethan sat on the floor by the coffee table doing his homework with Shiloh lying beside him. She leafed through what was mostly junk, then paused at an envelope from her attorney. What was he sending her? She hadn't been expecting anything. A flutter of anxiety stirred in her gut. She tore open the flap and unfolded the pages.

It was the divorce papers, signed by Derek…his name neatly scripted on the paper. *Derek David Jensen.* The perfect D boldly written with no hesitation. His name shouted off the page, and she felt short of breath. There had been no phone call ahead of time telling her he was signing them. The only time she'd spoken to him in the past few weeks was when he'd called to ask her about an insurance bill. He'd been all business, no small talk. Didn't ask her how she was, no mention of the divorce either—just right to the point of why he had called. It was as if a switch had flipped after their talk at the Bigfoot Inn.

Now she stared at the paper in her hand, feeling strange. She was officially divorced. A giddy feeling rose inside her, but at the same time, a grip of sadness tugged at her. She was a single woman, but the words felt foreign to her. This was what she wanted, wasn't it?

Scenes flashed through her head—running down Corral Canyon Road beside Jillian on her two-wheel bike without training wheels—Derek on the other side, afraid to let go of the back. Laughing as Jillian shouted, "Dad, I can do it myself!" Christmas Eve, after Jillian had gone to bed, getting Derek to slow dance to the song "Please Come Home for Christmas."

Was she better off now? She lived alone in a rented cabin, worked as a waitress, and would be spending Thanksgiving with four people who three months ago had been total strangers. But then another image flashed in her mind—driving home late from a Pampered Chef party years ago. Derek standing in the doorway, berating her the minute she walked in. Questioning her as to why she was late, grilling her as if she were one of his perps. It hadn't been an isolated incident. For weeks after she'd arrived in Willow Bend, if she was driving home late to the cottage, a knot would form in her stomach as if on cue. That was gone now.

She was a divorcee. Was that even a word anymore? She still hadn't fully grasped the reality of it. For months before she'd left Phoenix, she'd imagined being divorced, thinking she'd feel free and happy. But the reality was almost anticlimactic. She didn't feel joyous. She didn't know what she felt.

She picked up her cell phone, which was sitting on the edge of the table, and noticed she had a voice mail: it was Will, asking what time dinner was on Thursday. She felt a pang of frustration from the other night when Will had been called away. She stared at the divorce papers again, thinking she was free to do whatever she wanted. But was she just running straight into another relationship? Maybe it was better to wait.

"Watch this!" Ethan shouted. He stood in the middle of the tiny living room playing air guitar to Jimi Hendrix's "Purple Haze," while Shiloh danced around him. Rory laughed and got up to join in.

19

The sun had set over an hour ago, and Marlena's living room was bathed in a golden light from the amber-shaded floor lamp in one corner and another on the end table by the front door. Numerous candles flickered about the room. They'd eaten at Marlena's larger cottage, even though Rory had done most of the cooking at her place, but the Thanksgiving dinner hadn't gone exactly as planned.

While the turkey was roasting, Rory's oven had broken down, and by the time she'd discovered it, the bird was barely halfway done, and it was too late for it to be ready with the rest of the meal. She'd cursed the tiny 1960s worn-out piece of crap that passed as an oven and silently chastised Mr. Danvers for not upgrading his cabins. She felt like everything was ruined. All day she'd been trying to stay positive, pushing away the homesick feeling that tugged at her gut, telling herself the day was going to be special. But when the oven broke, it had reinforced all the frustrated envy that had been festering as she thought of Derek with Jillian.

When she made the announcement that they were having a meatless Thanksgiving, she had worried that everyone would be disappointed, but when no one seemed to mind, relief replaced the pressure that had been mounting inside. They'd finished cooking the turkey in Marlena's oven, and the aroma of turkey stuffed with cranberries, sage, and rosemary lingered in the air.

Contentment filled her as she poured more wine into Will's glass and then added a little more to her own. She smiled as she studied the group gathered around the coffee table eating pie and playing charades. Rory was impressed with how good Will was, practically guessing everything she acted out in less than two words. But Mr. Danvers stole the show. He had them in hysterics with his melodramatic portrayal of the characters; instead of acting out the words in the titles, he would act out the actual movie or book.

Now Mr. Danvers was imitating what looked like a strangely awkward ballet dancer or maybe someone afflicted with Tourette's.

"One Flew over the Cuckoo's Nest!" Will shouted.

Rory frowned at him. Where did he come up with that? "How many words?" she asked. "Is it a book or a movie?" Rory's questions fell on deaf ears as Mr. Danvers just continued with his jerky movements.

There was a knock at the door.

Shiloh lifted his head from under the coffee table and gave a muffled bark. Marlena looked out the darkened window and shrugged toward the group.

Before she had the door fully open, it suddenly flung wide, pushing Marlena against the end table. A man burst into the room. Everyone stared in silence until Ethan shouted, "Dad!" Rory looked at Marlena, completely baffled. *Dad?* The man's fists were clenched at his sides, and he scanned the room, ending on Marlena.

Rory's eyes darted to Will, who sprang from the sofa to a standing position. She glanced over at Mr. Danvers, still rooted to his spot at center stage on the living room rug, his arms held out frozen in their depiction of something, looking confused. Rory's head snapped back to the man while she watched in bewilderment as Ethan jumped up from the floor by the coffee table and ran toward his father, but Marlena caught his arm and pulled him to her, keeping her arm protectively around him. Ethan looked at his mother but didn't say anything.

"I knew I'd find you." The man slurred his words. He was a few inches taller than Marlena but with a stockier build. Rory could see the resemblance to Ethan; they had the same-shaped face and eyes.

"Max, get out." Marlena's words were calm but firm.

"Not without my son," Max said through clenched teeth, like an animal ready to pounce.

Will took a couple of steps toward Marlena. "Why don't we sit down and…"

"You stay the fuck out of this," Max replied without taking his eyes off Marlena.

"Marlena, do you want him to leave?" Will asked.

Marlena nodded.

"OK, buddy, let's go outside and talk." Will stepped toward Max and touched the side of his arm.

Max flicked his arm up and told Will to fuck off. Will reached out again, and this time the man flung himself at Will, knocking him backward. Rory cringed as the two men scrambled across the room, knocking over a chair and some candles. She grabbed her phone from the coffee table and punched in 911 with shaking fingers.

"*Dad!*" Ethan screamed. Marlena dragged Ethan into the bedroom, slamming the door behind her.

Rory jumped up from the sofa as the men crashed into the coffee table, spilling the wineglasses, and then the two ended up on the braided rug, rolling back and forth in a bear hug. She ran into the kitchen, her heart racing as she searched for something—what, she didn't know. She wanted to help Will. Instead she just stood in horror with her arms wrapped around her chest, watching the two men wrestle, with Shiloh nipping at their pants.

"That's enough!" A booming voice from across the room was followed by the distinctive sound of a gun cocking. Rory turned to see Mr. Danvers, a shotgun pressed up against his long gray beard, aiming straight at the two men. Both of them stopped their scuffle, and Will scrambled to his feet. Max remained on the floor, staring blankly at Mr. Danvers.

"Don't you move. You hear me?" Mr. Danvers said in a steady voice.

Max held up his hands. "I just want to see my son! He's *my* fucking *son*! She stole him from me."

Mr. Danvers, with his cheek pressed against the barrel, shouted, "Shut up!"

Rory's heart thumped against her ribs. She smelled the alcohol reeking from the man on the floor. Will brushed his hair back off his face and adjusted his pants and shirt, breathing heavily. Rory gave him a questioning look, wanting to ask if he was all right, but she couldn't form the words to speak.

"I'm OK," Will said, as if reading her thoughts. The four of them remained stationary, like actors on a stage waiting for their cue. Rory felt her knees getting weak, and she sank into a kitchen chair. Within minutes, the sound of sirens in the distance grew closer. The front door was still open. The crunch of screeching tires on the gravel outside followed by car doors slamming echoed inside.

Rory watched the bizarre scene of the police questioning Will and Mr. Danvers, while another officer handcuffed Max and led him out of the house. Then the first officer looked to her, asking about her connection to Marlena. She told him she lived next door.

"Have you ever met this man before?" She noticed the officer's thin neck and prominent Adam's apple that moved up and down when he spoke. He couldn't be more than eighteen, she thought. "Ma'am? Have you ever met him before?"

She hesitated, wanting to say, *I thought he was dead*, but she just shook her head.

The officer got Marlena from the bedroom and began questioning her. Rory listened while Marlena softly answered each question. Her face showed no signs of distress as she stared straight ahead at some distant object.

⸺⸱⸲◦◦◦⸲⸱⸺

The room was quiet except for the ticking sound of the clock in the kitchen and the muffled voices on the television coming from Marlena's bedroom, where Ethan was watching a movie. Everyone else had left, including Will, who had decided to follow the police down to the station. He told Rory he wanted to make sure Max got locked up for the night. He said he'd call her later. Rory was curled up on one end of the sofa, and Marlena sat rigid at the other end.

She studied Marlena's profile, partially in shadow from the amber lamplight. The smell of sage and rosemary hung heavy in the air. The turkey sat on the counter. Rory finally broke the silence. "Why'd you tell me your husband was dead?"

"To me, he *is* dead." Marlena's face was like stone.

"What about Ethan? Did *he* think his father was dead?"

Marlena shook her head.

Rory had felt a bond with Ethan for losing his father, and all this time he was alive. She felt strangely betrayed. "You could've told me the truth." She felt hurt that Marlena hadn't felt she could confide in Rory, especially since Rory had unloaded all her issues with Derek on Marlena. Rory studied Marlena's stoic profile, but Marlena remained silent. "I'm sure you have your reasons, but why would you keep Ethan from seeing his father?"

Marlena slowly turned toward Rory. "Not all fathers are good. I know you loved yours." She stared off toward the darkened kitchen and continued, her voice void of emotion. "Even Derek, when you told me about his verbal attacks, that was nothing compared to…"

She stopped and looked down at her hands. "Those stories you told me of Jillian and him, trips you took together…"

"You could've confided in me. I would've listened." She was hurt by Marlena's deceit.

"Maybe I wanted to believe he was dead." Marlena looked away again.

Rory stared at the stout candle on the coffee table, misshapen from the fall. "You thought he'd taken Ethan…that day in the meadow," Rory said. She was referring to a day that Marlena had pounded on her door in a panic, saying Ethan had disappeared. She remembered the look of terror on Marlena's face. But then Ethan had shown up with Shiloh a minute later. "Why didn't you tell me about Max then?"

Marlena shrugged.

She wanted to comfort Marlena somehow, realizing Marlena must have been living each day in fear that her husband might show up. "Well, at least he's been arrested. You won't have to worry about him now."

Marlena made a little snorting sound and shook her head. "If that were only true. This isn't the first time." She paused. "I'd hoped things would be different. This was the longest I've gone without him finding me."

Ethan called Marlena, and she rose, walking robotically to the bedroom. Rory scraped up the spilled wax from the floor, refilled the vase of flowers, and blotted up the water and wine on the rug, trying to erase what had happened, all the while thinking of the lie Marlena had been living. But hadn't she been living a lie as well back in Phoenix? Pretending to have had the perfect marriage? She remembered the hurt look on Kelly's face in Temecula when she told her that her marriage had been troubled. How many people had secrets? Living the lives they wanted others to think that they had, posting pictures on Facebook and Instagram, sharing all the wonderful things that they did. Was everyone living a lie?

Wandering around the open living area of the cottage, she eyed the warmth scattered about—a photo by the front door of Marlena and Ethan dressed in full Native American attire, headdresses and all, smiling into the camera; a necklace Marlena had made, with an intricate pattern of silver and lapis lazuli, lying on a small table in the corner of the room. She smiled at a picture taped to the refrigerator with Ethan holding up a fish, a proud grin plastered across his face, and the anger and betrayal she had felt melted away. This woman was a survivor, continuing to forge on through adversity or whatever life gave her. Rory admired that, and she forgave Marlena for lying to her.

Marlena came out of the bedroom and poured them both more wine.

"How is he?" Rory was worried about Ethan.

"He wanted to know why his dad had hit Will and what was going to happen to him. I told him that hitting people was bad and that his dad needed to be punished." For a fleeting second, Rory saw a crack in the steely facade Marlena wore. A look of sadness escaped across her face but then was quickly locked away.

"I can't imagine what you've gone through."

She told Rory briefly about her life with Max—the physical abuse, his drinking problem, the divorce, and how she'd gotten full custody of Ethan, had even gotten a restraining order against Max, but that hadn't stopped him from threatening her. She said she didn't want to have to keep moving and changing schools for Ethan.

All Rory wanted to do was put her arms around Marlena, but she wasn't sure if Marlena would want that. She felt a separation between them, something that hadn't been there before. The tiredness in Marlena's eyes was evident, and Rory knew she must be exhausted, emotionally and physically. She asked her if she wanted her to stay, but Marlena said she was fine.

Rory walked into her empty cottage carrying the uneaten turkey wrapped in foil. Marlena had insisted she take it home. What was she going to do with a whole turkey? She felt numb, completely drained. Alone. Missing Jillian now more than ever. Kicking off her shoes, she hit the switch on the wall that turned on the lamp by the couch and then went over and lit the lamp by the bed and the kitchen light. She needed light.

She shoved the turkey into the fridge and stood facing the cluttered mess in the kitchen, pots with dried food on them, a bag of flour on the counter, bowls piled in the sink. Too tired to do anything about it, she poured herself another glass of wine and then turned off the kitchen light, hoping to hide the disorder. She went over to the sofa and put her feet up on a throw pillow.

The day played back in her head. It had definitely not been a run-of-the-mill Thanksgiving, she thought. A nagging feeling tugged at her. She had been trying so hard to make this place her home, believing she and Marlena were close, like family, because she needed family. But she had created something that wasn't there. Marlena was her neighbor, a friend—that was it. A pang of sorrow filled her, wondering what Ethan's childhood had been like.

She thought about her own childhood—did anyone have a normal childhood? Maybe Jillian, or so she hoped. But what if the battles between Derek and her had scarred Jillian? She'd received an e-mail from Derek yesterday asking about the assets they had divided. It was all very cordial and professional sounding, as if he were talking about dissolving some venture he'd gotten into with a distant business partner. There had been no animosity in his words, and she was surprised. She hadn't answered him back yet, mainly because she hadn't a clue what she wanted to do with anything. When she had left almost three months ago, her thoughts had never gone past the initial leaving. Had it been that she had never really expected to go through with it? What did she want to do with the house, her furniture, all the odds and ends they'd amassed over the years? She rubbed her forehead, feeling a headache coming on, and decided it was too much to think about tonight.

She sipped her wine and picked up her cell. Will hadn't called. Her phone read 10:02 p.m. He'd left several hours ago. She called his cell, but it went straight to voice mail. She set the phone back down, not leaving a message.

Her phone rang.

She was about to say it must be mental telepathy when she noticed it wasn't Will but Jillian. That warm, comforting feeling spread through her when she heard Jillian's voice. She wished she could wrap her arms around her daughter.

"You don't want to know how it went," Rory said with a snort after Jillian had inquired about her Thanksgiving.

"What do you mean?"

"I wouldn't even know where to begin." Rory took a deep breath and then clued Jillian in on the day's events, assuring her that she was OK. She then asked Jillian how it had gone in Phoenix.

Jillian told Rory how Aunt Carrie had taken over, just like Rory had suspected she would, and that Jillian had been relegated to the menial tasks of chopping onions and cleaning up after her aunt. Rory pictured them in her kitchen. The depressed feeling seeped back in, and she tried to push it away, but it only grew as Jillian talked about her boyfriend, Joe, who hadn't come, wanting to spend the holiday with his parents in Florida. Once they were in London, they probably wouldn't be able to come home for the holidays, Jillian said, so he wanted to spend some time with his family. Rory felt the familiar knot twisting in her gut whenever she thought about Jillian in England. She swallowed a large gulp of wine.

Jillian continued with an account of her grandmother Jensen and her aunts, who grilled her about what Rory was up to, and Jillian assured her mother that she made it clear to them how great Rory was doing. "I told them you had this really cool place near the mountains and how you were working and taking classes. Grandma wants you to call her."

Rory stared across the room at the close-up photo of her and Jillian, their cheeks pressed together. Tears stung her eyes. Hearing about the family made her feel more isolated. She liked Derek's mom, but she knew she wouldn't call her. She would try to persuade Rory to come back.

Jillian was on her fourth or fifth tale, this one about her grandfather falling asleep at the table. Rory could tell there was something on Jillian's mind. She had sensed Jillian's hesitation each time she'd started a new account of the day. What was Jillian keeping from her? Had Derek blown up, and Jillian was afraid to tell her? "OK, Jillian, what's going on? You haven't said one word about your dad. Was he even there?"

"Of course." She paused. "What do you want me to say?"

"It's what you haven't said. You mentioned everyone else but him." She picked up her wineglass.

Silence, and then Jillian said, "He had a woman over."

"What?" She set the wine down on the coffee table.

"I'm sorry, Mom, but I thought you should know."

"What do you mean he had a woman over? You mean a date? A woman was at my house on Thanksgiving with *Dad?*" Her exhaustion was gone. She felt adrenaline pump through her veins. She'd been so consumed with wondering what direction her life was taking, it had never dawned on her that Derek would be starting a new life as well.

After hanging up with Jillian, she paced the entirety of the cottage and then went back to the couch, but within seconds she was back up, walking the floor as her mind replayed everything Jillian had told her.

Her name was Donna. She was thirty-six and had auburn hair. Jillian figured she was around five-four with a petite build. Pretty, but not as pretty as Rory, according to Jillian. She worked at the station as a clerk of some sort. No kids. Bicycled, like Derek. They'd raced together before. What kind of woman would go to a man's house for Thanksgiving when he'd only just divorced his wife? As soon as she thought the words, she realized how ridiculous they sounded. There was nothing wrong with what the woman had done. Derek was a free man. Why was this bothering her so much?

She felt claustrophobic. On impulse, she grabbed her purse, slipped on her shoes, and headed out the door. She got in the car, telling herself she just needed to drive and clear her head, but she knew what she was doing.

As she backed out of the driveway, she snorted a disgruntled laugh. She'd thought Derek's mom wanted to talk so she could convince her to come back, but maybe she was wrong; maybe she wanted to thank her for leaving her son. She imagined Derek with his arm around Donna, listening intently as she chatted with Jillian, inviting Jillian to go bike riding with them. The whole family gathered around Donna while she entertained them with her witty tales.

Twenty minutes later she was driving fast down the dark dirt road. Her headlights shone on the tall pines that bordered both sides. A deer bolted out from the woods, and she slammed on her brakes, swerving to the right, her left fender barely missing the hind leg of the deer that disappeared just as quickly through the trees on the other side. Her tires skidded on the grassy shoulder as she steered back onto the dark road, trying not to spin out of control. It was over in a second, but her hand shook as she brushed her hair away from her face. Her senses now on full alert, she scanned the line of trees as she continued down the road.

She needed to see Will. Last week had gotten messed up, but she didn't want to wait any longer. She played the scenario in her head. She'd knock on the door, he'd answer, and then he'd pull her inside and hold her like he'd done in the parking lot. She needed to feel his arms around her.

Was it because of Derek?

When had Derek started seeing this woman? Was it before Rory had left? She'd really been duped. Here she'd felt so guilty about her affair with Ben, and all along Derek had probably been cheating on her. Well, she had no reason to feel guilty now. So what if she'd vowed this was her time to be independent. It didn't mean she had to take a vow of chastity.

She pulled up to Will's driveway, but just as she was about to turn in, she noticed another car parked next to his Jeep. She turned the car so that her headlights shone on a Prius with Colorado tags. Her heart beat faster as her mind raced—he *had* met someone in Denver at the convention. But why had he come over for Thanksgiving?

She continued driving down the dirt road past his house, looking for a place to turn around. It was pitch black except for the beam of her headlights. She smacked the steering wheel so hard her fingers stung. Why hadn't he been honest with her? Instead, he'd made her believe he wanted to be with her. Anger rose up inside as she turned into another driveway a little farther down and then headed back in the other direction.

As she passed by his house again, she slowed down, staring at the A-frame, lights on inside, smoke coming out of the chimney. He'd made a fire. How cozy. What an idiot she'd been, believing he really cared about her. Her mind flashed to a vision of Derek in their den in Phoenix, flames crackling in the brick fireplace, nestled on the suede sofa next to Donna.

I'm the outsider looking in, she thought. She glanced down at the illuminated dash of the Falcon and dropped her head onto the steering wheel, thinking how life sucked. The molded plastic of the wheel dug into her forehead, but she pressed harder. No, men sucked. Why had she come running over here? She didn't need Will; she didn't need any man.

She lifted her head and shoved back her shoulders. Her hands gripped the wheel as she hit the accelerator. The tires spun, trying to grab traction in the dirt. She kept her foot pressed down, veering around the bend in the road, knowing she should slow down, but she kept increasing her speed. It felt good.

The next afternoon she headed out to the dumpster with a bag of trash, breathing in the crisp air tinged with a hint of burning leaves. She smiled, thinking she would invite Marlena and Ethan over to eat the leftover turkey. But when she glanced over at Marlena's cottage, she noticed Marlena in the driveway, placing a small suitcase in the car. Worry rose up inside as Rory wondered if Max had gotten back out of jail. Was Marlena running away again? She set the trash bag down and hurried across the damp grass. Marlena saw her and waved. Ethan was already in the car by the time she got over.

"Going somewhere?"

"My grandmother's." Marlena tucked her long black hair behind her ear as she stared down at the graveled drive. "Just for a couple of days."

Rory nodded. Her worry turned to hurt. Would she have left without saying good-bye?

"Look, Rory, I'm sorry—"

"You don't have to apologize."

"I should've told you the truth."

"It's OK."

A large crow dipped out of one of the pines and cawed. The sound echoed across the meadow.

"They've charged him with stalking. It's a felony. Maybe he'll finally get locked up." Marlena's hand was on the car door, ready to open it. "I really enjoyed yesterday, you know, up until—"

"Yeah, it was fun," Rory said with a smile that masked a sudden sadness creeping in.

"We'll see you in a few days." Marlena opened the door and got in. Ethan waved to Rory from the passenger side as Marlena pulled out of the driveway.

Rory trudged back over to the bag of trash, sitting in the walkway. Throwing the plastic bag in the dumpster, she felt as if her life was being thrown in with it. Why did seeing Marlena leave hurt so badly? Was it because she felt she'd been deceived? She'd poured her heart out to Marlena, thinking they were close friends, believing she was a widow who'd lost someone she loved. She realized she knew nothing about Marlena *or* Will. She'd thought he was one of the good guys, honest, caring, but it had all been a sham. Maybe her life in Phoenix hadn't been as bad as she thought. Maybe what she'd been searching for didn't even exist.

The sky was a brilliant deep orange with streaks of blue-gray clouds against the hills, but all she saw was the empty gravel lane where Marlena's car had been just minutes before. Her shoulders slumped as she wrapped her arms around her chest. She wanted to run away…just get in the car and drive. But what was she running from this time?

20

I don't know why it bothers me so much. Do you think I'm crazy?" Seated at the small outdoor café in Carmel, Rory wrapped her bulky knit sweater around her as a gust of wind blew by. She glanced up at the tall metal heater near their table, wondering if it was even turned on. It had been a week since Thanksgiving, and she had been having intermittent waves of melancholy. She had hoped Charlie's birthday weekend would lighten things up for her, but she couldn't get Derek out of her mind.

Charlie jabbed a forkful of salad, not seeming the least bit cold in her designer suit. "Why *does* it bother you? Because she was at your house for Thanksgiving or because Derek's seeing someone else?"

"All I could picture when Jillian told me was her eating off *my* china, sitting at *my* dining room table, and probably sleeping in *my* bed!" Seagulls cawed beyond the vine-covered arbor that hung overhead, partially blocking the afternoon sun. "I guess I've got to stop thinking of it as my house."

The aroma of fennel wafted by, and Rory's eyes followed the tray a waiter carried past their table. "There's more to it than that, though. I know you're going to think this is insane." She leaned forward, staring down at her bowl of soup and swirling her spoon across the thick liquid for several seconds. When she looked up at Charlie, her fork was poised midair. "I know I cheated on Derek, but a part of me felt justified because of the way he'd treated me over the years. So is it crazy that I'm hurt that he started dating someone else so soon? I mean, I really tried to be the best wife, and I feel like he's just moved on, like he didn't even care."

"Do you want him back?"

"No!" Rory shook her head. The muffled street sounds of cars driving by filtered through the café along with the smell of sea air.

"But you don't want him to see other women?"

"No. I mean, yes. I don't know." She brushed a strand of hair behind her ear. "I told you it was insane." *Was* she jealous that Derek was seeing someone else? The thought made her feel uneasy. Her eyes drifted to a couple seated across the patio, the man's hair gray around the temple like Derek's. The woman was gesturing as she spoke, and their eyes were locked on each other, as if no one else existed. Sadness washed over Rory. What was it that she wanted? Another gust of wind blew by, and she hugged her arms around her. "I want him to be happy, but I guess I wanted him to want me more. Is that stupid?"

Charlie gave a half smile but didn't say anything. She had a puzzled expression.

"What? You think I'm an idiot."

"I guess I'm a little confused. I mean, I get it…you expected him to fight for you, so it took you by surprise. But you gotta admit this is better than if he was refusing to let you go, isn't it?"

Rory laughed wearily. "I told you it was crazy." She stared down at the brick floor, swept clean except for a piece of smashed tomato next to another table. She was surprised the waiter hadn't picked it up; there had to be a law against trash being left on the ground for more than a minute in Carmel. The town was like something out of a children's picture book, with Hansel and Gretel–looking houses, quaint shops, and beautiful gardens everywhere.

"Do you think he was seeing her before?" Rory's eyes drifted back to the couple across the patio. Their hands were now intertwined. "What if he was having an affair?"

"Does it make any difference?"

"It's just not fair. I'm the one who's had to disrupt her whole life, move to a new town, and he gets to stay in our house and just replace me with someone else." She knew she sounded whiny, and she also knew it had been her decision to leave in the first place.

"Sounds like you wanted him to suffer more."

Was that what she wanted? Rory watched Charlie as she deliberately picked out the olives from her salad and gathered them on her fork, the shaft of light catching the diamond of her engagement ring. From the minute Rory had gotten off the plane, she'd noticed the change in Charlie's appearance. Even her skin appeared flawless, as if it glowed. Was there some mysterious formula to perfect skin that only the rich knew about? Now that Charlie was living in San Francisco in the fold of the Binghamton empire, she must be privy to the secret.

Rory brushed the crumbs of french bread from her lap and noticed that the white line that had been etched on her ring finger was now completely faded. Just three months to wipe away twenty-four years. She didn't know how to answer Charlie, not wanting to admit that maybe she *did* want Derek to suffer.

Waves crashed onto the giant black rocks outside the wall-to-wall windows of the Binghamtons' expansive living room. Rory was curled up on the deep-cushioned sofa, sipping chai tea and feeling blissful after her day at the spa. She closed her eyes, reliving the stone massage. The sound of a harp that had played in the background still resonated in her ears. The smell of rose and lavender from the aromatic oils lingered on her skin.

She hovered in a semiconscious state with random images flashing before her like a slideshow on a screen—gliding across the floor in dance class, the music acting as the strings and she the marionette; playing cards with Ethan; her dining room in Phoenix—Derek at one end of the table and the woman she'd never seen but had a complete picture of in her head seated at the other. She had to let it go. Her thoughts moved to Will and the Prius in his driveway. She felt herself tensing up and quickly erased the thought.

She opened her eyes and stared out at the misty gray afternoon sky. An image of Ben appeared in her mind—sitting on the edge of his bed, a rare rainy afternoon in Phoenix. He was picking his guitar, playing no song in particular, while he told her how he wanted to take her down to the Bayou Courtableau, where his grandmother Lucie Boudreaux lived, so that she could experience the smell of crawfish boiling in the big pot, mixed with the sweet smell of summer jasmine, his favorite scent. Remembering his distinctive drawl sent a rush of warmth through her chest.

Charlie walked into the room, her hair wrapped in a turban-style towel. An apple in one hand and a glass of water with lime in the other, she sank down into the large overstuffed chair. Her magenta silk robe stood out against the beige and white décor.

"I now know the secret you rich people have of looking so great: you just go to the spa once a week." Rory ran her hand over her cheek. "My skin has never felt so fantastic!"

Charlie laughed. "I'm not one of the rich people yet." She took a bite of the apple. "So what should we do tonight?"

"I'd be content just to lie here and look out at the ocean." Rory watched two seagulls soar by. "I can't believe the Binghamtons don't live here all the time."

"You should see their place in San Francisco." Charlie set her apple down and picked up the newspaper that was lying on the glass-

and-stone coffee table. "Let's see what's happening around here. We need to do something exciting." She flipped through the pages of the paper. "There's a jazz band at one of the clubs in Monterey." She continued scanning. "How about a karaoke bar?"

Rory shook her head and laughed. "You don't want to give me a microphone. Have you heard me sing?" She gazed back out the window. "Ben's here."

"What?" Charlie's brow furrowed.

"His band. They're playing in Monterey this weekend."

"No way! We've gotta go!" Charlie jumped up from her chair, and the towel fell from her head.

"I don't know." Rory leaned back on the sofa.

"What do you mean you don't know?"

"I don't know if I want to open that back up." She pictured standing on the sidewalk outside the breakfast place, seeing the hurt in Ben's eyes.

"Now I *know* you're crazy. Look, you said before that you really liked this guy. You're *divorced*, for God's sake! Derek's dating; what's stopping you?"

———

Bernie's was packed. Rory and Charlie were tucked in a corner toward the back of the room. She felt like she was burrowed in a cave of darkness: black walls and carpet, ebony granite-topped tables. The only source of illumination came from the bright spotlights that shone onto the stage. She'd been staring at Ben from the minute he'd walked across the raised wooden floor with his guitar slung over his shoulder, watching the way he put his guitar pick between his teeth while he adjusted his strap, studying his wavy brown hair, which brushed his collar, with some strands falling inside. Her eyes pored over him as if she were admiring a Rembrandt. She focused in on his blue eyes, how they turned down slightly and crinkled when he smiled.

Ever since Thanksgiving, she'd blamed her discontent on Derek having a woman over, on seeing the car in Will's driveway, on feeling distanced from Marlena—but deep down she knew they weren't the true source. She felt stagnant, like something was missing.

But on the drive to Bernie's, her breath had shortened from the excitement that welled over her, and she'd even let it spill out, telling Charlie how she felt, that this had to be a sign. It was too coincidental that Ben was playing in Monterey the same time she was here. She told Charlie how she'd been trying to push Ben out of her thoughts, wanting to stay focused on her journey, but now it all made sense. There was no reason why she shouldn't be with Ben.

"This next song is one I wrote a while back." Ben's words echoed through the microphone. His long fingers plucked at the guitar strings, followed by the haunting words. It was her song, "When Love Walked out My Door." Tears stung her eyes. She still couldn't believe he'd written a song about her. Why hadn't she realized how much she'd meant to him?

Toward the end of the song, Charlie leaned over and whispered, "Is that about you?"

Rory gave Charlie a sheepish grin and then nodded.

Charlie smacked her on the arm and said, "What's wrong with you? The guy's gorgeous. I can't believe you aren't with him?"

Rory glanced around the crowded room. Faces were fixed on the stage, everyone intently listening to the song. *Her song.* Her worries about what she was doing with her life seemed insignificant now. She'd found the missing puzzle piece—the picture was now clear. She couldn't wait for the show to end so she could tell Ben she was back. She tapped her foot while her hands fidgeted with her necklace. Eagerness bubbled inside, and she wanted to laugh out loud. Ben made her happy. Why hadn't she seen that before? But then an anxious wave washed over her. What if it was too late? What if he didn't feel the same? She'd left him twice. What made her think he'd still want her?

———————

She and Charlie squeezed through the people milling about after the show and weaved their way toward the backstage entrance. The lights were turned up; the black cave awakened with the noise of conversations and laughter. Rory was several steps in front of Charlie, moving with determination as if a force were propelling her toward Ben. Piped music blended with the hum of voices. She inhaled the smell of alcohol mixed with an assortment of colognes as she pushed past elbows and shoulders.

Less than twenty feet away, she saw him come through the backstage door. She smiled as her heart skipped a beat. She wanted to call out his name, and it took all her effort not to break into a run.

But then he made his way over to a tall woman with long blond hair and leaned down, kissing her on the mouth. Rory halted, feeling as if someone had just punched her in the gut. Charlie slammed into the back of her. Rory spun on her boot and began pushing her way back through the crowd, bumping into the bodies that impeded her escape. She heard Charlie shouting her name to come back. The sea of people melded together from the tears that blurred her vision.

"Rory!"

Charlie's voice rang loudly above the others. Why didn't Charlie shut up? She wanted to disappear unnoticed.

Charlie grabbed her and pulled her back. "Rory, what are you doing?"

"Didn't you see?"

"See what?"

"The woman. He's *with* someone."

Charlie glanced back toward Ben, who was now talking with some fans, his arm around the blonde. "So what if he's with someone? You haven't seen him for over a month. Did you expect him to become a monk?"

Rory shook her head. "I can't. Let's just go."

"No way. My God, the guy wrote a song about you. Isn't he worth fighting for? Hell, you think I didn't fight for James? Swallow your stupid pride, and go over to him."

Rory inhaled deeply. Maybe Charlie was right. The crowd was thinning out. She looked back over toward Ben and was about to just say, "Forget it," when she saw him look her way. His eyebrows rose with surprise. She had to go over now. She took another deep breath and walked the thirty feet toward him, her mind racing with what she would say.

"Aurora June." Ben's face lit up with a smile. His arm slowly slid from the blond woman's shoulder. The two other men who'd been talking to him turned toward Rory and Charlie.

"Hi." Rory smiled, feeling her heart hammer like a mallet, unable to say anything else. There were a few awkward seconds of silence, and then Ben introduced the woman. "Aurora June, this is Lisa. Lisa, Aurora June and…" Ben turned toward Charlie.

"Charlie Banya." Charlie piped in with a smile and shook Ben's and then Lisa's hands. "Rory's told me so much about you. And that song, 'When Love Walked out My Door'—it's really moving."

Rory looked over at Charlie. What was she doing?

Ben cleared his throat. He looked down at the floor for a split second and then said, "Thanks." His eyes went to Rory and then over to Lisa, whose gaze was locked on him.

Rory's eyes quickly scanned the blonde, from her long, thin legs to her perfect skin and whiter-than-white teeth. She was maybe thirty-five, maybe older; it was hard to tell.

The two fans who had been talking with Ben drifted away, and it was just the four of them.

"So what brings you to Monterey?" Ben asked. Rory noticed his ever-so-slight movement away from Lisa.

"Charlie's birthday." Rory glanced over at Charlie and then watched Lisa lean her body against Ben, wrapping her hand in his.

"You back in Phoenix?" Ben asked.

Rory shook her head. "Still Willow Bend."

"Isn't that near Six Rivers?" Lisa asked.

"You've been there?" Rory thought for sure that everyone could see her heart thumping against her blouse. She wanted the floor to swallow her up, but she wasn't about to let Ben or the woman see her pain.

Lisa smiled. "Kayaking—a few years ago."

After another few seconds of awkward silence, Rory said to Ben, "Looks like things are going well—with the music, I mean."

Ben nodded. "Yeah, we're on tour for the next two months."

"That's great." Rory felt short of breath. There were so many questions she couldn't ask. How long had he been with Lisa? Was it before Willow Bend? Was she traveling with him? She noticed the way Lisa casually stroked Ben's arm. She belonged.

"How's the journey?" Ben asked.

Rory took a second to process his words. "Good—"

An enthusiastic fan came up and shook Ben's hand, praising Ben for the latest CD. Ben directed his attention to the fan. Rory glanced over at Charlie with a nod toward the door, signaling that she wanted to leave. Charlie frowned at her with a look that said no.

The bass player from the band called to Ben from across the

room, waving his arm for him to come over. Ben looked in his direction and nodded, and then he turned back to the fan.

"We better go. It was good seeing you," Rory said, interrupting Ben's conversation with the fan. Mustering her best smile, she turned to Lisa and added, "Nice meeting you." Lisa replied the same to Rory and Charlie. Rory turned to leave before Ben could respond, but she caught his eye, and for a fraction of a second, she saw something in his expression. Did he still feel something?

They were about twenty feet across the room, and Charlie tapped her arm. "I'm going to the restroom. Be right back."

Rory gave a quick glance back toward Ben. He and Lisa were heading toward the bass player. Rory turned for the door, keeping her steps measured.

She punched the metal bar of the heavy door and stepped out into the cool night air. It hit her in the face as she drank it in with gulping breaths. She stood on the sidewalk, her arms wrapped around her body, clinging to herself. What a fool she was. Why had she thought he would still want her? Of course he had moved on, just like Derek had.

Rory stared across the street. A metal sign banged in the wind against the concrete wall of an abandoned building, each clang pounding deeper her humiliation. The streetlamp cast a circular glow around her.

A few minutes later, Charlie came up beside her.

"I'm an idiot," Rory said.

Charlie's arm went around her waist. "No, you're not."

The two began to walk down the sidewalk to the car.

"What made me think he'd still want me?"

"I guarantee you she'll be asking Ben about you tonight. If she'd been a male dog, she would've lifted her leg on him," Charlie joked.

"I don't know. She seemed nice." Rory felt a whisper of sadness brush over her. Across the street, a woman dressed in a heavy tattered coat and pushing a shopping cart filled with her possessions trudged along the sidewalk. A passing couple walked by arm in arm, sidestepping around the woman, not even noticing her, engrossed in their own conversation.

They stood by Charlie's BMW. A gust of wind blew the faint odor of fish from the wharf several blocks away. Rory grabbed the edges of her open jacket, securing it around herself. Charlie rooted for her keys in her purse. Rory stared down at the concrete, scuffing her boot against a crack, thinking how she'd been swept up in a fantasy. Maybe Charlie was living a fairy-tale life, but she wasn't.

She felt robotic as she walked up the steps, entering the small cabin of the private jet. She'd forced a smile as she hugged Charlie good-bye, just like she had done all morning during their trip to Big Sur. She hadn't wanted to ruin Charlie's birthday weekend, so she had acted like the whole incident from the night before hadn't really affected her. She'd pretended to brush it off, telling Charlie that she knew now it hadn't been fate. She wanted to forget about it and enjoy the day in Big Sur, but the whole time they were driving along the curving road high above the rocky coastline, the magnificent view was overshadowed by a feeling of despair.

Sitting on the plane, she tried to convince herself that she wasn't going to let what had happened upset her any longer, attempting to put her protective armor firmly back in place. She was heading back to Willow Bend, to the life she'd created. She had her dance class that she loved, her friend Caroline, her photography, and Marlena and Ethan. Maybe this was what was meant to be. Stay on her path for independence. She looked out the portal window into the blackness, the tiny lights along the wing illuminating the clouds that rolled past like smoke. The plane rocked with turbulence, and she gripped the armrest. She still couldn't get Ben out of her head.

———

Stopped at a traffic light on her drive back from the airport in Eureka, she turned her cell phone on and saw that she had three voice mails. The caller ID showed one from Jillian, another from Will, and one from Ben. She caught her breath, and her stomach knotted when she saw his name appear on the screen. Why had he called? Her finger hovered over his name, but she listened to the one from Jillian first.

Her daughter's familiar voice played over the speaker, wanting to know what Rory was up to and wanting to talk about their plans for Christmas in Maryland. It was only three weeks away. She went on to Will's message. He wanted to know how she was doing and asked her to call him. She hit the delete button and then glanced at the screen on her phone. Ben's name was the only one left. Her heart raced. She hesitated, knowing she had to listen to the message, but she stalled, afraid of what she would hear. She stared out the window at the tall redwoods that loomed beside the road, the tops disappearing into darkness.

She hit the button, holding her breath. His voice—"Aurora June. Please call me. I wish you'd told me you were coming to the show…" There was a pause, then, "Well, anyway, call me." That was it.

She didn't delete it. She wanted to be able to hear his voice again. She wanted to know about the woman. Was she a one-night stand? It hadn't appeared that way. His tone of voice had been ambiguous. He could've been calling just to talk, curious about why she'd come to the show, or maybe he had called to tell her he loved her. She'd never know unless she called, but her fear of finding out he was in love with someone else overpowered her curiosity. A battle raged in her head. *Call—don't call.* She set the phone down on the red leather seat, too confused to make a decision.

As her foot pressed the gas pedal of the Falcon, she remembered Ben's words on the sidewalk in Eureka—*I hope you find what you're looking for.* If she only knew what that was.

21

Her cowboy boots scraped across the stone steps of the Bigfoot Inn, hesitating at the top. Why had she come here? She'd told herself she needed food, having barely touched her lunch in Big Sur. Country music from the bar filtered her way while her hand rested on the cold iron railing. The double doors opened, and two couples came out laughing and talking, oblivious to her as they made their way to their cars. A whoosh of warm air brushed her face as the doors closed in front of her. Grabbing the rough wood handle, she pulled it back open.

She perused the crowded room, feeling more alone than before. A group of people at the bar shouted at the television, which was airing a Sunday-night football game. Her gaze went to the dining area, warmed by the golden light from the antlered chandeliers; the hum of conversations mixed with laughter rang from the tables filled with families and couples. Two tables were empty, one of them the one where she'd sat with Derek the last time she had seen him. She started to head toward it and then changed direction.

Squeezing between two people seated on stools at the bar, she signaled for the bartender and ordered a shot of Elijah Craig. The first sip of the amber liquid burned her throat as it made its way down. She took another sip. Then, staring at the small glass in her hand, she swallowed the rest in one gulp, pursed her lips together, and wiped her mouth with the back of her hand. The alcohol pumped through her veins, heating her blood. It felt good. Setting the shot glass on the bar, she motioned to the bartender for another.

Ben's bourbon. She remembered the first time she'd had it. They were at a small club, and he'd ordered it on the rocks for both of them and then proceeded to tell her the history of Baptist preacher Elijah Craig, the inventor of bourbon whiskey.

The bartender set the second shot in front of her. There was no sipping this time; she brought the glass to her lips and tilted her head back. A surge of warmth radiated out to her limbs and drowned out memories of Carmel. She closed her eyes. As she breathed in the smoky smell of barbequed ribs, her stomach rumbled, and she thought about ordering dinner. But instead she set the money for the drinks in front of the bartender.

"Crazy…" The voice of Patsy Cline crooned in the background as she crossed the pine flooring and headed toward a group of men in their late twenties, early thirties, playing pool in the corner. The Elijah Craig sang in her head—*fuck all men*. Who needed them?

They asked her if she wanted to play. One of the guys dressed in jeans and flannel, whom she'd met when she'd been here with Will before, handed her a cue stick. She picked up the small blue cube of chalk sitting on the edge of the table and ran it over the tip of the cue. Another guy racked the balls, and the guy in the flannel broke. No balls went in.

Leaning over the table, her head down next to the cue stick, she eyed her shot. It was an easy one. She smoothly slid the stick into the cue ball, hearing it click against the four ball, which rolled silently into the pocket. Piece of cake. She let a little smile escape her lips and then moved on to her next shot. The last time she'd played pool had been with Ben. She'd beaten him six straight games. When she was young, she and Nick used to go with their dad to Mike's Pub. They'd play for hours. Her father had been one of the best pool players in Takoma Park. She sank another ball, then another, one by one, practically clearing the table.

"You look like you've done this before."

She glanced up to see her photography teacher, Carter Bennett, standing near the table dressed in a faded blue cotton shirt, his sleeves rolled up, with a beer in his hand. She smiled and then finished her shot, missing the next one. While her opponent took his turn, Carter told her about some ideas he had for their last class tomorrow night. She nodded, half listening; she didn't want to talk. Why did he have to be here? Watching her opponent miss the ball, she walked around the table, discerning the best angle for her shot.

Light reflected off the balls from the pendants that hung over the table. Her eyes focused on the expanse of green felt between the cue ball and the eight ball. A difficult bank shot off the side rail into the corner pocket. She needed to make this one. Needed to win the game. She wasn't going to be a loser.

There was a round of applause as the black ball rolled effortlessly into the pocket. One of the guys asked her what she was drinking. They brought her another shot of bourbon. A distant voice in her head told her to stop; hard liquor and she didn't mix, just like her father. But Rory didn't want to stop; she felt pleasantly numb.

She played two more games. Carter sat on a wooden stool to the side, watching. She knew the men were eyeing her each time she bent over to take a shot. She felt their stares. It was like dangling a set of shiny keys in front of a baby, she thought, seeing the want in their eyes. The alcohol fueled a need to be desired, but at the same time, each click of the ball was like another fuck-you to men. Derek. Ben. Will. Again the whiskey shouted in her head—*they're all assholes!*

She sat the next game out and ordered some water. Her words were slurred; she knew she was drunk. Carter was asking her if she'd decided to enter the photography show in Eureka; the deadline was approaching. She didn't answer.

The din of voices and music sounded muffled as she mindlessly swayed to the beat. She felt Carter move in closer to her. He smelled of Old Spice, her father's cologne. She closed her eyes, picturing her father, and then opened them and gazed around the bar.

She saw Will standing in the arched entranceway, scanning the crowd. His eyes came around to her. She looked away and leaned in toward Carter, bringing her face next to his, which he took as a sign. He bent closer and kissed her. She kissed him back with her eyes closed as the room spun around in her head. When she glanced back toward the doorway, Will was gone. A sunken feeling pressed down on her. The waitress brought her water, and she ordered another shot.

With her hand on her brow, she tried to block the sun that streamed through the window. Her head throbbed. Where was she? She turned slowly to see Carter, his back to her, still asleep. What had she done? She partially sat up, resting on her elbow, feeling nauseated. They were lying on a mattress on the floor in a small room with dark-paneled walls. Clothes, books, and stacks of photographs covered the worn carpet. Slipping out of bed, she searched for her clothes through the clutter; finding her underwear tangled in the sheets at the foot of the bed, her bra on the floor, her jeans and top draped on a chair along with her purse. She dressed quickly, desperately needing a bathroom.

She was relieved to see Carter still sleeping when she returned from the bathroom in search of her boots, discovering one under some clothes on the floor. The red numbers of the digital clock beside the bed glared at her: 8:02 a.m. No! It couldn't be. She was supposed to be at work two hours ago. Scrambling around the floor, she frantically searched for her other boot. Carter stirred in the bed.

She froze on her hands and knees, holding her breath. Silence. He hadn't woken. She found the other one, slung her purse over her shoulder, gathered the boots in her arms, and tiptoed out of the room, softly shutting the door behind her.

She glanced around the main area of the small house, which she had no recollection of from the night before: a worn sofa, two small armchairs, a floor-to-ceiling bookcase filled with books stacked in a haphazard fashion, a kitchen off to one side, and hundreds of photographs hanging on the walls, propped against the walls, stacked on tables. As she slipped on her boots, a picture caught her eye: a large black-and-white photo of a nude woman, artfully done with light and shadow.

She walked over to where it hung in a black frame with a wide white matte. Her eyes drifted back toward the bedroom. An image of Carter's hand tracing her face flashed in her head. She remembered him telling her how beautiful she was. How he wanted to photograph her. Her stomach made a rumbling sound as a pang of hunger gripped her, followed by another surge of nausea.

Stepping outside into the chilly air, she breathed in the scent of damp pine needles. Carter's Subaru was parked in front of the house, but her Falcon wasn't. She felt dizzy and grabbed the metal railing on the porch. Where was her car? Glimpses of last night flashed in her mind. She remembered leaving the inn and Carter saying something about driving her home.

Now she stood on the porch, shivering from the cold. Her stomach ached with another gripping pain. She could call a cab. *Were* there any cabs in Willow Bend? She'd never seen any. Desperation seeped in. She called Marlena, hoping she wasn't already at work.

Looking up at the cloudless blue sky above the slight mist of fog that hung low in the air, she exhaled when she heard Marlena's voice. After figuring out where she was from the map on her phone and relaying the information to Marlena, she began walking down the street, lined with houses, out of sight of Carter's. Marlena hadn't asked any questions; she said she was already in the car on her way to the winery and would be there shortly. Rory then called Astral and told her she'd accidentally overslept. The frustration in Astral's voice, telling her to get in as soon as she could, came through the phone. Rory heard the clamor of the morning rush in the background. Would Casey fire her? She'd never been late for work before, but she'd seen the way he'd blown up at the cooks when they showed up late. An anxious feeling fought with the hunger in her belly.

The sound of her boots on the pavement echoed as she crossed Devers Bridge Road. Wishing she hadn't left her North Face jacket in her car last night, she huddled down on a large rock on the corner of the street with her arms wrapped around her knees and waited.

The rock felt as cold as a block of ice that sent shivers up her spine. She'd fucked up. More flashes of the night ran through her head. Slow dancing with Carter in the back of the bar. Challenging him to a game of darts and practically stabbing a guy in the arm as he walked by. Leaving the inn; stumbling down the steps, Carter holding her up; sitting in his car in the parking lot, making out; lying on his bed naked. She cringed, not wanting to remember. Bile rose in her throat. The alcohol felt like it had burned a hole in her stomach. She needed food, coffee, warm clothes. She wanted to cry.

A gust of wind whipped around her. Her body shook. A woman and two children with backpacks came out of the house across the street, the little girl's voice echoing through the mist. They got into an SUV. Rory lowered her head as they backed out of the driveway and drove by. She felt dirty, cold, and degraded.

She walked into the luncheonette, quickly slipping behind the counter, and grabbed her apron. Astral came out from the back with a tray of food and glanced up at the clock. It was five minutes to ten, and the second breakfast shift was dying down. "Thank God you're here. Casey got in about ten minutes ago. I told him you ran down the street for a minute to pick something up."

"Thanks; I'm really sorry about this morning."

"You all right? You look bad."

Rory's hand went up to her face. She could feel the puffiness under her eyes. "Rough night."

Astral nodded and then headed off with the tray, saying over her shoulder, "You can take table six. They just got here."

The huge cup of coffee, fried egg sandwich, and three Advil she had taken when she got back to the cottage were finally kicking in. Her headache had subsided, and her stomach had quieted back down, but the mental pain still lingered. She had stood in the shower earlier, her eyes closed, the hot water pelting her body as she tried to wash away the despondent feeling, but it remained.

Riding with Marlena to pick up her car had been only a five-minute drive, but it had felt like an eternity. Marlena hadn't questioned her about why she had been sitting on the side of the road at eight o'clock in the morning, miles away from her house. When they'd pulled up to her car at the inn parking lot, Rory felt she had to say something. She'd told her about seeing the car parked outside Will's house Thanksgiving night, about Derek and the other woman, and then briefly mentioned Ben. Marlena had just nodded as Rory rambled, trying to defend herself, make sense of it to herself. Marlena had told her she didn't have to explain; she wasn't judging her.

Now heading over to table six, she eyed the two women, who looked to be in their midsixties and were engrossed in a conversation. One of the women, with a mass of curly gray hair, reminded her of her mother, before she'd gotten sick. Rory stood beside the table for a second, not wanting to interrupt their conversation. The curly haired woman stopped talking and smiled at her. Rory took their orders, and as she walked back to get their coffee, she felt as if the woman knew what she had done last night—as if the words 'fuck-up' were printed across her forehead.

She stood at the coffee pot filling the white ceramic mugs and was reminded of that day in Phoenix, her possessions packed in her car, stopping at the roadside diner. She'd been filled with apprehension, but she'd also been filled with hope. Hope for a better life, a chance to find her potential. She thought of Derek's words at the pub: "Is this your dream, to be a waitress in a small town?" Was that all she was capable of?

22

A-21. She checked her ticket, glanced at the overhead numbers again, and then squeezed her way to the portal window past an elderly man in the aisle seat, then a woman, bordering on morbid obesity, who was crammed in the middle. Rory shoved her purse under the seat in front of her and buckled the lap belt. Exhaling, she rested her head back, feeling exhausted from the ordeal of getting through the crowded security lines.

The large woman next to her asked her where she was going. Rory wasn't in the mood for conversation. She wanted to close her eyes and forget about the past few weeks. She considered retorting, *Where do you think I'm going? We're on a nonstop flight to Baltimore, you idiot.* But instead, she smiled and told the woman she was going to see her family in Takoma Park. The woman relayed her itinerary to Rory, not leaving out any details.

The few times Rory had flown, she'd enjoyed talking with other passengers; it helped pass the time and distract her from her nervousness. But this time was different. She stared out the oval window watching the crew throw the luggage onto the conveyor belt that ran into the belly of the plane and thought it was a miracle that anything breakable ever survived. There was a lull in the woman's chattering, and Rory realized she was waiting for her answer.

"I'm sorry, what was that?" Rory asked.

"Do you have any children?"

Rory nodded and told her she had a daughter, knowing that would probably open up another topic of conversation. The woman's scent wafted across each time her arm jiggled. Grandma Harper's perfume. What was the name of it? Rory closed her eyes trying to recall. As a small child, she had loved squeezing the soft, cushy skin of her grandmother's underarm.

It was a full flight, and people were still struggling down the aisle with their bags, stuffing them in overhead compartments. Rory pleaded silently for everyone to hurry up and sit down. She was beginning to feel claustrophobic. As the woman rambled on, telling her about some strange skin ailment her son had been battling, Rory envisioned riding on the Binghamtons' private jet, the whole plane to herself. She remembered how she'd almost chickened out getting on the Cessna Citation, thinking of all the small-plane crashes—JFK Jr., John Denver, Buddy Holly—the list went on; but right now she would have given anything to be back on the Cessna.

After several minutes that seemed like forever, the flight attendant began her spiel on safety procedures, and the woman next to her finally stopped talking. Rory put her earbuds in, hoping the woman would think she was listening to something on her phone and leave her alone, but instead the woman patted her arm and whispered to her that she wasn't allowed to turn *that thing* on. Rory nodded and smiled, with visions of grabbing the woman's face and smashing it against the back of the seat. Feeling contrite, she glanced at the woman, who was listening intently to the flight attendant; she didn't need to take her moodiness out on the woman.

The hustle of the holiday had kept her busy: shopping, matting and framing pictures she was giving as presents, and then wrapping them securely to ship to Nick's. Between that, going to work, and watching Ethan, she'd had little free time, but an underlying dissatisfied feeling had been lingering in the background. Ever since her night at Carter's, she'd kept to herself, too embarrassed to face anyone other than Ethan, who helped her forget.

As they taxied out onto the runway, she thought back to the e-mail she'd received from Carter. He'd forwarded her information about the photography show in Eureka and added that he hoped she was going to enter; he didn't mention their night together or the fact she'd missed the last class. She never submitted anything to the contest, and as the deadline slipped by, tentacles of regret wound their way around her. She should've gone. But deep down she'd been afraid, thinking there had been an ulterior motive for Carter's praise and that her work wasn't that good.

She wondered if Carter had spoken with Will. What would Will think about her night with Carter? Did she care? She hadn't spoken to Will since Thanksgiving either. He'd left numerous voice mails that went unanswered, and he'd eventually stopped calling.

One day last week, on her way from the luncheonette to the bank, she'd seen him walking out of the post office, his head down, leafing through his mail. She'd quickly ducked into the bookstore and stood behind a rack of paperbacks, peering out the big front window until he was out of sight. She'd built a whole scenario in her head about Will: that he'd been in a long-distance relationship the entire time she'd known him but had kept it secret just in case he wanted to step things up with Rory. Keeping his options open.

She knew she was being crazy; she had no idea who'd been at his house, and she had no real reason to believe he'd been in a relationship with someone else. So why was she avoiding him? They'd been friends. Why couldn't she have left it like that?

She felt like a loser. She'd been on her own for four months now and still had no better sense of herself than before she'd left Phoenix. Her big quest to find her independence, and what did she do? Start a relationship with the first guy she met in the new town. Then she fooled herself into believing Ben and she were some cosmic couple meant to share their lives together, and then she fully

BENDING TOWARD *THE* LIGHT

degraded herself by sleeping with Carter. She slumped down against
the padded seat of the plane.

The thought of seeing Jillian, Nick, and Cass was the only thing
that had kept her going. A whole week together. Casey had closed
the luncheonette until after the first of the year, taking his wife and
kids to Mexico. He had given each of the employees a two-week
paycheck as a Christmas bonus the day before. Opening the envelope after she'd left the restaurant had temporarily brightened her
spirits, but it wasn't long before her sullenness had returned.

Now they were in the air. She'd silently said her ritual prayer
seconds before the wheels lifted and watched the earth get smaller
as they ascended into the sky. The woman next to her, who had
introduced herself as Beverly, struck up a conversation again. This
time Rory listened, deciding it was easier to give in.

By the time the flight attendant was handing out snacks and
drinks, Rory knew Beverly's life history—her successful battle with
breast cancer, how her husband was suffering from Parkinson's, and
that her thirty-three-year-old son was still living at home. Rory was
amazed at how cheerful the woman sounded as she recounted her
many misfortunes. But then it dawned on Rory that the woman
wasn't complaining. She didn't see her life as miserable. Rory wanted
to ask the woman how she did it. Her own problems seemed trivial
compared to Beverly's. She felt irritated with herself. She needed to
snap out of her doldrums.

Hours into the flight, cursing herself for having drunk so much
water, she felt as if her bladder was going to explode. But the task
of squeezing her way out to the aisle seemed daunting. The elderly
man was sound asleep, slack jawed with his head back. Beverly made
her best effort to move her legs out of Rory's way. She headed to
the back. Two people were already standing in the aisle waiting their
turn.

She glanced around at the other passengers while she stood in line. Two young children with headphones on were watching a movie on a tablet. A man in another row was furiously typing on his computer while the woman next to him read a book, but the majority of the plane was filled with people engaged in conversation. An air of excitement emanated from the crowd. It was three days before Christmas. Usually by this time she'd have caught the bug as well, humming Christmas carols as she went through her day, but so far she hadn't gotten in the spirit. The line moved closer to the restroom, and Rory watched a couple playing cards. She thought of Ben and playing gin rummy in his apartment last Christmas.

They had celebrated the holiday a week early. Derek had been playing golf in Scottsdale, and Jillian wouldn't be coming home for another four days. Rory and Ben had picked out a tiny scotch pine from a Christmas tree lot set up next to a gas station and taken the tree back to his apartment and decorated it with a strand of colored bubble lights and a box of red balls they'd bought at a dollar store. It had been nothing compared to the seven-foot tree that sat in her den, adorned with multiple sets of twinkling lights and ornate ornaments she'd collected over the years. But propped against the barren backdrop of Ben's sparsely furnished apartment, the little tree had looked like a sparkling gem in the desert.

Ben had lived in his apartment for a year, but there were still boxes lined up on the floor. Nothing hung on the walls. The only furniture was a futon couch and an old Morris chair with a green-and-brown plaid fabric he'd purchased at a yard sale. She'd questioned him the first time she'd been there, thinking he was getting ready to move, but he told her he'd just never gotten around to unpacking. She knew he had lived in a lot of places, and she remembered him telling her once that his home would always be the bayou.

While Ben was fixing dinner, she had stood at the sliding-glass door looking down from the third floor to the myriad Christmas lights that adorned the balconies of other apartments, reflecting onto the wet street, and was reminded of one rainy Christmas Eve when Jillian had been around six. She and Derek had taken Jillian out after dark with umbrellas. They'd watched, laughing, as Jillian splashed in the multicolored light-reflected puddles along the street, calling them fairy lights.

Rory had turned from the slider, glancing over at Ben, who had his back to her, and had been temporarily filled with nostalgia. Being with Ben was like an alternate universe, and when glimpses of her other life broke through, it was like slipping on a shroud of melancholy.

Now, a woman in line behind her tapped her shoulder, signaling it was her turn in the bathroom. Rory slid the bar on the narrow door, activating the fluorescent bulb and filling the tiny cubicle with a strange, glowing light. The bulb hummed beside the small mirror. The disinfectant smell permeated the air as she forced herself to breathe slowly in and out.

Why couldn't her life have been different? Why couldn't she and Derek and Jillian still be a family? She'd wanted it so badly. She needed to stop the what-ifs that were floating in her head. What if she'd never given up dance? What if Derek had been different? What if there hadn't been a woman with Ben in Monterey?

She pictured Lisa with her hand intertwined in Ben's. That could've been her. If she'd just gone with him to San Diego. She was doing it again: *what if.*

When she got back to row 21, she noticed that not only was the old man asleep, but Beverly had fallen asleep as well. She didn't want to wake them, but she didn't know how she could get to her seat without doing so. Take a flying leap over the two sleepers? The idea made her laugh. But instead of leaping, she lifted her right leg and placed it in the tiny space between the old man and Beverly. She was now facing the old man, her legs straddling his. An image of him waking suddenly and having a heart attack upon seeing her looming before him flashed through her mind. She stifled another laugh.

She looked down at Beverly's knees that jutted out to the seat in front of her, wondering how she was going to do this. She deftly raised her left leg, and in her best balletic style, swung it above their heads and spun around, placing it on the other side of Beverly. She was now straddling Beverly with her back to her while she hung on to the seat in front of her. One more hurdle to go: she needed to get her right leg over Beverly, and then she was home free. She heard a mumbling sound, and Beverly's knees began to shift position. Rory envisioned plopping on top of Beverly's voluminous thighs and Beverly wrapping her plump arms around her in a bear hug. Why hadn't she just woken them up?

Rory took a deep breath, closed her eyes, and jetted into her seat, escaping the fall. She blew out an audible exhale. Success! A clapping sound from across the aisle rang out. She saw a young man who smiled and gave her a thumbs-up. She smiled back, feeling her cheeks get hot.

She picked up her phone and put in the earbuds one more time, hitting the shuffle button. Peace at last.

Ironically, the first song that played was "I'm Gonna Be (Five Hundred Miles)." Sedona. Ben. She couldn't escape him. Ever since she'd seen him in Monterey, he'd been in her thoughts, cropping up unexpectedly like a persistent weed.

She turned off the music and leaned her head back. Last Christmas again. The smell of crawfish étouffée, Ben's favorite. Sitting on the floor in front of the sparkling little tree, the aroma of Cajun spices mixed with pine needles hung in the air. She'd been surprised at how good crawfish was. They'd eaten off paper plates and then exchanged presents.

Now she squeezed her eyes tightly, wanting to shut her brain off—erase the past like unsaved data and hit the restart button.

As the hours passed, the droning of the jet engines had lulled the plane into a hushed slumber. The only sounds were the occasional muffled clink as the flight attendants packed things away and the soft rhythmic snoring from Beverly, which, for some strange reason, gave Rory comfort. The cabin was dark. Rory pressed her forehead against the cold pane of the tiny window and looked out. Nothing but blackness.

She thought about Beverly's recitation of her sad life and her prevailing happiness. She needed to switch gears and focus on the positive. She needed a plan, some goal to attain. Should she go back to school? Her mind flipped through options. Paralegal? Accounting—no; nursing? Maybe. She continued to stare into the darkness. Then slowly, as if by magic, lights of red, blue, green, and white came into view, thousands of lights getting brighter. She thought maybe she was dreaming—fairy lights. She blinked several times, and the houses came into view, decorated for Christmas. She closed her eyes and inhaled deeply. L'air du Temps—that was the name of her grandmother's perfume. She smiled. The plane rapidly descended, and hope rose inside as the strip of blue lights came up to meet her, guiding her back to earth.

23

They'd gone out to get milk, but Rory felt it was a pretext. She suspected that Nick had been holding something in ever since he'd picked her up at the airport the night before. Driving along the once-familiar streets of Silver Spring, Nick asked, "Wanna see the old neighborhood?"

Rory was fumbling with Nick's heater. She'd forgotten how cold it got in Maryland, a damp cold that went straight to her bones. "Sure. Is everything—" Nick's cell rang, cutting her off. He pressed a button on his steering column and spoke to the unseen speaker. A man's voice filled the car, and Nick switched to the Bluetooth in his ear.

He turned off Bonifant Street onto Georgia Avenue. The few times she'd been back, she'd been amazed at the growth of the area and how close everything was. As a child she had thought going from Takoma Park to Silver Spring was such a long distance, but in reality it was only a couple of miles. They passed the Silver Spring Armory that used to be a firehouse, but now the sign out front read Fire Station 1 Restaurant and Brewing Co. The large bay doors on front that would open for the fire trucks were now just decorative.

She glanced over at Nick, studying his profile, his brown hair now flecked with gray, lines chiseled around his eyes. He'd always had happy eyes, but she noticed something different this time. A hidden worry behind his smile. She wondered why he'd wanted to go by the old neighborhood.

They edged their way to the next light. A sea of red taillights surrounded them. She was astounded at the level of congestion—the bustle of people, cars, and buses was such a sharp contrast to Willow Bend. Exhaust-covered piles of snow lined the side of the road, gray and dingy looking. The tires swooshed through the slush as they turned right onto Fenton off Sligo Avenue. Mike's Pub was still there, the squat brick building with the neon Pabst Blue Ribbon sign blinking off and on in the window. It hadn't changed, but everything around it had. Ollie's Hobby Shop was now a Dollar General, and the dry cleaner was now a Subway restaurant.

She chuckled, thinking how normal it had seemed as a child to be hanging out at Mike's, watching her dad shoot pool. Everyone had loved her dad. She remembered the circle of people he'd have gathered around him while he told a joke and the uproarious laughter that ensued when he finished. He made people forget their troubles.

As they veered left onto Philadelphia, the heater cranked out warm air, and she was finally able to release her huddled position. She wondered what it was like for Nick, still living in the same town he had grown up in. For years after she'd moved to Phoenix, she'd longed to be back home. She missed the change of seasons, the smell of burning leaves, crocuses popping their heads up in the spring, and family gatherings at her grandmother's. The feeling of belonging. Her roots were here, but would she still want to live in this place? The busy streets seemed foreign now.

They turned onto Ethan Allen into the heart of Takoma Park, past vintage shops and the Takoma Park Silver Spring Food Co-op. This was her mother's town. She smiled, thinking her mother would be proud. All her efforts years ago had helped shape the town into what it was today. Rory was aware of the moniker the critics used for the town, "The People's Republic of Takoma Park," but her mother had liked it. Her communal philosophy still lived on today.

Rory remembered the time her mother had taken her to a council meeting. Her father must have been out somewhere with Nick. She had been about nine. She'd sat on the linoleum floor in the back room of the plant shop where her mother had worked, which also served as the council's meeting room at night. Rory had been drawing with the new pack of Day-Glo markers her mother had gotten her. She'd never forget the feeling she had, watching her mother stand before the small circle of chairs filled with other council members, her face aglow with passion as her arms gesticulated her point. Rory had been in awe of her mother and at the same time sad. She had always sensed when she was with her mother, there was someplace else her mother would rather be; that night she knew where.

The green street sign that read Sycamore Avenue stood at the corner. Their street. Nick drove slowly up the big hill, passing the historic arts and crafts–style homes, some small, some large. The cherry trees with their bare branches lined the darkened street. She remembered when they'd first been planted, and now they were huge. She imagined how beautiful they must look in the spring. They drove past 7134 Sycamore, the Averys' house. They were probably long dead now. Mr. Avery had to have been in his seventies back then. He used to wave from the porch rocker he sat in every day. She had loved going up there to listen to stories of his childhood—how he used to ride his horse up to the Silver Theatre and tie it out front.

And then there it was. 7126 Sycamore Avenue. The tiny Craftsman home with its stone porch. Her house. Candles glowed in the window. The front yard was much smaller than she remembered. She pictured pirouetting up the walkway on her way home from school and turning to take a bow to her imaginary audience. She stared at the wooden arched front door, wondering who lived there now. Nick stopped the car.

"A lot of memories here," he said after hanging up the phone and staring at their old house.

"Yeah." Rory faced Nick. "Is everything OK?"

Nick nodded, looking past Rory.

Something was wrong; the spontaneous jokester Rory knew her brother to be was gone.

"Come on, Nick." She punched his arm. "Talk to me. Where's my brother who always has some crazy—"

"Cass has cancer."

His unexpected words threw her off balance. *Cancer?* No. She'd just seen them a month ago. Cass was too healthy. She'd always been into the natural-foods thing. "Oh, Nick…"

"Breast cancer, just like Mom." Nick was now staring straight ahead out the windshield.

"How bad?" Rory's hands suddenly felt ice cold. She rubbed them together, thinking how Cass had always reminded Rory of her mom. How odd that they would both get cancer.

"They're hoping it's contained in the breast. We're waiting on the results of the PET scan. They want to do chemo first and then possibly a lumpectomy. Cass just wants them to remove the whole thing now."

"How long have you known?"

"We just found out last week. She hasn't even told the kids yet. She didn't want to ruin Christmas for everyone." Nick humphed. "That's Cass for you." He looked at Rory. The slice of light from the streetlamp reflected the tears in Nick's eyes.

"Nick, just because Mom…you know, most women survive. I'm sure if they caught it early…" Rory's words sounded futile to her own ears. Of course Nick knew the statistics, but she didn't know what else to say.

She knew how much Cass meant to Nick, how much he depended on her. She shuddered, trying to imagine what he was going through. Guilt shot through her. There were times she had wished

Derek was dead. When his face was contorted with rage, his words spitting at her like pieces of glass, she would pray he'd have a massive heart attack.

She wanted to help Nick. She hated seeing him look so hurt. "When do they start the treatments?"

"January seventh. She has to go once a week for eight weeks, and then they'll check her progress. She'll probably lose her hair. She's already gone out and gotten a couple of wigs." He chuckled. "She said she never liked her hair anyway. It always drove her crazy."

Rory reached out and touched Nick's arm. "I'm so sorry, Nick."

Nick was still staring out the windshield, and she saw him grimace. He put his head in his hands. "I can't lose her."

"You won't." She stroked his back. "Cass is a strong woman. She'll survive this; I know she will." Rory spoke with conviction, trying to convince herself as much as Nick that everything was going to be OK, but in the back of her head, she thought about the fact that her mother had been strong too. An image of Beverly, the overweight woman on the plane, flashed in her head. She'd survived.

Rory's eyes drifted out the window at the sidewalk where Nick had held her hand while she learned to roller-skate, helping her up each time she fell. He'd always been there for her when she was young. "I can stay for a while. Help out with things."

"Thanks, but I think Cass is handling it really well. She wants to keep teaching." Nick pressed his lips together. "Actually, just telling you helped, Rory."

"Anytime you want to talk." She squeezed his hand.

Nick leaned across and hugged her. "Thanks." He put the car in gear. "We better get back."

They continued down the street in silence, turning onto Elm and up the hill past the playground. The day after her father's funeral flashed in her head—the first day the reality set in that her father was never coming back. She'd gone to the playground that day and sat on the swings, remembering when she was little her father pushing her and telling her she was flying like a bird. She'd loved that feeling, the thrill of soaring in the air, knowing he was right behind her. But when she had pulled back the chains that day and propelled forward, the pain had become too great. She had never set foot in the park again, purposely circumventing her route whenever she walked in that direction.

As Nick and she drove down the darkened streets illuminated by the twinkling lights of reindeer and snowmen anchored to the streetlamps, she thought about how she'd coped with the loss of her dad. There had been other triggers of pain after his death—things she'd loved in the past, but without him, they evoked a gnawing in her gut. She'd had to move her seat in history class because the boy sitting next to her wore Old Spice. For years, she wouldn't go into a flower shop, and when she walked by a florist's window, she would turn her head at the sight of a bouquet of roses. Her father used to give her six yellow roses after every recital.

The song "Born to Be Wild" had been their signature song, but afterward she would have to change the station if it came on the radio. From the time she was six, it had become a weekly ritual, dancing in the living room while her father played the air guitar with the stereo full blast. Without warning, her father would jump up from watching TV, turn off the set, and crank up the Steppenwolf song—which was Rory's cue to come running from wherever and join in, belting out the words, somewhat off key. Her mother used to hold her ears and shake her head as she walked through the room. Riding in the pickup truck with her dad, the windows rolled down, she'd put in the cassette and turn up the volume. The wind whipping into the truck, her long hair flying around her face as she shouted out the lyrics. She'd loved the song's feeling of adventure; it was the same feeling she had with her dad, a feeling of abandon. They were a team, partners in crime, like the time they had been riding back from her grandmother's, and her dad, without warning, had jumped the pickup over the curb in the neighborhood and had gone off-roading up the steep hill by the library. She'd never been afraid when her dad was around.

Now stopped at a light, she watched a man and woman, hand in hand, cross the street in front of them. The woman laughed loudly at something the man said. The sound carried into the closed car. Life went on, she thought. She glanced over at Nick and for a split second saw her father, working in his wood shop.

She had refused to enter the basement of the Sycamore house after his death. It had been the place where he made his magic, transforming ordinary pieces of wood into something enchanted. She would stand beside him for hours in his workshop, her safety goggles strapped to her head just like his, watching the tiny shavings fall away as the wood spun on the lathe. She'd be mesmerized as the chisel he gripped in his strong, steady hands carved the block into an intricately curved shape.

She thought about a day, about six months after he was gone, when she had been home alone and needed a hammer to hang a picture. For ten minutes, she had stood at the door to the basement staring at the knob, telling herself she could do it. It was just a basement. She had turned the knob and slowly opened the door, hesitating at the top as if she were opening the lid to his casket. Her pulse had quickened, and she had felt the sweat of her palms as she gripped the railing. She forced herself down the open wooden steps, but as she got to the bottom, the thick, dry smell of the lumber almost cut off her air supply. She turned and ran, tripping on the steps and scraping her shin against the bare wood.

Nick turned the car onto Second Street into DC, past the building where she'd taken dance for so many years. The sign on the second-story studio above the market now read Ji Kim's Karate. The lights were on, and she could see children inside dressed in white uniforms, punching and kicking in unison. She wondered where Ms. Petrova was now. She used to think Ms. Petrova had been ancient, but she'd probably only been in her early fifties back then, not that much older than Rory was now. That room had held Rory's dreams. She now understood the frustration Ms. Petrova must have felt when Rory had given it all up. "Wasting your potential..." Ms. Petrova's words echoed in her head.

Her past was smacking her in the face, fortifying the discontented feeling she thought she'd shed on the plane. Like a bug in a box, continually bumping into walls, she seemed unable to find the right path. Her life had traveled by in seconds, but where had it gotten her? She felt like she was still standing at the starting line.

They drove past the cemetery where both of their parents were buried. She thought back to the morning of her father's funeral, lying in bed, not wanting to wake up—sleep was where her father was still alive. Riding in the back of the black Town Car, her eyes swollen and red, boxes of tissues placed strategically about. She remembered staring at the reversed script of the decal on the window, Collins Funeral Home, thinking how much sorrow the car must have carried over the years. Then, glancing at her mother, she wondered how her mother remained so calm, never shedding a tear, not realizing until years later how much pain her mother had been in.

Death. Nick's face flashed in and out from the passing headlights as a feeling of dread crept through her.

Before Nick had come to a complete stop in the driveway, Rory swung open the car door, jumped out, and ran past the two cars parked behind Cass's Volvo. Jillian had texted her a few minutes ago to say she'd arrived. Rory entered the small foyer of the two-story brick house, almost a replica of her grandmother Harper's that had been just four blocks away, and slowed her step. The smell of pot roast drifted through the air and sent her back to her childhood—going to her grandmother's for dinner. She smiled, remembering how her grandmother used to say she had to keep eating until her belly button stuck out.

Voices clamored from the kitchen. Rory hurried down the hall and pushed open the swinging door. The adult bodies dwarfed the small room. How had they all gotten so big? Nick's boys were both over six feet tall, and Chelsea, his middle child, dressed in a long flowing skirt and knitted poncho, had transformed from a skinny little girl to a beautiful woman.

The counters were filled with cookie tins, pecan pie, and several casserole dishes. Rory stood momentarily frozen in the doorway, eyeing the scene, filled with an overwhelming joy. Jamie, Nick's oldest son, stepped to one side. And then she saw Jillian, standing in the circle of her cousins, her long blond curls framing her face, her cheeks flushed with excitement. Her eyes caught Rory's.

"Mom!" She ran over to Rory and hugged her tightly around the neck. Rory drank in her scent, the smell of Dove soap that Rory loved. Tears filled her eyes as she wrapped her arms around her daughter, not wanting to let go. She felt as if she hadn't seen Jillian in years.

"It's so good to see you!" Rory said as she reluctantly released her hold. She gave the others a hug, amazed at how much Michael, Nick's youngest, looked like her dad. Michael had always had her father's eyes, but now he had the same lean build and wore his blond hair in a ponytail just like her father had.

Rory glanced over at Cass, who was standing at the stove and stirring something in a big pot. Steam rose from the top, and Cass swiped her unruly hair with the back of her arm. "Dinner's almost ready," she said. "Did you all get the milk?"

"Nick has it." Rory walked over to Cass and placed her hand on her shoulder. "Is there something I can do?"

"Just grab your brother, and tell him it's time to eat."

24

The metal glider used to sit in the backyard on Sycamore and was now painted green with colorful cushions that melded with the retro-chic style of the décor in Cass and Nick's sunroom. Rory was alone. The quietness seemed odd. Dinner had been filled with lively conversation, everyone updating each other on what was happening in their lives.

Curled up on the glider, she set her book on her lap and listened to the silence. The muffled sound of laughter from a television drifted into the sunroom. She glanced at the small round table beside her and picked up a figurine of Santa Claus. As she turned it in her hands, light from the electric candles in the windows glinted off the porcelain. It was the same Santa that had sat on the mantle at the Sycamore house. She smiled, remembering how she used to think that after she went to sleep, the little red-and-white figurine would turn into the real Santa.

She sighed and set the fat little man back on the table. The melancholy she'd been harboring off and on for the past few weeks was back full force. Earlier in the evening, she'd been in the dining room putting away a soup tureen when she overheard Jillian in the kitchen, telling Chelsea that Derek was spending Christmas in Hawaii with his new girlfriend. She heard Chelsea say, "That must really be weird." She'd waited, her breath held with her hand resting on the swinging door between the two rooms, wanting to hear Jillian's answer. "It's not as weird as I thought it was going to be, but…"

But *what?* Rory anxiously waited, finishing the sentence in her head—*but I wish my parents were still together...but I don't like the woman he's seeing.* And then she heard Jillian say, "I worry about my mom. I hope she's happy." Rory quietly backed away, short of breath. Jillian's comment hadn't been what she'd expected. Did she appear unhappy? The words stung. She didn't want Jillian worrying about her. After waiting a few minutes, she straightened her shoulders, briskly marched over to the swinging door, and breezed into the kitchen with a chiseled smile that she hoped hid the hurt churning inside.

Now her eyes drifted to one wall of the sunroom that was filled with pictures of the kids in various stages of growth. There was one of Michael when he was about ten hanging upside down in a tree, another of the whole family gathered in front of the house. She pictured Nick and Cass in the future with their kids and grandkids living close by. What would her future be like?

She envied the life Nick and Cass had, but as soon as the thought entered her head, she was assaulted with shame—Cass, the cancer. She stared at a picture of Cass and Nick on their wedding day: a candid shot of Nick carrying Cass in his arms, her dress trailing on the ground. Cass had to survive this. The pictures solidified how much they had to lose.

She thought of all the pictures she'd left behind in Phoenix—the wall in her den with the collage of the past twenty-odd years. Would looking at those make someone think she and Derek had had the perfect life? After the holidays, she needed to call Derek and line up a date to sort out their possessions. They also needed to decide what to do with the house, half of which was hers. It felt odd; almost as if the past twenty years had never existed. She thought about the things she had left behind in Phoenix. None of it would fit in her tiny cabin. Maybe it was time for more permanent living arrangements.

Jillian walked into the sunroom and plopped down in the cushioned rocker across from Rory. "I was wondering where you were. Chelsea and I just got back, and I couldn't find anybody."

"Did you get all your shopping done?"

"It was insane out there." Jillian slipped her boots off and curled one foot underneath her. "I got everything done, except for Dad's. I figured I can ship his after Christmas."

"Jillian...about Dad. I hope you don't think I'm upset because he's with Donna."

"What made you say that?" Jillian played with the fringe on her long scarf.

"I just want you to know I'm all right with it. I want your dad to be happy."

Jillian stared out the darkened window. Rory followed her gaze, the glow of the candle reflected on the glass in a halo of light. Rory continued, "And I also don't want you worrying about me. I'm going to be OK."

"Going to be?" Jillian looked back at Rory with concern.

"I *am* OK." Rory smiled.

"I don't like thinking of you all alone." Jillian stared down at her scarf as her long fingers braided the fringe.

"I've got friends. I'm not alone."

"Why don't you come to London with me and Joe?" Jillian looked up, her blue eyes bright, the same look she used to get as a child when she thought she'd come up with a brilliant idea.

Rory laughed. "The two of you do not need your mother tagging along. Jillian, you don't always have to fix everything. What happened between me and Dad is between me and Dad. It's not up to you to make sure I'm taken care of."

"I know. It's just—"

"Believe me, I would love to be with you in London, but it

wouldn't be best for you and Joe. I'll visit, though. Maybe I can come out sometime in the summer, and we can go to Paris. I've always wanted to see France."

Jillian gazed across the room. The rhythmic creak of the rocker echoed softly. "What are you and Dad going to do? I mean with the house and everything."

"I don't know yet. I've gotta call him. We're probably going to sell the house." Rory studied Jillian's face. "Would that bother you?"

Jillian shrugged. "I don't know. Strange, maybe, but I don't think it would bother me." She went back to her scarf, undoing the braiding. "Do you think Dad and you will ever be friends?"

Rory tilted her head with a puzzled look.

"I remember Alexa Adams's parents were divorced, and she had to have two of everything. Two birthday parties, two Christmases, two graduation parties. Her parents couldn't be in the same room together."

Rory glanced over at the smiling Santa. Would she mind being around Derek? She pictured a scene: Jillian, Joe, Derek, and she together for a farewell dinner to see the two off to England. She wouldn't have a problem with that. "I guess it would be up to your dad. I could handle being together." But as soon as the words came out, she pictured the scene again, this time with Donna added to the group. How would she feel now? A green swell of resentment rose inside. She took a deep breath, not wanting to admit that maybe she couldn't handle it. At least not right now.

"I think Dad would be OK, too," Jillian said. "If Joe and I get married—" She put up her hand. "I'm just saying hypothetically, but *if*, I'd hate to think you both couldn't be there."

"Of course we'd both be there. Don't be ridiculous." Rory laughed it off, but inside, cold fingers of jealousy wrapped around her. She didn't know why she was feeling that way. It wasn't because

210

of Derek. Was she worried that one day Jillian might have a step-mom?

———◈◈◈———

Staring at the ceiling, she listened to Jillian's rhythmic breathing from across the room. When Jillian was little, Rory used to stand over Jillian's bed and study her angelic face while she slept, imagining her all grown up. She recalled their conversation earlier. She'd never thought about Derek married to someone else. Another woman in the family—would it be someone whom Jillian got really close to?

Rory rolled on her side in the twin bed and peered at the outline of her sleeping daughter. They were sharing Michael's old bedroom. Her eyes drifted through the darkness. She could make out the shape of a giant stuffed dinosaur that sat slumped in the corner. It seemed like yesterday that Jillian and Michael were just little kids. A part of her wished she was back there. She suddenly felt lost. She needed some kind of direction. If they sold the house in Phoenix, was Willow Bend where she wanted to live? Would she like it as much if Ethan and Marlena didn't live next door?

Rory had stopped by Marlena's the night before she had left for Maryland to exchange presents. Rory had given Ethan the book *Nop's Trials*, a story told from the point of view of a border collie. She remembered how much Jillian had loved it years ago. Ethan had made her a white-and-coral feathered dream catcher, and then he'd handed her a small box. Inside was a turquoise-and-silver bracelet that Marlena had made. Tears had come to Rory's eyes; she hadn't expected such a beautiful gift.

Later that night, after Ethan had gone to bed, the two women had sat on the sofa sipping wine and reminiscing about Christmases past. Marlena had told Rory about one Christmas she'd spent on the reservation with her grandmother when she was around eight. They'd celebrated Soyal, a ceremony to bring back the sun. They'd made prayer sticks and practiced purification rites, focusing on achieving inner peace. Marlena had laughed, saying that the only thing she recalled attaining was inner anger because the children had to be silent the whole time, and she hadn't gotten any presents.

But then Marlena's laughter had stopped, and the spark in her dark eyes had dulled. She had studied Rory's face, and Rory had felt Marlena was searching for an answer to some mystery. Then Marlena had said softly that she was considering moving at the end of the school year to San Diego to be near her parents.

Rory hadn't been surprised. After what had happened at Thanksgiving, she'd wondered if Marlena was going to stay, but hearing the words had filled her with sadness. What would it be like in Willow Bend without Marlena and Ethan?

Now she threw back the covers, unable to shut her mind down for sleep, deciding that maybe a glass of milk would help. She slipped on her robe and silently padded out of the room.

Seated at the red-painted table in the darkened kitchen, the only illumination from the dim light over the stove, she listened to the ticking of the old cuckoo clock in the hallway, the one that had formerly hung on her grandmother's wall. The lingering aroma of cinnamon and cloves made the small kitchen feel snug and cozy. She tucked one foot under her as she felt her limbs relaxing, her sleepiness returning. She dipped a peanut butter cookie into her glass of milk and then leaned over and took a bite. Cass made good cookies. The clock chimed once. She inhaled deeply, thinking of Cass. As if on cue, the swinging door to the kitchen opened, and Cass softly entered, her hair disheveled, her robe hanging off her shoulder. She jerked when she saw Rory, letting out a gasp. "You scared me."

"Sorry. I couldn't sleep," Rory said.

"Me either." Cass rubbed her eyes as she walked over to the cupboard and got a glass. She poured some water and then grabbed a bottle of Tylenol on the counter and popped two pills in her mouth. "Tylenol usually works for me, but I may have to join you in some of those." She opened the metal tin on the table and sat down across from Rory.

The two ate their cookies in silence for a few minutes, and then Cass said, "Nick talk to you?"

Rory nodded.

"I knew he would. But it's OK. I just don't want the kids to know yet." She drew in air and then exhaled audibly. "I want to have the results from the PET scan first."

"When is that?"

"Probably the day after Christmas or maybe Friday."

"Cass, I..."

"I know." Her sister-in-law smiled at her. "It sucks."

"If there's anything, anything at all."

"Thanks. Right now I just want to put it out of my mind, if that's possible." Cass bit into her cookie and wiped the crumbs from her face. "So what's going on in your life? Tell me something fun and exciting."

"Derek and I are officially divorced." Rory didn't know why that popped out; it wasn't something fun *or* exciting.

"Are you happy with that?"

Rory hesitated, thinking about the question. "It's what I wanted. Derek's happy. He's going to Hawaii with this woman, Donna." Rory knew her words sounded caustic, but it had been simmering in the back of her mind. Why, she didn't know. It wasn't like she wanted to be in Hawaii with Derek. "I'm sorry. I know that sounded childish." She brushed a strand of hair behind her ear.

"No, I can understand how you feel. He's having all the fun."

Cass smiled and then gazed across the darkened room. "I always liked Derek."

Rory raised her eyebrows.

Cass held her hand up. "Don't get me wrong. Liking someone and being married to him are two different things. I remember when I first met him, Nick had told me how he didn't think Derek was right for you, but there was something about him…I don't know…a rugged quality. *Capable*—that's the word. Like when we all went on that camping trip, there wasn't anything he couldn't do." Cass stared down at her hands that were clasped together on the table. "He made you feel safe…" Her words trailed off.

Rory sensed the fear in Cass's voice. An anxious wave washed over Rory. What would she do if she got news like Cass's? Would she want Derek back?

Cass looked at Rory and then said, "I think what you did was brave. I'm sure it wasn't an easy decision to leave someone you've been married to for so long. It must've been scary."

Rory thought back to that first day, driving away from the house on Corral Canyon, not knowing where she was going. "Scary would be putting it mildly."

"How do you like Willow Bend? You seemed happy there."

Rory sighed. "It's nice."

"That didn't sound convincing."

Rory looked down at the cookie crumbs floating in her milk. "When I first got there, I was really excited—starting a new job, having my own place—but lately I feel…I don't know. Stagnant, Unfulfilled." She shook her head. "I don't know what's wrong with me. I feel like I don't know my place in the world."

Cass reached out and stroked Rory's arm. "You're going through a transition. It's understandable you'd feel confused."

She smiled at Cass. It felt good to talk with someone about her thoughts, but at the same time, she felt chagrined—she should be the one giving Cass comfort, not the other way around. "I don't need to bore you with my neurosis."

"Don't be silly. There's nothing I can do with my problem, but maybe I can help you with yours."

Rory leaned back in her chair. "It's funny—when I first left Phoenix, I was filled with this urgency, like I only had this finite amount of time to do something with my life. I felt like Derek had been holding me back, and if I broke away, my problems would be solved. But now I have no excuses." She wrapped her robe tightly around her. "It scares the hell out of me, thinking, what if there isn't anything? You remember the movie *As Good as It Gets*? What if that's what I had, and now I don't even have that?"

"Rory, you're an intelligent, beautiful woman; there isn't anything you can't do." Cass pulled at a tangled curl. "Do you like your job?"

"I like the customers, but…"

"You're taking dance again. Have you ever thought about doing something with that?"

Rory frowned. "Like what? I'm forty-two. I don't think there's a big calling for ballerinas in their forties."

"Not like that. But what about teaching? Didn't you used to teach?" Cass opened the tin of cookies and rooted out a second one. "You know, that reminds me—an old sorority sister of mine runs a school for the arts in North Carolina. Maybe she could use some help."

"I haven't taught dance in years." She shook her head.

"It can't hurt to see, and besides, she owes me. I'm the one who introduced her to her husband. Who knows? I could call her."

Rory scrunched up her face.

"Oh, come on, Rory, what have you got to lose? And wouldn't

it be nice living back on the East Coast, especially since Jillian will be in London?"

Cass had a point. What ties did she have to the West Coast now?

"Let me find out more about it," Cass said.

Rory felt a bubble of excitement rise up. But then she began questioning the idea: she hadn't taught dance in years—there was no way she'd get the job. It was nice of Cass to suggest it, but she knew Cass had to be doubtful too.

"Rory…"

"Yeah?"

"I know this may sound selfish, but I wish you lived closer for Nick's sake. I'm worried about him. I think after what happened with your mom, he's convinced that's what will happen to me." Cass paused, pushing the cookie crumbs around on the table. "You make him laugh…I guess what I'm trying to say is I'm glad you're here."

"Hey, we're family."

Cass smiled, but Rory saw tears welling in her eyes. "I feel like I have to be strong. That if I give in to the fear, everyone else will fall apart. But I can't help think what if…"

Rory reached across the table and squeezed Cass's hand.

Cass looked at Rory. "The strange thing is it's not that I'm scared of dying. I worry about the kids and Nick—how will they survive? Will Michael finish college? Will Chelsea meet the right guy? Who will be there to give her advice when she's a new mom?" The tears spilled over and ran down Cass's cheek.

"Oh, Cass…" She got up and put her arms around Cass's shoulders and leaned her head down next to hers. "You're going to beat this. I know it." Her emphatic words got muffled in Cass's thick curls. She inhaled the smell of lemons as her tears dampened the frazzled locks.

Cass nodded and patted Rory's arm. "Thanks. I have to believe that." She swiped the tears away with the back of her hand. "I went to church the other day."

Rory sat back down across from Cass. Cass chuckled and then continued. "I didn't tell Nick. I don't know what made me do it. It was Tuesday, and I sat in one of the pews for an hour, just thinking about my family, my life…things I wanted to say to my kids, things you think you'll always have time to say later…I remembered your mom; right after she was diagnosed, I was taking her for her treatments…" Cass hesitated for a second. "She'd talk for hours about the past. Like she was collecting memories of things she wanted to resolve. She talked about you a lot. She said she regretted not insisting you get help after your dad died. She worried about you not being happy."

Tears stung Rory's eyes as she gazed across the room at a red-and-black ceramic rooster that sat on the counter. In the darkness, the bird looked as if he was staring back at her. She needed to start believing in herself again, she thought sadly. Knowing what Cass was facing reignited her sense of urgency. The cuckoo clock chimed twice. Two in the morning. The quiet house was tucked safely in bed, but Rory felt a drumming expectation with each beat of the ticking clock.

25

Driving down Interstate 40 on their way to Wilmington, North Carolina, Rory and Jillian leaned toward each other as the chorus to "Born to be Wild" approached, belting out the lyrics in unison. When the song had come on the radio, Rory realized for the first time it had lost its dreaded feeling. She felt happy, as if her dad was with them on the journey.

Rory hadn't wanted to leave Silver Spring; she wanted to be there when they got the test results. But she'd sensed that Cass and Nick wanted to be alone with the kids when they gave them the news. Cass had contacted her friend Jennifer Madden at the school in North Carolina, and she had told Cass she had a few positions open and would love to meet with Rory. Rory had wanted to say no, feeling foolish for even thinking the woman would hire her. She knew Jennifer was only doing it for Cass's sake, but at least Rory would get a few days with Jillian alone.

The long stretch of highway that ran southeast was practically empty. The landscape felt alien: flat land, scattered pines mixed with an occasional scrubby palm, a few billboards along the way, but no sign of life. She'd only been to North Carolina once before when she'd visited Nick at school in Greensboro.

She had been eighteen, had just gotten in a huge fight with her mother, and had borrowed money from a friend down the street for bus fare. She'd shown up unannounced at Nick's apartment. That had been the first time she'd met Cass, and Rory had known the minute she saw them together that Nick was going to marry her. She remembered the look Nick had when he was around her—enraptured. Rory had teased Nick, telling him that he was whipped, but she'd been happy for him.

She wished he'd felt the same about Derek and her. Nick and she had been alone in the kitchen at the house on Sycamore the night before her wedding. She was nervous and jittery, and she'd wanted Nick to tell her everything was going to be OK, but he hadn't. Instead he had told her it wasn't too late; she could still back out.

She glanced at her daughter's profile. Jillian hummed to a Beatles song on the radio, her thumbs rapidly hitting the keys on her phone, texting Joe. Maybe being a single parent, struggling to survive, wouldn't have been the best thing for Jillian. She smiled with pride, thinking Jillian was at least one thing she and Derek had done right.

The brilliant cerulean sky filled the windshield of Cass's Volvo. Carolina blue. *Maybe things happen for a reason*, she thought. They drove under the large green sign that read Wilmington—Carolina Beach—Fort Fisher. A fleeting thought popped into Rory's head, and she found that she was picturing herself working at the school. Was this something she wanted to do? She had done some research on the school and found out that they held regular dance classes, along with acting and singing, but they also specialized in dance therapy for children with special needs. It sounded great, but she didn't want to get too excited about it—the whole thing was a long shot anyway. Her focus shifted back to Jillian—three days together, what more could she ask for?

Reclined in beach chairs that they'd pulled out of the storage closet of the rental, Rory and Jillian were soaking up the warm afternoon sun. It was their last day together. Jillian was flying out from the Wilmington airport the next morning to meet Joe in Florida, and Rory was heading back to Maryland to spend New Year's with Nick and Cass. They had the beach to themselves. Jillian had found a small transistor radio in the cottage that now played in the background against the lapping sound of the near-nonexistent ocean waves. With her jeans rolled up to her knees, Rory made circles in the sand with her toe while she listened to Jillian, whose face was lit up as she described the gallery where she would be working in London.

"They have one of Monet's early works at Sainte-Adresse and one from Picasso's Rose period. They also have several Nigel Cooks." The enthusiasm that emanated from Jillian spilled over to Rory. Jillian told Rory how she and Joe had been searching online for places to live. They had a few prospects; one was a flat in Notting Hill. Jillian tilted her head back, laughing as she said the words with an exaggerated British accent. Rory smiled. She was happy for Jillian. The ache in the pit of her stomach that she'd had every time she thought of Jillian in England was gone, and she wasn't sure why. She felt content.

While Jillian searched the web on her phone to show Rory one of the flats, Rory thought about the day before, crossing over the bridge back into Wilmington with the USS *North Carolina* towering in the dark waters of the Cape Fear River on her way back from her interview with Jennifer. A marshy smell had filtered into the car, and as she had driven past the large Georgian-style historic homes, she'd let out a scream as a bubbly feeling rose inside. What had started out a whim was now becoming something she wanted. She had been impressed with the school and could see herself teaching there.

Now Jillian handed the phone to Rory to show her one of the flats. She tried imitating Jillian's British accent and told her it looked *very posh.* Jillian laughed and then slipped her phone back in her bag. She began digging in the sand in front of her beach chair.

"Mom, I'm really proud of you." Jillian brushed her long curls away from her face with the back of her sand-covered hand.

"What made you say that?" Rory smiled.

"Just everything you've done. I know it must've been really hard to leave Dad." She swiped her sandy palms on her pants and hugged her knees, leaning forward in her chair. "I just want you to know that you're a great mom."

Rory smiled as Jillian went back to making towers of sand.

"I'm glad you pushed me to be independent. I remember you always telling me to question authority." Jillian laughed.

"I sometimes thought I may have gone too far, but I didn't want you to have the fears that I had." Rory glanced down the beach at an old cottage sticking up from the dune. "I remember these coffee mugs that Grandma Jensen gave me one Christmas about ten years ago, each with a different scene painted on them of the four seasons. My favorite was the spring one, which had a picture of this tiny cottage covered in ivy with flowers along a path leading up to it." Rory smiled; her eyes were far off. "Each morning I drank out of that mug, I'd stare at the picture of the cozy little house and be filled with this incredible peace." Rory laughed. "There were times I thought maybe I was going crazy; I wanted to live in that cottage. I guess I didn't know how to fix what was wrong with me, so instead I just wanted to escape." She reached down and picked up a small iridescent shell, turning it in her hand. "I blamed your dad for a lot of my problems, but that wasn't fair. For the first time, I'm beginning to see a future." Two seagulls soared above the glassy water. Rory stared at their graceful bodies and how effortlessly they moved. "I hadn't expected to really want this job, but I feel like it's stirred something inside me. Last night, I started reading one of the books I got at Barnes and Noble yesterday, and the whole idea of dance therapy is so fascinating." She dropped the shell in the sand, still staring at the birds in flight. "I gave up dance years ago, and it probably was the one thing that could have helped me." She glanced over at Jillian. "But even if I don't get this job, I know I want to go back to school; I'd love to get a degree in psychology."

"I remember when I was a kid, you were the mom all my friends wanted to go to. You were like the neighborhood shrink. Samantha used to say that she wished her mom was more like you. I never realized how lucky I was."

Rory smiled. Jillian's words shot straight to her heart. She was glad Jillian hadn't thought it silly that she wanted to go to school.

"I remember you taught dance when I was little." Jillian dug a tunnel in the sand. "Why'd you give it up?"

A breeze blew Rory's hair across her face, and she gathered it together, twisting it in a long spiral. She didn't want to tell Jillian that it was because Derek hadn't wanted her to work, that he had used Jillian to make her feel guilty about working. "There were different reasons. I don't think I had a whole lot of self-esteem. I doubted my abilities." She smiled at Jillian. "It's weird; I can't really explain why I feel so different now. Nothing's really changed, but I don't feel like I'm running away anymore."

Jillian's cell phone rang. She swiped the sand off her hand and picked it out of her bag. Rory saw the love on Jillian's face and knew it was Joe; that look filled Rory with joy.

She sat back in her chair, breathing in the salty air, and closed her eyes, letting the warmth of the sun caress her skin. She listened to Jillian's playful banter with Joe, and a smile spread across her face. The rhythm of the lapping waves lulled her, and she felt herself slipping into a dream state. The radio played an old Motown tune but all she heard was Ben's voice, singing her song. The lyrics tugged at her heartstrings. She pictured Ben's face, his long fingers strumming the guitar. The searing pain she had felt in Monterey came back. She shuddered and opened her eyes.

Jillian was still on the phone engrossed in her conversation with Joe. Rory stared out at the endless water. The past year and a half flashed before her: the affair, the disintegration of her marriage, leaving Phoenix, waiting tables at the luncheonette, Will, and now North Carolina. Was she moving forward?

Her cell rang, and she wrestled it out of her jeans pocket. Nick. A grip of panic made her heart race. Had they gotten the news? She held her breath as she punched the button, but his voice sounded almost joyous. The results had shown that the cancer hadn't spread. The doctors were confident that with treatment and a mastectomy, Cass should fully recover.

After hanging up, she felt the sandbags of tension that she hadn't even realized were sitting on her shoulders lift away. She looked up at the sky, so intensely blue it didn't look real. Then her eyes drifted back down the beach to the tiny cottage peeking over the dunes, and she was filled with that same euphoria she'd felt from the little house on the mug.

26

Tearing off the brown wrapper that held the stack of napkins together, she shoved a handful into one of the spring-loaded metal holders lined up on the counter. A week had passed since Rory had been back in Willow Bend, and she'd received an e-mail the day before from Jennifer saying that she was still working on her decision. Rory couldn't believe she was actually in the running. On her flight back from Maryland, she'd finished the book on autism and dance therapy that she'd bought in North Carolina, and she wanted to learn more.

The disposable rain ponchos that hung by the glass door to the street rustled as Pops walked in, dressed in his usual navy-blue chinos and work shirt with his name embroidered in light-blue script under the words Popeye's Auto Repair.

Pops reminded Rory of her uncle Jimmy. Both men were around the same age, and they both wore the lingering smell of gasoline and grease on their clothes. He had her uncle's hands too—no matter how much hand cleaner Uncle Jimmy used, the cracks of his roughened fingers seemed to be permanently stained.

The lunch crowd had gone, and there was only one other occupied table. Rory headed over with a menu and glass of water to where Pops was seated.

"How's that Falcon running?" He asked her that every time he came in.

"Great." Rory handed him the menu. "I may need an oil change soon."

"Bring her in anytime." He glanced at the menu and then handed it back to Rory. "Give me the cheeseburger, extra pickles. And a—"

"Coke." Rory finished his sentence. She didn't know why he liked to look at the menu; he always ordered the same thing.

Filling the glass from the soda tap, she thought about her uncle Jimmy and last Tuesday, New Year's Eve. They'd gone to Mike's Pub to celebrate, and her father's old haunt had made her think about the night he had died. Mike's had supposedly been his last stop before crashing his motorcycle. After several beers, she'd gotten up the courage to confront her uncle. She needed to know if what Nick had told her was true. Had her father really killed Kirk Lucas?

She'd just beaten her uncle in a game of nine-ball. He had teased her, calling her a pool shark, and then he had squeezed his burly arm around her shoulder, laughing, saying she was almost as good as her dad.

She had smiled, but she hadn't been able to get the nagging question out of her head. Her father had been the epitome of love, kindness, everything good, so how could he have killed someone? She finally screwed up her courage, and the words came out.

By the change in her uncle's expression, she knew she had taken him by surprise. He had stared into space for several minutes as if seeing her dad across the crowded bar, and then he had said, "Rory, whatever your dad did, he did it because he loved you. You were like sunshine to him." Her uncle paused and gave her a puzzled look. "What brought that up now?"

Rory shrugged. "I don't know, I guess being here made me think of that night…" Rory gazed at Nick, who was laughing across the room, his arm around Cass.

Uncle Jimmy squeezed her closer to him. "Hey, you need to forget about all that. It was a long time ago." He smiled at Rory.

Rory smiled weakly, but something in her expression must have gotten to Jimmy.

"All right." He faced her with his hands on her shoulders. "I'm only telling you this because maybe if you know the truth, you can put the whole thing out of your mind. Your dad came to my shop that night. I could tell he'd had a lot to drink, and he wouldn't stop talking about Kirk and how he'd been a worthless piece of shit. Your dad kept saying he'd screwed up but that he'd made things right. I asked him what he meant, and then I saw the cuts on his hands. His knuckles were all beat up. I asked him what he'd done, but he said I didn't need to know. And then I got a call, and I went into the office, and while I was on the phone, your dad left." Uncle Jimmy looked across the bar. Tears welled in his eyes. "I should never have taken that call. I shoulda taken the keys to his bike the minute he came to the shop."

"Hey, you didn't know. It wasn't your fault." Rory hugged her uncle.

How different things would've been if that day had never happened. Such a seemingly normal day had, in an instant, changed the course of their lives forever.

At the stroke of midnight, she'd stood alone toward the back of the bar, observing the crowd: Nick and Cass had been locked in an embrace, and a woman who'd had more than her share of tequila had been dancing on the bar while a group of people below the woman, oblivious to her gyrations, sang "Auld Lang Syne." Rory had raised her beer bottle in the air, toasting the image of her father's smiling face, and silently vowed that this was going to be her year.

Now she walked across the restaurant with lightness in her step as she placed the cheeseburger in front of Pops.

"I told you you'd forget something," Rory said without looking up from the counter she was wiping, thinking it was Astral coming back in for the second time. When she glanced up, though, it was Will standing by the door. She felt her cheeks warm as she looked down at the circular streaks of moisture her rag had made on the green Formica. Will hadn't been in the luncheonette since before Thanksgiving. She wondered what had brought him in today. It was almost closing, and Rory was the last one left in the restaurant.

"Too late to get a cup of coffee?" He strode over to the counter and slipped onto a stool.

Rory glanced at the clock. It was five of three. "I just rinsed the pot."

"How 'bout a Coke?" He smiled.

"Sure." Rory reached for one of the tall soda glasses lined up on the glass shelf behind the counter, bumping into one with the back of her hand and knocking it over. She caught it before it hit the floor. Her heart thumped in her chest. She was glad to see Will, but at the same time, she felt awkward. She'd acted ridiculous before, getting upset because he'd been with someone else. Her mind raced with what to say.

But he said it for her. "For days, I racked my brain trying to figure out why you wouldn't take my calls." She set the Coke in front of him on the counter, and he continued, "And then I ran into Marlena the other day…" He looked up at her and smiled.

Rory knew her face had to be crimson; it felt like it was on fire. What had Marlena told him?

"Thanksgiving night—"

She cut him off. "You don't have to explain—"

"I think I do. When I got back to my place, there was a car parked in the driveway."

No shit, Rory wanted to say.

"It was Rachel, my ex-wife. She'd driven from Colorado."

Rory nodded. *OK*, she thought, *he's being honest.* But she couldn't help thinking she'd been right; he probably had been seeing her all along.

"I'd run into her when I went to that convention."

Aha, right again, she thought, as she remembered how distant he'd acted after returning from Denver.

"Her husband recently died. Aneurysm. It was real sudden, and she was pretty devastated."

Rory was confused. This wasn't the story she had expected.

"Anyway, she kind of lost it and needed someone to talk to. She ended up at my place. She stayed for a few days and spent most of the time telling me what a great guy her husband had been." Will laughed. "Just what every ex wants to hear, right? But I felt bad for her. She was a mess. I slept on the couch and gave her my bed. She woke up after the third night and thanked me for listening to her, and then she got in her car and left."

"I didn't know—I mean, I thought—"

"I'm sorry if you thought—"

"No, it's OK." She came around the counter and sat on a stool next to him. She smelled the woodsy air that permeated his clothes and studied his face as if seeing him for the first time. He wasn't the cad she'd made him out to be; he *was* one of the good guys. "That was nice of you to be there for her."

"What else could I do?"

Rory nodded. "Life can really take unexpected turns. I just found out that my brother's wife has cancer."

Will nodded. "Sorry to hear that. Just when you think you've got it all together, something can come along and knock you right off your feet." He sipped his Coke and then picked up the paper wrapper from the straw and rolled it in his fingers.

Rory felt the awkwardness between them. Their words felt stilted.

"How was your Christmas?" he asked.

"Good. I got to spend time with Jillian. How about yours?"

"Crowded." Will chuckled. "We're the cliché of a Mormon family. I've got more relatives than the population of Willow Bend, and they were all at my parents' house."

Rory laughed. The easy feeling, like slipping into a comfortable pair of shoes, was coming back.

Will stared at the paper wrapper, now in the shape of a ball, as he rolled it around in his fingers. "I got a transfer offer…in Utah."

"What?"

"About eight months ago, I'd put in for a transfer. I'd been in Willow Bend six years, and I was looking to move on, but nothing was available, and I kind of forgot about it. But then about a week ago, I got a letter from the forest service saying there was an opening in the Wasatch Mountains."

"Are you going to take it?"

"I don't know. I'm supposed to go in two weeks to meet with them and check it out." He looked at Rory.

She smiled, trying to hide the strange feeling inside, but she knew he could see it in her eyes. It didn't make sense—she had been thinking of leaving Willow Bend herself. Why did it hurt to think he might be moving to Utah?

"I figured I should at least go take a look. I might tell them forget it."

Was he saying this because of her? Worry slipped under her sadness. She didn't want Will to leave, but she didn't want him staying on her account. What was wrong with her? She needed to be honest with him. "I may be leaving Willow Bend too."

Will's eyebrows rose.

Rory told him about Jennifer Madden and the school. "Who knows; I probably won't get the job, but it's funny—I've become fascinated with the studies on autism and dance therapy." She leaned forward at the counter. "I always pictured someone rocking in a corner, out of touch with the world, when I thought of autism, but I've learned so much more." She glanced across the room out the big front window to the street, where two boys went running by with backpacks flailing, raucously shouting to someone farther down. "I don't know what it is, but I feel a connection to it. As a kid, I spent a lot of time alone. After my brother Nick started school, my dad would be down in his workshop, and I'd be upstairs in this imaginary world I'd created. Even when I was in school, I was always a loner." She placed a strand of hair behind her ear and looked back at Will. "Dance became my outlet. It was where I felt alive. And studies show that dance can help handicapped and autistic children express themselves and open their world. It's really interesting…" Rory paused and looked down at her hands. "I would love to be a part of that in some way. I want to go back to school."

Will chuckled.

"What? Do I sound crazy?"

"No. I've just never seen you so pumped about something. I think it's great." Will tossed the balled-up wrapper over the counter, where it landed in the trash can by the cash register. "I hope it works out for you."

"Like I said, I'd be surprised if I get this job, but I'm going to start taking some online courses and maybe teach dance again."

Will nodded.

Rory couldn't tell what he was thinking. Had he wanted her to tell him not to leave Willow Bend? "What are the Wasatch Mountains like?"

Will looked at her and smiled. "I used to go there when I was a kid. It's kind of like God took all of his masterpieces and put them in this one museum." He paused. "So Willow Bend was your stepping-stone."

Rory frowned with a puzzled look.

"On your journey," Will added. "This wasn't your destination."

"I guess I haven't figured out what that is yet."

"If you don't get the job, do you think you'll still leave?"

Rory pondered the question. "Maybe." She stared across at her own reflection in the mirrored wall behind the glass shelves, feeling like she was just getting to know the person staring back at her.

She caught Will studying her profile; then he said, "After Rachel left, I thought about us. You and me." He motioned his hand in her direction. "When Rachel and I divorced, I vowed I would never go through that again. I figured the best way to avoid another divorce was to not get married. I dated, but I always made sure things didn't get too serious. Which wasn't always easy." He grinned. "Why is it that when you don't want something, that's the one thing the other person wants? For a while it seemed like every woman I dated had marriage on the brain. But when you came along, I thought it was perfect—you'd just ended a marriage and didn't want to be in a relationship. I didn't have to worry."

Rory wondered where this was going. Was he telling her he liked the fact they weren't serious? But the tone of his voice said something else. An uneasy feeling tumbled inside.

"When you didn't take my calls after Thanksgiving, I began to think I wasn't going to see you again, and I didn't like the feeling. There were days I wanted to stop by here while you were working and ask you what was wrong, but I fought it." He sighed. "I never expected it would be me that would want something more. I didn't think I'd feel this way again."

No, don't say it; don't go there, Rory implored in her head. An anxious swell swept through her stomach. She needed to stop him. "Will—"

He chuckled. "Don't panic; I know it's not going to work. We're in different places right now. I just hope we can stay friends at least."

Relief washed over her. "Me too. The past few months have been hard for me…I knew it wasn't going to be easy when I left Phoenix, but having you as a friend helped." Rory turned back to her reflection. "I guess no one really knows what lies ahead. I feel like I'm going through some kind of metamorphic change. I'm just not sure what the outcome is going to be."

"Things never stay the same." Will's straw made a slurping sound as he sucked up the last of his Coke. He set the glass on the counter. "So we both may be leaving Willow Bend."

"And Marlena's moving to San Diego after Ethan finishes school." Rory picked up his glass and took it around to the other side, placing it in the sink.

Will gave a nod. "Whatever happened with her husband?"

"They charged him with stalking, so I assume he's locked up somewhere."

He nodded several times. She sensed the gears shifting in his head and wished she could read his mind. He smiled at her from across the counter and said, "Willow Bend just won't be the same without us."

27

Rory dropped the hot pan onto the counter. The chicken soup splattered down the pine cupboard. *"Shit!"* She grabbed her hand and then turned on the cold water, letting it run over her already reddened palm. She rested her elbows on the edge of the sink and hung her head down. It would probably blister, but that was par for the course. Nothing seemed to be going right today.

Her faucet had broken in her shower this morning, and Mr. Danvers had said he couldn't get to it until tomorrow; her envelope containing her week's tips that she was going to take to the bank had disappeared from her purse at work. And then to top it all off, she'd gotten the phone call.

Rory wrapped a paper towel around her hand and then scuffed her wool moccasin slippers over to the kitchen table and slumped into a chair. The overhead kitchen light glared down on the coffee stains that ringed the brightly colored tablecloth. She ran her forefinger around one of the rings, and the news she had pushed out of her mind began weighing her down again.

As she had driven home from work, her heart had beaten a little faster when she'd seen the 910 area code show up on her phone, knowing right away that it was Jennifer Madden. She'd held the phone in her hand, and a glimmer of hope had shot through her, a distant, anticipative voice saying, *just maybe...*

On the third ring, she hit the button.

Five minutes later, she'd dropped the cell onto the passenger seat. The gray asphalt blurred before her. She hadn't expected to get the job, but at least before the phone call, there had been that tiny sliver of possibility.

Now, she tried boosting herself up, channeling Beverly's upbeat aura—the overweight woman on the plane had become Rory's symbol of positive energy—telling herself there would be other opportunities. "Life can take strange turns"—that's what Caroline had said the other day.

She had stopped into Caroline's shop a couple of days ago to tell her that their dance instructor had asked Rory if she'd be interested in teaching a Saturday ballet class for five- and six-year-olds, starting in March. Caroline had been behind the counter, folding silk scarves and arranging them in a wicker basket. Rory had flipped through a rack of dresses, holding a few up to herself in the process.

"Are you going to do it?" Caroline had asked.

"I want to, but a part of me—and I know it's a long shot—is hoping I'll get the job in North Carolina."

Caroline had nodded.

"I know what you're thinking—I'm deluding myself. I'm probably only in the running because Jennifer's a friend of my sister-in-law." Rory had gone over to the small leopard-printed chair by the counter and sat down. "I wish I'd never given up dance years ago."

"What makes you think if you'd stuck with dance, your life would've been perfect?" Caroline had set the purple-and-blue paisley scarf into the basket and then picked up the basket and come around to Rory. "Look at me." She leaned against the counter. "I pursued dance and made it in New York. Then there was Portland, and now I have a dress shop in Willow Bend. Life can take strange turns, and nothing's guaranteed." She placed the basket on a display shelf. "You need to accept your life for what it is now and enjoy it. So what if you don't get the job in North Carolina. Start teaching here, and continue with school. You said you love the classes you're taking."

Rory had enrolled in two online college courses—one was Autism 101, a study of the levels and treatments for autistic children, and the other was an introductory psychology class. Every break she got at work and in the evenings, she was focused on her textbooks, finishing her assignments well in advance.

Now seated at the kitchen table, she thought about Will. He had left for a week to check out the new job possibility; he still hadn't made his mind up. He had become a regular at the luncheonette again, dropping by right before closing and making her laugh. She'd miss him if he did decide to leave, and now she was wondering if Willow Bend was where she should be. She closed her eyes. Things would work out. She took a deep breath, channeling Beverly again.

It was Friday. Tomorrow she would call Marlena and see if she and Ethan would like to go hiking. She could take her camera. She hadn't taken any pictures since her photography class had ended in December, over a month ago. Maybe she'd ask Caroline if she'd like to go to a movie tomorrow night. She felt the dejectedness fade as she headed over to the stove and heated the soup back up.

Something brushed against her side, and she pushed it away as she crept down a dimly lit hallway. She knew it was a dream, because she wasn't afraid, even though the place had an eerie quality to it. Closed doors lined both sides. Each knob she turned was locked. She was nearing the end of the hall, and a strange light spilled out from the cracks in the door that faced her. And then there was a knocking sound. It was coming from the other side of the door. The pounding got louder and louder.

Her eyes opened. She stared at the dark ceiling, disoriented. Her heart beat against her ribs. She sat up and ran her hand through her hair, thinking, *What a crazy dream*, but then she jerked at the sound of frantic knocking. The noise hadn't been a dream.

There was someone at her door.

She glanced at the bedside clock—2:43 a.m. Confusion followed by fear jumbled her thoughts. Then she heard Ethan's voice, screaming her name.

She stumbled out of bed with her foot tangled in the covers and fell on her knees. Scrambling to her feet, she raced to the door. As soon as she opened it, Ethan ran in with Shiloh by his side. From the porch light, she noticed his flannel pajamas with cowboys and horses on them, and in her discombobulated state, she thought of Nick, years ago, having a pair just like them. But then she saw Ethan's face and noticed that he was crying.

"Ethan, what happened?"

"It's...my...dad." His words came out fragmented between sobs. He was shaking.

"Your dad?"

He nodded. "He's...he's..." He sucked in air between sobs.

"He's what?" Rory stroked Ethan's hair, trying to calm him down. She knelt down beside him.

"He's going to...k-k-kill my mom."

"How could—he's in jail—"

"*No*, he's not; he's *here*!" Ethan shouted.

"OK, OK." She put her arm around Ethan, trying to comfort him while she collected her thoughts.

"He's hitting her...and she was screaming...I snuck out...he said...he..." Ethan's voice shook between gasps. "He said he wanted to kill her."

Running her fingers through her tangled mass of hair, she

thought, *Focus!* She stared across the darkened room as the gears in her head begin to churn. "OK," she repeated. Adrenaline pumped through her veins.

Robotically, she ran over to the kitchen counter, where her cell phone was plugged in, and yanked it from the cord. She pressed it firmly in Ethan's hand. "Call 911. Tell them what you told me."

She grabbed her sweatpants and sweatshirt that were lying on top of the hamper and threw them on over her nightgown. Then she ran over to the closet, pulling hats and scarves from the top shelf. In the dim glow from the bathroom nightlight, she saw the black case.

Derek's words echoed in her head—if you're going to use the gun, make sure it's ready to shoot. Just like he'd shown her at the shooting range, she checked the chamber, made sure the safety was on, then shoved the Beretta into the pouch pocket on the front of her sweatshirt. She ran toward the front door, then stopped and went over to Ethan, who was still standing in the same spot, his body heaving up and down. She put her arm around him. "I want you to stay here. I'm going to lock the door, and don't open it. You called 911?"

Ethan nodded.

"Help is on the way. Your mom's going to be all right, OK?"

He nodded again.

She jogged across the damp grass; it chilled her bare feet. Her sweatpants hung loose on her hips, and she had to hike them up as she ran. The racing beat of her heart made it hard to breathe, and she had to force the air in and out of her lungs. A distant voice in her head asked, *What are you doing?* The darkened outline of Marlena's cottage loomed before her. Was she really going to go in there? It was a clear night, and the moon was nearly full. The soft, steady chirp of crickets droned in the distance. She hesitated at the bottom of the steps to Marlena's front porch and glanced around. Only Marlena's car sat in the driveway. Was he gone? She looked up at the house; the door was sitting ajar, and it was dark inside.

Silence.

She hesitantly climbed the three steps and then tiptoed across the wood slats of the porch and stood by the door for several seconds, listening. Three low hoots of an owl echoed from the forest, breaking the silence.

She glanced around the porch, feeling the stillness of the night as her breath made puffs of air in front of her. Sliding her hand into the pocket of her sweatshirt, she flipped off the safety with a soft click. Her fingers grasped the cold metal of the barrel, and she wrapped her blistered palm around the plastic grip. The thump of her heart pounded in her ears as she gently pushed open the door and stepped into the living room.

A sliver of moonlight shone through the parted curtains on the side wall. Rory spotted the bottoms of two bare feet sticking out from beside the dining table. Her breath caught in her throat. She glanced around the room, her eyes adjusting to the darkness, and then stepped cautiously across the rug.

Marlena lay on her side, a pool of dark liquid puddled under her head.

"Marlena!" She knelt down and gently touched Marlena's arm. "Marl—"

Her words were cut off as her head snapped back.

Someone yanked on her hair, pulling her upward. She felt hot breath against her neck and smelled onions, cigarettes, and alcohol. An image of Kirk Lucas flashed in her head as the taste of bile filled her mouth.

"You must be her dyke friend." The words spat against her cheek. "Well, aren't I lucky—I can get rid of two for the price of one. Are you the bitch she's fucking now?" He whipped her around to face him. "You're better looking than the others." His voice was low and deliberate. His black eyes bored into her, and she looked away.

"The police are on their way." Rory heard the words coming out of her mouth and was surprised at how calm they sounded.

"Is that so? Well, then I better work fast."

She saw a flash of something shiny whiz past her face. What was it? A knife? Without thinking, she shoved him hard in the chest. He stumbled backward, but before she could even move, he lunged at her, knocking her over as they both fell to the ground with a thud. Her breath was sucked out of her lungs, and her head reeled. She wriggled her body, trying to slip out from under him, and then she saw the flash again.

He waved the blade back and forth over her face.

"I hate to ruin such a pretty face."

28

He ran the tip of the knife along her jawline. Rory felt the flow of blood run down her neck. She saw the blade coming at her again, this time toward the other side of her face. His weight was heavy against her. She flailed back and forth, trying to get him off, and then with a raging force she heaved to one side as she let out a guttural scream. It was enough to get her hand in her pocket.

The metal tip of the blade touched her skin just as she wrapped her finger around the trigger and pointed the gun up.

She felt the rush of air pressure whoosh over her face from the blast that rang out in the room. It was louder than Rory had expected.

A residual echo rang in her ears as she lay there, momentarily stunned, Max slumped on top of her. The smell of his sweat filled her nostrils. She scrambled her way out from under him and got to her knees, gasping for air. The gun was still gripped in her hand and she stared at it as if it was alive, then dropped it on the floor. There was a stinging pain along her jaw. Warm liquid seeped under her collar. She reflexively reached her hand up and then quickly drew it back. Her fingers were covered in blood. She slumped onto her haunches feeling dizzy but she knew she had to concentrate. Max's body lay face down on the braided rug. With one leg outstretched, she nudged him with her foot. He rocked slightly and then lay still.

Was he dead? Then she remembered Marlena. Was she dead?

She crawled over to Marlena's body and sat beside her. She tried searching for a pulse but felt nothing. *No.* The room began to shift as if the floor was moving. Her vision became blurry, and she had to hold on to her head, feeling weak and nauseous.

Hands clamped around her arms, lifting her. She looked up to see bodies in uniforms, so many of them. A stretcher was being wheeled in. Someone led her by the arm over to the sofa. Suddenly the room was bathed in bright light. Rory squinted, shielding her eyes with the back of her hand. She looked down at the dark circular stain on the front of her sweatshirt. Max's blood or was it hers? A woman with short, curly hair pressed something against her neck. She winced, and then the room began to spin.

Distant voices. "Ma'am, ma'am."

Faces loomed above her. Was she lying down? Something cool touched her jaw. Warm hands pushed up her sleeve. She remembered Ethan in her cottage.

"Ethan."

People were talking to her, but she was having a hard time hearing them.

"Ethan."

Then she heard a voice say, "Who's Ethan? Ma'am, who's Ethan?"

She whispered, "Next door," before slipping into a swirling black tunnel.

Her mouth was dry with a salty, metallic taste. She went to open it, and there was a sharp pain on the left side of her face. Reaching her hand up, she felt a thick bandage along her jaw. She opened her eyes and scanned her surroundings—an enclosure of white curtains. Machines beeped and hummed beside the bed; they were connected to her. A cuff wrapped around her arm, a clamp on her finger. She heard muffled voices on the other side. Someone laughed. More talking. From the slit in the curtain, she caught a glimpse of a nurse walking by. She tried sitting up, but a woozy feeling forced her back down. She stared up at the acoustic-tiled ceiling. Then everything came tumbling back. Marlena. Tears filled her eyes.

The curtain pulled back, and a man dressed in a black T-shirt, tan corduroy jacket, and jeans stepped into the small cubicle. He had a clipboard in his hand, and a stethoscope stuck out of his jacket pocket. He smiled at Rory.

"You're awake. I'm Dr. Youngren." He stood beside her bed and placed his hand on her forehead. His hand felt warm and dry.

"Where am I?" Her voice sounded raspy, and it hurt to talk.

"Mad River Hospital in Arcata. Do you remember anything from last night?"

She nodded.

"I've got some paperwork I need you to sign. Are you allergic to any medications?"

Rory shook her head.

"I'm going to start an IV of antibiotics; you're running a fever."

"Marlena...the other woman...is she..." Rory couldn't finish the question.

"She's fine. She's been admitted for observation."

She felt a rush of relief as she closed her eyes and thanked God.

He stared down at her. "How are you feeling?"

"The man. The one I shot—"

"There's someone waiting outside to talk with you. Do you feel up to it?"

She nodded.

The doctor jotted something down on his clipboard. He stopped at the edge of the curtain. "Is there anyone we could contact for you?"

Her first thought was Derek, but something stopped her. She pondered the question. Will was in Utah until next Thursday. There was Jillian, but she didn't want to scare her; she wanted to call Jillian herself. Nick? Again, she didn't want to scare him; he had enough to deal with.

She shook her head.

Alone in the curtained cubicle, she stared at the blinking machines beside the bed. She felt the blood-pressure cuff tighten and was reminded of Max's firm grip on her arm, his face so close to hers, and she was surprised that instead of fear, she had only felt anger.

A few minutes later, the curtain parted, and a gray-haired man slipped through. He was dressed in dark-green uniform pants and a tan shirt. Rory gazed at the bear emblem on his shirt sleeve, and then her eyes fell to the shiny black holster that carried a gun and handcuffs. He introduced himself as Deputy Wallace of the Humboldt County Sheriff's Office. Her breath hitched as her heart rate increased. Now there was fear. Was he here to arrest her?

29

Rain sprinkled the windshield of the Humboldt County patrol car. Rory stared at the intermittent swipe of the rubber blades. The passenger-side blade left a wide smear of water across the glass, distorting her view of the road. Deputy Wallace slowed the car down as he turned onto the gravel lane, passing the weathered sign that read Willow Resort Cottages. It had been a forty-five-minute drive from Arcata, and Rory had spent the time reliving the nightmare over and over in her head.

She had killed someone.

Justifiable homicide. That's what Deputy Wallace had called it. He'd questioned her for over a half hour and then told her he'd be back after he'd talked with Marlena. He said they'd already questioned Ethan, who'd been taken to the Hoopa station. The deputy had left her when a nurse had come to start her IV. It had been eight more hours before they had released her. She had wanted to see Marlena before leaving the hospital, but the nurse had said Marlena was sleeping.

It was Saturday evening—5:38 p.m. according to the clock on the dash. The gray sky darkened in the gloomy dusk. She rubbed her hands down the goose bumps that had spread over her bare arms. They'd taken her sweatshirt and given her a hospital scrub tunic to wear home. Deputy Wallace had offered her his lined jacket right before the automatic glass doors of Mad River Hospital had swooshed open in front of her, but she'd told him she was fine.

Now, hugging her arms around her sides, she wished she hadn't declined.

The tires of the patrol car crunched on the gravel as it pulled up behind her Falcon. Deputy Wallace offered to walk her in, but she said she could manage on her own. He reminded her about Monday; she needed to fill out some paperwork at the station. She clutched the bottle of antibiotics along with the hospital release papers and stepped out of the car, wearing the blue paper booties the hospital had given her.

Her feet treaded timidly over the gravel that dug into her soles. As she crossed onto the wet grass, she glanced over at Marlena's cottage. Yellow crime tape formed an X pattern on the front door. A shiver coursed through her body. The booties soaked up the moisture and clung to the bottoms of her feet. Rory opened the front door and then turned and waved to Deputy Wallace, who nodded as he backed out of the driveway.

She slipped off the soggy paper shoes and flipped on the light switch. Everything appeared strangely normal, as if it had been happily awaiting her return: the pictures on the wall by her bed smiling at her, the colorful quilt over the couch, the grouping of plants clustered on the small table under the side window.

She stood in the center of the room, unsure of what to do. Shower. That was what she needed. Her emotions felt as if they were buried under layers of gauze with just traces seeping through. If someone were to ask her how she was feeling, she wasn't sure what her answer would be. Her fever was gone, and the ibuprofen had taken away the pain in her jaw. But waves of apprehension kept cresting and then subsiding like a gathering storm.

She had killed someone. The words kept repeating in her head.

She went to the kitchen drawers and pulled out plastic wrap and tape, and then she took them into the bathroom. Standing in front of the mirror, placing the makeshift waterproof cover over her bandaged jaw, her hands shook slightly. It wasn't her reflection.

Her eyes were puffy and red. The thick layer of gauze distorted her jawline. She gingerly patted the tape in place, trying to push away the thought that she'd almost died—just one swipe of the blade.

She pulled back the flowered shower curtain and almost cried. Mr. Danvers must have stopped by while she was at the hospital. A shiny new pulsating showerhead stood before her.

The hot water pelted her skin but was unable to reach the chill that ran deep. She kept her head tilted away from the water, letting the warm liquid run down her side. A vision of the knife painlessly slicing through her skin and the feel of warm blood running down her neck flashed through her mind. Her body felt numb, and so did her brain—muffled as if it was all too much to process.

———————

Curled up on the sofa under the down comforter she'd dragged from her bed, with her hair wrapped in a towel, she sipped herbal tea. Her skin felt clean. She started to read her book but eventually put it down because the words weren't connecting. She turned on the television and watched the old classic *Dark Victory*. Bette Davis's distinctive voice soothed her.

She jolted from the jarring ring of her phone and glanced out the darkened window, trying to orient herself; she must have fallen asleep watching the movie. Her hair was matted to one side of her head; the towel had fallen loose. She staggered over to the night-stand to her cell phone. The bedside clock read 8:22 p.m.

It was Marlena. She told Rory that she had a concussion, fif-teen stitches in her head, and two cracked ribs. Ethan was with her grandmother, and she said her parents were on their way up from San Diego. She asked Rory how she was. Rory told her she was fine, considering, and then there were a few seconds of silence.

"Marlena…" Rory wasn't sure what to say. She'd killed Ethan's father.

"You saved my life."

"I thought you were dead." Rory's voice cracked as Max's words echoed in her head.

"I can't remember much about last night," Marlena said softly.

"What about Ethan? Does he know?" Rory wondered if he would hate her for what she'd done.

"He knows Max is dead, but he doesn't know how it happened. I told him the police shot him. He never needs to know the truth."

"Max was going to kill me…I didn't have a choice."

"I wish I'd done it years ago. I just never had the guts."

Rory stared at the television screen. Bette Davis again. *Must be a Bette Davis marathon*, she thought. Marlena's words were bumping around in the outer region of her consciousness. She heard Marlena say that she should be released tomorrow but was probably going to stay at her grandmother's for a few days, and then she heard her say, "The police questioned me…they're not charging you with anything, are they?"

"No. Justifiable homicide." Two words she'd heard so many times before, never imagining they'd apply to her.

30

Sunday afternoon, 4:30 p.m. Ever since she'd awoken at Mad River Hospital, time seemed to have elapsed in slow motion. She had slept almost twelve hours, and the minutes since then had been moving as if she were in a time warp. Seconds ticked by at a slower pace; she was sure of it. She wanted to see Marlena, hoping it would erase the image of her lying on the floor in a pool of blood.

Earlier, Rory had gently removed the thick bandage on the side of her face. She needed to see the damage. An incision about five inches long ran along her jawline. It had been closed with twenty-six stitches that made her look "Frankensteinish." She re-taped some new gauze back over the wound.

Since then, she'd done the few dishes left over from the days before; vacuumed the cottage, which took all of fifteen minutes; watered her plants; and dusted every surface in the room. She'd watched two movies, both of which she'd seen before: *When Harry Met Sally* and a Nick and Nora Charles film.

Now she sat at the square kitchen table with a cup of tea, her cell phone in front of her. She wanted to call Will, just to talk, but she didn't want him to feel compelled to come back from Utah. Before leaving the hospital, she'd called Jillian. Lying in the hospital bed, she'd suddenly been overcome with a feeling of loneliness. She'd assured Jillian she was all right, but Jillian had wanted to fly out anyway. It had taken insistent pleading on Rory's part to convince Jillian not to come. Rory knew how busy Jillian was in school, and Rory really was OK.

From the window, she watched a flock of birds circle around the meadow, darting in unison in a sweeping arc before settling in the grass. It seemed like a hundred years ago that she had been in the luncheonette talking with Will at the counter, excited about starting classes. She felt as if she was hovering in limbo now. She turned her head at the sound of a car pulling into the driveway. Maybe it was Marlena.

She stood and glanced out the front window. A dark sedan was stopped behind her Falcon. More police? And then she saw his face.

Derek.

He got out of the car dressed in jeans and a windbreaker jacket, his head down as he walked across the lawn and up the steps to her porch. She was frozen, her mind racing with questions: What was he doing here? Did he know what had happened? Had Jillian called him? The loud rap on the wood made her jump.

Her pulse beat in her throat as she took the six steps to the door. She stood in the entrance, and her eyes scanned his face for some answer to his surprise visit. But his blue eyes gave nothing away.

"Derek. What are you doing here?"

"I talked to Jillian yesterday. I thought I should come up."

"Why?"

"Why?" He gave a short laugh. "Hell, Rory, you shot a man who was trying to kill you. Jillian's concerned, and so am I."

"I'm fine, really. I told Jillian that."

"You don't look fine." He pointed to her bandage.

Rory's hand went to her cheek. "Looks worse than it is." She tried to make light of it. Why, she didn't know.

"Are you going to let me in?"

"Sure." She stepped back from the doorstep. The scent of his Drakkar Noir drifted behind as he passed by. Rory reflexively scanned the room, making sure the place looked presentable.

Derek walked over toward her bed and studied the wall of pictures. She noticed his eyes lingering on the picture of Ben. She held her breath, waiting for some remark about the photo, but he didn't say anything. He glanced around the rest of the room before sitting on the sofa. "Nice place." He unzipped his jacket and crossed his foot over his knee as he leaned back with his arm stretched out along the top of the sofa.

It felt strange, seeing him on her sofa, looking at home. He didn't belong here.

She went over to the sink and filled the tea kettle, needing something to do. "You should've just called me. I really am fine," she said over her shoulder. "Would you like some tea or a beer? I think I have some." She went over to the refrigerator and searched for a beer.

Derek came up behind her, moved her hand off the fridge door, and shut it, and then he turned her by the shoulders to face him. "Hey, you're not fine."

She saw the concerned look in his eyes. "I *am*." She smiled and then looked away.

"Rory, Jillian told me everything that happened. It's not easy to get it out of your head. I've known guys on the force who've had to kill or be killed. It sticks with them."

Rory backed away from his arms and shrugged. "I guess I'm different." She spun around to get two mugs out of the cupboard and then remembered that she already had a mug of tea on the kitchen table. She turned and brushed past Derek.

"Rory." He lightly touched her arm. "You're not different. You've gotta face what happened; that's the only way you're going to get past it."

Visions of the attack flashed in her head—the knife blade waving back and forth—his breath in her face.

She shuddered.

Derek's arms were around her. She felt her body give way. Tears blurred her vision. His familiar arms felt comforting, but at the same time, the embrace unsettled her.

The tea kettle whistled, the shrill pitch rising in intensity. Derek released his hold, and Rory hurried over to the stove, wiping away the tears with her fingers.

"I'll take that beer if you've got it."

"Sure, help yourself."

They sat at the kitchen table.

"Look, Rory, I know this isn't going to be easy on you. Killing someone can haunt you. And I know the way you are. Hell, you cried for days when you ran over the neighbor's cat." Derek took a sip of his beer.

Rory stared at the steam, rising from her mug. "I don't feel like I have the right to decide when someone dies."

"Well, in this case, you didn't make the decision—he did. He made it when he held that knife to your throat."

"Justifiable homicide." Rory looked up from her mug. "That's what they called it."

"Because that's what it was. Look, in this world you can either be the victim or the victor. You had no choice; it was his life or yours." Derek rolled the green bottle in his hands. "So they've already decided not to charge you?"

Rory nodded. "I'm supposed to go to the sheriff's office tomorrow."

"I'll go with you," Derek said matter-of-factly.

"You don't have to. I can handle it."

"I know you can handle it, but it wouldn't hurt to have someone in law enforcement on your side. And you never know what the wife is going to do. I've seen so many cases of women with busted faces, broken bones, battered by their husbands…and then they show up in court looking like the creep is the love of their life. She could change her story about what happened."

"Not Marlena. I know her." Rory shook her head. But did she? Max's words echoed in her head again. Was Marlena gay? She looked at Derek. "She won't change her story."

Derek nodded. "Still, I think I should go with you."

"Fine." She stared back at her mug but felt Derek's eyes on her.

"You wanna get some food? They don't feed you on the plane anymore," Derek said.

"I don't really feel like going out."

"You got anything we could fix here?" He glanced over toward the cupboards.

She shook her head. "I usually go to the grocery store on Saturday…"

"I guess they don't have Chinese in this town."

"Actually, they do, and it's pretty good. They even deliver."

They ordered moo shu pork, beef lo mein, and egg rolls, their usual order. Derek told her he had booked a room at the Bigfoot Inn, joking about the crazy town that she'd moved to where they worshiped an imaginary monster. Rory defended Willow Bend, saying how nice everyone was, even though some were unique and a bit eccentric. She told him she liked the fact that it had originally been a gold rush town and that it still had that adventurous spirit.

By the time the food arrived, they'd covered topics from who was going to win the Super Bowl to Jillian moving to London. Derek dished out the food onto paper plates, and Rory took small bites because it hurt to chew.

Derek laughed, his chopsticks poised in his hand, recalling the first time Jillian had seen chopsticks—she'd stuck them in her nose at the restaurant.

Rory chimed in. "And remember the look on the woman's face

next to us? She thought we were the worst parents. And you encouraged her. Didn't you stick them in your ears?"

"It made Jillian laugh."

She shook her head. "You'd have done anything for her."

The laughing subsided, and Rory stirred her chopsticks around the noodles. "I hear you went to Hawaii for Christmas. Was it nice?"

Derek nodded. "Yeah, it was beautiful."

"So are you serious about her?"

He raised his brows.

"Jillian told me. I mean, Hawaii—it sounds serious."

"I don't know. I guess it is."

Rory knew she shouldn't ask the next question, but she couldn't stop herself. "Were you seeing her before I left?"

He glanced up from his plate. "Look, Rory—"

"Forget it. You don't have to answer." She knew from Derek's hesitation that the answer was yes, but did it matter? She'd had an affair. But would she have broken it off with Ben if she'd known? A strange feeling roiled inside. She told herself it made no difference. But then a green trickle of envy pushed its way in. "I'm glad you're happy," she added.

"What about you? Are you seeing anyone?"

"I'm just curious about one thing." Rory pointed her chopstick toward him. "Why did you come up in October and want me to come back?"

Derek leaned back in his chair and ran his hand through his closely cropped hair. He looked across the room, his eyes focused on some distant object. "I didn't want our marriage to end. I knew things weren't right between us, but I guess I don't like change." His gaze moved to the darkened window. The lamplight shone on his face, spotlighting the rugged lines that were etched on his forehead and around his eyes.

He hadn't said he'd wanted her back because he loved her. Had she expected him to say that? She'd left him—she'd told herself she didn't love him anymore. Why would she think he would still love her? "It sounds like you two have a lot in common…the bike thing," she said as she stared down at her food, poking at it with the wooden stick, thinking about the times Derek had wanted her to ride with him. She'd gone once, but she'd hated it; the torturously tiny bike seat was uncomfortable, and the cars on the road had made her nervous. "We were just too different, I think."

"We're opposite ends of one long spectrum of differences," Derek added with a chuckle.

Rory pushed the plate of food away from her. "We need to decide what we're going to do with the house. Do you think you'll want to sell?"

"Donna and I talked about that. She wants something smaller, I think."

Hearing him coupled with someone else sounded odd. "I'd say things are serious." Rory was surprised at how quickly Derek had moved on. Maybe he needed to be with someone more than she did. "So you want to move?"

"We're never home. Donna signed us up for this bike tournament that takes place every other weekend, and you race at different locations. She wants to do one next year that goes cross-country. She likes traveling."

"I've been thinking about moving…maybe back to the East Coast…" Her words drifted off. Derek's voice echoed in her head—Donna liked to travel. Why hadn't he cared what *she* liked? She started to tell him about Jennifer's school and her interview, but she was afraid he'd say something to reinforce the fact that it had been a silly fantasy. She didn't tell him about the classes she was taking either, feeling protective of the whole thing. "I'd like to split up our things.

And maybe we could talk to an agent. Get the house listed."

"Sure. I can make some phone calls." He poured more wine in both of their glasses and then tilted his head and said, "The East Coast?"

Derek's jaw twitched as he sat next to Rory on the wooden bench. She knew he was agitated. They'd been waiting for Deputy Wallace almost a half hour at the Humboldt County station, a small stucco building located on the Hoopa reservation. She wanted to tell Derek to just leave, that she didn't need him, but she knew that wasn't true. Having him beside her eased her anxiety. They weren't going to arrest her; she was only here to fill out paperwork. So why was she so nervous?

The fluorescent lighting glared onto the scuffed linoleum. It needed to be cleaned. She wound her finger around her hair as her foot nervously tapped the floor. Her gaze followed the hum of the busy office: a woman on the phone, another typing, and two men in uniform huddled in a conversation toward the back of the room. Had they forgotten about Derek and her? And then Deputy Wallace finally came through the front door with his holstered gun strapped to his side.

Rory watched him brush his hand over his thinning gray hair. She nudged Derek and nodded in Wallace's direction. Derek jumped off the bench and cut the deputy off on his path, introducing himself with a handshake.

Rory listened to Derek explain his reason for being there, cluing the deputy in on his position with the Phoenix police force. Deputy Wallace nodded and then glanced over at Rory. She smiled, feeling a lump in her throat as her fingernails dug into her palms. She needed to calm down, but she was shaking inside. What if something had changed? What if they wanted to charge her with murder?

Deputy Wallace motioned for them to follow. She slowly stood up and walked behind Derek, staring at his leather jacket that was stretched taut against his back muscles. She liked the buffer he created between her and Wallace.

Derek pulled a chair out for her beside the deputy's desk and then grabbed another one and sat next to her. She felt as if she was hyperventilating, unable to catch her breath. Forcing the air slowly in and out, she chanted in her head to relax, but the reality of the whole nightmare was crashing in on her. She'd killed someone. Had her father purposely crashed his motorcycle, unable to deal with what he'd done?

Justifiable homicide. She heard the words again, and her focus returned to the deputy. He laid some paperwork in front of her, telling her to read it and make sure everything appeared accurate, and if so, she needed to sign at the bottom.

The words stared back at her, the events spelled out exactly as they'd happened. Why had she gone to Marlena's cottage and not just waited for the police? She'd put her own life in danger to save Marlena. Maybe she was stronger than she thought.

She signed the papers.

While the deputy and Derek talked shop for a few minutes, Rory stared at Derek's profile, and her mind drifted to the night before. They'd talked about the past and about Jillian. He'd helped her forget the nightmare. She'd asked him to stay and watch a movie. She hadn't wanted to be alone. But not long into the movie, she'd fallen asleep, and she remembered he'd helped her into bed. Then she'd watched him turn out the lights, lock the door, and leave.

They walked out of the station; it had been over in less than twenty minutes. She was free; not that she had ever *not* been free, but she felt lighter. They drove away with the gun wrapped in a plastic bag between them on the seat.

Derek's cell rang. She glanced over and saw the lines around his eyes deepen with his smile. She listened to him say that his flight was booked for this evening. He was talking to Donna. He looked happy. She wondered if he used to smile like that when she would call him. He laughed. She couldn't remember him laughing on the phone with her. Then she heard him repeat his flight information and what time he would be back in Phoenix.

Was Donna upset that he was here with her? A thought struck her: she was the other woman now. It felt weird. And then she realized that this was the first time in years Derek and she had been together for this length of time and not argued.

31

Wednesday. Less than a week since her life had been altered. She'd been surprised when Casey had called Monday morning, before she left for the sheriff's office, and given her the week off. He'd heard the news; everyone had heard the news, which had spread like dust in a desert wind.

Derek was back in Phoenix. He'd called yesterday to see how she was doing. If people had been listening in on their conversation, they would've described her tone as cheerful. She'd told him she was doing great and had a million things she needed to catch up on.

But after hanging up, she felt deflated, like it had taken all the air she had in her to keep up the sunny demeanor. She'd repeated the process with Jillian and Nick each time they called. Jillian had called her at least five times since Derek had left. Rory wondered if Derek had told Jillian something that made her think her mother wasn't OK. Maybe she was fooling everyone, including herself, into thinking she was fine.

She'd kept busy—paying bills, grocery shopping, working on an assignment for her psychology class, reading from her autism textbook—and she'd almost convinced herself she was all right. But now she felt like there was a gaping hole in her chest, filled with emptiness. Derek's words echoed in her head—*this will haunt you.* Each morning in that semiconscious state between sleep and waking, she'd think the whole thing had been a dream. But then as the sleep slipped away and reality slithered in, the dreaded feeling would return.

She sat in the wooden rocker on her front porch, staring at Marlena's cottage. One strand of the yellow tape had broken loose from the front door and was rippling up and down in the breeze, like a May Day ribbon. Field day at school when Jillian was eight—Rory had made May Day ribbons. She pictured Jillian running through the playground with the ribbons sailing behind her.

The distinctive broken-muffler sound of Mr. Danvers's faded black pickup rumbled down the lane. She watched him pull into her driveway. He killed the engine, and it let out a loud bang in protest. Rory jerked; at the same time, a flock of birds shot out of the pines with a rustling sound that echoed through the meadow. The truck door creaked open.

Mr. Danvers had called her earlier to see how she was doing and told her that Marlena, who was now staying at her grandmother's, was coming by later to get some of her stuff. He said he wanted to clean the place before she got there. Rory had offered to help.

Mr. Danvers pulled a bucket and mop out of the back of his truck. "You sure you want to do this?" he called over to Rory.

She nodded, feeling compelled to go. Every time she looked in that direction, a swell of anxiety rose inside. She thought maybe if she went over there, she'd get some kind of closure. She followed him across the yard.

"I had a bad feeling the minute I laid eyes on that man. He looked like nothing but trouble." Mr. Danvers walked slowly with an arthritic gait. "Some people are just no good. The world's a better place without that kind, if you ask me." He climbed the steps to the porch and set down the bucket; then he turned to Rory, stroking his long gray beard.

An eerie wave washed over her. She shuddered and then rubbed her hand along her arm.

"You don't have to do this, you know."

"No, I'm fine. I need to see it."

"Suit yourself." He picked up the bucket, pulled the rest of the tape off the door, and wrapped it into a ball. "I never would've taken you for a gun person," he said as he opened the front door and flipped on the light switch.

"My husband gave it to me years ago for protection. He's a cop. There had been some break-ins…" She hesitated on the porch as her voice trailed off.

Mr. Danvers turned around, holding the door open. "You comin'?"

"Yeah." She inhaled deeply and went inside. Her heart rate increased. She felt the adrenaline pumping through her veins like it had that night. Her eyes went to the dried pool of blood on the wood floor by the table. She pictured the bottoms of Marlena's bare feet. Then her gaze dropped down in front of her to the dark stain on the worn, multicolored rug. Her hand covered her mouth, and she swallowed hard, trying to force back the bilious feeling in her belly.

"I guess this might as well be thrown out. That stain'll never come clean. Place could use a new rug anyway." Mr. Danvers dragged the coffee table off the braided rug and then knelt down, rolling it up.

Rory stood frozen, watching him. She noticed the wood underneath the rug was several shades lighter than the rest of the floor, except for one spot where the blood had seeped through in a criss-crossed pattern.

Mr. Danvers lifted one end of the cumbersome rug and began to drag it toward the front door. Rory snapped out of her stationary spot and grabbed the other end.

"You don't need to do that. I've got it."

"I want to help." She picked up her end, and the two carried it across the street to the dumpster, heaving it over the side. Rory brushed her hands against her jeans as the rug fell in with a resounding thump. Her breath was heavy from the exertion, but it felt good. Liberating.

She followed Mr. Danvers back into the house. While Mr. Danvers set about scrubbing the wood floor with hot soapy water, Rory went around the room straightening things that looked out of place: an overturned plant, some books scattered on the floor. She rooted under the kitchen sink, found some floor polish, and then grabbed a mop from the broom closet. She sat on the couch waiting for the now-clean floor to dry and looked around the cottage.

Ethan's backpack hung on the back of a chair. Marlena's jewelry case was opened on the dining table, with a partially made necklace laid out in front of it. A normal night had gone so awry. Would she see that vision of the blade hovering over her face every night before she fell asleep?

Once the floor had dried, she poured the polish over the wood and then made careful sweeps along the grain, buffing it to a glistening shine. The variation of color from where the rug had been was less visible. She moved the coffee table back in its spot in front of the couch and then glanced over at Mr. Danvers, wanting approval that everything looked all right for Marlena.

"Washing the floor is not going to erase it from your head, you know." He came over and took the mop from her, went over to the sink, rinsed it out, and put it back in the broom closet.

Rory stood by the sofa watching the polish fade into the wood. Was that what she'd been trying to do?

"I killed a man once." Mr. Danvers said matter-of-factly, as he stepped out onto the porch.

Rory stopped in the doorway, surprised at how nonchalantly he'd spoken the words.

"Back in seventy-two." He sat down in one of the rockers on the porch and looked out across the meadow, chuckling in his gravelly voice, and pulled at his beard. "They thought they were badasses."

Rory sat down in the rocker next to him. "What happened?"

"Some bikers passing through town tried to rob Crawley's bar while I was there one night. I slipped out to my truck and come back in with my old Browning. One of the guys had a gun aimed at Crawley, so I set my sight on the guy"—Mr. Danvers held his arms up holding an imaginary gun, re-enacting the scene—"and I yelled to him to drop it, but did he listen? No, he's gotta be a badass, so I shot him." He stroked his beard as he rocked. "It was over in a second. But I relived that night over and over in my head for years."

"Were you charged with anything?"

Mr. Danvers chuckled again. "Hell, no. The sheriff at the time was my cousin, and he knew those boys were no good. In fact, we never had any trouble at the bar after that."

"Did it ever stop haunting you?"

He nodded. "Give it time. You'll get over it." He stood and picked up the bucket. "Well, I better head out. If you need anything, let me know."

Rory watched him walk across the grass to his truck. She rocked back and forth, the rungs creaking on the wood slats of the porch. The afternoon sun cut a shaft of light across the meadow, spotlighting a Canada goose silently landing on the surface of the pond. The black pickup rumbled its way back down the lane. She continued to rock until the muffler sound was gone. Her gaze drifted back to the meadow. She remembered when she'd first arrived here, how breathtakingly beautiful she'd thought the scenery was—lush green foliage, so different from the desert terrain. She closed her eyes and breathed in the rich pine smell that she'd gotten so used to she didn't even notice it anymore.

32

After leaving Marlena's cottage, she'd taken a long shower, but Mr. Danvers was right: she couldn't wash away what had happened. She then called Casey and told him she wanted to come back to work tomorrow, needing something to keep her mind occupied. She slipped on a clean pair of jeans and a sweatshirt and then headed into the kitchen to make a pot of tortilla soup. Chopping the celery felt therapeutic; she liked the crunching sound of the vegetables as they fell onto the cutting board in tiny uniform pieces.

The aroma of chicken stock mixed with cilantro and onions filled the air, and for the first time since the attack, her stomach actually felt hungry. She sat at the kitchen table, yellow highlighter in hand, and studied a chapter entitled "Chemistry of the Brain." It talked about the wiring of the brain and how through therapy a subject could learn to reroute the circuitry, allowing them to accomplish new things. They used an analogy of athletes in the Tour de France who were able to block out pain and overcome horrendous obstacles.

She looked up from the book and stared across the room, wondering if you could block out mental pain as well as physical. The sound of a car driving down the lane made her glance out the window. The sun had already slipped behind the hills, leaving only a dusky orange sky as a white SUV drove by. She went over to the side window and saw Marlena and a dark-haired man get out of the car. Rory slipped on her UGG boots, turned off the gas burner, and headed out the door.

Marlena was at the bottom of her steps as Rory approached. Her usual ruddy complexion seemed paler. Her eyes looked tired.

Rory smiled and felt tears sting her eyes. She walked over to Marlena and gently put her arms around her. She felt Marlena's strong hands press into her back with a little extra squeeze. "Rory, this is my father, Joseph."

Joseph smiled at Rory. He was a small man, a few inches shorter than Marlena, with a slight build and kind eyes. "We are indebted to you. Your act of courage will never be forgotten," he said softly.

His words surprised her. She looked down at the ground, feeling her cheeks warm. "How's Ethan?"

"He's doing better than I'd expected." Marlena smiled and then frowned. "Your face." She reached out and gently touched the bandage. "I'm so sorry. How bad is it?"

Rory shrugged. "I'm hoping it looks better once the stitches are out." She paused. "Mr. Danvers was here earlier…" Her eyes went to the front door of the cottage. "It's clean."

Marlena nodded.

The three went inside. Marlena stood in the center of the room, as frozen as Rory had been earlier. Rory knew she was reliving the scene. Marlena then turned and smiled at her. "It's over." She looked at her dad. "I'll be all right, if you want to go to the winery."

He nodded and then left the cottage.

"He's going to go pick up my things that I left at work."

Rory frowned. "You're not going back to work?"

Marlena shook her head. "I'm moving to San Diego."

"When?"

"Next week. I just decided last night. My grandmother's moving with me, and she'll take care of Ethan while I'm working."

Rory felt a swirling eddy of emotions course through her. "It's so sudden." She dropped down on the sofa and wrapped her arms around her waist. "Will I get to see Ethan before you leave?"

"I was hoping you could come to my grandmother's for dinner on Sunday. She wants to meet you, and so does my mother."

"Sure." She wanted to say, *But Max is dead now, so why do you have to leave?* But rationally, she understood Marlena not wanting to return to the cottage.

Marlena sighed. "I wish things could've been different. We'll miss you."

"I'll miss you guys too." This was happening so fast. She felt as if the world had tilted, and everything was off kilter.

"I'm just taking a few things right now to get us through the week. My dad and I are coming back next week for the rest. It's not much." Marlena gave a weak smile. "We've moved so many times—I've learned not to hang on to too many things. Hopefully, we can finally settle down, and I can give Ethan a real home."

Rory nodded, watching Marlena gather the loose stones off the table and put them back in the tackle box case.

Marlena went into her bedroom, and Rory glanced around the small cottage, realizing how much she was going to miss them.

Driving through town, she thought about the somewhat celebrity status she'd achieved over the past month. People were coming into the luncheonette wanting to see the woman who had killed a man. With each week since the incident, the stories had grown. Pops had come in one day and told her a guy getting his tires rotated at his shop had asked him if he'd heard about the Annie Oakley woman in town who'd shot a guy right between the eyes from twenty yards away.

She'd tried to dispel the myths when customers asked her about that night, but she realized they weren't really interested in the truth;

they liked the makings of a good legend. As she passed by the Bigfoot Inn, she thought, of course they did—the town boasted a whole museum dedicated to the mythical beast.

Turning at the flashing yellow light, she caught a glimpse of her face in the rearview mirror. A nasty red scar ran down the side of her face. The doctor had told her it would lessen with time, but plastic surgery was also an option. It didn't bother her, though. It was her battle scar, and it reminded her to stay strong. The curving road out of town bordered by tall pines looked the same as it always had, but she felt like she was seeing it through different eyes. Was it that she'd faced death and beaten it?

Life had taken on a whole new meaning. She felt empowered, but there were still residual effects: she woke several times throughout the night, and her lamp stayed lit beside her bed; she kept the television on when she was home alone; and she was seeing a psychiatrist. She'd been five times, and it was helping, not only with the shooting but also with her past traumas.

As she pulled into her driveway, she glanced over at the now-empty cottage next door. Marlena had called a few days ago and told her about her new job at a winery in San Diego and that she and Ethan were settling into their new lives. Rory thought about the morning Marlena had left. As Marlena had pulled away with Ethan, Rory had watched the red taillights round the lane out of sight, and something had ignited inside her, like a wind that fueled a fire; energy swept through her, prodding her to move on as well.

She picked up the mail on the passenger seat and noticed the edge of a postcard peeking from the stack. She pulled it out and saw a picture of Charlie with her fiancé, the two arm in arm and leaning against a large oak tree, with a caption that read, "Save the Date." Charlie looked happy. But Charlie always looked happy, she thought. She flipped it over and read the information about Charlie's wedding. July 26. Almost six months away. Where would she be by then?

Caroline had told her about several schools that specialized in dance-therapy training, and she'd made some inquiries. She had made up her mind to leave Willow Bend, and now she was trying to decide where to go to school in the fall. She had picked out several schools with good psychology programs, but she hadn't made a final decision yet on which one. Two were on the East Coast.

She glanced at the red hands of the clock on the dash—4:45 p.m. Two hours before she had to leave for her farewell dinner with Will. He had taken the job in Utah.

They met at the Italian restaurant on the outskirts of town, the one where they'd kissed in the parking lot, a night that seemed an eternity ago. Tony Bennett crooned from the speakers in the corner of the room. A candle stuck in an empty bottle of Chianti served as the centerpiece atop the red-and-white-checkered tablecloth. She chuckled and then said to Will how the numerous deer heads hanging on the wall gave the room the Willow Bend version of a romantic Italian atmosphere.

Will poured more wine in her glass.

She looked up from the dessert menu and caught Will staring at her. She knew he was looking at her scar. He shook his head. "Every time I see that, I can't imagine what you went through, and I still can't believe you didn't call me right away."

"I didn't want you worrying about me and maybe have it influence your decision about taking the job."

"So you really do want to get rid of me?" Will teased.

"It's not that." Rory laughed. "I just didn't want you staying *because* of me."

"I've yet to figure you out."

"Why do you say that? I'm not that complicated."

Will nodded and sipped his wine. The server came to take their dessert order. Rory ordered the tiramisu for both of them.

Will changed the subject, talking about the work that was going on at the forest in Utah. She heard the excitement in his voice and saw the spark in his green eyes. Her gaze drifted toward the door as a young woman with long dark hair walked into the restaurant and then stopped beside the door, looking as if she was waiting for someone. Rory recognized her from her photography class. She tried to remember her name…Brittany, B-something…Belinda, that was it. Rory started to signal her with a wave, but then she saw Carter come through the door and place his hand on Belinda's back, and the two of them walked toward the hostess stand.

Rory's gaze went back to Will, who sat with his back to them, still talking about Utah. She nodded at something Will said, but her thoughts were focused on the couple across the room. She hoped they would be seated on the other side of the restaurant, but the hostess grabbed two menus and led them down the aisle by Rory's table. They were fifteen feet away…ten…five. Carter spotted her.

"Rory, Will." He patted Will on the back and then leaned down and gave Rory a hug and a kiss on the cheek. "Wow, that's some scar. I heard about what happened," he said. "I've been thinking of you." He stepped back and placed his hand on Belinda's arm. "Rory, you know Belinda?"

"Yes, hi," Rory said.

Belinda smiled and nodded and then said hi to Will.

Rory felt uncomfortable and wondered if her whole face was as red as her scar. Visions flashed through her head of scrambling for her clothes off the floor of Carter's room and sneaking out of his house while he was still asleep. She was at a loss for words.

"We missed you at the show." Carter's gaze was locked on her.

She averted her eyes. "Things got busy. I never got around to signing up for it."

"A shame. I think you would've done well."

"Another time, maybe." Rory fidgeted with her fork.

Carter and Belinda said their good-byes and then moved on to their table. The red-and-white checks of the tablecloth blurred before her. She felt Will's eyes on her.

"You OK?" he asked.

She nodded and glanced up at him, smiling, trying to mask the awkward feeling inside.

"That night at the inn…" Will didn't finish the sentence.

"That was a bad night." She focused on the tines of her fork as she flipped it over on the table.

"You know, when I saw you with Carter, I…it surprised me. I didn't know what to think."

"Neither did I. I'd really like to forget that night."

Will nodded and, after a few seconds of silence, asked, "How are your classes going?"

"Good." She wanted to hug him for not pushing her about the night at the inn. "I've gotten all As so far," she said proudly. "I've decided to go full time next semester; I just don't know where I want to live."

"Utah's nice," Will said with a gleam in his eye.

She laughed. "I'm sure it is, but I think I want to go back east. There are a couple of schools that the American Dance Therapy Association recommends for undergraduate work." The server brought the tiramisu, and Rory stabbed her fork into the dessert. "They say you need a master's to become a certified dance therapist, but I can't think about that now." She glanced up at Will, her fork held midair. "You know, for years I felt my life had been decided. I had made my choices: getting married, raising a child. I'd sometimes look at other women around my age with college degrees and careers, and I'd be envious, never thinking I could do that as well."

"My grandfather used to tell me that people should never stop learning, because once you do, you'll die." He popped a bite of tiramisu into his mouth and then said, "It actually freaked me out when I was a kid—I used to think if I skipped school, I might drop dead."

She laughed, studying his face. "Was that supposed to make me feel better?"

"No, I'm just saying—it's never too late."

She smiled. "It's going to be different here without you."

———

She entered the cottage feeling sated, tired, and slightly melancholy. As she kicked off her boots, she thought about after dinner, leaning against her car in the parking lot. She'd vowed to write to Will every week and made him promise to do the same—she didn't want to lose him as a friend, feeling as if everything she got close to slipped away. She'd hugged him, and he'd kissed her, a lingering kiss that made her not want to let go.

She threw her purse on the couch as she wrestled with an ache that seeped all the way to her bones. She'd miss Will.

Her cell rang; it was Nick. She glanced at the time on her phone—the middle of the night in Maryland. Her stomach did a little flip. Good news never arrived late at night.

33

Nick's voice came over the line in a hushed tone.

"Is everything OK?" Rory asked.

"Just wanted to know how you're doing. Are you still seeing the shrink?"

"Nick, it's one o'clock in the morning there; you didn't call to see how I'm doing. What's wrong?"

"I needed to talk with someone."

She dropped onto the couch. "Is Cass all right?"

"She's having a bad reaction to the treatments. Her hands..." Rory heard the crack in his voice before he continued. "The drugs are causing her skin to burn. Her hands look like they're on fire. The pain is excruciating."

"Oh, Nick, that's horrible. What are the doctors saying?"

"They need to stop the treatments and try another drug. She's been holding on so well, but when this happened, I think it really set her back. She hasn't been able to teach, and with her hands as they are, she can't do much of anything. She can't even dress herself. Chelsea said she was going to leave school and come take care of Cass, but we...she'd miss...we don't want her to drop out of school. I've been staying home for the past week, but the medical bills are multiplying—I just want this all to be over for her. We thought she only had four more weeks of treatments, but now the doctors don't know."

"I can come."

"That's not why I called, I just—"

"I know, but I want to be there." Rory's mind flashed with things she would need to do. Tell Casey, Mr. Danvers. She could fly…or maybe she should drive.

"Rory, you don't have to. We'll work something out."

She heard the pain in Nick's voice, and it brought tears to her eyes. "I'll call you in the morning and let you know my arrangements. I'm coming, Nick."

It was after midnight. Her flight had been delayed in Chicago due to the weather, so she'd told Nick to just leave the door unlocked. Sitting in the back of the cab, she thought of the phone call she'd made to Charlie while she was stuck at the airport. Ironically, Charlie had been at the airport in San Francisco, whizzing past security lines on her way to the private terminal. Rory chuckled, recalling their conversation.

"I'm meeting Cruella DeVil and then flying to Paris for my dress fitting," Charlie had said in her throaty voice.

"You better be careful; one of these days you may accidentally call her that to her face." Rory knew Charlie was referring to her mother-in-law to be, having heard her say it before.

"She knows how I feel. I swear, I think she'd wear her sable on the beach."

They talked about the wedding, and Charlie insisted Rory had to be there, adding that there would be tons of rich bachelors, and with Rory's looks she could have the pick of any one of them.

"Wait till you see the five-inch scar on my face. I'll probably scare most of them away."

Charlie had been amazed at Rory's tale of the shooting and added that Rory was now at the top of her list of people who were cool.

She was like the avenger, Charlie had joked. Rory had laughed, but on the inside she felt there had been nothing cool about it.

Now the cab turned onto Sligo Creek Parkway on the way to Cass and Nick's. Staring out the car window, she thought about her last day of work in Willow Bend—driving through the sleepy town just before sunup; past the market, Caroline's, and Tanoak Books; taking mental snapshots of them, wanting to capture the memories. Willow Bend would always be special. She almost felt like she'd grown up there. Of course it wasn't like Takoma Park, with all her childhood memories, but in Willow Bend it was like she'd had a crash course in independence.

Stepping-stone. She smiled as she thought of Will's words. He was right. Willow Bend had been a stepping-stone toward her future. It made her feel like she was moving forward.

Through the darkness outside the cab, she could see the rippling current of the black creek as they drove along the winding road. She was reminded of the time when she was about eight, standing on a rock in the middle of Sligo Creek. Nick had already crossed the eight-foot span of water, and she had been following him. She'd stopped, unable to move as she stared at the swirling eddy of dark water rush around her feet, afraid to take the next step. Nick had stood on the bank, urging her to continue. "You can do it. Don't stop now." And then, sucking in air, she'd leaped to the slippery bank, grasping with all her might to stay on dry land. She'd made it, her shoes never getting wet.

Minutes later, the taxi pulled up to Cass and Nick's two-story brick home. The house was dark except for the porch light. She paid the driver, got her bags, and headed up the walk. She was glad they hadn't waited up, but as she put her hand on the knob, the door swung open, and Rory stifled a gasp.

34

Cass stood in the doorway, and the change in her appearance was shocking. She'd lost most of her hair, along with about ten pounds. Her hands looked raw, and her eyes were sunken, stripped of their usual zest, reminding Rory of photos she had seen of Holocaust victims' hollow gaze.

Cass's hand went to the tufts of hair that sprang from patches on her head. "Sorry, I forgot my scarf."

"No." Rory knew Cass had seen the stricken look on her face. "You just surprised me; I hadn't expected anyone to be awake." She gave Cass a hug, and her fingers felt the bones in Cass's back through her thin nightgown. Rory breathed in the same smell she remembered from her mom, a strange, almost chemical smell.

"What a pretty scarf. I love the color," Rory said as she squeezed past Cass, whose patchy clumps of hair were now covered. Cass sat in a rocker in the middle of the small kitchen. Rory had changed into flannel pajamas and thick wool socks.

"Chelsea got me this and a few others before she went back to school after Christmas break." The long coral-and-blue-flowered scarf wrapped around her head hung down by her side. She chuckled, patting the arm of the rocker. "Nick brought this into the kitchen for me so I could watch him cook. He's like a lost lamb. I kind of guide him around. This is where I sit most nights when I can't sleep. For some reason, the kitchen calms me."

Rory put the tea kettle on the stove. She wasn't tired. Her eyes drifted to the counter by the sink that was now filled with medicine bottles.

Cass caught her eye and said, "I know—it looks like a pharmacy."

"Do you take all of this?"

"Not all at once. The doctors have prescribed so many different things I can't keep track. Pills for sleeping, another for anxiety, nausea, diarrhea. Then there's all the herbal stuff that Chelsea got me."

"Does any of it help?"

"Some of it. But I prefer this." Cass held up a small plastic bag. Rory's eyebrows rose.

"Michael brought it over the other day. You want some?"

"What? Now?"

"I usually smoke a little at night. It helps me sleep, and it helps with the nausea too." Cass pulled a pipe out of the pocket of her robe. She chuckled. "I feel like I'm a teenager again, except instead of hiding it from my parents, I have to hide it from my husband."

"Nick?" Rory said with surprise.

"I think Nick would give me cocaine if he thought it would make me feel better, but Nick's never liked any drugs, even when we were in school. It probably has something to do with your dad." She filled the small bowl of the pipe. "I wanted him to join me the first night Michael brought it over, but he wouldn't. I think it bothers him to think Michael smokes pot." Cass lit up the pipe and then closed her eyes while she held the smoke in her lungs for several seconds before exhaling. "You know—your dad—all his issues— Nick worries Michael will go down the same path." She passed the pipe to Rory.

Rory hesitated. She hadn't smoked pot since before Derek, but she didn't want Cass to think it bothered her. The smell sent her back to her senior year, Jimmy Waters's basement, sitting on the couch listening to Metallica. She grabbed the pipe and thought, *Why not?* She brought the pipe to her lips and inhaled and immediately began coughing. With watery eyes, she handed the pipe back to Cass and got up, barking several times as she poured a glass of water.

"Whoa. I forgot what that was like," Rory croaked.

Cass laughed. "Yeah, it takes some getting used to. And the stuff they have nowadays..." She rolled her eyes. "No comparison."

The tea kettle whistled. "I think I'll stick with the Sleepytime tea." Rory brought her mug to the kitchen table. She looked over at Cass. "What did you mean about my dad?"

"What?"

"His *issues?*"

Cass held up her hand. "That's coming from Nick—you know I never met your dad."

"What did he say?" A slight numbing wave washed over her as the marijuana snaked its way through her bloodstream.

"I don't know—just stuff like how your dad never really had a job, that your mom was the one who supported the family and had to be the responsible one."

"My dad was a woodworker—he made beautiful things."

"I know; I've seen some of them. But Nick said he only worked when he felt like it. He said he could remember your mother and father arguing because your dad wouldn't give up smoking pot. I guess with her political career, she felt it put her in jeopardy."

Rory started to interject, to tell Cass she was wrong, but then she realized that what she'd said wasn't a lie. Rory could remember those same arguments, but for some reason she'd blocked them out. She had practically canonized him, made him into some idyllic father figure.

She thought about all the times she'd made decisions based

on what she thought her father would've thought—staying in her marriage longer than she should have because her father would've thought she was giving up; breaking it off with Ben, on the anniversary of her father's death no less—her father's disappointed face looming in her mind.

But her father hadn't been the saint she'd made him out to be; he'd just been human, with faults like everyone else, maybe more than most.

She noticed Cass's gaze go to her cheek. The scar. Rory ran her finger over the welted line on her jaw.

"What a nightmare you must've gone through."

"A nightmare is putting it mildly."

"I can't imagine how you get over something like that."

Rory looked at Cass's cracked and reddened hands and wanted to say, "It was nothing compared to what you're going through," but instead she said, "The shrink has helped."

Cass nodded.

She wanted to confess something to Cass, something she'd only discussed with her psychiatrist. She hesitated, feeling awkward admitting it, but at the same time, she wanted someone to reassure her it was all right to feel the way she did. Cass was a professor of sociology. Maybe she could help her figure it out. "This may sound strange, but in a weird way, I've never felt as good as I do now. It's like I have my confidence back. Some kind of inner strength has taken over. Like it awakened something in me that I hadn't even known existed."

Cass nodded. "It's not strange at all. You've gotten back something that was stolen from you years ago."

"That's what the shrink said. But there's a part of me that feels guilty. Why did taking someone else's life make me feel better about myself? Isn't that kind of sick?"

"I don't think it was the act of taking someone's life that did it. It was that someone was going to take your life, and you stopped him; you overpowered him. That's a heady thing."

Rory glanced over at the ceramic rooster, now hidden behind the menagerie of medicine bottles. The black eyes, like a watcher of the night, peered out above the containers. "I've decided I want to get a degree in psychology."

"What about dance therapy?" Cass stroked the edge of her silk scarf.

"I'm still in the planning stage."

"I feel bad if I messed up your plans. I told Nick he needed to call you back and tell you that you didn't have to come. I'm not as bad as he makes me out to be. He worries about me."

"You didn't mess up my plans. I wanted to be here."

Cass smiled. "It'll be nice to have some company other than Nick." She shook her head. "I love your brother, but he can't hide the fear in his eyes. Every time I look at him, I'm reminded of the cancer. I need something to take my mind off of it. So how long can you stay?"

"Till you kick me out," Rory joked. "I quit my job. I left my stuff in storage and my car with a mechanic in town, but I don't think I'm going back to Willow Bend." She told Cass about Marlena and Will leaving. "Who knows? Maybe I'll stay in Maryland—Goucher College was one of the schools the ADTA recommended for undergraduate work." Rory sipped her tea. "Once I pick a school, then I'll find a place to rent, but eventually I want to buy another house. We're selling the one in Phoenix. Derek's putting it on the market this week."

"So things are better between you and Derek?"

"I think we can be friends."

"Is he still with that woman?"

"Yeah." Rory curled her legs up into the chair. "I think he was seeing her before I left him."

"What makes you think that?"

"He didn't come right out and say it, but I knew."

From the hallway, the cuckoo clock chimed the hour. The small lamp by the kitchen table cast a soft light onto Cass's face, giving her skin a warm glow. Rory thought for an instant that Cass looked healthy again, like her old self. Rory gripped her mug of tea and looked down at the table. "I had an affair." She waited for Cass's reaction, but when there wasn't one, she glanced up.

Cass was smiling, and Rory gave her a puzzled look.

"What?" Cass asked with a smile. "You want me to look shocked or say how could you?"

"I don't know. I felt wrong about it. Ashamed. Other than my friend Charlie, you're the only person I've told. It's strange…now that I know Derek was having an affair, I don't know what to feel."

"From what you've told me in the past, I think things had died between you and Derek a long time ago. There's nothing to feel guilty about. So what ended your affair?"

Rory gave a sheepish look. "Guilt?" She told Cass about Ben, the places they'd gone to, the songs he'd sung to her, the fun they'd had together.

"He sounds like a great guy. Any chance of getting back with him?"

Rory told her about Monterey, the other woman. "I probably blew my one chance of finding the right person."

"Just because he was with someone? Rory, come on—why not call him? What have you got to lose?"

"My pride?"

"To hell with pride." Cass waved her raw-looking hand at Rory. "Life's short. You've got to take chances."

35

Propped against pillows atop the antique spool bed—the same bed that used to be in her grandmother's house, the one she used to have to climb up into before her grandmother would tuck her in and read the Reddy Fox stories—she gazed out the upstairs window of Chelsea's room. The gray March sky looked dismal against the black branches of the bare trees. It was the sixteenth of March, her birthday.

Living in Phoenix, she'd forgotten how much she'd hated the month of March growing up. She used to wish she'd been born in another month. March was cruel, teasing everyone into thinking spring had arrived with warm days that smelled of new growth, only to take them away, turning cold and bitter, colder than any day in January.

She'd been at Cass and Nick's for two weeks and had fallen into a routine: up each morning to fix Cass's breakfast, and then the two of them would sit at the kitchen table and make a list for the day. Some days it was laundry; others they went grocery shopping or took Cass to the doctor.

Cass had started a new course of drugs. There were bad days that Cass spent not far from the bathroom or in bed, but others were good, like yesterday, when they'd gone to the nursery where Rory's mom used to work and bought pansies to put in pots on the front porch.

But the doctors had said things could get worse before they got better. They were going to do another PET scan in two weeks to see if anything had diminished. The air of not knowing was like a thick fog, hovering over the house, weighing them down.

Rory tried to keep busy so her mind wouldn't conjure up worst-case scenarios. She was still taking her online classes, but she was also auditing a class called Alternative Approaches to Therapy at Montgomery College, where Cass taught. Cass had contacted the woman who ran the class, and she'd agreed to let Rory in as a favor.

The first day she'd walked across the campus, she'd felt out of place. The faces of the nineteen- and twenty-year-olds loomed before her like a glaring reminder of her age. But she'd shoved the feeling aside; she wasn't going to look back with regrets anymore. Four years of schooling seemed daunting, but she needed to take it one day at a time.

Now, sitting on the bed, she'd just finished reading an e-mail from Will. He loved his job. She pictured him walking through the mountains with Jasper at his side. Someday that would be her, doing something she loved. She set the laptop beside her and picked up the *Washington Post*. Jillian and Joe were coming down the following weekend to celebrate Rory's birthday belatedly. It was the soonest they could come.

She scanned the Style section, flipping the pages, trying to come up with something fun to do. Her eyes fell on a picture of a local band. She was reminded of Ben and what Cass had said about taking chances.

She picked up her cell on the nightstand and punched the text icon; then she hit the letter B, and Ben's name appeared. Her blood pumped. She tapped on his name and then began typing—*How are things going*. She erased it and then typed again—*What are you up to?* Then she stared at the screen, deleted the text, and set the phone down, gazing out the window. What was she doing?

She watched a robin fly past the window, a piece of twine hanging from its mouth, settling in the large oak tree in the backyard. The bird repeated her actions several times, building her home strand by strand.

She picked up her phone. Her thumbs rapidly typed: *Wondering what town you're in. I'm in Maryland. Thinking of you.* She hit the send button before she could change her mind. Her pulse beat in her throat.

She stared at her phone for several minutes and then jumped off the bed, threw on some workout clothes, and headed out of the room. She crossed the hall and quietly pushed open the door to Cass's room. She was asleep; her patchy head lay on the pillow. Rory pulled the door closed and headed for the stairs, but then she stopped, went into her room, and grabbed her phone off the bed. No response.

She turned on the treadmill that sat in one corner of the unfinished basement. The far corner was Nick's workshop area, so different from her father's. Instead of wood tools like chisels and routers, it was filled with carburetors, gaskets, and other grease-filled items. The smell of dirty oil hung in the air. A square rug delineated the other corner that used to be Michael's band area, with an old drum set and several guitars hanging on the wall.

She hit the mountain course button on the treadmill. She wanted to sweat. Twenty minutes into the grueling pace, she was awash with perspiration. She used the bottom of her T-shirt to wipe the moisture off her brow that trickled down and stung her eyes. The staccato clapping of Santa Esmeralda's "Don't Let Me Be Misunderstood" pounded from the ear buds into her brain, pushing back her qualms about sending the text. Her lungs burned, but it felt good.

Thirty-five minutes in, drenched in sweat, she was over the hump. Her body felt energized. Endorphins coursed through her veins. Her phone lit up in the cup holder on the treadmill, and she saw his name on the screen. She stopped the treadmill and jumped off, picking up her phone and reading the text: *Happy Birthday—been thinking of you too. How long are you in MD? I'm in NY next week. I could come down.*

Her breath hitched, and her lungs expanded, holding in air. He remembered her birthday. He wanted to meet with her. She smiled and let out a laugh.

36

In the dim light of the small club off P Street in DC, Rory thought no one would be able to tell that Cass was wearing a wig. She'd never seen her with straight hair before, but the long brown locks were attractive, Rory thought. Glad that Cass had decided to come to her birthday celebration, she smiled at Nick, whose arm hung around the back of Cass's chair. The last few months had aged him. Worry lines were permanently etched around his eyes.

Michael was on stage playing his guitar for open-mic night. He was good, Rory thought. Her mind drifted to Ben. He'd called her a few days ago. The conversation had been brief—he was in New York and on his way to a recording session. She closed her eyes, remembering his voice. She'd felt awkward, talking with him over the phone, like she was speaking to a stranger, but at the same time, she felt as if her soul was being stretched across the line. They didn't talk about the past or about seeing each other in Monterey. He'd asked her what she was doing this weekend, and she'd told him about the club. He said he would probably be in the studio all weekend, but he'd call her if he could get away. That was the last she'd heard from him.

She pushed the thoughts of Ben out of her mind. This was her night. Jillian was sitting next to her, and Cass and Nick were here; she shoved her shoulders back and smiled. Michael was still on stage; his voice had a bluesy edge to it. She wondered if Nick realized how talented Michael was. Tapping her boot to the beat, she sipped her beer, eyeing the scene. Joe had his hand intertwined with

Jillian's; Cass was resting her head on Nick's shoulder. Everyone's attention was on Michael.

He ended with an intricate run on the guitar, and then the audience broke out in applause. Rory glanced around the small room, feeling proud of Michael; everyone seemed to have liked him. And then her eyes fell on Ben, standing by the door. He wore a dark leather jacket and he hadn't shaved. His hair brushed the collar of his jacket as he scanned the room. Her heart pounded against her thin blouse.

Her eyes darted to Jillian; she hadn't had a chance to tell her about Ben. Michael was back at the table, and Jillian was hugging him. Rory then flashed a look to Cass, but Cass was talking with Nick. Excitement poured through her, but at the same time, she felt nervous. She hadn't seen Ben in months, and now her whole family was about to meet him.

"What did you think, Aunt Rory?"

She looked up at Michael, who was standing beside her chair. "I think you were great." She stood and gave him a hug. "I loved it." Over Michael's shoulder she caught Ben's eye. He smiled, gave her a wave, and then began making his way toward the table.

Her palms were sweating; she wiped them on her jeans. She hadn't thought this whole thing through. Was it because she hadn't really expected him to come?

And then he was right in front of her. She could smell him, that musky scent of his Tom Ford cologne.

"Aurora June." His voice sent shivers up her spine. He leaned in and gave her a kiss on the cheek. "Happy birthday." His touch felt like an electric shock.

"Thanks." Her cheeks burned.

"You look great." His eyes were riveted to hers.

Without even realizing, she brushed her hair from behind her ear, letting it fall over her cheek, hiding the scar that was already covered by makeup. She glanced at the table, and all eyes were on her. Jillian and Nick had puzzled looks, but Cass gave her a wink.

"Everyone, I'd like you to meet a friend of mine, Ben Colter. Ben, this is my daughter, Jillian, and her boyfriend, Joe." Ben shook their hands, commenting on Jillian's resemblance to Rory, and then she introduced him to Nick, Cass, and Michael.

"I heard you play. Nice job," Ben said to Michael.

"Thanks."

"Ben's a musician too," Rory said, feeling as if her voice was several octaves higher than normal. Michael pulled an extra chair over to their table. Ben sat down next to Rory.

"Are you in a band?" Michael asked, seated on the other side of Ben.

Ben nodded and then asked Michael about his guitar.

Rory listened to them talk about the tone and depth of the instrument. She felt Jillian nudge her thigh. She glanced over, and Jillian raised her eyebrows with an approving nod.

Rory felt as if this was a dream, because she'd had this dream before. The year before, when she was seeing Ben, she'd sometimes wake early in the morning, not wanting to open her eyes, wanting to keep the dream going and return to the place where she was with Ben, openly; Jillian and Nick were there too, and no one was judging her.

The waitress came for another drink order, and Cass began the third degree on Ben in a playful way that had everyone laughing. Her faded southern accent sounded more pronounced as she asked him what part of Louisiana he was from, if he was a Saints fan, and how long he'd been playing music.

He told everyone that he'd been playing music all his life, and then he looked at Rory and said, "But it wasn't until I met this woman that my songwriting really took off. She was a big inspiration for me."

"*Really?*" Jillian commented with a devilish edge to her voice.

Rory felt the heat rising to the surface of her cheeks again.

As soon as the bathroom door swung closed behind them, Jillian shoved her mother's arm. "Mom! The guy wrote a song about you? Why didn't you tell me?"

Rory scrunched her face and shrugged.

Cass walked past Rory and said over her shoulder as she entered one of the stalls, "Because your mother's an idiot. She thought you'd hate her."

Jillian frowned at Rory. "What? Why would you think that?"

"Because I was seeing him while I was still with Dad."

A flicker of surprise flashed on Jillian's face, but then she said, "So what? I knew things were bad between you and Dad years ago." Jillian went into the stall beside Cass and called out, "I want to hear all about it."

Rory went into the third stall. Was Jillian really OK with this?

The three stood at the sinks while other women filed into the restroom.

"He wants me to go with him for a drink." Rory stared at Cass and Jillian's reflections in the mirror.

"*And?*" Jillian coaxed.

"You and Joe are only here till Sunday; I don't want to miss seeing you."

"It's just for tonight. You can bring him over to Aunt Cass's in the morning."

"I don't know." Rory's eyes pleaded with Cass. In the bathroom light, Cass's wig looked less natural, and a pang of sorrow shot through Rory's gut.

"He can come for breakfast. Joe and I can make omelets, if that's OK?" Jillian glanced over at Cass.

"Of course." Cass stared back at Rory's reflection. "Follow your heart."

Rory sucked in air and studied her own reflection. The makeup had worn off slightly, and the scar looked brighter against the fluorescent light. "All right. I'm gonna do it."

"Yes!" Jillian exclaimed as she fist-pumped the air.

Rory and Ben walked along the sidewalk to his car, their boots clicking on the pavement. Ben stopped in front of an old VW beetle, the paint having disappeared years ago, replaced with a rust-colored primer.

"Is this yours?"

Ben shook his head. "A friend of mine in New York let me borrow it."

"I thought *I* drove a relic."

The passenger door squeaked on its rusty hinges as Ben opened it for her. The backseat was piled with clothes and sheets of music.

Ben started the engine.

"Where do you want to go?" He glanced over at her, his face cast in shadow from the streetlight. "I'm staying at a hotel around the corner. We could go back there for a drink."

"Sure." She stared out the windshield at the row of brick buildings, clutching her hands in her lap.

Stopped at a red light at Wisconsin Avenue, she noticed Ben glancing in her direction. His hand reached over and brushed her hair back behind her ear. "What's this?" His finger traced her scar.

She looked out the side window to a group of people walking down the cobblestone walk. Their laughter echoed into the night. For the first time, she felt self-conscious about the scar, wishing she had opted for the surgery to correct it. She wondered what he thought of it. "It's a knife wound."

"What? Have you joined a street gang?" Ben chuckled. The light turned green, but she could feel Ben's eyes staring at her. A car horn blared behind them.

"You better go," she said, pointing toward the light.

He stepped on the gas. "You want to elaborate?"

"I was attacked."

Ben hit the brakes, and Rory heard the screech of tires behind them.

"We're going to have an accident."

"I thought you were joking about the knife. What happened?"

Rory inhaled, feeling she'd repeated the story so many times it was beginning to feel scripted, but she had to tell him. "How far is the hotel?"

"Just a couple of blocks."

"Why don't we wait till we get there? It's a long story."

37

The small brick courtyard was shielded from the street by a half wall and a row of evergreens. Ben had gotten a hotel clerk to light one of the fire pits, and Rory was huddled against the big cushions of the sofa, thankful that she'd borrowed one of Cass's winter coats before leaving the house. The hum of traffic filtered through the buffer of trees.

Ben was lounged against the couch, his leather jacket open to the cool night air.

He smiled, not saying anything, just studying her face.

"Aren't you cold?" Rory asked.

"You warm me up."

There it was. The way he used to talk. She remembered how she had loved it, but at the same time, she had been leery, wondering if it was sincere…was that the way he talked to all women? A server came with their drinks. The scent of apples and cinnamon wafted from her cup. A dollop of whipped cream sat on top. "What is it?"

"Hot apple cider with bourbon," Ben said as he picked up his glass of bourbon on ice.

"Elijah Craig?"

"You remembered." He ran his finger along her jaw again and asked her about the attack.

She relayed the events, which no longer brought a pang to her gut, more like she was reciting a scene from a movie.

He looked at her with shock and disbelief without saying anything. After several minutes of silence, she wondered what he was thinking. "Say something."

He looked down at the drink in his hand. "I'm stunned. I can't imagine what you've been through. How do you ever recover from something like that?"

Rory gazed into the fire as she wound some of her hair around her finger. "I've been through worse."

Ben raised his brows and gave her another incredulous look. "You're full of surprises. What could be worse than someone almost killing you?" He leaned back against the cushion and studied her face as if he was seeing her for the first time.

"I was almost raped." She saw the pain on his face and added, "It was a long time ago." She unwrapped the hair from her finger and picked up the warm mug of apple-scented liquid. She took a long sip and then opened up her past to him. Her therapist had encouraged her to do it. It felt good. After Derek's reaction years ago, she'd never been able to share the attack with anyone. She had also kept her guilt over her father's death hidden from Ben. But now everything came spilling out.

He reached over and pulled her hair back, exposing the faded scar at her hairline. "Was this from the attack?"

Rory nodded.

"I always thought it was from Derek."

"He never hit me. In fact, he was the one who kept me from going off the deep end back then." She sipped her drink, feeling the warmth swirl around her limbs like a soft blanket. "With therapy, I've been able to see myself more clearly. I think for years I was afraid to let myself be happy." She stared into the blue-tipped flames that leaped like a Cossack dancer flinging his arms about. "I made excuses for staying in a marriage that wasn't right, but I think the real reason I did was because it felt safe." She turned her eyes to Ben. "When I met you, I felt joy I hadn't felt in ages, but I think it scared me. I think deep down I was afraid to feel that way, afraid it might all be stripped away again, and the pain would be too great to bear."

"You deserve happiness." Ben reached over and held her hand. "I was surprised when I got your text. After Monterey, when you never answered my call, I assumed I wouldn't see you again."

She thought back to Monterey, seeing Ben with Lisa. It felt like a million years ago. "What brought you to New York?"

"I'm working on an album for a friend." He stared into her eyes. "I like your family."

She smiled, thinking the whole thing felt surreal. Ben had always been her secret, and seeing him talking with Nick and Jillian had felt odd. This was real.

The waiter came out to settle the tab. The bar was closing.

After the waiter walked away, Ben said, "Want me to take you home, or do you want to come upstairs?"

She didn't want this moment to end.

She lay across the king-sized bed, one leg wrapped around the white sheets, stretched out like a cat, purring in the sun. She'd forgotten how euphoric the feeling was after being with Ben; like each fiber of her body was reverberating with the beat of a melodic rhythm. A shaft of light from the partially opened bathroom door cut a narrow white swath across the darkened wall.

Ben's cell rang from the nightstand. She sat up and glanced at the name *Lisa* lit up on the screen. The programmed ringtone repeated several times. Ben came out of the bathroom, and she quickly lay back down.

"Was that my phone?"

"Yeah." She wanted to ask him about Lisa, but she couldn't. She watched him pick up the phone and then set it back on the nightstand. He slid into bed, slipping his arm under her head. He stroked her hair with his fingers. They lay in silence for a few minutes, and then she said, "Can you come to breakfast tomorrow at my brother's house?" Deep down a part of her wanted to see him in Nick's kitchen, as one of the group, but at the same time, she wanted to walk away, not liking that niggling feeling in her gut of wondering who else was in his life.

"I've got to leave first thing. I have a session at noon in New York. I can drop you off, but I can't stay."

Rory nodded and felt his chest hair tickling her cheek, but her thoughts were on the phone call. Why had Lisa called?

"You want to come?"

It took a minute for his words to register. "To New York?" She propped her head up to face him. "I can't. My sister-in-law…and Jillian…" her voice trailed off.

"I can come back here. I have a few days before I have to head to Nashville."

She brushed her hand over the dark hair of his chest, feeling the warmth of his skin. She didn't want to think about tomorrow or two days from now.

The next morning, Rory, dressed in Ben's denim shirt, sat by the window that overlooked Wisconsin, watching the city come to life. Ben was taking a shower, and the muffled sound of the running water filtered into the room. As if by some prescient knowledge, she glanced over at his phone, and within seconds it began to ring. She went over to the nightstand. Lisa. Her eyes darted toward the bathroom. The steady patter of the shower continued. The call went to voice mail. She wanted to listen to the message, but instead she walked back toward the window, telling herself it didn't matter.

But she could feel it building, the curiosity taking over. She turned from the window as if hands were nudging her toward the nightstand.

She picked up the phone and noticed he had three new text messages. They were all from Lisa. The newest said, "Call me." The one before it said, "When are you leaving NY?" And the first text, which had been sent the day before, about the same time Ben had arrived at the club, said, "Just left Montecito, reminded me of that night…"

She set the phone back on the nightstand, then picked up the hotel phone and asked the front desk to call her a taxi. Her adrenaline pumped as she threw off his shirt and quickly got dressed, her mind racing with theories of why he'd come. If he was still with Lisa, why had he slept with her last night? Was she just a fling to him?

She heard the squeak of a pipe, and the water shut off. She went back over to the window, scanning the cars on the street below for the taxi. A few minutes later, he came out of the bathroom, shirtless, wearing only jeans; his hair was wet and tousled as if he'd just rubbed a towel through it. Seeing him sent tingles across the surface of her skin, and she turned back to face the window. He walked over and slid his arms around her from behind, resting his chin against the top of her head. She closed her eyes and drank in his clean, soapy smell. She wanted time to freeze right now and this moment to last forever.

Then, without even realizing the words were actually being spoken out loud, she heard herself say, "Why didn't Lisa go with you to New York?" She felt his hands ever so slightly tense around her middle.

"What made you ask that?"

She shrugged. He turned her around to face him and then cupped her face in his hands. His eyes gazed into hers so intently she had to look away—out the window, where they settled on a woman taking boxes out of the trunk of her car. Rory watched her struggling as she stacked them one on top of the other, gripping her chin over the top box and balancing them in her arms as she headed down the street. Rory wondered what was in the boxes, and then her eyes drifted back to Ben.

He stared back at her and said, "You never answered me last night when I said I could come back down in a few days."

"Cass has her PET scan this week. I'm not sure how things will go." She turned back toward the window.

He nodded and went over to his black leather satchel, pulled out a clean shirt and slipped it on. He then grabbed his phone from the nightstand along with the shirt Rory had been wearing and shoved them in the bag. "I've gotta get on the road. I can't be late for this session. You ready?"

"I called for a taxi."

"Why? I could've taken you."

"That's OK." She tried to sound light and casual even though she was swirling inside with emotions.

"Call me if you want me to come by on my way to Nashville."

A lump formed in her throat. She couldn't speak. He was leaving. A part of her wanted to grab her purse and go with him... forget everyone else. But she knew she couldn't. This was too hard. She wasn't cut out for the one-night-stand relationship—at least not with Ben. He put on his jacket and then came over and kissed the top of her head.

"Lisa and I are friends..." He paused and touched his finger to her lips. "She's not you."

38

Rory hammered the last nail into the compost bin and then stood to brush the dirt off her bare knees. She swiped her hair with the back of her gloved hand. "What do you think?"

"It looks magnificent," Cass replied from her lounge chair under an umbrella in the backyard. A magenta scarf was wrapped around her head. "I didn't know you were so handy with power tools."

"Neither did I." Rory sat down in the grass, admiring her project, which was almost an exact replica of the one her father had built for her mother, and feeling the warm breeze caress her skin.

It was one of those days that had to be spent outdoors—mid-seventies, low humidity, not a cloud in the sky—and the distant hum of a lawnmower droned against the chirping of birds. The garden was a kaleidoscope of color. Just as Rory had forgotten how much she'd hated the month of March in Maryland, she'd also forgotten how much she'd loved May.

She wanted to drink in the air, the smell of cut grass and rich dirt reminding her of when she was young, and she'd lie on the glider in the backyard, looking up at the trees, the blue sky, wanting to soar with the birds.

She tapped the hammer against her palm. "I forgot to tell you—Derek called last night and said someone signed a contract on the house. They want to close in four weeks."

"Do you have to go out there?"

"No. He said they can scan the papers and send them to me."

"What about all your stuff?"

Rory stared off in the distance.

"I'm fine, if you want to go now," Cass continued. "And besides, Chelsea will be home by the end of the week. She only has one final left."

Rory looked over at Cass. She did look better—not well, but better. The last scan she'd had in March had shown little improvement, but the doctors were hopeful about the new course of drugs. They'd told Cass on her last visit that if the next scan showed significant shrinking of the tumors, they would probably perform the surgery once she'd gotten her strength back.

"I don't want to go out there right now. Just thinking about going through all that stuff feels strange, and it would be weird with Donna there. I made a list of the things I really want to have. It's not much, just a few pieces of furniture, some pictures, and my pottery. I guess a part of me wants to start new. I don't need any reminders of Phoenix." She pulled a dandelion from the lawn and twirled it between her fingers. "I also got a call from Jillian last night. She sounds like she's on cloud nine." Rory glanced over at Cass.

Cass's scarf blew across her face, and she reached up to pull it down. Her hands looked normal again, the skin no longer raw. "I knew she'd love it there." Cass gazed off into the distance. "The kids are all grown up." Her eyes settled back on Rory. "Did Michael tell you he sent his demo tape to Ben?"

Rory nodded.

"Have you talked to him recently?"

"Ben? He called last night. He's leaving for Japan in a few weeks." She focused on a fat bumblebee that was buzzing around the roses. "He still wants me to go with him."

"Do you want to go?"

"A part of me does."

"Like I said before, you don't have to stay here on my account."

Rory's gaze was still on the bee. "What if things don't work out between us? We've never really spent more than a couple of days together at one time. What if we've both built up this fantasy relationship that doesn't really exist?"

"You'll never know unless you try."

Cass was right. Rory knew she was stalling, making excuses in her head for why she shouldn't go, because she still feared she might get hurt. She hadn't seen Ben since her birthday celebration, but they'd talked almost every night on the phone, sometimes well into the wee hours of the morning, sharing stories of their childhood.

He told her how his parents had both worked on the *Louisiana Hayride*, a radio show in the late fifties, but had given up music to run the family store in Arcadia. She remembered the picture she'd seen of him as a little boy wearing baggy shorts and holding a guitar that appeared enormous against his skinny arms and legs. He'd said music was in his blood.

Their late-night talks made her feel closer to him than any of the nights they'd spent together in the past. He'd call from whatever town he was in, describing it in such detail she felt like she was there: places like Wichita, Gatlinburg, and Cripple Creek. A part of her ached to be with him.

Her cell rang on the small table by Cass's chair. A North Carolina number appeared. Jennifer Madden?

It was. They exchanged hellos, and then Jennifer jumped right in, saying, "I wanted to check with you first before I called anyone else. I know this is short notice, but we've got a bit of an emergency at the school. One of the instructors has broken her foot and will be out all summer, and I have classes starting up in three weeks." Jennifer continued, telling Rory she had a place for her to stay—a small house her family owned on the Cape Fear River. It needed some fixing up, but if Rory wanted to put in the work, she could stay there rent-free for the summer.

After telling Jennifer she'd call her back with her decision, she stared at the phone in her hand.

"What was all that about?" Cass asked.

"Jennifer. She wants me to teach at the school for the summer."

"That's fantastic!"

"Did you have something to do with this?" Rory looked skeptically at Cass.

"I haven't spoken to Jennifer for at least two months."

"I can't believe this." Rory sat dazed, wondering if Cass was telling the truth.

"Are you going to do it?"

She rose from the ground and went over to the newly constructed compost bin, running her hand along the wood frame. "I don't know."

She had finished her online classes and had decided to enroll at Goucher College in Baltimore. Did she want to move to North Carolina? She'd been so excited about it last winter, but now she didn't know. She liked being close to Cass and Nick and living back in Maryland. It was just for the summer, though. She could always come back to Maryland. She turned the crank handle on the side of the compost bin, and her mind spun along with the wire cage inside. Or should she go on tour with Ben?

<hr />

The next week seemed to drag on. Her mind was riddled with questions and decisions. Her head was telling her one thing and her heart another. She wished she could take a poll, survey people as to what they would do, but she knew the decision was something she had to make on her own.

She was seated alone on Cass and Nick's sunporch; the windows open, letting in the evening air heavy with the aroma of lilacs and roses, and the occasional whiff of barbequed chicken from the neighbor's grill next door. Her cell buzzed on the table. She had been expecting his call, but her heart did a little skip when she saw his name appear on the screen. This was it. Ben needed an answer tonight. The last time they had talked she had told him about the offer from the school, but it was as if he hadn't heard, or didn't want to hear, instead he had continued to entice her into going to Japan.

"Did you know that Japanese cows are massaged daily and fed a diet of sake and mash beer?" Ben asked when she answered the phone.

She laughed. "I'd like to be a Japanese cow."

"Except you'd eventually be eaten. I was thinking maybe we could stop off in Hawaii on our way back. You said you'd always wanted to see Hawaii."

"Ben."

"I don't like the sound of that."

"It's not that I don't want to be with you. It's just—what I mean is—I can't let this opportunity with the school go. I know it's just for the summer but it's what I'm hoping to eventually do and if I don't try—

"You don't have to explain." She heard the frustration in his voice.

She wanted to say to him that if she went on the tour instead of taking the job offer, she'd be tempted to stay with him and never go back to school, but the words never made it out. "I'm sorry, Ben."

"Don't be sorry. You made your choice."

His words hurt and there was a voice screaming inside her, wanting to take back her decision.

They continued with a few more minutes of conversation that felt as stilted as a meeting between two strangers; she wished him luck on his tour and asked him to call when he got there. But she knew from the tone of his voice that he probably wouldn't call. She had turned him down too many times. Why couldn't she have both: a relationship and a career? After hanging up, she sat in silence for what seemed an eternity with the phone still in her hand. Her body felt raw and exposed, like skidding on concrete.

39

She turned onto the dirt lane, crossing over a ditch bordered by scrubby pines. The Jeep jerked and rocked as she traversed her way along the rutted path. She glanced out the car window to the brown remnants of what had once been neatly rowed cornstalks, now hidden beneath a field of overgrown weeds. A long black snake lay in the middle of the lane, basking in the warm sun. She slowed the Jeep down and watched as it slithered its way into the tall grass. She hated snakes and wondered if it was a sign that maybe she'd made a mistake. She had been telling herself on the drive to North Carolina that she had gotten too comfortable at her brother's house and she needed to move on, be on her own again. But as she rounded the curve of the battered road lined with a thick layer of trees, she thought maybe staying at Nick's hadn't been so bad.

Jennifer had told her that the house had sat vacant for years and would need some fixing up, but Rory had not expected this. She tried to keep an open mind as she got out of the old Jeep Wrangler that Nick had lent her for the trip. The small Cape Cod–style cottage had probably been charming at one time, but now faded blue paint peeled from the broken shutters that hung askew from the dormer windows above the front porch.

She carefully crossed the tall grass, scanning for more snakes as she made her way toward the house. She lifted the silver rock beside the wooden steps and found the key Jennifer had said was there. She hesitantly turned the lock, half afraid of what she would find inside.

She held her breath as she turned the knob of the weathered wooden door but was pleasantly surprised once she entered. The interior was in much better shape. A shaft of sunlight streamed onto a thick coating of dust on the old pine floors, but the few pieces of furniture were covered with white sheets. A staircase ran along the side wall to a loft above.

She sneezed a few times as she made her way toward the kitchen, which she immediately fell in love with. Her eyes scanned the room to the large fifties-style O'Keefe and Merritt range, a white porcelain farm sink, and a long, free-standing butcher block table that ran along one wall. She could picture making dinners at the vintage stove. She opened the side door that led to a screened porch. Several of the screens were torn out completely, and one was hanging from the top, billowing in the breeze.

Her gaze drifted to a wide opening in the trees about twenty yards away that looked onto the river. She pushed open the screen door and stepped onto the sun-worn gray boards of the attached deck. A few boards had buckled and would need replacing.

The Cape Fear River snaked its black water around a sharp bend. She spotted a stone path through the tall weeds that ran from the porch down to the shoreline. She wanted to walk down and get a closer look, but tall boots and a lawnmower were needed before she did anything in the yard. From this vantage point, the twenty-acre property was completely secluded.

Across the thirty-foot expanse of the river, gnarled tree trunks rose from the banks, their branches reaching out over the water. The only sound was the rustle of the leaves and the rippling current, splashing over the rocks along the shore.

Two weathered Adirondack chairs faced the river. She brushed the seat of one and sat down. The air was thick with the smell of white jasmine that surrounded the porch. Ben's favorite smell. She closed her eyes. Days after their last conversation she had been angry with him, wishing they could have kept their long-distance chats, wishing he had understood her reasons for not going to Japan. She felt he wasn't being fair to her. But then there were nights, alone in bed, where she wished she had gone. As the days passed, though, the wound of knowing it was probably the end of their relationship was slowly healing. She kept telling herself that she had made the right decision.

Beads of sweat dripped off her forehead as she tacked the last screen in place. She wiped her brow with her forearm and then climbed off the ladder to admire her work. She smiled. The house had been transformed, and she'd accomplished it all on her own. She slipped the hammer into the pouch on her tool belt, thinking the past month and a half had flown by. She walked around the neatly trimmed grass to survey the improvements.

The shutters had been scraped, painted a sky blue, and rehung. The planked siding had a fresh coat of white paint. She'd replaced several boards that had rotted on the front porch and the deck, and the shrubs around the house had been cleared of weeds and pruned back.

Each morning, she woke with energy and purpose, ready to tackle the day. The days were nonstop from dawn to dusk: teaching classes, renovating the house, and taking an English class at the community college for the summer.

She loved working at the arts school, where she taught two ballet classes and two modern dance classes and assisted in dance-therapy classes for autistic and handicapped children. The work was not only rewarding but enlightening. She'd never spent time with disabled children before, and she felt that she learned something from them every day.

Her favorite was a little girl named Adelaide who'd been born with moderate cerebral palsy. She had extreme weakness on her left side and had trouble balancing, but she always had a smile on her face and something kind to say. After class, she'd hug Rory around the waist and thank her for such a wonderful time.

After putting her tools away in the small shed beside the house, she headed inside. A warm feeling washed over her as she pulled open the antique screen door with scrolled detailing at the top that she'd found at a flea market and was now sanded and painted to look new.

While fixing up the house, she had discovered that she loved working with wood. As a child, she'd spend hours helping her dad in his workshop, but ever since her father had died, she hadn't even walked into a lumber store.

She poured a glass of wine and went out back to sit on the deck. It had become her ritual. Every evening around eight thirty, when the heat of the day was just a warm reminder, she would sit in one of the now-refurbished Adirondack chairs and watch the blue sky transition to amber. Then, as if the sun was shouting its farewell, the sky would ignite with an intense coral before fading to indigo. During those tranquil minutes, she'd reflect on her day and her life.

She felt as if her mind, body, and spirit were humming in tune with each other. Her arms and legs were now burnished gold and toned to perfection from afternoons and weekends working out-side, and she felt healthier than she had in a long time—not just physically but mentally as well.

She held the photo she'd received that morning in the mail from Jillian. It had been enclosed in a card that had a picture of a Labra-dor on the front. The dog looked almost identical to Daphne. Jillian had written a short note: "Couldn't resist the card! Miss you and love you. XOXO Jillian." Rory stared at the photo of Jillian and Joe standing in front of the ivy-covered Georgian-style brick building where they lived in London. The look on Jillian's face said it all; Rory knew she was happy, and just seeing her daughter's elation made her heart soar. She flipped the photo over and read the back again: "Our new place! Can't wait for you to visit!"

Time seemed to be moving so quickly. The summer was halfway over, and Charlie's wedding was just a week away.

The light show in the sky was over, and Rory got up to fix dinner.

On her way home from work the next evening, she thought about the conversation she'd had with Jennifer earlier. Jennifer had told her that several of the parents had raved about Rory, saying their children loved their teacher Miss Rory, and were eager to go to class each week. She went on to say that the enrollment for fall was growing, and she was hoping Rory could stay on as a permanent addition to the staff. Rory had accepted without a moment's hesitation.

Now, stopped at a traffic light on College Road, she glanced over at the brick entrance that read University of North Carolina Wilmington, and an exultant current rippled through her body. Maybe she could go to school there in the fall. She made a mental note to call the school and talk with an advisor tomorrow.

As the light changed and she drove past the large expanse of grass on the campus that was shaded by tall pines, she noticed a woman walking a dog that looked identical to her old dog Daphne. If she was going to stay in North Carolina maybe it was time to get a dog. She missed having a dog.

Her cell rang. It was Nick and Cass, together on speaker. Cass's tumors had shrunk significantly, and the doctors had scheduled the mastectomy for August 7. Nick said she wouldn't need any more chemo. A swell of relief washed over Rory, and she told them she wanted to be there for the surgery.

"She's going to beat this," Nick said. Rory heard the hope in his voice.

"How's it going down there?" Cass asked.

Rory told them about her decision to stay. "I can't believe how much I love it here. It's strange—I've only been here a month or so, but it feels like home."

"Cass has always wanted to go back to North Carolina," Nick said.

"Maybe you guys need to move down here too," Rory said jokingly. She shifted down the gears of the Jeep as she stopped at another light, picturing Nick and Cass living in the same town. She turned off the highway onto Shady Lady Lane, wondering about the origin of its name every time she drove by the green sign, passing the pasture filled with black-and-white dairy cows, their ropy tails swishing back and forth as they grazed. She told them about the renovations she'd done on the house. "Dad would've been proud of my table saw skills."

"Maybe we'll come down for a visit after this is all over with," Cass said.

After hanging up, Rory turned onto the long drive leading to the house. The overgrown field now had neatly planted rows of corn. She'd gotten the OK from Jennifer to allow a neighboring farmer to lease the land. He'd even plowed a few rows for her to put in a vegetable garden. Her tomato plants and yellow squash were thriving.

She rounded the bend past the line of trees that separated the field from the house and slowed the Jeep down, studying the improvements she'd made. Flowers bordered the path leading to the front steps, and morning glory vines wrapped around the square columns of the porch. She had done this all on her own. Pride mixed with joy swirled inside.

40

Rory stood beside the rail, eyeing the magnificent view from the rooftop of the skyscraper hotel that overlooked the city and the bay. She sipped her Cabernet, needing a break; her smile felt like it had been permanently plastered to her face after mingling through the crowd of strangers for the past two hours. She'd only been able to say a brief hello to Charlie, who'd been surrounded by a constant stream of guests and photographers. Rory thought back to her wedding—hurriedly put together, with just a few friends and family, gathering back at their house afterward. Even though her mother had tried to convince her to wait until after the baby was born before getting married, telling her there was no need to rush into it, Rory had been insistent. She had told her mother that she wanted to spend the rest of her life with Derek.

She slipped off one of her heels, releasing her toes from their torturous chamber. She knew she shouldn't have worn new shoes. They'd looked great in the store, but after standing in them for most of the day, she wished she could kick them both off and rub her aching arches. She closed her eyes, feeling the warm bay breeze blow through her hair and picturing the night at the hotel in DC—Ben's long fingers massaging her feet.

At the airport in Wilmington while she was waiting for her flight she had clicked on The Lost Riders website. Ben's band. A collage of photographs appeared of the band onstage at various concerts. She had stared at a close-up of Ben and felt the familiar warmth swirl through her, followed by an ache deep down. She knew she shouldn't be on the site, but instead, she had continued scrolling through the pictures, and her eye caught one of Ben standing with a group of people; next to him was Lisa. The caption read, Stillwater Wine Festival. It had been taken just last week. Now, she glanced back out at the San Francisco skyline, wishing she hadn't gone on the website. She needed to put Ben out of her mind. She didn't need a man. A dog was what she needed. As soon as she got back to North Carolina she would get a dog.

"Great view."

A man dressed in a dark, expensive-looking suit stood beside her. Charlie had been right—there was an inordinate amount of gorgeous-looking men at the wedding, and this was probably the twentieth one who had struck up a conversation with her.

She snapped her smile back in place and slipped her foot back into its satin-covered cage from hell. The chit-chat began again. Number twenty was an investment banker, forty-three, and single, and he loved sailing. She laughed at his droll banter, but inside she longed to be sitting on her deck in North Carolina, watching the sun set.

The man was telling her about one of his sailing trips when she blurted out, "Do you like dogs?"

Her question clearly took him by surprise. He appeared baffled. "Dogs?"

Rory nodded.

"Not particularly. Don't they shed a lot?"

She remembered Derek's constant complaints about Daphne's hairs on the sofa. She smiled, thinking she'd rather be curled up on the couch with a dog then spend another minute listening to this guy. "Yeah, they do."

Number twenty grimaced. "Too messy for me." He went back to his dissertation on sailing.

She glanced across the expansive deck and saw Charlie seated alone. Rory quickly excused herself and made a beeline across the stone floor. A jazz band was set up in one corner, and the saxophone trilled over the hum of voices as she brushed past women in designer gowns, hoping Charlie wouldn't be grabbed by someone before she got there.

"Rory! Oh my God, I thought I'd never get to talk with you." Charlie gave her a big hug. "You look fantastic, as usual." She pushed Rory's hair back and checked out her scar. "It's not that bad."

"Thanks, but I know what you're really thinking—why didn't I have plastic surgery?"

"No! But I do know a great doctor." Charlie laughed. Her face glowed in the sparkling light.

"So what about Ben? I feel like I've lost touch with everyone getting ready for this thing. The last time I talked to you, you were contemplating going to Japan with him. *So?*" Charlie had a gleam in her eye.

Rory shrugged. "It's over. I think there were only so many times I could turn him down." She told Charlie about her decision not to go to Japan.

"Why didn't you call me? I would've made you go."

"You sound like Jillian."

"I knew she was a smart girl. C'mon, Rory, *Japan?* With a cool guy that you love. It's a no-brainer." Charlie waved her bejeweled hand at Rory. "And don't give me that look—I know you love the guy. You didn't fool me in Monterey after that night at the club when you tried to pretend it didn't bother you that he was with someone else. You were in love with him then."

"OK, I admit I was in love with him, but there's more to it than that."

"What else is there?"

Rory scanned the elaborate scene. The tiny white lights laced onto the potted trees reflected off the shimmering gowns as couples slow-danced. "I let Derek run my life for years. I put my own needs behind everyone else's—and I wanted to—but not anymore." She twisted her wineglass back and forth on the gold tablecloth. The red liquid swirled inside. "I gave up so much, and I don't want to do that again." Her gaze drifted to the night sky, aglow with the twinkling lights of the city. "I'm determined to finish school. I know it sounds silly. Why is it so important to get a degree at my age?" She absentmindedly ran her finger along her scar. "But it's something I have to do to prove to myself that I can do it. And I love teaching at the school…" Rory looked over at Charlie with her perfectly done makeup and bouncy curls that framed her face, but all Rory saw was the compassion in Charlie's eyes. "I still love Ben. I still dream about him—and it hurts—but I guess I can't have both."

"As long as you're happy, that's all that matters."

Rory smiled. "I am, except for my feet. These shoes are killing me!" She laughed as she kicked off her shoes under the table.

The plane taxied down the runway after landing safely in Wilmington. She watched the other passengers whipping out their cells, bringing them to life, anxious to be reconnected with the world. She didn't need to turn hers on—no one was meeting her at the airport. But she rooted in her purse for it anyway and turned it on out of habit. To her surprise, she had a text from Charlie. She should be in Fiji by now on her honeymoon, why was she texting? It read, *Thanks for the gift. I love it! PS: I got a gift for you, too. XOXO.* She wondered what Charlie meant by that. Why would she have gotten Rory a gift?

After making a salad for dinner, she went onto the back deck. Listening to the low croaking of the bullfrogs down by the river and the gentle hum of the cicadas, she inhaled the jasmine-scented air, feeling as if something was missing. This was what she had longed for in California. She couldn't figure out why she was feeling odd. As the darkness settled she got up and went inside.

Slipping under the cool sheets, she lay on her back, and stared at the whirring ceiling fan, wishing she hadn't gone to California. It had been good to see Charlie, but she'd been left with a lingering feeling of discontent. She replayed the conversations she'd had with the people at the wedding, their lives sounding like they were straight off the pages of a Danielle Steele novel. But she'd had an opportunity to travel around the country and even to Japan if she had wanted to. Was it foolish to be sticking to her goal of going back to school?

She pictured the numerous men who had flirted with her—attractive, wealthy men—but none of them compared to Ben. Maybe Charlie and Jillian were right; maybe love was more important than anything else.

Sleep eventually took hold, but she woke the next morning with the sheets in a tangled mess on the bed as if she'd spent the night wrestling demons.

Later that day on her lunch break, she contacted the local shelter and set up an appointment for that evening. The irksome feeling from the night before still tugged at the corners of her mind, like an unwanted visitor, but she convinced herself that having a dog would make things better.

41

The Bose speakers were turned up full blast, and Rory sang about Bobby McGee along with Janis Joplin's raspy voice. Lucie lay on the kitchen floor, nudging a ladybug across the wood planks and cocking her head to one side as she watched it crawl. Rory had gotten the dog just hours before the dog was to be euthanized. The minute she saw Lucie she knew she was taking her home. The attendant at the shelter had said they didn't have a history on the dog other than it had been found wandering the streets and they believed she had been abused in some way. She was timid around people, especially men. Her fur was a mottled brown and she was missing part of one ear, but it was the look in her eyes that drew Rory to her. She felt connected to the dog, knowing they both had endured past traumas.

It was her one-month anniversary with Lucie and the dog's nervousness had diminished. All she had needed was love. Rory had named her Lucie after Ben's grandmother. She liked the stories he had told her about Grandma Lucie on the bayou.

Now Lucie watched as Rory, with her hands full of lettuce, carrots, and a cucumber made pirouettes from the fridge to the counter. A pot of gumbo simmered on the stove as she prepared the salad. She smiled, thinking about the Skype session she'd had earlier with Jillian.

Rory looked forward to the mother-daughter time they shared every Sunday. It was like having Jillian right there in her living room, even though each time the session ended and the screen went black, a slight melancholy feeling tugged at her. But this time it hadn't been just the usual chit-chat. Jillian told her that she and Joe were getting married the following spring in Cornwall. They had yet to set a specific date, but they would let her know when they did.

Rory's eyes fell on the bookcase she had recently refinished, now filled with cookbooks, along with her pottery collection and photographs of Jillian as a child. Derek had shipped her things from Phoenix.

Jillian was getting married. She pictured the gothic stone chapel that Jillian and Joe had discovered on a recent trip to Cornwall and had described in such detail—the elaborate stained-glass windows, filtering in a kaleidoscope of color across the dark-paneled walls. She knew Derek and Donna would be there next to her in the pew hand in hand—they'd gotten married a few weeks ago. When Derek had called with the news, she'd at first felt strange. Derek was married to someone she'd never even met. But the odd feeling subsided. She was happy for him.

Rory sang into the olive oil bottle that doubled as her microphone and then poured it into the dressing vial with the vinegar and water. She added the seasoning packet and then shook the bottle while she danced barefoot across the kitchen in her tank top and cut-off shorts.

Glancing out the open window over the sink to the backyard, she surveyed the profusion of flowers and shrubs, thick from the end-of-summer season. She smiled with pride at the new beds she'd dug that were now filled with yellow coreopsis, purple coneflowers, blue *Angelonia*, and white Grecian roses. Then her eyes drifted to the Ansel Adams calendar on the wall—a wide-angle shot of a redwood looming into the sky—SEPTEMBER.

A year ago, she had been driving down Poplar Street in Willow Bend, filled with apprehension about starting a new life alone.

And then she'd met Will, Marlena, and Caroline. And then Ben had walked into the California Roadhouse—shot back into her life like a bullet. She pictured standing on the street outside the club in Monterey after seeing him with Lisa—it had felt like the bullet had gone straight to her heart. But the wound had healed. She was happy now. Cass and Nick had just left two days ago after spending a week with her. They'd even gone house hunting for a vacation home nearby.

She poured the dressing over the salad and stuck it in the fridge. There was a knock, and Lucie jumped from her spot on the floor, barking as she ran into the living room. Rory wiped her hands on the dish towel and followed Lucie, wondering who was at the door. She never had visitors.

The front door was open, and as she stepped around the corner of the kitchen, the evening sun cast a shadow across the room. Lucie made a low growl at the darkened silhouette of a man through the screen. Even before Rory's eyes could make him out with clarity, her body sensed who it was. She felt her heart race in her chest and her breath catch in her throat. It couldn't be, but it was. The wooden screen door squeaked as she pushed it open.

"Aurora June." Ben gazed down at her with a grin on his face.

She was speechless. What was he doing here? How did he find her? And then without thinking, she threw her arms around him. He hugged her back, and she closed her eyes, drinking in his familiar scent.

She released her hold and stood back. "What are...how did you...what?"

"Can I come in? Something smells mighty good in here."

Rory laughed. "It's gumbo. I'm trying out a new recipe. How did you get here?"

"I drove from Tennessee."

"I mean how did you know where I live?" Rory felt the heat

rising to her face. Excitement, surprise, and confusion all swirled inside her.

"Who's this?" Ben said as he knelt down and tousled Lucie's fur. Rory was amazed that Lucie allowed him to touch her. She still was shy around strangers. Her tail thumped against Ben's leg.

"Lucie."

Ben's eyebrows rose.

Rory felt her cheeks warm. "Yes. I named her after your grandmother." She shrugged. "I liked the name and she sounded like an amazing woman."

"She is. I like it."

He stood, and she couldn't believe he was actually here, in her living room. "So how *did* you find me?"

"A friend." Ben had a devilish grin on his face.

Rory looked puzzled. A friend? Maybe Cass? "What friend?"

"You wouldn't by any chance have a cold beer?"

"Sure."

Ben followed her into the kitchen. "Cool place."

"Thanks. I'm renting it from the woman I work for." She grabbed two beers out of the fridge and turned around to see Ben looking out the door to the screened porch. "Nice view."

"I know. I love sitting out there every evening. The sunsets are spectacular."

Ben pushed open the door, and Rory followed him outside to the deck. They sat in the Adirondack chairs, and Lucie settled herself down on the now dark-stained boards.

"OK, what friend told you I lived here?" Rory felt a bubble of laughter rising up inside. Was Ben really here, sitting beside her? How many nights, sitting alone on the deck, had she envisioned this?

Ben took a sip of his beer and gazed out at the river. "About a month ago, I got a phone call." Ben proceeded to tell her that Charlie had called him. She had insisted that Rory wasn't aware of what she was doing, but she felt it was her duty as a friend to push the universe into action. "I can't remember exactly what she said, but after talking with her, I knew what I had to do. Things became crystal clear to me. It was as if I'd been wearing blinders, and somebody had finally removed them. I had to wait till the summer tour finished, and then I drove straight here from Nashville."

"What are you saying? What did Charlie get you to see?" Rory thought about the text she'd received from Charlie right after the wedding that said she'd gotten her a gift as well. Had she meant Ben? Had Charlie somehow brought Ben to her?

"I'm in love with you, Aurora June. I've loved you since the day I met you. But I put my music first." Ben stood and walked to the edge of the deck, picking off a ginger blossom and twirling it in his hand. "It's been an incredible year for me, but most of that was because you inspired me to write some beautiful music. It finally dawned on me that all that success doesn't amount to a rat's ass if I can't be with you."

He sat back down and slipped the blossom behind her ear. Rory's heart felt like it was swelling out of her chest.

"I admit I was pissed you didn't go with me to Japan, but I understand why now. What I'm trying to say is I'm here, if you'll have me."

"What about the band?"

"I'm taking a break for now. I haven't liked the way things have been going lately anyway, and I think this is a good time for me to regroup, get back into writing, maybe do a solo album."

"You mean you can stay? Live here with me?"

"If you want me."

"Are you kidding? I dream about you every night."

They watched the sun slip behind the trees and the sky turn from amber to indigo, and then they went back inside, ate gumbo, drank beer, and danced in the kitchen, until finally making their way to the bedroom.

———

Several weeks after Ben arrived, he went to Nashville for three days to do some session work, and while he was gone, Rory called Charlie to thank her for the gift. She asked her exactly what it was she'd said to Ben. Charlie laughed, saying the hard part had been getting Rory's phone out of her purse at the wedding to get Ben's number. Talking to Ben had been easy. She said she hadn't told him anything he hadn't already known.

The days slipped by like cool water sliding over rocks, effortlessly tranquil. Rory went off to school each day, either to teach or take classes, while Ben worked on his music.

Evenings were her favorite time. Ben and she would make dinner together while Lucie watched their every move, and then they'd sit out back, talking about their future. They talked about spending Christmas with his mother and grandmother on the Bayou Courtableau.

Once the sun had set, the night sky sprinkled with the ephemeral light of fireflies that danced on the lawn, they would reminisce about their childhoods, each one trying to top the other for best memories. Eventually, they'd head back inside and settle on the big sofa in the living room, where Rory would study, she had enrolled at the university, and Ben would work on his songs.

———

By November, the nights had gotten cooler. Nick and Cass were down for Thanksgiving and had brought the whole clan. They'd recently settled on a house not far from Rory in Hampstead, close to the beach at Topsail Island. It would be a vacation home for now, and maybe one day they'd retire there.

After the big meal, Rory went into the kitchen to get more wine, and as she rounded the corner, she paused at the archway to the living room, eyeing the scene. Michael and Ben were picking their guitars while Chelsea sang along with them. Lucie was curled up on the sofa and the smell of pumpkin pie hung in the air. Jamie and Nick were playing cards at the temporary dining table that had been set up in the living room.

Cass came up behind Rory and slipped her arm around her waist, resting her head on Rory's shoulder. Her hair had reached a short pixie length, and the color was back in her face. The cancer was gone. And even though they knew there was a chance it could return, no one wanted to think that way. They were all taking each day as a blessing.

"He's a great guy," Cass said.

"I know." Joyful tears filled Rory's eyes; she'd wanted this for so long, and now it was here.